B4/23

I'M NOT SUPPOSED TO BE IN THE DARK

PRAISE FOR *I'M NOT SUPPOSED TO BE IN THE DARK*

"Family secrets, broken friendships, spirit possession, and natural magic. This book will haunt you until the very end and long after you finish."

—Rachel Menard, award-winning author of
Game of Strength and Storm and *Clash of Fate and Fury*

"In Neilson's hands, a ghost story is never just a ghost story—teenage rebellion and friendship troubles are woven together with captivating imagery, compelling characters, and yes, ghosts. This book is a study in the lengths we will go to in order to protect those we love. A study in knowing when to let go and when to hold on—even if it means risking ourselves in the process."

—Lillie Lainoff, author of *One for All*

"In her mesmerizing and atmospheric second book, Riss M. Neilson blends themes of family and love with an undercurrent of the supernatural to create a story that is both vivid and beautifully told."

—Lyndall Clipstone, author of the World at the Lake's Edge duology and *Unholy Terrors*

"Stirring, raw, and beautiful, like a dream that stays with you all day, *I'm Not Supposed to Be in the Dark* will haunt you long after the conclusion. Here is a book about the power of magic, love, and feeling seen in the face of tragedy."

—Mads Vericker, co-owner, Heartleaf Books

ALSO BY RISS M. NEILSON

Deep in Providence

I'M NOT SUPPOSED TO BE IN THE DARK

RISS M. NEILSON

HENRY HOLT AND COMPANY
NEW YORK

Henry Holt and Company, *Publishers since 1866*
Henry Holt® is a registered trademark of Macmillan
Publishing Group, LLC
120 Broadway, New York, NY 10271 • fiercereads.com

Our books may be purchased in bulk for promotional, educational,
or business use. Please contact your local bookseller or the Macmillan
Corporate and Premium Sales Department at (800) 221-7945 ext.
5442 or by email at MacmillanSpecialMarkets@macmillan.com.

Library of Congress Control Number: 2022920241

First edition, 2023
Book design by Aurora Parlagreco
Printed in the United States of America.

ISBN 978-1-250-78853-5
(hardcover)

1   3   5   7   9   10   8   6   4   2

For the *weird girls* and anyone who's always felt a little different.

And for my mother, Angie, whose love knows no bounds.

PART ONE

A LIST OF PROBABLE CAUSES

ONE

Steps to keep away the dead (a family remedy):
1. Crush tea leaves
2. Add to cup of boiled water
3. Drink every single drop within thirty minutes
4. Repeat twice a day, every day . . . forever.

Except it doesn't keep them out completely. Most nights when sleep finds me, so do the spirits. They don't interact with me, but I can see their shadows lurking in the void space of my sleep. Mom says it was bad before the tea. *They would talk to you in your dreams, touch you, and worse: find you while you were awake.*

I'm not scared to dream, but she says I should be.

I put my cup on the windowsill and listen to the sounds of night while I wait for Derek Johnson to come out of his house across the street. He's late. Twenty minutes past the time he's been coming out the last couple weeks. Maybe he'll stay in. Maybe . . .

His front door opens.

Nerves steal my breath. I hide behind my blackout curtains to peek at him through my binoculars. He's wearing a yellow hoodie under a jean jacket and sunglasses. Sunglasses with dark lenses, even though it's night. But stranger than that is what he does. How he stands on the top step, so still and unmoving, for so many seconds I remind myself to breathe. When he finally moves, he glides down the steps like a phantom, otherworldly, but then he does something different. He walks over to the rosebush crawling up the side of his house. It's an everblooming rosebush that brushes his bedroom window and has for well over a decade. He just stares at it.

I squint through the binoculars to get a good look. Maybe there's an animal hiding between the branches. Maybe something is wrong.

Minutes pass before he turns and walks across the lawn to the sidewalk and up the street, fading into the distance and darkness as he goes.

My hands shake as I hang my binoculars and prepare for sleep. Not that I want to. What I want is to find out where Derek goes on these late-night adventures. Does he meet up with someone? There's an urge in my body to know, to find out, and it's hard to quiet. Each night, I consider going after him to see for myself, and the urge turns into a deep ache somewhere down in my bones, in my marrow. I can't pretend he doesn't exist the way he pretends I don't exist, but I shouldn't go after him. He'd catch me, I'm sure of it. And I can't ask him what's going on because he won't speak to me at all. Not after he ended our friendship two years ago.

I try to bury the urge while scribbling in my journal, hoping the street wakes to distract me. My neighbors usually give me something to write about with their late-night arguments, the pit bulls barking from backyards and their outdoor cats making hellish breeding sounds. They make a movie for me many nights, but not this one. I consider watching *The First 48*, but my eyes are too heavy. Mom is working an overnight shift, so I lock my bedroom door and put a chair against it. I'd never tell her that sometimes I'm scared to be home alone because she'd tell me to stop watching the gruesome things I watch. She has no choice but to work.

My room goes hazy as I crawl into bed, the tea fast at work, but before sleep pulls me under I pray that whatever Derek's doing he's being safe.

The world tilts. Dulls and darkens. My fingers are in front of me, manicured nails painted white even here. I have ten of them. Not eleven, not nine, but this is still a dream. I'm conscious of it, even though I shouldn't be. My eyes flick around. This is nothingness. It's not pitch-black but a dark gray, as if dense storm clouds strung together to suffocate out all of the daylight. A shadow space.

With each step I take on this gray plane, my feet make ripples on its moving surface. I open my mouth, try to use my voice, but haven't mastered speaking here yet. My throat hurts—tingles and burns—but if I could call out, I don't think the spirits would answer. My limbs feel too thick to move on my own, but suddenly

I'm lifted and dropped again. I'm hanging upside down, or right side up, then I'm floating. Gravity moves how it wishes here so I don't fight trying to control my body anymore. But then I feel my skin prick all over. My stomach squeezes before I see them slithering. The spirits are wisps of white and black wafting through this world, circling me. They slide through the crevices, the open spaces between my body parts. They could almost touch me, almost. I try to move away from them, but there are so many of them and only one of me and the gray space between all of us goes darker.

But then . . . something new happens. I'm dumped into a different dream where I'm falling from a sky that looks like the one of my waking world. My stomach is ripped away as I drop, drop, drop. The wind burns my lungs and . . .

I think. I might. Die.

Until I hit the ground with a thud, and there is no more darkness. An anomaly. This has never happened when I dream of the gray. Here, it's a bright day, the sun hurts my eyes, but I blink the world into view, my house sitting across the street. I can smell . . . roses.

"Where have you been?" Derek's voice calls, and I twist my body to him. He is younger. Fifteen, and climbing out of his window while the branches of the rosebush grow like they're trying to climb inside of it. He jumps down, his arm scratching against the leaves and thorns. He plucks a pink Pippin rose off its branch to hand to me, smiles. "They're in full bloom now."

The rose is yellow around the edges and beautiful in my palm. I bring it to my nose, inhale the sweet fragrance as he watches me.

But then the smell starts to change. Rancid, rotting. I gag and hold it away from my body.

"What's wrong, Aria?" Derek says, and when I look up at him, his dark skin goes pale until it starts to fade. He tries to touch his face, but his hand goes right through it. "Aria." His voice is thin, scared. It makes my heart thrum. Before I can reach for him, he is nothing but wisps of black, and the world around us both goes gray.

I try to scream, but it's no use.

This is how I wake: holding my throat, trying to speak, but gasping for air instead.

I sit up, reach for the glass of water on my nightstand, drink it until my throat stops hurting and I can whisper some words. It was just a dream.

No, it was a memory changed.

Derek is okay. *He's fine*, I tell myself. But goosebumps trail my arms and there's sweat at the base of my neck and my shirt clings to my back. I dream of him sometimes. But never when I'm dreaming of the gray space, never with him in it.

And the stench of decay . . . it's still here. Once a mouse died on a sticky trap behind the fridge, and Mom and I forgot we put a trap there. This is that smell, but more intense, potent. The same smell as the dead rose in my dream. My hands spread over my sheet, getting ready to search, to tear apart my room, but the stench billows through my open window in a rush and has me blinking until I'm out of bed. Death is the kind of thing I spend nights wondering if I'll ever see. My love of murder mystery makes me imagine one of my neighbors is dragging a dead body across the concrete, blood trailing as it gets loaded into a trunk.

But all I see through my window is smoke rising from the rosebush near Derek's.

A fire? No. It's something else.

I'm about to leave when I notice the teacup on my window-sill and a knowing wave washes over me. It's unfinished. I forgot to drink every last drop.

Is that why my dream was different?

The benefit of being alone is that I don't have to slink by my mother's room or be careful to avoid the wood planks that creak as I walk down the hall. As soon as I open my front door and step outside, the smell catches in my nose and makes me choke. I cover my face with my sleeve, hesitating on my porch, trying to see the rosebush with nothing but the moon and what the dim streetlights provide. Finally, I force myself down the steps. In this moment of curiosity, my heart races for another reason: It's been so long since I've crossed this street. Derek wouldn't want me to, but I do it anyway.

His porch light blinks on as I creep over to his window. I freeze, counting several seconds before I start to take slow steps until I am standing just a foot from the rosebush. And there's no other confirmation I need to know this is where the smell is coming from. It's not the same rosebush I saw before I fell asleep just hours ago. The one that has lived so long people call it unbelievable, a gift, a rarity. It is a dying thing, shriveling right in front of me.

I use the flashlight on my phone to examine it, to make sure I'm seeing what I think I'm seeing. And I am. But I can't be. This rosebush has been alive longer than I have. It has drawn blood from me and Derek with our playful finger-pricking games and double dares more times than I can count. It has drawn blood from us when we climbed in and out of his window too. But now, it's withering and dying in the darkness, crumbling like it's being burned, but there's no fire. The leaves are black, the petals are almost there. They fall against the side of the house; some stick there like tar. One rose falls and I catch it, but it soon turns to dust in my palm.

I blink, shiver, and swallow. Remember the dream, the rose dying in my palm then too. Derek going gray. Suddenly it feels like I'm back there. My limbs are not my own, the world around me dulls, and I feel something pulling, grasping at my back. I reach for one of the stems in front of me, but it's too weak. It cracks under the weight of my fingers before I can grab it.

Other stems fall with it, and I am sliced by a thorn. The pain makes me wince, but the world returns to its normal inky black. My body is mine again. Then, in a matter of seconds, the whole bush starts to crumble from the top. Rotted leaves and branches and flowers fall from the sky and land on me. I shield my face, step back, coughing at the smell just as the light in Derek's room blinks on.

Another step back, two. I don't see him, but I can feel him looking at me. The rosebush isn't okay, but he is. A feeling brushes against my bones, though. It isn't the same feeling as when we were young, when I'd knock on his window and wait for him to open up for me so I didn't have to be alone at night. The feeling now makes the hair on my arms rise.

Slowly, I walk backward across the lawn, onto the sidewalk, but when my feet hit the curb, I stumble into the street. Luckily, I catch myself before my body hits the pavement, then I run.

When I'm safe through my front door, I lean up against it to catch my breath, willing myself to wake up from whatever this is. But there are blackened leaves in my hair and blood begins to trail from my finger down my wrist and the smell of death sticks to my skin.

TWO

The sound of Mom's car door slamming shut stirs me awake. I'm on the sofa, still in my shoes and sweatpants, halfway off the couch, the smell of rot on my shirt. My body is stiff.

So is my finger.

I sit up quickly. See that it's swollen with two red pinpricks in the center: proof of what happened last night. The rosebush, the sinking feeling, Derek's light coming on. There are several seconds when I can't do anything but breathe before I get up and rush to the window. A small crowd is gathered across the street, surrounding Mr. Johnson and Derek's younger brothers. And I can still smell it, not just on my clothing or in my hair. It's stronger now: wafting through the crack under my front door, seeping through the shut window, polluting the block.

From my front porch, I can hear the complaints. The smell alone would've pulled my neighbors out of bed, but the climbing rosebush has also rebloomed and reached for the sky for a rare twenty years. *Why so suddenly? How? It doesn't make sense.* Nosier than me,

Karina Wilson from a house over pretends to weep while talking to Mr. Johnson, then she moves and blocks what little view I had of the messy pile of black leaves. The man who lives upstairs from us is pulling on a leash to keep his dog from sniffing and licking at what's left of the rosebush roots.

It's torture not knowing what Mr. Johnson's theories are, and not being able to walk over there and examine things myself. But my mom is there, staring at the side of the house before reaching to touch the tar-like substance sticking to the vinyl siding. A breath gets caught in my throat waiting. When she pulls back like the substance stung her, I flinch too.

Mr. Johnson sees my mom staring at her fingers and moves toward her. I try to read their lips but fail. My mom gives him a hug, and for the briefest second I remember hugging his son. There's an ache in my chest when she walks away from Mr. Johnson, from the rosebush. She sees me, and I use my eyes to tell her to stay where she is and soak up information.

She doesn't listen. She heads up the steps and onto our porch, and before I can ask her anything she shakes her head, says, "Come inside," and walks through the front door. I move to stalk after her, but then that sinking feeling from my dream last night grabs my stomach. The back of my neck tingles; so do my legs. I shift to see Derek walking down the steps of his house with his eyes locked on me instead of the crowd, instead of the dead rosebush.

He's okay. He's not turning gray or disappearing. He's not a shadow.

I can't remember the last time he's looked directly at me, and suddenly I'm conscious of it. I tuck a curl behind my ear, then the contact is gone; he turns away. Heat replaces the prickling in my neck and crawls to my cheeks. My eyes dart from Derek to the remnants of the rosebush and back. But he strides past the people gathered under his bedroom window, ignores his dad calling out to him, and starts walking up the street.

I'm tempted to cross now that I know he's gone, but something tells me Derek will know it if I do.

He didn't always hate me. We played while we were in diapers, dared each other to eat bugs when we got bigger; we climbed trees to build forts and helped his mom prune that rosebush every winter. We wrote *Derek and Aria best friends forever* in permanent marker on each other's legs freshman year and I believed it with my soul. The first person Derek would've called about the rosebush dying was me, but things are different now.

Mom is already heading for the shower when I walk inside. "Please, Aria," she says, pulling the elastic out of her straightened hair and letting it fall over her shoulders. "Can I answer your billion questions later? I just want to wash away the smell of work and go to bed."

I still smell like death from the rosebush, but I'm not ready to wash it away. "Talk while you shower," I say, following her into the bathroom. "Please, I'll cook beef sinigang for dinner."

"You're slick." She sucks her teeth and begins to undress. "*Have kids*, they say. *They'll grow up and you'll get your privacy back*, they say."

I arch an eyebrow at her. "Who says that?"

"Everyone."

"Well, too bad I'm still a child."

"If that's the case, you should definitely do as I say and leave me in peace after the shit I had to clean off the walls at work. Besides, you could always go talk to Mr. Johnson yourself." After she says it, she sees the look on my face and mumbles an apology. She knows why I won't go over there. She turns on the water and gets in the shower, pulling the curtain closed.

I brace myself against the bathroom sink and wait. But not long. "What are the findings?"

"There's nothing significant to report to you, Aria. The findings are inconclusive. Yesterday the roses were still in full bloom and today . . . well, you know. They're the opposite of blooming. And Mr. Johnson doesn't know why. No one does. Happy with those deductions?"

"Negative." I lean into the sink until I hear it creak under my weight. "Does Mr. Johnson feel broken up about it? You know how much Mrs. Johnson used to love that rosebush."

Steam starts to fill the bathroom; I breathe it in while she speaks.

"He seems more clueless than sad, but what do I know? I could hardly get more than a few words in with everyone out there," she says. "And you should stop calling her Mrs. Johnson before you offend that family. You know he doesn't ever want to talk about Shelley."

Shelley. Derek used to call her by her first name, and I'd joke about how my mom would never let me call her Helena.

Memories of Derek and Shelley fill my mind. They'd tend to their garden in the backyard while I watched them grow basil and blueberries and watermelon. Shelley telling me and Derek which branches to remove from the rosebush while we helped get it ready for the season change. Derek smiling, always smiling when his mother was around. But that was before she left him and his whole family two years ago.

I make a mental note: She's no longer Mrs. Johnson. She's Shelley, always has been. And Shelley never came back, not even once. Now the roses are gone with her.

Mom snaps me from my thoughts. "It's weird," she says. "The rosebush. It seems like . . ."

Seconds pass. My heart beats hard in my ears. My skin is warm. "Like what, Mom?"

She doesn't respond. I turn toward the mirror, watch it fog out my features. "There's something strange about it," she finally says, even quieter now.

The black tar substance. The smell. The way it crumbled over my head. That pulling feeling right before. I look down at my swollen finger; the pricks are still bright red and burning at the slightest touch. "Do you think . . . there's something other-worldly about it?"

The silence is maddening before she laughs a little. "Aria, come on. It's just . . . Maybe it had a disease. We should leave it alone." I want to tell her about my dream last night and how it felt like a premonition, but she says, "Please shut the door on your way out. I'm finishing, then going to bed for a few hours. Don't forget . . ."

"To make my tea," I mumble. How could I forget? She reminds me like clockwork.

"And," she stresses, "that you have to meet with your titi Evelyn in an hour."

I sigh and slip out of the bathroom, shutting the door. Senior year doesn't start for two days and Mom insists I get my college plans settled like she hasn't already settled them herself: me living at home and going to Rhode Island College. Titi Evelyn isn't even an academic advisor, but Mom keeps saying, "She has a PhD from RIC. Doesn't owe much in loans; she'll convince you to stay at home." Neither Titi Evelyn nor Mom ever ask what I want.

There's only one bag of tea leaf left in the cabinet, but it should last another month. With a mortar and pestle, I crush the leaves until they are almost as fine as dust and boil some water. But I'm feeling off-center thinking of the dream I had after not finishing my tea last night.

While watching the steam rise from the kettle, I call my sister. Adelia is in her first year of college and lately she's been too busy for my calls, but to my surprise, she picks up this time. Her voice sounds breathy, like she's walking up the URI campus hills. She lives there, forty-five minutes away, even though our mother expects me to stay at home. Adelia tells me I have four minutes and twenty seconds to talk her ear off before she has to hang up. So I speed through the story about the rosebush dying and tell her about my dream too.

Her breathing is even now. She's stopped walking for this.

"You saw it before it happened?" A hypothetical question. She doesn't wait for my response. "Interesting."

I'm not sure if she's teasing. "Will you just come take a look at the rosebush?"

She hums, which means a no is coming. Adelia hasn't been home since she left for school a month ago. "Maybe soon, but if there is something . . . strange going on, you already know of a certain shop owner who could tell you what it is better than I can," she says.

I roll my eyes because I've been trying to push away all thoughts of the shop owner she's referring to, and because I know she's right. "You know I'm not allowed in the shop anymore."

"What I know," Adelia says, "is that you're immature and need to apologize."

"For what? He's the one . . ." A loud whistle breaks through the room and interrupts me.

"Is that the tea kettle?" Adelia asks. Then, "You're still drinking that stuff?"

Her emphasis on the words *that stuff* makes something stir inside of me. "Twice a day," I tell her. "Same as the last time I saw you. Same as the past decade."

"No, I mean . . . even though not drinking all of it gave you a vision last night?"

"What if it wasn't a vision exactly, and what if the tea isn't connected?"

"Hmm," I can tell she's smirking, "well, you're the one who presented it that way."

"What if I'm wrong and . . ."

"Aria," Adelia interrupts. "Are you looking for me to tell you to take your tea today?"

I chew my lip, say, "Maybe that's partly why I was calling. You're always saying I'm rash, and I'm not sure if this urge warrants a reaction. I mean, the tea protects me, right?"

"Does it really?" Adelia says, and we both fall silent for a few seconds. "We never talked much about your tea. But aside from wanting to know about the *vision* you had, do you ever think about what it would be like if you decided to face the ghosts?"

"Why would I want to face them?" I eye the kettle and the teacup on the counter.

Then my sister says, "To ask what it is they want from you." Even though the thought has nagged me for years, hearing her say it causes a shiver to crawl up my spine. "For all your curiosity about everything else, I wouldn't be surprised if you ache to know more about yourself and the spirits. Especially now that you had that dream of the rosebush dying. I'm sure you're anxious, mind running, curious with what else you might see without the tea."

"But I can't be." The words come out in a whisper. I clear my throat, speak louder. "You know Mom and our little shop owner wouldn't let me stop the tea. Not if it keeps me safe."

"Something I've always found intriguing about you is how you usually do whatever you want," my sister says, "consequences be damned. Except when it comes to this." Her words bite into me, but before I can respond, she says, "The four minutes are up. Talk to you soon."

"I have twenty more seconds," I say. Then, "You didn't try to convince me to drink it."

"You didn't really want me to," she says, and hangs up.

But part of me did want her to convince me—because why would I want to be tormented by the things I used to experience when I was younger? Right now, my dreams are only gray void, wisps of shadows. They're bearable, but without the tea they wouldn't be. And worse: neither would my waking life. That's what I've always been told, and yet, I'm never scared to dream. I've always been curious. It can't be a coincidence that last night's dream was different; the foreshadowing was visionary.

But it wasn't just the rosebush that faded away, it was Derek too. He's been acting strange. What if something in my dreams can tell me why?

My throat is so thick, dry. I pour water from the kettle into the cup and drink a few sips. Out of habit, or maybe fear. Because Mom's always saying, *We should leave it alone. Not now, Aria. Drink your tea, Aria. Don't forget to drink your tea.* But the conversation with Adelia reverberates in my mind as well, and all of my curiosity clouds Mom's constant warnings.

I stare down at the warm cup in my hands. The fragments of crushed leaves have settled at the bottom, and before I can think twice about it, I pour the liquid down the drain. Blood rushes in my ears, and I can barely breathe, but there is something else: a buzzing in my bones. Adrenaline coursing through me. I reach into the cabinet, grab the last bag of tea leaf and inhale before dumping all of it into the trash.

My chest is hot when I walk toward the bathroom. Mom

will know what I did by hearing my voice. She will. The shower isn't running anymore. She must be getting dressed. I knock, clear my throat, say, "Mom, can you tell Titi I'll talk to her after church tomorrow?"

"What?" Mom says. "No, you've already canceled on her twice. You're going."

I try to calm my racing heart in fear that she'll hear it somehow. "I accidentally spilled the last bag of tea on the floor and I need to go get more."

"Aria," she groans, then opens the door. She has a towel wrapped around her head and is pulling on her pajama pants. "You know how rare those ingredients are. You know you need it."

"Accidents happen, Mom," I say. "I'll go to the shop."

Her nostrils flare. "You sure will. Right now." I nod and turn, but she calls out to me. "Did you get to drink your morning cup?"

I'm too nervous she'll see the lie in my eyes so I don't look back at her. "I did," I say.

She doesn't speak for a few seconds, then, "Good. That's good, Aria."

Adelia's challenging words may have further sparked my curiosity, but this isn't just about the tea or defiance or asking the ghosts what they want. This is about the rosebush. What happened to it wasn't ordinary; it's not something of this world. And the only person who might be able to explain it needs a good enough reason to see my face.

THREE

Zackary Cayetano: age seventy-one, husband of Felise Cayetano, father of deceased Arlindo Cayetano, grandfather of Adelia and Aria Cayetano—deals in magical objects.

He runs his shop in a small white house with blue shutters on a very quiet dead-end street. I park my bike beside one of his garden gnomes on the lawn. He has a dozen of them, rooted in random places in the ground. They're ancient, cracked and decaying, but he won't get rid of them. As children, Adelia and I would make bets on who could pull one of them free from the dirt, but neither of us ever could. And we only stopped trying when Lolo Zack told us if we managed to pull one of them out it would follow us home and hide under our beds, consuming bits of our flesh while we slept at night—much like the duwende creatures that would steal children in Filipino myths.

Even though I know he was trying to scare us, I avoid getting too close to them on my walk up the stone path to his house. It's been months since I've knocked on his door, and when he opens it, he pushes silver hair out of his eyes and makes a sour face.

"Don't look so disappointed to see me," I say.

"I thought it was the milkman." He frowns. "A grave disappointment, indeed."

I try not to look bitter about it. "Well, are you going to invite me in?"

"Tell me what you want." He doesn't look at me, too busy scouring the street.

"I need another bag of tea," I say. This catches his attention. He scans my face, squints, but doesn't ask *why so soon*, doesn't say anything at all. "Please let me in."

"I'll drop some to your house later," he says, then fans both hands out and tries to shoo me away. But a dark blue car with tinted windows pulls up in front of his house and his mouth goes slack. He stutters out something in Tagalog, but I only understand a few of the cuss words before he pulls me by the arm into the house and shuts the door behind us.

"Suddenly I'm allowed in?" I shoot him a look, fix my jean jacket. The living room is a mess. There are scraps of metal on the floor, dozens of plants crowded together in every corner, and boxes stacked upon boxes, leaving no place to sit. "See, if you hired me to work I could make sure this house is organized, make it look like you actually own a couch."

I'm expecting to be met with sarcasm, but Lolo Zack isn't even looking at me. He's peeking out the blinds, his shoulders high. I come up behind him and peek too.

"What's wrong?" I ask before a light-skinned man with a clean-shaven face gets out of his car and starts walking on the lawn toward us. "Lolo, are you hiding from him?"

My grandfather shifts to look at my face and there's a flicker of fear on his. "Go to the kitchen and fry some garlic. Stay there until I come back inside." He punctuates each word. My pulse begins to pick up, but I don't move a muscle. I've never seen him this way. "Now, Aria."

He doesn't need to tell me again. I'm in the kitchen taking garlic out of his pantry before I hear him slam the front door. My breathing is uneven, trying to figure out why he looked so scared. When I go to the stove, there's a pan on it and the garlic has already been fried.

Lolo comes back inside the house, limping into the kitchen because he doesn't have his cane. He tries to act unfazed by what just happened, even smiles with one side of his mouth. "Thought you wouldn't be coming over anymore. Thought you were done with me," he says.

"I thought so too," I tell him. "But anyway, who was that outside? Are you okay?"

Lolo limps over to the stove. With his back turned to me, he says, "An old business partner I no longer associate with."

I grab his cane from where it's leaning against the wall and tuck it beside him at the stove. "Why is that?"

"Because he tried to use me," Lolo says, his voice shaking a little. "He's trouble and I don't want my family anywhere near him. You understand?"

"I do," I say. I'm surprised he's told me this much already, and I decide not to push it with more questions. I don't even tease him about the fried garlic when he cracks an egg into the pan. "There's another reason why I'm here . . . besides the tea."

"Of course there is." He adds rice, stirs. "I'm guessing a plea to work for me?"

My blood heats because of the laughter in his voice. I tell him no, then explain what happened with the rosebush. He stops stirring the food in the pan, his hand stills.

But then he shrugs. "And?"

"Did you hear what I said? It's gone. The whole bush, crumbled and blackened. It stinks. The roots are dead. Before I left to come here, there were flies already circulating."

"Rosebushes don't live forever. Guess it needed its eternal rest. Are you hungry?"

Instead of an answer, I whip my phone out and push it into his face. The oil pops on the pan and singes me.

"Ha, a quick comeback from God for your disrespect," my grandfather says.

"Tell me you think this is normal," I say, and show him again. This time I'm careful not to get too close. "Last night, it crumbled in my hands. Just crumbled. But it also cut me? How?"

He flinches at the word cut. I watch him. I see it. Even though he's pretending to be unaffected. "Why are you asking me this?"

"Why don't you seem that surprised? Why are you not upset over this?"

He puts down his big fork and grabs hold of my hand, examining my finger where the skin broke. Then he pulls open a drawer beside him and takes out a tube. Smears some blue liquid on my skin. I hiss at the pain. "Don't be a baby cry," he says.

I tilt my head to catch Lolo's eyes, say, "I dreamt that a rose crumbled in my palm before it happened." The two things I don't tell him: that I didn't finish my entire cup of tea (must be slick about this) and that Derek was also in the dream (Lolo would tease I have a crush when I don't).

His mouth twitches as he stares at me. "You dreamt of this?"

"I did," I say. "That must mean something, right? Or am I . . . do I have psychic abilities?"

He lets go of my hand and moves to take a dish out of the drying rack, fills the plate with longsilog and hands it to me. "We can eat out back if you'd like."

My Cape Verdean family from my mom's side shows their love with food as well, but it always feels deeper with my Filipino side. Still, I say, "I don't want to eat."

Lolo smiles, his false teeth overly white. "More for me. And I wish you were a psychic. Maybe I'd have a chance at winning the Mega Millions."

We sit in the backyard on a small round table while he eats, while the sun starts to climb higher in the sky, while my stomach rumbles and the chickens in his small coop begin to chirp. I'm not sure why Lolo Zack keeps animals in his shop when they're biologically close to humans and he *never spells humans*, but he won't give me the details about his business unless I work for him. The things I already know: Lolo lives in an even smaller house with my grandmother a few miles away, but he's never there. He's always here, making balms and salves and potions with pig's feet and growing plants entirely too quick to be normal, same with the chickens and birds and the insects he whispers things to while I watch them grow big before my eyes. Before he hands them off for pay.

I was seven the first time I noticed customers coming to him with wounds and diseases. He'd try to usher me somewhere out of sight, but I'd peek and see him creating concoctions in the kitchen while customers screamed in agony over their open flesh. And I noticed he never did the work of rubbing the balm on their wounds; he'd hand them the concoction and they'd hand him cash before he'd wish them well and watch them limp back out the front door.

Lolo Zack is how I found out that magic exists. If there's anyone who knows what kind of supernatural madness is happening on my block, it's him. But he just wants to eat.

My stomach rumbles for a third time and he puts down his spoon and pushes his plate in front of me. He makes the best longsilog. I hope to perfect mine like this someday, but I'm annoyed that he thinks he can use food to silence me.

More annoyed that he's not wrong.

He sits back, eyes tracing my face, watching as I eat. "You've come here after all of these months just to ask me about a rosebush that has nothing to do with you?"

I swallow my food, look toward the coop because the chicks won't stop chirping. "Don't you want to see it for yourself? It's something in your field."

He laughs so loud I startle. His belly jumps as he leans back in the chair. The chicks chirp louder like he's scared them too. "My field?"

"The magic you do. The things you can see."

Both of his brows raise into his high forehead before his silver hair flops down and covers them. "I'm not a medium. I don't do the kind of magic," he stretches the last word like it's silly, "you're referring to."

I cut my eyes at him, take another bite, and wave the fork in the air. "Yes, I know. You put spells into objects, but you'd know something is off about it. You'd be able to tell."

My phone goes off as he reaches across the table to grab a ball of fried rice from my plate. With a mouth full of it, he corrects, "Not all objects. And you need to learn to mind your business. That's what I do in my *field*." Another text message comes through and I silence my phone. "You should answer that. Might be one of your friends. Be a kid, Blue."

Lolo's called me Blue forever. Says it's the color I gravitated toward as a child, and I've always imagined me running around his house with blue markers and drawing all over the walls, but he says it was deeper than that.

I peer down at my phone. Two text messages from my friend Brianna.

1: So today is Saturday and before you say you don't want to come out just think about how we're going to be seniors and this is the last time we can party as juniors.

2: You'll have fun. If you don't, I'll watch crime TV with you for the next two Saturdays.

I smile at my phone, ignoring Lolo's peering eyes while typing back.

Bri, I can't tonight. Too much happening. Maybe next weekend.

You're insufferable. I guess I can hang out with my other friends tonight.

Let me know how that goes. Tell them I said hello.

She sends me an eye roll emoji and I click out of the conversation.

Lolo's eating more rice when I look at him. "Be a kid, Blue," I mimic, and the corners of his lips turn up. "Well, Lolo, you're the one who said I should grow up the last time I was here."

"Because you annoy me," he says, tone flat, "but I changed my mind. You *should* be a kid . . . before it's too late."

His words cause the pit in my stomach to stretch, make me feel like there's some other meaning besides the fact that I'm aging. "Is that why you don't want me to work for you? You let Adelia work for you when she turned fifteen, and she didn't even have friends. At least I have friends."

Adelia has always been Lolo's favorite. I tell Mom that Adelia's really just partying on the weekends and that's why she hasn't been home, but according to everyone Adelia can do no wrong. Before she went away to college, she worked for Lolo Zack after school and sometimes spent whole weekends with him. I would spend weekends too, but while I was out playing with the kids on the block, climbing trees and chasing squirrels, Adelia was helping Lolo Zack in his garden. Adelia was cleaning his weird animals and watering his grass. Adelia didn't have to leave the house when his customers came looking for whatever he cooked up for them. But when Adelia went to school and I wanted to learn more about whatever they were doing, Lolo Zack only taught me how to cook.

"So why aren't you with your friends now?" Lolo says. "Why are you here asking questions?"

I push the plate of longsilog back toward him and sigh. "You're saying Adelia never asked questions? She just worked for you and kept her mouth shut?"

"I'm saying Adelia stayed out of what didn't concern her. In my line of work, I have to stay out of what doesn't concern me or it'll eat up my soul, and worse, my time. That is not you, Aria. Never has been. You carry notebooks around to study people for God's sake. Leave the rosebush alone and go get a regular job."

My chest grows warm. I shift my butt because there's a notebook in my back pocket. Lolo Zack has told me that magic can darken the soul, and that I'm too nosy for his line of work, but I know there's something else. Something he's hiding from me and he has always wanted to hide from me, but not from my sister.

Then suddenly he says, "You've been drinking the correct amount of tea, right?"

This is why I have to be slick. Maybe the tea does more than keep the ghosts away. Another secret. "Yes," I lie. "Two teaspoons, one cup of water, twice a day."

There's a stifling moment of challenge between us before my lolo Zack smiles again. "Would you like to feed my chickens while I get a new batch ready for you?"

"What if I don't want to take it anymore?" I ask. Another challenge. "What then?"

He grips the sides of the table. "I'd say that's too bad. Without the tea, the spirits will be able to see you better, clearer, and for your own well-being we can't let that happen." He gets up to head into the house. "Have fun feeding the chickens, Blue."

While he's gone, I imagine a night where those shadows in my dreams turn to solid bodies. I imagine the silence turning to whispers. I imagine being able to keep my two feet on the ground while looking into the face of a spirit and asking what they want.

No one ever asks me what I want.

Lolo Zack is in his kitchen, putting a spell on some tea leaf for me, but I've decided I'm not going to drink another drop of tea unless I want to.

FOUR

Notes in my journal of the first forty-eight hours with no tea:

-Wired. Feels like I've had two Red Bulls and a shot of soy sauce and vinegar.

-Derek leaves his house at two A.M. His long hair is out (different).

-The smell of the rosebush makes me gag when I open the window.

-The sun comes up, so tired, but still can't sleep. Horrible tea detox effect?

-Getting ready for church with a kick of adrenaline. Feels like I slept thirty-six hours straight but wasn't even an hour. Will I fall asleep while Father Duncan preaches about sinning?

-At church, Titi Evelyn lectures me about my lack of college plans and compares the many extracurricular activities she did to my none. My head feels too heavy for all the nodding. One of my cousins says I look like a bobblehead. Titi stole my adrenaline.

-Derek and his father sit in their usual places in a pew in the back row, but neither of them talk to anyone. They slip out before the service is over. Avoiding questions about the rosebush and prayers for their household? I would.

-It's dark out again. Tempted to drink my tea, but I pour it into the snake plant by my bookcase in order to avoid gulping it down for the sake of sleep. Snake plants are resilient, but I hope it doesn't die.

-Mom is at work, but I wish she were here to keep me company.

-Gross how my brain automatically remembers Derek keeping me company.

-The birds are happy before sunrise. That annoys me this morning.

-I am a senior.

FIVE

The spectacle of the rosebush seems to die down, but no one is happy about the lingering stench. It's sweet-and-sour and rancid all at once. As if a garbage truck trailed trash juice up the street. Mr. Johnson is already outside with someone who pulled up in a pickup truck at six this morning. Earlier, I watched them dig up the soil and rip out blackened roots, leaving a crater of empty where life used to be. The worst part is the whole mess of the rosebush—what was once monstrous in size—fits into a single black garbage bag, and tying it shut doesn't stop the smell.

I'm fully dressed for my first day of senior year and need to leave for the city bus soon, but I also need to see what's happening across the street. Minutes pass; my alarm goes off again. I'm frustrated that this is the last time I can silence it, but finally the man reaches into the bed of his truck for a gallon of some sort of chemical. He puts on a mask, then motions for Mr. Johnson to stand back before he pours the entire contents of the bottle where the rosebush roots were. While Mr. Johnson is coughing, a sickness washes over me. There's currently a chemical eating at the earth and the past and whatever is trying to linger here.

When I step outside, I think the rotten smell is finally gone. Replaced with something sharp and sterile, antiseptic, the kind of smell that says nothing will ever grow there again.

But then . . . there it is. Underneath the chemical clean, the rot starts to rise.

I get to the bus stop first, but see Derek coming. His thick hair is tied up in a bun and he's wearing a *Death Note* shirt, so I hide my own anime T-shirt under my arms. Not that he looks at me anyway. Standing at the bus stop together has been the most awkward part of us not being friends now, and today is no different. He stares right through me while he walks over, and it brings me back to tenth grade. We said it would be the greatest year of our lives.

Derek had his hair faded back then and he was only six inches taller than me instead of a whole foot and a half. The night before our first day of school, we couldn't be together physically so we performed murder skits for each other through our windows. I remember wishing we were both staring out of his window, side by side, our shoulders touching. I thought about those small touches for too long that night, so when he got to the bus stop the next morning I was worried. He was Derek, my forever platonic best friend Derek, but something was happening. Every time he was close, a warm feeling spread through my stomach. I think I was developing a little crush, or maybe teenage hormones were to blame. But I'm glad I never told him. It might've made me feel even more awkward now that he doesn't speak to me.

I'm bitter thinking of it, but then his eyes meet mine. For a second, there's a flicker of something inviting, and I'm not prepared for the way my body tries to remember him close, sitting beside me on the city bus, his thigh touching mine, him occasionally finding my wrist like he was searching for a pulse to make sure I was real, still near him.

When his eyes dart down to my backpack and he sees all the pins there, the ones *he* gave me as gifts throughout the years, I panic, open my mouth and instead of trying to make normal conversation, I say, "Yeah, I still have them." And then, flushing because he looks startled or something, I add, "And I'm sorry about the rosebush. I know your mom loved . . ."

He frowns and pulls on his backpack straps. "Please don't talk to me about my mom."

"Alright," I say, too stunned to say anything else. He hasn't strung that many words together for me in years, and he probably won't ever again. He puts in his headphones, shifts his body away from me, and stays that way. When the bus pulls up, he nearly leaps onto it to put distance between us, then he takes a seat at the back with some of his gamer friends while I sit up front alone.

I should've just said hello.

⁕

Thankfully, Brianna's waiting for me outside of the school. She's beautiful in her flowy miniskirt and the three anklets that compliment her golden skin. She has her hair in a high bun, her edges brushed in pretty shapes on her forehead, and she's wearing platform Converses. People are looking her way: boys wondering if she'd ever give them a shot and girls hoping to have a chance with her this year. Bri stands like she knows it, but she squeals when she sees me, runs over, and throws her full force into a hug.

"You look adorable, darling, exhausted but adorable." She says it in a fake British accent that I know she'll keep most of the year. "Have I mentioned how I love, love, being a senior?"

"Seven times over the phone yesterday," I say. Compared to Bri, who is planning to go premed and already has her college life mapped out, I'm not excited about being a senior. And compared to Bri's, my style is quirky. My hair falls in loose curls right above my shoulders and I have two braids in the front that are studded with wildflowers from the woods. I'm wearing pink overalls with a *Demon Slayer* T-shirt underneath and limited-edition Adidas sneakers I thrifted a few months ago. "Also, is adorable a compliment? Or an insult? I can never tell with you."

She smiles. "Today it's a compliment, but I can't promise it'll be that way tomorrow."

Brianna Lewis has been my only other real friend since freshman year, and we got closer after Derek and I drifted apart. She's fun to talk to and only complains a little when I go on and on about murder mysteries. I tell her about my dreams, about spirits and strange things happening, and I can tell she doesn't believe any of it. Still, she never calls me crazy or weird. The most important part: She never stops listening, even if it's not what she wants to hear. We walk into the corridor, stopping at our lockers before homeroom, and talk about the rosebush.

"I fact-checked on Google," she says. "Maybe it was an aggressive form of root rot? Maybe gopher damage?" She hangs a mirror in her locker while theorizing. My favorite: "Maybe some dudes had beef with Mr. Johnson and poured toxic chemicals on it Friday night?"

The school speaker cuts in, interrupting her nonsense only for the principal to start talking about how we seniors have to set a good example for the rest of the school. He mentions SATs and prom and says he wants us to make him proud. Bri grins and twirls in her dress, says it all feels like a dream. But I'm busy thinking of what it would be like to learn magic and travel to different countries, to work for Lolo and be surprised each time a customer knocks on the door with a strange request. Having some unpredictability in my life, that's what I dream of.

I make it two thirds through the school day without a single class with Derek. Last year, I had to suffer with seeing his face in most of my classes while he made sure to sit as far from me as he could get. But during gym, while I'm rubbing my eyes from lack of sleep, I can't stop wondering what he's doing, if he's drawing characters in his notebook, if he's laughing with his friends, if he's worried about the rosebush. If there's someone who's caught his attention. My stomach clenches. I shouldn't care about who he likes; I shouldn't wonder.

A dodgeball flies right by my face and Bri smacks my arm. "Pay attention."

Our gym teacher blows her whistle, points at the other team. "I said no balls to the face."

While we're all on time-out, Bri whispers "Look," and I follow her gaze across the room. "The new kid keeps staring at you. He was in my last two classes. His name is Sean. Oh, oh. He's definitely looking at you. *And* he's cute too."

I find him in the crowd and our eyes lock. He flashes me a smile, but then the teacher blows her whistle and he cocks his arm back and hums the ball at me. The sting startles me, but I'm so tired it takes me an extra second to react. When I look up, he's still smiling at me.

Brianna sucks her teeth. "Damn. It's the bullying-on-the-playground-because-he-likes-you game. I hate how guys flirt."

"We are playing dodgeball," I say, rubbing my thigh, "and he doesn't even know me."

While I'm walking to the back of the room where the eliminated students wait, Bri calls, "He might not know you, but he has two eyes. He can see how hot you are." Half the class turns our way, but I don't want to kill her until Sean looks too. He runs a hand over his faded hair and winks at me. I need energy because when I get back in the game, I'm coming for him.

⁓✻⁓

Mrs. Dolly's class is sixth period English and I'm here before anyone else. I lay my head on the desk, look at my watch. Too many hours without sleep. Too quiet in here. Too . . .

Sleep grasps me and pulls me under. I am back in the gray

space. But this time when my feet move on the surface, the ripple sparks a color I've never seen here. Bits of green break through the surface. I take a step back from the shock of it, step forward again. The ripple reminds me of walking through a field of grass.

Grass . . . here in the gray?

But I have no time to truly register this change because the shadows come, swirling through the air, below, above; one stops right in front of me. I am facing this shadow and it is facing me and I can't remember this happening before.

When I shift to the right, it mimics me. Then I hear it. Sounds I've never heard in this dreamscape. A whisper. A voice. One. Three. Five. All around me, coming from nowhere and everywhere, but I can't make out the words. The shadow in front of me comes closer, its wispy form bends and widens and thickens until it becomes a shape.

The shape of a human, cloaked in darkness.

We are an inch apart and I choke out a word. Just one.

"Hello," I say.

I'm shaky, trembling. And then the spirit lifts its shadowed limb and touches my arm, sending a spark from my toes to the tips of my fingers, making my corneas burn.

I wake with burning eyes, choking on air, skin tingling all over.

It was a dream. Only a dream. I'm fine. But my eyes itch and water and I . . .

"Sorry," a voice says, and my head snaps up to see Sean looking down at me. "Sorry for tapping you. I hope I didn't scare you, but the teacher was staring, so I figured . . ."

The spirit touched me in my dream. Or did Sean touch

me and I imagined that the spirit touched me? I don't register his words until someone clears their throat. *Shit.* The room is full, and they're all staring, so I focus on Sean's face, wipe my mouth with the back of my hand and mumble, "Thanks." I refuse to be embarrassed for falling asleep, but my eyes still hurt and there's a sharp feeling in my fingers. I hide my shaking hands under my desk.

"I wish I could say it's a pleasure to have you back in my class this year, Aria," Mrs. Dolly says. "But we're off to an interesting start. Let's keep the sleeping for your bed. Okay?"

"I'll try my best," I say, my heart still beating so fast.

The class laughs and Mrs. Dolly rolls her eyes, then waves a hand at Sean to find a seat. And when he moves, my eyes land straight on Derek. He's in the front row and he stares at me for too many seconds. He looks concerned. He always knew when something was wrong without me having to say anything. Does he know what I was dreaming about? Can he see it on my face? They touched me, I want to tell him. But his lips turn down as his eyes shift from me to Sean a seat over, then he puts his wall back up, blocking me out and turning to face the front.

Mrs. Dolly's voice is big in that high-pitched, peachy kind of way, but it never matches her words or tone. "I wish summer vacation was much, much longer, yet here I am with all of you. I'm just hoping we can get through the rest of the year as quickly as possible."

She sits on her swivel chair, says more things, but it's like I can hear the spirits whisper again, faint, so faint, the words blending and blurring, coming from the vents in the walls, seeping through the ceiling, and blocking her out.

They whispered, they touched me. I felt it. It wasn't just Sean, it was a spirit.

"Aria," Mrs. Dolly calls, "since you're still in a daze from the nap *I* could use, you can be the first to share with the class something weird or exciting that's happened this summer."

It takes me a few seconds, but I stare at Derek's back and swallow. "This really old rosebush in my neighborhood died out of nowhere," I say, and watch his shoulders rise. "I mean dead-dead, rotted out at the root, and it left this reeking smell on our street."

He may not have been looking at me a second ago, but he is now. His eyebrows are scrunched together and his eyes are low. He opens his mouth like he's about to say something, but his friend beats him to it. "You talking about Derek's rosebush?"

Everyone looks at Derek, then back at me, making the connection. Some of them already know we live on the same street, that we were once best friends, but those who didn't know do now. Sean tilts his head and gives me a curious look, smiles without showing his teeth.

"Yeah," Derek mutters, cutting his eyes at me, "it's my rosebush to worry about."

A few oohs erupt in class, but Mrs. Dolly hushes them away. My cheeks burn; I couldn't care less what anyone else thinks, but I am angry. Yesterday, I could say Derek spent two years avoiding me, but he never treated me badly. Not until today. It might be delayed, but I don't care. "I'll mind my business when you get that smell under control," I say.

Everyone in the class laughs, including his friend; even Mrs.

Dolly gives me an admiring nod. I watch Derek's shoulders stiffen again, but he makes no moves to look at me.

"That is strange," Mrs. Dolly says, "but I think even stranger is this tension in the class . . . so let's move on to a different story, shall we?"

SIX

"She's a brave soul because I ain't going near that boy alone ever again."

My neighbors would swear they're whispering, but I don't even have to strain my ears to spy what they're saying from a porch over. The brave soul they're talking about is my sister. She needed to pick something up from Lolo's house and decided to come spend time with me and Mom too. The boy my neighbors are talking about is Derek, who came outside right in time for Adelia to walk across the street straight over to him. I never wanted their friendly relationship to change just because I wasn't friends with him anymore, but I'm jealous to see them talking near Derek's window now. While she's looking at the vinyl siding, he's staring at her.

"You see the way he's looking at her," Karina Wilson says. "He was looking at me the exact same creepy way in my yard that night."

There's a quickness in the way my mind turns over her words to make sense of them. Forget creepy, why would Derek be in her yard in the first place? I tilt my head toward the two women, but then I hear it again: whispering. Not coming from them or from across the street, coming from nowhere but settling around me like a bubble. The dream I had in class earlier is still messing with my head, but I need to concentrate on what my neighbors are saying.

Except Karina stands up, shakes out her shirt, and says to my other neighbor, "Enough of this. We're missing *Family Feud* and it still stinks out here."

When they go into Karina's house, I try to pay attention to Derek's body language, wishing for telepathic powers to see into his mind. But Adelia nods at him, bends over once more to touch the fresh soil they laid on the ground and starts to walk my way. Derek follows her with his eyes, burns a hole into her back. It doesn't even seem like he notices me sitting here. The look on his face makes my stomach squeeze. He doesn't snap out of it until Adelia sits beside me on the porch. He hops on his skateboard and rides it up the street.

"What'd you find out?" I ask my sister.

"Well, no way it was root rot," Adelia says. "I thought you were exaggerating, but . . ."

The sky goes dark above us. I lay my head on her shoulder for a second, close my eyes, and sit with the fact that I've missed her before I say, "I never, ever exaggerate."

She snorts, then says, "Derek seems different too. Something is off about him." I lift my head, look into her eyes, but she shrugs. "Teenagers."

"You're still a teenager," I say, but my brain is doing backflips.

I'm about to tell her about him sneaking off in the middle of the night and what the neighbors said, but she leans forward to look at the teacup beside me. It's probably gone cold by now. Mom brought it out for me when Adelia arrived, then went back inside to get dinner packed for us to all go to my father's resting place and eat.

"I haven't seen you take a single sip of that tea," Adelia says, tilting her head at me.

I pick up the cup and toss the tea into the bush to my right, then point a finger at her. "I stopped drinking it after our call, but don't take credit."

"I'd never," she says, a slick smile creeping up.

"Mom would not be happy if she knew you were a part of this," I say, smiling back just a little.

Adelia shifts so she's no longer facing me and watches a streetlight flicker in the distance. "Mom wouldn't be happy about a lot of things," she says.

"What wouldn't I be happy about?" Mom asks, startling me from behind.

My sister seems unfazed. She stands to give Mom a hug, her wavy hair swaying just above her butt. "I was telling Aria that I'm struggling in science class," she says.

My sister is a bad liar. Science of all subjects. She could mix chemicals in her sleep.

I don't know if Mom believes the BS, or if she's just so happy Adelia's here, but she doesn't argue. She tells Adelia to study harder, that college is different than high school, then pats her bag. "I packed us the good leftovers. Take us to go see your father."

There's a small shrine behind our church. It's white, made of battered brick, and missing a sculpture of Mary that is said to have once dwelled inside. The sculpture might not be there anymore, but my family says that part of my father's spirit is. That it's watching over his family on earth while he's in heaven. Mom says he had a calm, pulsating energy when he was alive, and it's easy to feel near the shrine. We'll lay a blanket on the grass, bring a battery- operated lantern if it's dark out, and sometimes we eat here with him.

Mom hums while chewing today. "This picadillo is really good, Aria," she says, "almost as good as your grandfather's."

"I'm going to tell him you said that," I say, swatting away a mosquito. "He'll be so mad. The thought pleases me."

"Hey, don't swat the mosquito my way, you mischief-maker," Adelia grumbles.

Mom swallows a bite, fixes me with a serious stare while poking at her food. "So you're on speaking terms with your lolo again? It wasn't just a quick tea run the other day, then?"

"I guess we're fine now, but it's annoying that he treats me differently than her." I point a finger at my sister, but she just shrugs and keeps chewing. "I'm going to keep harassing him until he lets me work for him."

In the past it was because I'd always wanted to learn the business, but it's not just that anymore. The closer I am to him now, the closer I am to the secrets he's keeping from me.

Mom wipes her mouth with a napkin. "You know, you're

lucky he tolerates how hot and cold you are with him. Your father used to say that when he was young even the slightest edge to his tone was considered disrespect. But your lolo lets you walk in and out of his life like it's nothing. I think you take advantage of how untroubled that man can seem."

A pit grows in my stomach and my heart pricks. "I don't mean to disrespect him."

"I know, but sweetie, did you ever stop to think that maybe he sees something different in you than he does in Adelia?" She looks into my eyes, really looks. "Possibly it's so different it's special. You might not have the same relationship, but maybe accepting that will bring you closer to having your own type of bond with him."

I roll my eyes, fighting off a smile. "When did you get so wise, woman?"

"As soon as I laid eyes on you, Aria. I was still so naive when I had Adelia, but you woke something inside of me." She's quiet for a moment; her words feel weighty around us. For some reason, they make me think of secrets and tea and the spirits. "And I'd prefer you get a regular job than work with your lolo, anyway."

"Why? It's a family business. Dad worked for his father, Adelia worked there, I . . ."

"You're both just going to keep talking about me like I'm not here, huh?" Adelia asks.

"Probably," I say.

Mom pats Adelia's head but speaks to me. "It's not the type of family business I want *you* involved in," she says, and I wonder if she knew what she was getting into when she married my father Arlindo and his magical family. "You should concentrate on solidifying college plans. Take an extracurricular to look good on the RIC application."

"I'm going to be eighteen soon; what happens when you can't tell me what to do?"

Adelia wiggles her brows. "Yeah, Mom, what happens when you can't tell this adventurous little rascal what to do?"

Mom closes up her food container and says, "I'll hope you'll still respect my decisions as a parent, Aria, and know that I'm always thinking of your best interests." She looks between us. "Adelia, You're different. You have a sense of direction, but your sister is always searching for something, and I'd like to think I've helped lead her in the right direction over the years."

"No one is arguing with that," my sister says. "But she's growing up."

"I am," I say. "Mom, are you saying I can't be independent? That I'm not capable? You work all the time; I'm home alone and I think I do a pretty good job taking care of myself."

It's too dark to see her wince, but I hear it in her voice. "You're right. You have a lot of freedom, but I always trust you to stay close to home. I'm just scared that you'll run out into the big world and find things in it you're not ready for." She smiles at me, puts a hand on my knee. "You remind me so much of your father. You even look like him with that dimpled smile. I wish I would've asked him to stay closer to home."

Her words make the backs of my eyes burn. I know she loves me. She's made sacrifices and has been so strong while raising

Adelia and me on her own. She was only twenty-six when my father was murdered on a work trip in Florida. And though they arrested the guy who did it, he never said why he killed my father. No one ever uncovered the reason. I've searched old archives and articles trying to find information on him, spent years inventing stories and scenarios of why, but I've never really considered what those stories could be doing to Mom.

I don't say anything, just stand and extend a hand to help her up. My sister wants me to pull her up too, but I psych her out and make her stand on her own.

We look up at the band of clouds illuminated by the bright gibbous moon before putting our hands on the brick shrine to speak to my father. We tell him about our week, how good the food is, Mom sings a song. But while she goes to fold up the blanket, Adelia and I stay.

I close my eyes for a second and imagine he hears what's inside my heart about my hopes and dreams. I hope he hears me asking him if he could do a little something to ease Mom's fears about me. And then, I feel something. A vibration that deepens to a burning sensation that runs from the tips of my fingers to the knuckles.

I flinch back, but my hands are fine. They're not sore. The burning disappears quicker than it came. "Dad? Is that you?" I whisper to the shrine, to the atmosphere, to whatever realm is between us.

"What?" Adelia's voice cuts in. "What'd you say, Aria?"

I open my mouth to tell her about the feeling, but then my body turns heavy, dense; the air thickens and the whispering comes again. The sound creeps through the grass and slithers up my spine. I turn to look for the shadows, for spirits. But my sister grabs my shoulder.

"Are you okay?"

"I . . ."

"You girls ready?" Mom calls. "I'm getting sleepy."

Adelia ignores Mom and waits for me to speak; she won't take her eyes off of me.

"I'm fine," I whisper, then shake her off and run my eyes over the brick one last time before letting Mom lead us through the dark.

SEVEN

"I'm sorry I can't stay longer," Adelia says, parking in front of our house, "but I have to get back to school for something. I promise I'll come visit soon. I love you."

Mom sighs and kisses Adelia's cheek. "I love you too, baby. Soon, please."

Before I follow Mom out of the car, Adelia turns in her seat and tells me to stay back. When we're alone, she asks about my dreams. I tell her how there weren't any when I first stopped taking the tea, then pause and pull my hoodie down so it's stretched over my bare knees.

"But I had one in class today and I think . . . I think a spirit touched me. I felt it, Adelia."

My sister's doll-like eyes shrink as she studies me from the front seat. "Did it hurt?"

I swallow. "You believe me?"

"You never, ever exaggerate," she mimics me from earlier, but she's still looking so serious. "Well, did it?"

"Not exactly," I tell her, "it felt like a static shock through my body. And I can't say I'm not nervous to feel it again, or worse, but I need to know."

Adelia chews her top lip, then looks out the window toward the space where the rosebush was. "And you felt something at Dad's shrine too?"

"His energy, at first, but then," I swallow, "whispers. Sounds that feel . . . dark? Spirits."

The grasshoppers are loud in the bushes outside. We quietly listen to them before Adelia reaches into her military jacket and hands me something. I study it, run my finger along the raised edges, the button at the bottom. It's our father's old pocketknife. Lolo gave it to Adelia when she went away to college. She cried the first time she held it. But I don't feel the same heavy emotion holding it now. It's weird, but it's always felt as if that grief doesn't belong to me because our father died when I was three. I'm only a year younger than Adelia, but it feels like he was stripped away from my memory while her memories still cause pain.

"Why are you giving this to me? It belongs with you."

"It belongs with us," she says. "Don't let anyone or anything fuck with you. Okay?"

When I turn on the light above me and open the knife, I see the blade is black, serrated in the middle. I didn't remember it looking this way. "Do you mean the spirits? You want me to use *this* to protect myself from them? That sounds illogical."

"Our family makes magical objects, Aria. Is anything really illogical? And anyway, I just had this feeling since I arrived here . . . ," she starts, shaking her head. "Then seeing you by the shrine . . ." She breathes out. "Listen, you don't need to be scared, but something tells me you should have this. You said *dark* and what I heard was *dangerous*." Her words thicken the air between us. "I want you to learn things, but keep your guard up, keep your trust close."

"I will," I say, flicking the knife closed. "But is there something you know about me that I should know? Something you might've learned from Lolo?"

"Lolo's never told me a thing, but there were whispers about you around the shop," she admits. My heart leaps into my throat, but then she says, "Nothing I've ever understood or can explain. But I'm a call away if you keep looking and need help putting the pieces together."

My fingers flex around the knife; my disappointment comes out in deeper breaths. "So that means you'll actually pick up your phone?"

"Anyway," she rolls her eyes, "years of watching all those documentaries and horror shows hopefully taught you how to use a knife." I can tell by her face that she's not joking. "But if you need a lesson, I got you on that too."

As soon as I step inside the house, I'm hyperalert in a way I only get after a murder mystery leaves me with bone chills. Mom is in the kitchen washing dishes. She left the living room light off, nothing is out of place, her Dunkin' cup still sits on the coffee table, and the curtains are open because we forgot to shut them. It's quiet. Maybe it's a residual feeling after what happened at the shrine, but I'm still cautious. I switch on every light I pass.

In the kitchen, I open the closet door, the big cabinets, look out the window.

"Why are you acting strange?" Mom asks, and the sadness in her voice makes me stop.

"I'm fine," I say, even though my heart is thrumming. "Are you okay, Mom?"

She puts a dish in the drying rack. "You're fine, and I'm okay. I just hope Adelia is too."

I lean against the counter. "Why wouldn't she be?"

"Never mind." Mom sighs, then says, "Can you turn on some music, please?"

My cue to leave her alone with her overbearing worry. This time, I actually give her the privacy because I'm still feeling anxious. I put music on for her and walk through the house opening more closets, the bathroom door, peeking behind the shower curtain, finding no one.

I walk over to my bedroom, but something in my peripheral vision catches my attention. Adelia's bedroom is across from mine and the door is cracked open, even though she didn't come into the house earlier. The thumping in my chest picks up as I tiptoe across the hall to peek through the crack, but I don't see anyone in her half-lit room. I inhale, straighten my back, push the door open with my foot, and take a few steps inside. The room looks the same as it's always been: a perfectly made bed, art prints framed on the wall, photo albums on a dresser, the window screen pushed up, leaving the window . . . open.

Fear squeezes my insides; my eyes flick to the mirror on the wall.

There's someone standing right behind me.

But I have no time to react, to scream, because the person moves forward and clamps a hand over my mouth. The contact sends a rush of cold skittering across my skin.

Then a whisper in my ear: "Don't be scared, it's me."

Derek.

He lets my mouth free and turns me toward him in a fluid motion. Our bodies are only inches apart. His fingers feel like lightning and ice and so strange on the small of my back. Like the touch could burn right through my shirt. He smiles but lifts a finger to his lips, says, "Shh."

Derek Johnson broke into my house and was in my sister's room and I'm silent. Shaken while he backs away from me and climbs out of her window into the night.

I'm breathing hard, so fast. There must be an imprint of his hand on my back, and my lips . . . I trace them with trembling fingers, feeling the ghost of his hands all over me.

My eyes dart around the room after I switch on her light. What was he looking for? Why was he here? Everything seems like it's in place until I notice something I hadn't seen in the dark: lying on her bed is a stem lined with what look like flowers.

But they are colorless. These flowers are gray. Lifeless as my dreamscape.

I hesitate before reaching for the stem. When I pick it up, a spark kisses my skin, the same feeling of Derek's hands on me. It sends me skidding back on the hardwood floor, stem still in hand. I wait for the feeling to settle, twist it one way, then another. And within seconds something happens that steals my breath: I watch it come to life in my hand.

Color seeps into the flower, purple and pink spreading through the banners and wings.

Wisteria.

EIGHT

Drip. Drip. Drip.

It's a steady sound. Louder than a leaky faucet, like sitting on the porch after a rainstorm while water drains from the gutter. It's coming from above me in the gray space and I imagine rain soaking my hair, making my shirt stick to my skin, but I can't feel anything, can't see it. Only can hear it. Same as the whispers, they're louder now, closer.

"Tell me," I say. My voice doesn't sound the same here, it's crackled like static on a phone call. The shadows are near, forming shapes, brushing by me. "Talk to me."

"Aria," they say. My name comes out in a low rumble of thunder; the sound of water falling gets louder. Goosebumps dance across my arms. "Aria."

"Aria, wake up." My heavy eyes open to Mom's voice. She's standing above me, shaking my shoulder. "You're going to be late for school." She tilts her head. "What were you dreaming about? Sounded like you were talking to someone."

My head hurts; this world is too bright, the sounds too loud.

There are still goosebumps on my skin. I close my eyes and lie to her. "It was a nightmare from murder TV."

"Hmm, maybe less of that before bed?" She smacks my arm lightly and sends another set of shivers through me. "Shake it off and get dressed. I'm leaving for work. See you tonight."

She walks out of the room and I reach for the wisteria stem on my nightstand. The purple is deeper today, small slices of yellow breaking through the center, and it doesn't smell sweet; it smells of damp grass. It smells of rain.

Derek's already on the pavement in the distance down the street when I step outside for the bus. While watching him go, my fingers find my lips again, memories of last night flooding my mind and making it hard to move. But I can't follow after him right away anyway.

Karina Wilson's doorbell makes the sound of a cow mooing and I know it's going to be stuck in my head the rest of the day. The worst part: She doesn't answer the door, and I wanted to ask her about her run-in with Derek before school.

By the time I make it up the street, winded from running, Derek's already getting on the bus. He turns back and looks me dead in the eye, then lets the doors close behind him.

I'll have to take the next bus.

I don't see him until lunch. He's in the line, picking his usual safe selection: cardboard-tasting pizza with an orange on the side, and

I cut everyone in line, ignoring it when they complain, just to get behind him. The shepherd's pie is the riskiest choice here, and that's the tray I grab. Derek looks down at me. There's a smile working on one side of his mouth, but he forces it away. I wasn't prepared for the space between my body and his to feel like a live wire.

I swallow, say, "We need to talk."

Derek picks up chocolate milk. Another safe choice. "Is that right?"

Cutting the line worked in my favor for more than one reason. "Yes. But first, can you please pass me the last strawberry carton?"

His eyebrows cinch together. "I guess," he says, then does. Someone behind me groans about my win, but I don't care. "What could you possibly want to talk about now?"

"You know what we need to talk about."

"Actually, I don't." He steps out of line and walks toward his lunch table.

I'm right beside him, walking extra fast to keep up with his big ole steps. "Don't play dumb. Last night . . ."

But Brianna's voice booms at me from behind. "Girl. Where were you?"

When I stop to look back at her it gives Derek a chance to put distance between us. He takes a seat with his large group of loud friends and Brianna mouths an apology. She didn't realize I was talking to Derek. She pulls me by the arm to our table while making me explain why I missed first period and what Derek and I were talking about.

We're alone at the table when I explain everything that's

happened. Brianna uses a notebook to block herself and catch peeks at Derek like she'll be able to see the strangeness on his face. "Maybe he was trying to steal something." She turns back to me, wiggles her brows. "Or maybe he has a crush on Adelia. She is perfect, after all. Do you think she has a girlfriend?"

"He was definitely searching for something," I say, using the plastic from Bri's sandwich to wrap the wisteria stem for safekeeping. "And your obsession with my sister needs to stop. I tried calling her three times this morning to ask if there's anything special hiding in her room and she texted me, *busy Aria, busy*. Do you really want to have a crush on someone like that?"

"She's dreamy," Bri says. "Especially when she doesn't let you bulldoze. Are you going to tell her about Derek?"

"I don't want to blow his cover yet," I say. "I just wanted a possible lead, but by the time I talk to her I'll have found out what he was looking for on my own."

"I bet you will," Bri says, and nods to the wisteria. "What are you going to do with that?"

"I don't know, but I think . . . maybe it's magic." After I say it, the corners of her mouth crinkle. I wonder if she believes me sometimes, or never at all. "If it's a spelled object, my grandfather should know."

"Too bad he'll never tell you," she says, and starts flipping through the flyer our guidance counselor gave me last period to find a job. "Aren't you supposed to be looking at these?"

"How can I worry about a job search at a time like this?"

"Do you have much of a choice?" She scans the pages. "What

about this desk job at Neighborhood Health Plan of RI. It'll look so good for your apps, and it seems easy enough."

"You sound like my mother," I say, adjusting the pearl clips I made for my hair. "And they'd probably put me by myself in a back room assorting files with no one to talk to."

"No one to examine, you mean." She shoots me a look. "You're not going to give up on working for your grandfather, even after your mom said she doesn't want you to, are you?"

I tuck the plastic-wrapped wisteria into my pocket. "I'll be able to make money to help my mom with the bills, put it on my college apps, investigate the Derek situation, and find out about myself. I had another dream last night. They feel like they're starting to . . . come alive."

Brianna's lips turn down; she runs her hand along the paper while I lay my head on the cafeteria table. From under my arm I could see Chris Somata and Macy Avery fighting over something. Nothing interesting there. They fight every day.

"Sit up," Brianna says, tugging on a strand of my hair. "I think I have an idea to get your grandfather to hire you."

"Hmm . . . Interesting, keep going."

"You have to make it clear to him you'll be a good worker and follow his rules. The rules that are specifically for *you*, *Aria*."

"I see where you're going with this," I groan. "But you know how hard it is for me to mind my business, *Bri*. I have an ugly little confession. Earlier, I asked our counselor what Derek was doing for college. She didn't tell me a thing, said I should ask him myself, but . . ."

"I'm surprised the guidance counselor still speaks to you

after all these years of harassment." Bri smiles. "Why are you worried about what Derek's doing for college?"

"Stop looking at me like that," I say, heat cutting across my cheeks. Brianna doesn't know that Derek and I planned to go out of state to college together, or at least to URI, to travel the summers and spend mornings watching the sun rise, to save each other seats in the crowded cafeteria and cook ramen noodles on a little electric stove before we studied because we were still hungry. It's already senior year and it's never felt like an impossibility the way it's starting to. "Anyway, there's no way I can mind my business the way my grandfather wants me to."

"You're a mess," she says before sliding a thick layer of lip gloss on. "I guess we can go back to looking for jobs. I saw one at a concession stand. You like to cook. How about being cramped in a tight space and slapping hot dogs on buns? I think you'd be perfect for the job."

"How do I get him to agree?"

She taps her fingers against the table and says, "A contract."

"Oh. I'm not going to like this one single bit."

NINE

After school, I take the bus straight to Lolo's. A customer walks out as soon as I make it up his steps. They look startled to see me, shove their brown paper bag under their arm, and avoid my gaze. But at least they leave the door open for me.

Lolo Zack is lining up glass jars that have purple-colored goo inside them. "My customer let you walk right in?" he asks without looking at me. "Making a mental note to charge him extra next time."

"Or you could charge him less seeing that I'm your darling granddaughter."

"Darling?" He laughs with his belly. "Falser words have never been said."

He walks over to the window and plucks a snail from the ledge. The snail is large, bigger than any I've ever seen, and its shell is iridescent: changing from a shimmering yellow to a purple as he shifts it in the light. Its slime drips down and lands on Lolo's shirt, but he doesn't seem to notice. He opens the top to one of the glass jars and places the snail inside. It should sink, but instead the snail glides over the goo slowly. And somehow the snail's shell seems smaller, like it shrunk to fit the size of the jar better in two seconds.

"What are you making with them?"

"Something like a cataract cure," Lolo says, sticking his tongue out at me. "Snail slime to supercharge the eyes." I bend low to look at the snail's shell, at the muted blue color of the slime pooling under it and sinking into the goo. "Clients say it's delectable if ingested. Care to try?"

"Absolutely not." I move away from the jars and touch the wrapped wisteria in my pocket. I won't show Lolo until he lets me work for him. Any sooner and he'll just take it from me. He goes to the sink to wash his hands, then starts to slice up a mango for me to eat.

"I have something to give you. Something important," I say. He looks suspicious but keeps slicing. I take the contract out of my pocket and open it up. "Are you ready to listen?"

He shrugs just one shoulder. "Not really, but you'll run your mouth regardless."

I roll my eyes, clear my throat, and begin to read. "This contract is for Zackary Cayetano from Aria Cayetano for the job position of assistant for the Cayetano business." I don't dare to look up from the paper to see his face. I read as fast as I can before he asks me to stop. "Aria Cayetano agrees to do any work necessary for the position in a timely, orderly fashion with the utmost care for Zackary Cayetano's workspace. Aria agrees to treat the customers with respect, dignity, and most of all, *privacy*. She agrees to mind her business and only get into matters that

Zackary Cayetano deems okay. She also agrees not to disclose any of the things seen or heard to anyone outside of said business. Failure to comply with these rules will result in permanent termination, possibly from the family. Attached is her cover letter and resume."

He's not amused; his face is expressionless when I finish. I lay the paper on the table in front of him. "If you agree, we can both sign here."

I point to the signature section at the bottom of the page where it reads:

Zackary Cayetano x _____ Date:

Aria Cayetano x _____ Date:

Lolo lifts his head from the paper to examine me but doesn't say a word so I keep speaking. "There's not much on my resume. I had that one job at McDonald's and worked a temp position at an ice cream shop last summer. But I think I'll be a hard worker, and my availability is pretty open after school and on weekends. I can even give you some refer . . ."

"Blue . . ."

My stomach clenches. "Don't answer right away if you're going to say no. Tell me tomorrow. But, Lolo, I want to be a part of this. I want to learn." He starts to shake his head and I rush to say, "I'm getting older and so are you. What if I need to make my own tea? Who's going to teach me?" A trick. A trick I didn't realize I had until the very second I said it.

A smile splits his face. "I'll be alive forever, Blue. Immortality juices flow through me."

I can't tell if he's lying. "Still, I should know myself. Please let me learn with you."

He takes a mango slice off the plate, chews it. "You'll wait till tomorrow for a *no*?"

"I'll wait because you have to think about it. You're going to think about it."

"Very well," he says, putting the plate of mangoes into my hand, "if you prefer to suffer in silence until the inevitable, that's fine with me."

"You're horrible," I say, but I'm satisfied while eating every mango slice on the plate.

Fate must be on my side because I don't have to hear Karina's doorbell moo again. She's already on her front porch when I get home.

"Got this from my daughter." She adjusts the sunflower crown on her head. "Cute, huh?"

"Extremely cute," I say, smiling. "I wanted to ask you something. About Derek."

She scrunches up her nose, then waves me up the steps to sit on the porch with her. She looks over at his house, then around the street like he's hiding somewhere, listening. Chills crawl their way up my back. "That boy." Karina shudders.

"Why are you upset with him?"

She clicks her tongue, looks at me like I'm silly. "Upset?

Scared is more like it. The other night, there were noises in my yard and I went to take a look, and when the back porch lights flicked on I noticed that boy was standing by my door waiting for me."

There is only so fast my heart can beat. I lean forward. "Waiting to say what?"

"It's not what he said, it's what he did." Karina wraps her arm around herself. "That boy ran a tree stem along the side of my face. I screamed because I thought it was a knife, but thank goodness it wasn't. After he ran the stem over my skin, he stared at it, then stared at me. I tried talking to him, but he just jumped off my porch and ran. And I heard he did something similar to old Felix who lives up the street. He's been creeping around everyone's yards. I don't know if he's bored or needs therapy, but his daddy asked me to leave it alone. Said Derek won't bother me anymore. All I know is I made my daughter set up a security cam yesterday."

I lied. My heart is erratic in my chest. Beating too fast to be healthy. I take a breath, try to slow it, then hold the wisteria stem up to Karina with a shaky hand. "Did it look like this?"

She takes it from me, stares at it for a while, but says, "Nah. It had no flowers at all."

Gray. My stem was gray-looking yesterday, but it still had flowers. "Are you sure?"

"Positive. He held it to my face, pulled back slowly. It didn't have any flowers."

"Was it this color?"

"I can't be sure, girl." Her brow furrows; she looks me up and down. "Why?"

"It's . . . ," I start, then shake my head. "I was just being nosy."

Karina narrows her eyes, then pats her thighs with both hands. "Don't tell me the two of you are in it together, playing stupid pranks on people like back in the day."

"We're not friends," I say, standing up, wishing we were. "Sorry for asking."

"You can't help yourself, never could." She shrugs. "Tell your momma she should set you up with a security cam too."

11:00 p.m.: Derek's out earlier today. He runs his hand over the skateboard propped against the side of the house, then squats low under his bedroom window. He's there a while, touching the soil, I think. His back is to me, but I imagine that's what he's doing.

11:05 p.m.: I dip my finger in the tea Mom brought me before she went to work and swirl it around. Derek has been motionless for three minutes and twenty seconds.

11:06 p.m.: Suddenly Derek stands, turns, and looks straight at my window.

My finger goes still inside the tea. I'm behind the curtain, but he can see me. I know it. I feel needles at the back of my neck. After a deep breath, I push open the curtain, stare back at him. Blood is rushing in my ears as he smiles. Derek Johnson broke into my house and was in my sister's room and now he's smiling at me. It feels like a challenge, a bet that I'll get creeped out and look away. But then he pulls out his phone and two things happen: 1. My phone vibrates on the windowsill. 2. I jump and spill the tea. It slides down the wall, splashes onto my socks, and stings my skin. Derek's eyes are locked on me when I pick up my phone. He's still smiling, and I've got two text messages.

I don't even know how he got my new number.

401-555-7988: *kinda creepy how you watch me, but cute too.*

I read the text three times, begin to type, then erase, type again, but my phone rings.

I stare at it for a few seconds before pressing it to my ear. "How'd you get my number?"

Derek waits. All I hear is breathing on the other end. Each breath brings a wave of chills to my bones. "Aria," he finally says. My name sounds like a song in his mouth. "Would you like to keep me company tonight?"

"Excuse me?" I laugh. "Is this a joke? I thought you wanted nothing to do with me."

He smiles, and I can hear it in his words. "You have no idea what I want, Aria."

I flush, the heat traveling from my neck to my cheeks, but I hold his gaze out the window. He's not flirting with me. He can't be. "I'd know if you told me."

"Maybe I will," he says. "You coming?"

"Is this because you don't want me to tell anyone you were in my sister's room?"

"What if it is?" Forty seconds. Forty-five. Neither of us seems to be breathing. "Wear something comfortable," he finally says before hanging up the phone.

TEN

There's one other rider on the bus and they're sitting all the way up front. Derek stretches his long legs across the back seat, and I curl up in the aisle seat next to him. I can't believe this is happening. Bri's not going to believe it when I tell her that I suggested Thayer Street because Derek's hungry and he couldn't think of anywhere to eat that was open in our neighborhood. For a while, there's only the sound of the engine, the clanks and rattling the bus makes as it stops and goes, but Derek starts to sing a song I don't recognize.

"What is that?" I ask him. "It's pretty."

Derek's eyebrows shoot together, he cracks a smile at me. "You don't know 'At Last' by Etta James?" I shake my head. His smile widens. "Shame. Music was at its prime in the '60s."

I lift an eyebrow. "You listen to '60s music?"

The bus jerks to a stop and the only other rider gets off. When I turn back to look at Derek, he has changed positions. He's only a few inches from me, staring intently. He doesn't answer my question, instead he says, "Has anyone ever told you your eyes are different?"

We're close enough to share the same breath, but I don't move away. Even though it's Derek, and he hasn't explained why he was in my sister's room, I don't want to scare him off. I also have no idea what he's talking about. "You mean, that my eyes are light brown with . . ."

"They're different." He cuts me off and leans closer. Our noses are nearly touching and I stop breathing. As he examines me, his own eyes seem to get darker before they widen like he sees something that surprises him. Then he sits back, eyebrows low, and air finds my lungs again. "Take a good look in the mirror when you get home," he says.

I laugh a little. Derek is truly acting strange, but mostly I'm just happy there's some distance between us again. "Okay. Now, let's talk about Adelia's room. And about what you were doing in Karina's backyard the other night too."

He doesn't ask how I know about Karina. "Maybe before the night is over," he says.

I cut him a look. "You know what, I'm not playing these games. I can just . . ."

"You won't tell anyone," he says. A command? A challenge?

My throat tightens. "What'd you do after Adelia's room? Did you go home?"

He shrugs, his face still dancing with something. "I went hunting," he says.

I tilt my head at him, my heart hammering. "Hunting?"

"Yes, you know. For prey." One second. Three. He grins. "I slept, Aria. Didn't you?"

The way he asks makes me shiver. I glance out the window,

thinking of the whispers in my dreamscape, everything that's been new since stopping the tea. And I think of the wisteria stem he left on my sister's bed. I wonder if he knows I know about it, if he's waiting for me to give it back to him, but I left it at home on purpose. Our stop is ahead; I stand and pull the cord.

He stands too, but then he grabs my arm to spin me toward him. It's a gentle hold, gentler than the other night, but his hand on my skin still feels like static.

"You'll have to trust me, Aria. Can you do that?"

I pull away from him. "Maybe. Guess we'll see before the night is over."

The corners of his lips turn up and he waves a hand at me to walk ahead of him.

⚘

Derek doesn't seem to remember how live Thayer Street can be at this hour. He stares at the people sitting on top of their cars, he makes faces at the Brown University students who cross the street without looking both ways. He's amazed by how many food choices there are, and I let him be amazed while I make mental notes. Derek was just skateboarding with his friends on Thayer a month ago. I know because Bri and I were eating Antonio's Pizza while he was here.

We decide on burritos from Baja's. When we were younger, Derek didn't care much for Mexican food. A fact that I constantly teased him about because what normal person doesn't like tacos? But today he orders three hard tacos on the side of his steak burrito. More mental notes.

It's narrow in Baja's. A one-person lane, and sometimes when you sit in the booth and someone walks by, you can feel their jacket brush up against your arm. But Derek wants to be in here instead of outside. He watches people while he eats, he watches me while I eat, and he savors his food like he's never eaten before. He even pops a finger into his mouth to lick the hot sauce off of it and hums while drinking his soda.

After, he looks at my quesadilla. "Going to eat all of that?"

"You're greedy," I say. "Order your own."

Derek laughs and passes me a napkin. "You have sour cream on your face."

I look in the mirror on the wall to wipe it off, and Derek grabs a napkin for himself. But the napkin in his hand floats down onto his plate when he looks into the mirror with me. He's so still, staring at himself with a curious expression. And then something changes. The light around us goes dark. Everyone in the restaurant behind us disappears. Everything goes to the gray. It is only me and Derek. His eyes are wide and so black they're startling. As black as the inky shadows that appear behind both of us. The shadows start to pull at my back, the same feeling in my dreams when gravity goes the wrong way, and then . . .

Tap. Tap. Tap. I blink, breathe deep, and break free of the mirror. Derek's tapping on the table. "You okay over there?"

The lighting is normal in the room; the colors have returned. Baja's is as busy as it was a few seconds ago. There are no shadows. Derek picks up his napkin.

My heart is running ragged. "I'm good," I say, then again, "I'm good."

He tilts his head. His eyes are still dark, but not like they were. "You don't look so good."

"Neither did you," I say, studying him too. "You didn't look so good in the mirror."

"Hmm," he says. "I feel fine."

"Do you really?"

I see the frown on his lips before he flips it. "I said I'm fine. Now, how about you tell me something about yourself. Something only your closest friend would know."

I want to push and ask him if he saw something in the mirror, but I'm still trying to figure out what it was I saw. The whispers, the spirit touching me, all of that has only happened in my dreams. Derek clears his throat, waiting for me to answer, but my mind is too foggy and my thoughts are thick. Everything feels sticky, and when I think of his question again, I find it odd. Why would *he* ask me something like that? But then, suddenly I'm sad that there's stuff he doesn't know about me after the years we'd spent together. If I did ask him about the mirror and he didn't see what I saw, would he think I'm being weird?

"Do you want to get out of here?" I ask. "We can walk and talk. I need some air."

"Some air sounds nice," he says, and stands to take both of our plates to the trash.

When I stand and he comes back, he slips his hand into mine.

I feel the lightning of his touch through my limbs as he pulls me through the crowd.

ELEVEN

My hand is still pins and needles minutes after he touched it. I'm not sure what it means that he held it several blocks. Or that I was overly conscious of how intimate it was. Or that it didn't feel like a normal touch. But I make mental notes of what I'll write in my journal tonight.

> *Reasons why Derek Johnson might be talking to me:*
> *–He doesn't want me to snitch about him breaking into Adelia's room.*
> *–He's playing games with my feelings because he's bored.*
> *–He's ready to forgive me.*

The last one brings hope to my heart and warmth to my belly. Even more so when he starts to whistle as he walks beside me and it feels so right to be here with him.

"Still waiting for that secret," he says.

I snort. "Now it has to be a secret?"

"It's always had to be a secret."

Here it goes. I breathe in deep, let it go. "I'm not sure I have many secrets you wouldn't know from . . . when we were friends," I say.

"Were." He repeats the word. "What a curious thing that we're not anymore."

Am I really ready for the conversation, or am I rushing it? Is he? "What's curious about it?" I ask. "You're the one who didn't want to be my friend anymore."

"That's right," is all he says before he starts to whistle again. Maybe he's not ready.

We walk through the streets of downtown, heading uphill, and I try to think of something stupid to tell him to distract from the tension between us. Thoughts of the mirror and the inky shadows rise up, and then it just comes out. "I . . . I've been seeing things." When he slows his pace and looks down at me, tilting his head slightly with a curious spark in his eyes, I'm back on the porch with Karina and she's telling me she's scared, I'm back in Adelia's room and there's someone behind me in the mirror. All of that fear was because of Derek.

"What kind of things?" he asks.

I walk faster to put a few steps between us. "I've been seeing shadows and . . ." We're almost at The View. I don't know if he remembers my dreams, but something stops me from mentioning them explicitly now. Suddenly I feel exposed. "Never mind. It's stupid."

A few seconds later, he says, "It's not stupid. I see them too." His voice is soft, wispy. It feels like his words are circling me, and my mind snaps back a couple of years to us talking about spirits.

Me sharing secrets with him about my family and my dreams while we were lying on his bedroom rug at night with a flashlight between us. Him saying he'll always believe me.

We finally make it to The View, and if I thought Derek looked amazed by Thayer Street, I wasn't prepared for how he seems stunned silent by this hilltop. I catalog his reactions while he walks over to the metal fence that separates us from a steep drop downhill. He stares out at Providence and the bright lights of its city buildings and I make mental notes of the ways he doesn't seem like himself. He's been here many times. We've been here together. Then I remind myself that I don't really know him anymore. How do I judge his strangeness if I don't have anything to compare it to? Lolo Zack always says it can take five minutes to fundamentally change a person. Derek has two years' worth of five-minute moments I know nothing about.

He grabs the spokes of the iron fence and tips his head to stare up at the moon. It's huge, almost full, and hovering near the state house. From up here we can see the markings more clearly, the tinged-orange glow. Its light reflects in the body of water below us and . . . Derek touches his face. Is he crying? Why would he be crying?

I reach to touch the statue of Roger Williams in front of us. "Remember when we learned he was once buried here?" I say, and Derek looks over at me. "We dared each other to climb in the tomb and see if he still was, but neither of us ever did. Something about old bones and buried things and wondering if he would curse us from the grave made us chickens, I think."

Derek laughs. "Or it made us smart. If a spirit lingers here it might come to get you."

My face goes hot. "Are you teasing me now?"

"Do I look like I'm teasing?"

"I can't tell anymore," I say.

He smiles. "I like that," he says.

"I bet you do."

He looks out at Providence again. "It's beautiful here, puts me in a mood."

"What kind of mood?"

"I want to dance," he says, then glances down at my face.

"Dance?"

He's amused. "Yeah, you know, two people, music, body movements . . . like the prom."

Heat flashes across my face. "I knew what you meant." I shift away from him, remembering our promise for prom. Last year he went with someone else. "Are you going this year? To prom, I mean."

"Only if you'll be my date," he says, smiling smoothly.

I snort, but my belly is warm again. "Stop teasing me."

"I'm not." He lifts a finger for me to wait, pulls out his phone, and puts on a song. "This is 'Unchained Melody' by the Righteous Brothers. You'd be wise to remember them," he says.

I'm the one smiling now. "Would I?"

He holds out a hand, bows his head. "Can I have this dance?"

"What?" I laugh. "You're . . ."

"I would never tease you about this," he cuts in. "I want to dance with you, Aria."

There are warning bells in my head, but my body doesn't listen to them. I put my hand in his and let him pull me against him. "Are you sure?" I say, a few seconds and moves too late.

We both vibrate with his laughter. "You're a particularly funny human."

"I hear that a lot, actually."

The melody is sweet, slow. Derek sways us, sings the words softly. I wonder if he can hear how fast my heart is beating while he uses his thumb to trace circles into the small of my back. He sends me in a spin, then pulls me close to him again.

We smile and laugh as we dance in the darkness.

Maybe I need to add one more note to the mental list: Maybe Derek is talking to me again because he realized he likes me.

No, no. That can't be it.

But when he reaches for my falling sleeve and his fingers graze my shoulder, we both take a sharp breath. He stops lifting my sleeve just as the song changes.

"Your scar," he says.

I close my eyes to the memory coming. Let it take over. We were thirteen and puberty pimples and always getting hurt by messes of our own making: playing with pincher bugs, roller-skating over broken beer bottles on the concrete. That summer, our neighbor started leaving her food orders outside for hours and yelling from inside every time a kid wandered near her driveway, so I wanted to investigate. "She might be keeping someone in her basement," I said. But Derek said she was probably just sad. I couldn't accept this. Derek spoke about sadness making his mother quiet before, but I never understood sadness the way he had.

We climbed our neighbor's fence, but her German shepherd was loose. It came running at us and I fell before hopping back over. The dog towered above me, and I made a move, but it lunged forward and its teeth clenched down on my shoulder. It was just a warning bite. I knew because it let me go quickly and barked for me to leave. Still, its teeth broke skin and there was blood and swelling and I was screaming. Derek was back at my side, hauling me out.

After the emergency room, with stitches in my shoulder, I begged my mom to make sure the shepherd wasn't going to be put to sleep. She said she'd do what she could, but she wasn't happy about it, or with me and Derek and our *dumb decisions*. So that night, I didn't climb through his window like I wanted, but I was happy when he knocked on mine. He sat with me on the bed, told me how scared he was, how he should've done more to help. His voice was shaking and he could barely look at me so I held his hand and lied that it didn't hurt. Derek asked if he could see it, then helped take off the bandage. After examining my stitches with a frown, he went over to my desk, grabbed a box cutter, and used it to tear at his own shoulder. As the blood began to pool, he looked at me and said, "Now we have matching tattoos."

And even though our parents would soon find out what happened and he'd need stitches same as me, it was the closest to someone else I'd ever felt.

When the memory leaves me and I open my eyes, Derek is still looking at my scar. I want to tell him I missed him, and I'm sorry for whatever I did that made him walk away from me. I almost do. Until he runs a finger over my jagged skin and says, "Where'd you get this?"

It's not just his burning touch, but his words that send a shiver through me. I pull back slightly and lift the sleeve myself. "I . . ." It's hard to get my own words out; they feel wrong to even think. "You know where I got it, Derek. You were there."

I want to mention our *tattoos*, but I wait to see his reaction.

He blinks and lets go of me. His eyes narrow as he examines my face, my body. I wrap my arms around myself, but he doesn't stop looking at me.

"You're so clumsy," he finally says. "Let's get you away from this fence before you find a way to fall to your death."

The way home is eerily quiet. I don't ask about Adelia again, and when we reach our houses, Derek uses two fingers and salutes a goodbye. I hurry inside, take deep breaths at the door, touch my shoulder. Derek Johnson has a self-inflicted scar to mirror mine, but he doesn't remember it. The dream I had about him the night the rosebush died comes to me and so does the look on his face in the mirror tonight, how black his eyes were. Before I can think anymore, try to connect the pieces, my phone vibrates with a notification. It's an Instagram request from him, and a few seconds later he tags me in his story with a picture of me looking out the bus window. I didn't realize he took it. My brown curls are floating above my shoulders and my bottom lip is poking out. My breathing slows as I stare at myself. Something stirs in my stomach. I look beautiful from this angle. From his view. But there's something wrong with me, and now there's no denying there's something wrong with him too.

TWELVE

Hello, the spirits whisper. *Hello.*

Their whispers are soft, sweet. I'm not scared. I can hear the direction they're coming from and while I walk toward them, the gray under my feet turns shades of green and brown before bouncing back to gray. The whispers get louder, clearer, but the farther I get, the harder it is to move. My feet grow heavy, each step weighed down until I can't move at all.

And then I hear something behind me. Not whispers, but screaming.

Suddenly I'm being swept backward. My hair rises as if it's caught in the wind, my limbs flail, my body doesn't belong to me. It belongs to this space. The world around me grows grayer, deeper, empty. Except when I stop moving, I realize . . . it's not.

I'm on semisolid ground again and I can hear them close enough to touch me. Spirits. Hundreds of them. Maybe thousands, crying, moaning, *hello, hello.* I turn and see a black hole, a spinning vortex suspended a few inches off the ground and at least a mile wide.

It moves and ripples and pulls shadows through the gray, but it no longer pulls me.

The spirits speak from inside its dark belly. *Help*, they say.

It's been three days since I danced with Derek. I wash my face with warm water and look in the bathroom mirror. My muscles have felt weak since I woke up. I'm still tired, and I can't stop hearing the sounds of spirits crying and calling out for help. But why? What was the black hole in my dream? Has it always been there? Has the tea been hiding it from me? Was it there that night when I looked in the mirror with Derek and his eyes were as dark as an abyss?

His eyes. *Take a good look in the mirror when you get home.*

Derek's words have been haunting me. I lean forward to get as close to the mirror as possible. But my eyes look as they always did. They're chestnut brown, amber in the sunlight, and there is still nothing strange about them.

From the living room, I can hear Mom in the kitchen. She's on the phone talking in a hushed tone, and something tells me to creep near the door to listen. Most of her words are too low for me to understand, but then she sighs and says, "Of course I trust you, Zack."

Why is Mom talking to Lolo?

"I'm just nervous she'll find out. I don't know much about your . . . world, and I don't want to know about it. But Aria, she . . . Yeah, yeah. You're right. Keeping her close is better."

Me. They're talking about me.

Mom whispers more things I can't hear, and then she says, "Okay. She can work for you."

The doorbell rings and I startle back and bump the end table near the door. Mom stops speaking, and I take quiet steps through the living room and into the hall. My throat is dry when I call out, "I'll get it."

"Oh, okay, baby," Mom calls back. "I didn't even know you were awake."

A spark of betrayal flickers in my chest. She didn't know I was awake, and I didn't know how involved she was with hiding things from me. And the worst of it: Lolo only wants me to work for him to keep me close, not because the contract made him want me around.

When I open the door, Brianna is standing on my porch with bubble gum–pink glasses propped on her head. She looks me up and down. "You told me to be here early so we could go to the mall and get an outfit for the party tonight." Damn. I forgot all about tonight. Bri's annoyed. "Did you even wipe the boogers from your eyes yet?"

After a shower, I throw on biker shorts, a T-shirt and a baggy flannel, then Brianna does two big cornrows in my hair.

Lolo texts my cell phone four words while I'm lacing my Vans. *You can start tomorrow.*

This is a good thing, I remind myself. Lolo thinks keeping me happy will keep me from knowledge, but he doesn't know I stopped taking the tea and he doesn't know that I know what his plan is. And aside from all that, I'm finally going to be working for him, which is what I've always wanted. Not in the way I wanted, but I'll take what I can get. *I knew you'd give in, old man*, I text back, bitterness still on my tongue so I'm glad he didn't call.

Before Bri and I leave the house, I pack us a lunch that we can eat on the steps outside of Providence Place mall. She opens up her Tupperware container and brings it to her nose.

"Yum. I'm so happy food is your love language," she says. "How did I get so lucky?"

"I'm the lucky one," I tell her. "You helped me with the contract. You're brilliant."

"I am, aren't I?"

We're ready to go, but when we step on the porch we see Derek and his skater friends riding up and down the street and doing tricks off the sidewalk.

"Wait," I whisper to her. "Can we sit here a minute?"

She looks from me to Derek and sighs. "You mean, can we be stalkers for a while?"

"We are not going to be stalkers. We are just watching the entertainment."

"Tell me what's entertaining about watching *boys*," she gags, "skateboard."

I sit on the porch and look up at her. "So . . . we love the sunshine, right? We love the sound of cars passing on the street."

She starts to smile and sits down beside me. "True. And?"

"And I enjoy people watching, and you enjoy doing it with me sometimes, yeah?"

"Um . . . I guess."

"Well, right now, all of those things apply. Especially the people watching."

"The Derek watching," she clarifies, "while he's being goofy with his skater friends and his perfectly nice booty is jiggling for your enjoyment."

"You're gross," I say. "I just want to keep an eye on him. Find out what he's hiding."

"Okay, Harriet the Spy. But I'm pretty sure he'll notice you noticing him from here."

I haven't told her about the other night and how he didn't remember my scar. She'd probably say it's not a big deal, and she'd be more interested in how I felt when we were dancing, but I'm not sure how I felt when we were dancing. Warmth spreads through my chest at the memory of our bodies pressed close, his hand on my back, us smiling. Oh. That. I felt that.

"Oh shit," Brianna says, snapping me out of the memory and pointing to one of the boys who fell off the skateboard. We watch as Derek jogs over and bends to help his friend, but after we realize his friend is good we see that Derek isn't. His shoulders start to twitch. I stand on instinct to see better. Derek lowers his head as the twitching makes its way up his neck. "What the hell?" I can hear Brianna saying while Derek's limbs jitter.

His friends call his name, and one of them finally walks over and pats Derek's back. A few seconds later, he stops twitching and I start breathing. But when he lifts his head, his eyes catch mine. We stare at each other for just a moment before he drops his skateboard to the ground and walks straight over to us.

Derek blocks out the sun. We're at eye level because I'm standing on the steps; he doesn't even look at Brianna. "Are you serious, Aria?" he says. There's a heaviness under his eyes that wasn't there the last time we were this close. "Why are you always watching me?"

"Awkward," Brianna whispers.

We were just together three nights ago, and he's acting like this? I shake my head. "So you're back to being rude now? Wishy-washy because your friends are here?"

His eyebrows dip down. "What are you talking about?" His voice is hoarse, tired.

I soften at the sound. "Derek, are you okay?"

His jaw clenches. For a second, there is no one and nothing around us. It's just the two of us, and he tells me that he's not okay. I can see it in his eyes. But then he flicks his tongue over his bottom lip and looks away. "I need you to stay away from me. Please, Aria."

"I won't," I say. "I know something is wrong with you. You can talk to me."

Derek runs a hand over his face, then pivots on one leg and begins to walk away, but I reach out and grab his arm. A strong static shock pulls us apart. He looks down at where I touched him. I look at my hand, then back up at him. The lines of his face go rigid, and I know he's about to say something that will hurt before he does. "You don't know anything about anything. You didn't two years ago, and you still don't. We're done here. Stay away from me."

His words sting my heart. I reach for Bri's hand, pull her up, then give Derek a sharp look. "I'll stay away, but don't ever call me up at night to keep you company again."

Confusion flashes across his face, but I walk down the stairs with Bri and push past him before he can say another word.

THIRTEEN

We are seventeen and according to Bri we're supposed to party. But at this particular party, while blunts are being passed around the room and people are drinking shots with no chasers, I'm playing a version of *whodunit* in my mind. Is Adrianna still sleeping with Angel behind her cousin's back? Does Corey really do drugs with college kids? If I don't think of these things, then I'll think of the rosebush and my dreams and Derek telling me to stay away from him after what happened between us.

"Stop being a weirdo." Bri leans against me. "Can't you pretend to have fun?"

"For a little while," I say, tearing my eyes away from Corey. "And only for you."

But then a wave of kids comes through the door and they're so loud, bumping into everyone else, screaming ridiculous things. Gross Gary from our school is among them and he slings his arm around someone else and pulls that person inside the house.

The person is Derek, and seeing him here shocks me. Derek doesn't ever come to these kinds of parties; Derek doesn't ever hang out with Gross Gary and his gang of creeps.

I blink a billion times but he's still here, wearing a leather jacket and his long hair braided into two rows. There's a magnet connecting us; I know because he notices me staring at him from across the room before he notices anyone else. He gives me the same inviting smile he gave me the other night on the bus, and I shift away from his view.

"Damn," Brianna says. "Derek didn't look that fine this morning."

She's not lying, but I roll my eyes and whisper, "What is he even doing here?"

Brianna doesn't know how to whisper. "Looks like Gary got his grimy little hands on him." She nods toward the door. "The new kid Sean too."

My gaze flicks to the group again. Sean is sitting on the arm of the couch talking to a girl. "But isn't he Gary's cousin? That makes sense. Derek doesn't. He wouldn't hang out with someone like Gary willingly."

Gross Gary got his nickname because of the way he harasses girls for sex. Word in school is that Sean moved here from Texas over the summer. He might not know the truth about his cousin yet. But sophomore year, Derek let it be known how disgusted he was with Gary.

"The old Derek might not have. You don't know him anymore," she reminds me, then gives him another approving once-over. "Still, I truly can't believe you slept in that boy's bed and never made a move."

"You're ridiculous," I say. "You should make a move."

"Fortunately for me, I only like the superior species," she

says, then grabs my hand and squeezes. "And anyway, after what happened on the porch he's ugly in the heart."

"You're saying that to make me feel better."

"And I'll do it every time." She kisses my cheek and looks toward the kitchen. She begged me to be here because she was supposed to meet up with a girl she's been talking to from Central and wanted me as a wingwoman, but she hasn't exchanged two words with the girl yet.

"Yo." Some kid peeks his head into the living room. "We're playing spin the bottle, or was it seven minutes in heaven? I don't know, but if you're down, come to the kitchen."

"This isn't the '90s," someone calls out.

But Bri smiles, says, "This is my chance," and drags me behind her toward the kitchen.

"Or you can just . . . talk to her."

"I'm not listening to you, Aria Cayetano."

I've only ever played spin the bottle once in the seventh grade when Luis Price begged me not to tell anyone he was too scared to kiss me, and I'm dreading another incident like that. I lean in to whisper, "Aren't we too old for this?"

But Brianna isn't the only one who hears me. Twenty of us are gathered around the kitchen island, and one of them is Kiara Dion, who's hated me since the third grade for unknown reasons. "Don't be boring," she says, running her hand over the rim of her glass. "I know that'll be hard for you, Aria, but try hard."

"Yeah, Aria," Bri says, "let's be good sports. Kiara desperately needs this game since it's the only way she'll get some action."

Kiara and her friends cut glares in our direction, but the girl from Central who Bri is talking to smiles from across the circle. I look around at everyone else and my eyes find Derek's again. Right now, in this light, they look so dark. They bring me back to the sounds of spirits crying from inside the black abyss and I shiver. He doesn't stop staring at me when I look away. I can feel his gaze when the kid who presented the game says the rules go like this: Spin the bottle, but the couple has to go upstairs together and can't come out of the bedroom without a confirmation make-out video sent to his Snapchat.

"That's perverted," I say, and everyone laughs.

Sean gives me a small smile and says, "She's right. No evidence necessary."

The idea of a confirmation video is squashed right then, but there's still making out to be had. Sean is looking at me and so is Derek. One on my right, one on my left, both of my cheeks are on fire. I hope when I spin the bottle it lands on Brianna. I'm usually lucky with scratch tickets, guessing on tests, betting on who murdered the victim on crime TV. Pretty sure if I focus hard enough, I'll wind up with her and this will be easy. But Derek's turn is before mine and when he spins the bottle it lands on me—unlocking the most unlikely scenario.

While the knots in my stomach are getting tighter, Bri leans over and whispers, "You good with this? I'll make a big scene to stop the game if I have to."

I don't say anything, just wait for Derek to shake his head and walk out of the room or say he's going to spin the bottle again, but none of it happens. He only looks at me expectantly.

"I think this game is stupid," I say in my own effort to get out of it.

But then Derek, my ex–best friend who just told me to stay away from him, tilts his head and asks, "You scared?"

Laughter breaks through the room. They're all childish, but I don't care. Of course I'm scared. This is kissing, and this is Derek. But he doesn't look scared or upset, he looks entertained. He's definitely messing with me, and I refuse to be the one to back down in front of all these people. "Wished for someone else," I say, "but I'm not scared."

One time I was dared to jump into the water at Conimicut Point Beach when it was forty degrees and dark out. I left with fifty bucks and the experience of feeling like my heart stopped. I tell myself this is nothing compared to that, but I'm still shaking on the inside.

Brianna squeezes my hand right before I follow Derek out of the kitchen. My hypothalamus sends messages to my nervous and endocrine systems to be on alert as I walk into the hall and up the steps behind him. But when I reach the landing upstairs and Derek opens the bedroom door to our left, I hold his gaze before pushing past him to head inside first.

FOURTEEN

The door clicks shut behind Derek and he locks it too.

One second. Four. It's hard to find my voice, but I'm the first to speak. "The other day you wanted to dance with me, this morning you ordered me to stay away, now you want to kiss me? I'm getting dizzy with your hot and cold, Derek. What happened to *We're done here?*"

His eyes rake over my body, up then down, up again. I refuse to look fazed, even when he laughs. "I never said I want to kiss you. We played a game, remember?"

There's a patch on my pant leg; I run my fingers along the edges and he tracks the movement. "So this is for show, then? You want everyone to think you're cool?"

His face scrunches up as he moves toward me in a rush. There are only inches between us, and he bends his head lower and makes it hard for me to breathe. I can smell mint on his mouth. He lifts his hand and brushes his thumb over my lip. The top, then the bottom, lingering there, stroking softly until every part of me catches fire.

It's maddening the way my body bends to be closer.

"Just do it already," I manage to say.

He trails his thumb down my chin, grips it. "Aria." The way he says my name, like it's foreign on his tongue, sends goosebumps over my skin. His mouth is hovering just above mine. I can't think, I can't move. "You're in my way," he says.

But he pins me in place with his arm, and I hear the latch click on the window behind me. My body is buzzing, my brain a jumbled mess. I push him away and put distance between us.

He laughs an irritating laugh and opens the window.

"What the hell was that?" I ask, and Derek doesn't even acknowledge it. He lifts the window screen to stick his head out. When he straightens up and puts one leg through it, I almost choke. "What . . . What are you doing?"

"Trying to be cool," he says, before he climbs out the window onto the roof.

My phone buzzes in my pocket, but Derek pops his head back in. "You coming?"

"Where?"

"Somewhere special," he says. "Somewhere that'll answer both of our questions."

"I told you I'm not keeping you company again," I say. "And I don't trust you."

"You wound me for no reason." He puts a hand over his heart. "But we both know you can't resist. And I'll do more than tell you why I was in your sister's room. I'll show you."

Lolo's favorite saying rings in my ears: *Your curiosity will get you in trouble one day, Blue.* But I don't know another way to be.

I shoot Bri a quick text and follow Derek onto the overhanging roof. It's sturdy, but it slopes downward and my feet don't feel steady.

"We could've just used the front door," I tell him.

"And risk having your friend follow us?" He slides himself down the rooftop, turns around and lowers himself off the overhang. When I can't see him anymore, my stomach drops, but then I hear a thud when his feet hit the ground.

"Come down," he says. "I'll catch you."

There was a time I'd believe he could break my fall, but that was a Derek I could trust. I slide down enough to see the edge and the ground below. Derek is standing down there, adjusting his leather jacket. The grounded heels of my feet are the only thing keeping me from falling forward. I'm not scared of jumping, I'm scared of following Derek again only for him to disappoint me tomorrow. But there's only one way to find out.

"I don't need you to catch me," I say.

Derek laughs, stepping back so I can see him better now. There's an amused smile on his face; he raises his hands in the air. "Okay. If you fall and break your face, I'm not to blame."

I hate him. I'll tell him that after I land. I turn and catch the ledge and try to lower myself down, but my arms feel like they're going to break. I let go and the fall steals my air and pain shoots from my feet to my thighs. But my knees don't buckle, and I don't lose my footing because Derek's arms are around me. "You good, Bluebird?"

I push away from him. "I told you I didn't need you to catch me."

He ignores me and reaches for my hand just like that night. "Let's go get our answers."

The bus we're on is the same bus that leads us back home. I ask where we're going, but Derek keeps saying it's a surprise. "You're more than welcome to pull the stop cord and leave. I'm not keeping you here."

He's not. That pulling feeling in my stomach is. He's a magnet and I'm being sucked in.

I touch my fingers to my lips involuntarily, turn my face when he catches it.

The past twenty minutes replays in my mind till I hit a snag and tilt my head at him, narrow my eyes. "Did you call me Bluebird?"

He kicks his feet onto the seat in front of him, leans back. "I did."

"Why?"

He shrugs, his voice low and steady when he says, "You looked like a little bird up on that roof. You look like one in my mind too." It doesn't sound like he's insulting me. I briefly wonder if he remembers Lolo's nickname for me before he leans in to graze his pointer finger down my wrist and makes all of my thoughts fall away. "I take back what was said this morning." The corners of his mouth twitch. "Lately, I haven't been feeling like myself, but I don't want you to leave me alone."

He can hear my heart beating from where he sits, even with the bus making loud noises and the other people talking, I know it. My phone rings again, breaking the contact between us, allowing me time to regulate my breathing. I stare until it stops. This is the third missed call from Bri. There are fourteen text messages. I can feel Derek staring at me while I read them. They range from *You better not be doing nasty things outdoors* to *please pick up*. Derek stands and pulls the stop cord, and I, with the quickest fingers, text Brianna to tell her *I'm okay, I'll call soon*.

Derek doesn't look back to see if I'm following, but he does wait for me on the sidewalk. We're on Plainfield Street. Our houses are around the corner, but he leads us toward Neutaconkanut Park. Memories suffocate me as we move through it: sledding with Derek down these hills in the winter, running through the baseball field before games and getting yelled at by the coaches, jumping from one bleacher seat to the next to avoid lava.

We've taken the path up the hill that we're standing in front of now countless times. But there are things I know I'm not supposed to be doing and one of them is going into the dark forest. Bodies get buried in the forest at this hour. And there's something wrong with Derek. I know he wouldn't hurt me, but what answers can he give me here?

He grabs my hand, causing a burning cold to rush through my bones. "There's something up there you need to see," he says. "There's something I need to show you. It's safe. I promise."

"No more games?"

A row of white teeth flash when he smiles. "Cross my heart and hope to die."

The path is stone and the climb is steep. Derek uses the flashlight on his phone so we can see where we're going and he keeps asking if I'm okay. I hate it. I want to tell him I'm brave, that being under the dense canopy of trees in the dark doesn't scare me. I want to tell him during the years he's spent avoiding me I've jumped in waters darker than this. But the tree branches reach for one another like fingers, leaving only small slits of space for moonlight to break through. And everything about being in the forest right now makes the back of my neck prickle.

At the end of the path, we walk the stone steps that lead to a clearing. It's brighter when we break through the canopy. From this elevation we can see Providence, much higher than at The View, but Derek doesn't stop to look. He pulls me toward a marked trail and says, "How much do you trust me now, Bluebird?"

My mouth is dry. "The smallest fraction," I say.

"That's all I need."

As soon as we step onto the dirt trail, we're swallowed by darkness. I can hardly see my feet in front of me, so I keep close to Derek until he comes to a stop.

Between two big trees, something glows in the distance.

There's a snap, a click, a lock opening: Seeing it unlocks a door inside of me. My heart slows to a steady beat, my vision sharpens, I'm not scared anymore. My limbs pull me toward the glow like I'm in the gray and I don't fight it.

I step in front of Derek to be the first to walk through the trees. Twigs scrape against my legs, leaves catch in my hair, beetles click close by, but I keep moving.

When I make it to another small clearing, the air leaves my lungs. I stop short, the world spinning, Derek right behind me. He presses his body into my back, one hand snakes around my belly, and he leans in to whisper, "Do you see them?"

"I see them," I breathe.

Wisteria trees. So many wisteria trees twining together in the middle of this circular space, branching out in different directions, blooming with pink, blue, purple flowers. They are bright, glowing things in the dark, filling the air with a sweet fragrance. It's potent enough to swarm my senses and force my eyes closed. The light is warm behind my eyelids.

I lean into Derek and welcome the cold of his touch before looking again.

My face is wet; I'm crying and I don't know why.

Derek wipes my tears from behind. His fingers feel like tiny needles pressing into my cheeks, but right now I welcome that too. "I knew you'd see them," he says.

I open my mouth to ask him a thousand things, but then a group of moths in the trees unfurl their wings and fly around us. One flutters, lands on Derek's hand, its hind wing centimeters from my face. I hold my breath as he holds out his hands in front of me. That's when I notice they aren't moths. They're butterflies. Swallowtails with glowing green wings, bioluminescent the same as jellyfish or fireflies.

Derek backs away and walks around me to raise his arms in the air. A dozen swallowtails land on him like he's the light.

The sight burns into my brain and I know it'll be a memory for my deathbed.

I watch him walk toward the wisteria, and the butterflies remain in his hair, on his shirt, on the back of his neck. When he steps under a tree, they finally beat their wings and scatter off to find space on the branches.

Green swallowtails aren't common here. Butterflies sleep at night. None of this is normal.

The flowers brush the top of Derek's head. He reaches out to touch a branch and an image of him snapping off a stem and carrying it with him flashes across my mind. The stem he left on my sister's bed is between the pages of a book in my bedroom right now.

Before I can mention it, he says, "They've been growing for weeks."

"Weeks?" My feet move. One. The other. "This is a decade's worth of growth. Wisteria trees don't grow here. All the different colors. And the butterflies . . . This . . They're not . . ."

There's a strange look on his face. His mouth turns downward. "You're right. The wisteria aren't ordinary. But they grow here now and always will." His lips rise a little. "Except, not everyone can see them."

We are quiet for a moment. The wind moves and sends the leaves on the trees swaying toward me, a hook to pull me closer. I find myself under the tree with him, but I'm careful not to touch anything. The question is on the tip of my tongue. Why me? Why can I see them?

Derek responds like I've asked out loud. "Bluebird," he breathes, and it feels like that breath is in sync with mine. "You're special, and I need you to know."

My chest rises and falls.

He places one hand flat against the tree and brings the other to my cheek.

The touch is slight and still I burn.

My fingertips, my arms, up and down my legs, across my chest. The backs of my eyes sting while all the color leeches from the flowers above my head. The butterflies are no longer blinking in the branches. Everything around us goes gray.

We are under a lifeless wisteria tree and I am not dreaming.

"Tell me what you see," Derek says, but the color starts to seep from his face too.

The whites of his eyes go black at the same time as the abyss gathers behind him. His hand begins to shake. I can feel his fear seeping through my skin, simmering there, as the shadows slink out from the abyss and form ribbons around his wrist.

"What do you see, Bluebird?" He sounds nothing like himself.

Shadows wrap around his chest, crawl from his shoulders to his chin, darken his face. They tug him backward and tug me with him. Panic rises in my throat; I try to escape but can't break loose. Then my mind snaps to the pull I felt when the rosebush crumpled, how the spell was broken by being cut with a thorn.

I bite down on my cheek until the taste of copper fills my mouth and use the pain to pull away from Derek, stumbling backward and breaking the gray around us.

We're back in our world in an instant. With colorful glowing flowers over our heads and moonlight cutting through the branches and life beneath my feet. Swallowtails flutter all around us. Derek's eyes are no longer black and my breathing begins to slow, my heart tries to catch a steady rhythm.

But then the shadows slowly spill from the sky behind him, slithering down the trees, rising from the dirt. Our sky, our trees, our dirt. Not a dream. Not a vision of the gray.

Derek opens his mouth and says something, but I can't hear him.

He reaches for me and suddenly the shadows disappear.

"Aria," he whispers. His eyes are wide, he sounds scared.

But I turn and I run.

FIFTEEN

The burning in my lungs is the only thing that slows me down with my house up ahead. I push through the pain but can't ignore the tricks being played on my peripherals. Shadows are reflecting in the windows of houses, darkening the streetlights, crawling out from under cars. What I saw in the park is making my world feel distorted.

I grip my porch railing, pull myself up the stairs two by two, but I'm not quick enough. A feeling pricks from the base of my spine and I turn just enough to see Derek coming toward me in the distance. I stumble with my keys, drop them on the porch, curse out loud.

He's getting closer. What does he want from me? He's . . .

My front door opens. "Where the hell have you been?" my mom says. "I've called you twice. Sent an SOS text and everything."

I snatch my keys off the floor and push my way inside, pulling her through the door and locking it shut behind us. She's still talking when I walk over to the window and peek out. "What are you doing? Why are you breathing so heavy? Were you with a boy?"

Derek sits on his front steps and stares at my house. It feels like he's staring through me, into dark corners of my soul and calling to the spirits.

I duck away, lean against the wall, and cough some air into my lungs.

"Aria!" My eyes snap up to Mom's face just as the alarm goes off on her phone and surprises us both. She frowns, and I'm shaking but she can't see it. "Please tell me you're okay, Aria. There's an emergency at work. Not only did two people call out, but my regular client Billy fell and he won't let anyone else take care of him. I really have to get going."

I don't know if I'm okay, but she needs me to be. I nod and let her give me a hug, but part of me hopes she'll feel me tremble and change her mind, leave work for someone else and be with me. She pulls back. "I love you," she tells me. "We'll talk later, but you better stay home for the rest of the night. You hear me?"

"I'm not going anywhere," I say.

⁓⸒⸜⸝⸒⁓

Brianna says she wishes she could come over, but as soon as she got home from the party her parents put her on lockdown because they smelled beer on her breath. She said she only had one because she spent most of the night in a corner talking with Val from Central.

"Tell me exactly what happened to you. Be extremely exact this time," she says. We're FaceTiming and she has her phone propped up on her desk. She removes the topknot from her hair and throws on the furry pajamas she loves to wear even in the summer. I'm in the empty bathtub with the cold ceramic pressed against my skin, grounding myself the way my big sister taught me how. Adelia was my first call, but she didn't pick up. I'm trying to figure out what happened so I can explain it better to Bri because none of my words feel like enough.

She sprawls out on her bed. "Sooooo . . . he almost kissed you."

"No, he didn't," I say. "And that's not what we're focusing on."

"Right." Bri picks at her nails. "The spirit world. You sure you saw them in the park? Maybe you're drunk? Or maybe Derek tried to kiss you and you freaked out and ran?"

My mouth still tastes like metal from biting my cheek. I glance at the steam rising from the teacup on the sink. "Do you really believe that? Do you think I'm lying?"

"Hey." She softens her voice and picks up the phone so we're at eye level. "I don't think you're lying, but we were partying, it was dark out, maybe they weren't even wisteria. Also, there's the very real possibility that the butterflies you saw were actually moths."

"I know the difference," I say. "My grandfather raises both."

"Okay." Bri sighs. "All I'm saying is I'd probably feel a little weird if my ex–best friend turned enemy tried to kiss me. Especially if I were you and had a hard time being intimate with people for real. When it's not a game of truth or dare or spin the bottle."

"I didn't drink at all, there were definitely wisteria and

butterflies, and I don't have a hard time being intimate with people," I say. "I just won't do it unless I feel serious things for them."

I hate that I'm defending myself when all I can think about
is the way the world changed around Derek. How different he
was acting.

"Hmm," Bri says. "Well, you'll never feel serious things for
anyone if you aren't open to it." My head is pounding now. I let
her talk because I won't be able to convince her about the wisteria. She doesn't dream about spirits, she can't see them, but I can
show her the trees tomorrow and she'll know.

"I don't know what's happening," I say out loud. Thinking
of going to show her the wisteria makes me shiver.

She tucks her hand under her chin and puckers her lips at me.
"What's happening is Derek likes you."

In my mind, I tell her to stop and listen to the facts: Derek
has been acting strange. He suddenly wants me around after
ignoring me for two years. He left a wisteria stem in my sister's
room. My neighbor said he touched her with a stem too. And
he was in the gray space with me; I saw it. Guilt makes my heart
heavy. He sounded scared tonight. But I won't say any of this
again because I don't have the energy.

She laughs to herself. "Trying to imagine you running away
from him with your bowlegged self."

"I'm hanging up now," I say.

"Wait, wait, did I mention how dreamy Val is?" She's slurring now, half asleep.

"I'm happy for you, Bri," I say, "but it sounds like you should
be dreaming right now."

"You're right." She blows me a kiss. "Love you, and I promise to be a better listener tomorrow, okay?"

"Yeah," I say, trying to push down my bitterness. "Get some sleep."

"You too, darling."

My body aches from the whole night when I crawl out of the bathtub. My brain aches from the whole week. But what I saw in the forest was real. I don't know what that means for me or Derek, but it had to be real. I grab the teacup and count down from ten. I'll take the tea again; I'll take it if it means I won't see spirits in the world. If I can go back to knowing they're in my dream and there's a barrier between us.

Five. Four. Three. Two. One.

I bring the cup to my mouth to take a sip, but something catches my attention in the bathroom mirror. I lean closer, a little closer. The bus ride with Derek flashes in my mind. Suddenly the teacup is as heavy as an anchor.

My eyes are still brown, but the irises are stained with small strips of color like the glass of a church window. The flecks of blue burn brighter than the rest.

PART TWO

LITTLE RED HERRING

SIXTEEN

"You never miss church," Mom says, clapping her hand over my forehead. I'm in bed but didn't sleep last night. Too preoccupied with trying to dissect what happened at the park to find out what it's like in the gray space now. If it has changed. "You sure you're not sick?"

"Do I look sick?" I'm not being sarcastic; I wonder if she sees the color in my irises.

"You look a little silly." She smiles. "Why do you keep opening your eyes so wide?"

"You don't see anything strange about them?" I won't give myself away. If I tell her what happened she'll make me drink the tea again. But I have to ask somehow.

She squints. "Are you getting pink eye? It's been ages, but I hope not."

"I'm fine," I tell her. "I just don't feel like going to church today." Not with Derek there.

"But you still want to go to work with your grandfather later?"

"It's my first day. Can't give Zackary Cayetano something to complain about already."

She stands and smooths over her church skirt. "Alright, but be careful, Aria. Don't play with the poisons, listen to everything he says, and you're not allowed to bring home animals."

"This lecture couldn't wait? I won't be seeing you again before I go then, huh?"

"No, but I promise to take a day off of work soon so we can spend it together." She nods at the teacup on my nightstand. "Is the new batch your lolo made as good as the last?"

"It tastes a little better," I lie. I haven't had a single sip. "I love you."

When she leaves for church I make a mental list of things I have to do today: meet up with Bri to go to Neutaconkanut Park, work for Lolo, avoid Derek at all costs, be brave.

⁂

As soon as we step into the park my body knows it. The joints between my bones ache for me to move toward the hill. The wisteria trees are calling me. I'm sweating before Brianna and I head up the stone path. But I'm not as scared as I thought I'd be. I need to see them. I need to show Bri so I can have someone else to talk to about all of this. Earlier, we sat in the sunlight and she spent six minutes trying to see the different colors in my eyes, but she said they just looked like pools of honey. Maybe she'll be able to see them once she sees the wisteria trees. And I can't go another day without trying to figure out why they're here and why Derek wanted me to know. Whatever he did to me last

night changed something inside of me. No, I was already changing after I stopped drinking the tea, whatever Derek did to me
just helped it along.

Did he see the shadows swarming between us when the world
lost its color? Did he see them when they were still in our
world after? Does he know why I ran?

Bri clicks her tongue. "The effort this is taking is despicable.
Never drinking again."

"Appropriate," I say. "Especially for you."

But climbing to the top of the hill takes a lot of effort for
me today too, and the heat isn't helping. I'm sweating in places
I wish wouldn't sweat and my thighs are chafing together where
my shorts cut off. Once we reach the top and start on the dirt
trail, I don't know where to go or which trees Derek and I walked
between. But then I stop and concentrate on that buzzing in my
bones. It gets deeper as I do, and the hairs rise on my arms before
I lead Brianna between two big trees and through a narrow path.
We weave and duck fallen branches and wince as they scrape
at our legs. But the sweet smell starts to fill my nose the closer
we get. Brianna doesn't smell anything. Not even when I step
through the last of the birch trees and into the clearing.

"Look," I manage to say over the pounding of my heart.
"Look at them."

In the daylight the purple and pink flowers are at peak
beauty, and the blue flowers are a breathtaking shade of turquoise. Branches stretch and sweep the floor to touch the other
trees in the forest. I'm careful not to walk on them. The swallowtails are sleeping during the day, hanging upside down beneath

branches. And even though the glow of the wisteria has faded to a shimmer in the sunlight, there's no way anyone can say they're normal.

But then, from behind me, Bri says, "I can't see anything."

"What?" I spin around, thinking she's kidding, but she's looking at me like I've lost it.

"There's not a single wisteria tree here. It's just grass." A wave of sickness unsettles my stomach. She scratches one of her brows. "Aria, I . . . have to go do homework."

"Wait, you really don't see anything?" She has to. I need her to see them.

She's already backing away from the trees, from me. "I don't see anything, and I'd humor you, but I just can't. Maybe you should tell your mom what's going on. She can . . ."

My eyes burn with tears, I blink them back and swallow the saliva gathering in my throat. "Bring me to a hospital or something? I thought you believed me."

"I wanted to," she says. "But there's nothing here. Just like there's nothing different about your eyes. I'm tired, Aria. My feet hurt, I'm thirsty. I'm going home. Let's go home."

Last night resurfaces in my mind. I hope she can't hear the tremble in my voice. "Derek said not everyone can see them. Maybe I can see them because . . ." I trail off. She's still looking at me like my brain needs to be scanned. "Forget it. Sorry for bringing you out here."

She tries for a smile, and I can tell she feels bad when she says, "No, it's okay. Maybe this isn't the right area? Maybe they were white oak trees or something and you got confused? Or maybe you are just spiritualizing your refusal to give in to your feelings for Derek."

Oh. "Yeah. Maybe I just need some sleep," I say, and take one last look at the wisteria branch and the butterflies hanging over my head before following her back to the path we made.

SEVENTEEN

Lolo's house has transformed over the course of a few days. The door is unlocked and when I walk in, a sour smell smacks me in the face. There are strings of garlic hanging from the living room ceiling, but the smell of something festering is coming from the kitchen.

"Lock the door behind you," Lolo calls out. "The gnomes might follow you inside."

I lock the door and look out the window. All the gnomes are still in their places.

Lolo's by the kitchen sink. I feel at ease seeing him do magic work after what happened with Bri. "Trying to ward off a vampire with garlic?" I ask. "And what is that awful smell?"

Lolo's kitchen is filled with milk crates, stacked high to the ceiling. His table is unrecognizable. There isn't an inch that's uncovered by bottles, ointments, dead beetles in plastic cups, string of pearls spread over newspaper. And there are birds flying around, full-grown cockatiels I didn't see the other day. One makes a nest out of my hair.

"Don't swat him away," Lolo says, turning toward me with a respirator mask on his face. "He wants to keep warm, just came out of his shell last night."

"He should still be bald and scrawny, and I'm not thrilled he's keeping warm in my hair, but alright." With the bird on my head, I walk to the sink to see what he's doing.

Lolo points to a mask on the table. "Put that on before you come any closer."

I do as I'm told and the bird flies from my head as I hurry back to the sink.

Lolo laughs. "You would rush toward poison."

"Poison?" I repeat, remembering Mom's warning from this morning. Among other things in the sink, there are three small glass bottles—each with a liquid a different color and texture. The one in the middle is the color of snot and thick like it too. "Ew. What is that?"

"It's part of a tonic," Lolo says.

Bile rises in my throat. "Someone is going to drink that?"

"Yes. Would you like to taste test it?"

"If you go first," I say, and my eyes scan what else is in the sink. There's a clear vase filled to the brim with a sticky-looking liquid and a shrub with thick leaves and small purple flowers that don't seem to be in bloom. Toward the bottom half of one stem there are three black berries hanging. I recognize them and take a step back, watch as his gloved hand plucks one of the berries and rips off a small slither of the root. "Is that a . . . Lolo, is that a belladonna?"

"A spelled one," he says, before using a mortar and pestle to crush the berry. "By the way, I'd advise against ingesting anything you're unsure of while you work here. One time your grandmother ate a grape that wasn't really a grape anymore and she regretted it for days."

"Noted." I watch while he dips the crushed berry of death into the sticky substance, then drops it into the snot-filled jar. "How can someone ingest a belladonna? Won't they die?"

"Maybe so," Lolo says in a playful voice. "Get the door." I didn't hear anyone knock, but now I do. The corners of his mask lift as he smiles at me. "Keep her busy while I finish up."

Serena Bettencourt comes to my grandfather's house in tears. She refuses the tea I offer her and doesn't calm down even though I tell her Lolo is getting her order ready. I don't know what to do but stand in the corner of the room while she sobs on his couch.

"It's my husband," she says to me, "he's left me for another woman and my heart is so broken."

"Whoa." I put two hands up. If I could run out of here I would. "Please stop there; I'm only a kid. You don't have to tell me anything."

"Oh, that's right. Your grandfather doesn't like the details. But I just figured . . ." I shift in my stance, avert my eyes when I hear Serena suck in her snot. "I'm sorry. I just figured maybe you know how it feels when someone leaves you suddenly. You're not a kid, but you are young and still I sense that you've been left before. Have you?"

An image breaks through, blurring the room and making my

heart pound: Derek opening his front door two years ago and not being able to look at me. "I need more space," he said.

I wrap my arms around myself now. That was different. Derek wasn't my lover, my boyfriend, we weren't together like that. And now he's . . . What's going on with him? What's happening between us? And why is Serena sensing something like that coming from me? I make a note to work on my mental blocks in Lolo's shop, then watch Serena scrape her fingernails over Lolo's fabric cushion. "You want to make your husband come back to you?" I ask her.

She wipes her nose with the back of her sleeve. "Of course. He's the love of my life."

Another mental note: Never mess with Serena. I imagine it like the movies: Lolo comes in to tell this woman there are two rules in his shop. One of them is he can't make anyone fall in love, and the other is he can't kill anyone. But when Lolo walks in, he hands Serena a birthday gift bag with balloons on it and says, "Be careful, the glass bottle is filled to the top." Serena stares down at the gift bag. "It's the biggest one I had." Lolo shrugs, then wiggles his eyebrows. "Inconspicuous as well."

"Perfect," says Serena.

Lolo gives her a pen and a piece of paper too. "You know what you're asking for? I can't guarantee there won't be consequences when he drinks this for the spell."

She unfolds the paper and signs it without looking at either of us. "I understand."

"Let's just all pray it goes the way you want it to."

"It has to," she says, hands the paper to him, and takes a stack of money out of her purse. "A thousand dollars. You can count it if you want."

He doesn't, he slips the money into his back pocket and opens the front door before she even gets the chance to get off the couch. "I'm sure I'll see you again soon, Serena. Be safe."

"I always am," she tells him.

Lolo walks toward the kitchen as soon as she leaves. He reaches under a statue of a snake on the top of his fridge and takes down a key. "Since you're not allowed in my office without my company, pretend you didn't see that," he tells me, unlocking his office door. This is the most organized room in the whole house. There isn't even a book on the floor. He tells me to turn around and count to ten while he unlocks his storage cabinet. "You can look now," he says.

I watch him put the piece of paper Serena signed in a folder. "You keep records?"

"My own contract of sorts," he says, closing and locking the cabinet. "People make silly decisions, Blue. They won't blame me for the repercussions."

"Can you really make that woman's husband go back to her?"

Lolo laughs. It startles me. "I don't do any of the spell work for clients. I only give supplies for spells they choose to do. She needed a tonic that would make her husband . . . docile. But you should know now we offer a supply, we have some other services here too, but we do not get involved once the supply is out of our hands."

"So, she paid all that money for you to give her a tonic so she can use her own spell to brainwash her husband? Couldn't she have created the tonic herself, then?"

"Possibly." Lolo shrugs. "But I've been doing this for a really long time. People trust my supply; they know it's pure. Free of any other wishes, even their own, before they use it."

Hearing Lolo speak makes my heart race. He's never told me so much about what he does. There's another question on the tip of my tongue. It takes me a moment to ask, but Lolo waits patiently. "Don't you think it's wrong?" I finally say, thinking of the tea he makes me and the secrets he's kept from me. "For her to do a spell that'll keep him from his free will?"

"None of my business," Lolo says. "And it's not yours either."

"Got it," I say, realizing this is an opportunity to prove to Lolo I can handle every part of the job, even the morally questionable parts. But . . . "Will the berry hurt her husband?"

"Not if she does her spell right," Lolo says. "And the amount of berry in the tonic isn't enough to kill, if that's what you're worried about. May send him to the toilet, though."

I laugh. I'm happy to be here. Away from Bri and home and Derek and hours from tonight's dream. I haven't felt anything since I've been here. No stirring under my skin or seeing something wispy float across my vision, and I haven't heard a single whisper. I wonder if Lolo has wards up to protect him from spirits or if they just don't want anything to do with a badass old man who can send them away with some herbs the way he can. The thought makes me more anxious than ever to learn from him. "Will you teach me how to make a tonic?"

He tilts his head and stares into my eyes. So long my stomach starts to drop. For a moment, I think he sees the color in them. He would be able to see it even if no one else can. But all he says is, "I'll teach you, after we eat."

EIGHTEEN

7:15 P.M.: During dinner Mom gets mad when I tell her what I did with Lolo is classified.

8:35 P.M.: I stare in the mirror for twenty minutes and try to name every color in my iris.

8:55 P.M.: Attempting to capture them with my phone camera doesn't work. Maybe Bri is right. Maybe I'm looking for things because I stopped taking the tea and expect them to be there.

9:15 P.M.: Decide Bri is absolutely wrong. As a Gemini, it's in her nature to be practical.

9:16 P.M.: Google what happens to plants when herbal tea is dumped into their soil.

10:25 P.M. Studying for AP Calc requires all of my attention, but I'm itching to go back to the wisteria trees. Not now. I'd be alone in the dark.

10:26 P.M.: Derek must sense my thoughts. He walks up the street. Coming from the park? I duck behind my curtain, but he waves at my window like he's already seen me.

10:27 P.M.: He takes something from his bag, walks over to

the rosebush. It's not a rosebush anymore. Wonder if I should call it soil or plot. Maybe stick with rosebush for now. He drops to his knees. Confused. What's he doing? Wonder if he's planting something.

10:37 P.M.: Derek stands, wipes his hands on his pants, then blows me a kiss before going inside. Did he really just do that?

10:46 P.M.: My cheeks have finally returned to their normal color and temperature. Ugh.

11:16 P.M.: Sleep pulls me under a few seconds after the whispers start.

I'm beneath the wisteria again. It's daytime, and the flowers aren't pink. They're blood orange, close to crimson. A hungry ache grows inside of me. *Taste them*, it whispers. My mouth salivates as I reach for one, but it disappears under my touch and causes light to leave the sky. Darker, dull, all that's left is a blanket of gray, thick like ash. The shadows sweep through the space, come from below me, fill every crevice around me with darkness. They tug on my hair and touch my lips and set fire to my skin. They scream. *Help*.

"Hi, Bluebird."

Derek. I hear his voice, but the shadows still cling to me, prying my mouth open and slipping down my throat. I choke. I'm full of them. When I cough, something climbs up my esophagus and tumbles out of my open mouth. A fragile butterfly with black wings lands in my cupped hands before it gains strength to take off into the gray sky.

I can't see Derek, but he starts speaking again. "*I've been looking for you,*" he says.

I close my hand and an iridescent blue burst of light blinds me right before I wake up, sick to my stomach. Every muscle in my body feels foreign; my brain might be splitting. My throat is dry. I roll over on my side, push myself out of bed, and make it three feet to throw up in my wastebasket. The shadows crawled their way inside of me. A butterfly, it . . .

No, I was dreaming. It was just a dream. But my eyes flick around my room. Moonlight creates cascading lines on the wall and reminds me of dark things, but I see something else too.

There's a wavering glint in the air and it distorts the color behind it, making my wall darker. I try to trace the edges of the glint with my eyes, but there are none.

I step closer, squint, and that's when I notice the glint is a transparent-looking layer. Much thinner than Saran Wrap or the white of an egg, filmy like a bubble but reflecting no color. It separates me from the wall. A barrier. Some type of delicate barrier. I reach for it with a trembling finger but can't feel anything at all. And just like the shadows in the park last night, the barrier disappears and the glint fades in front of me.

NINETEEN

I scribble long delicate branches in my notebook. Small green petals, pink, turquoise, crimson flowers, butterflies with blackened wings. Mrs. Dolly comes up and taps my desk. "Would you like to share your sketch with the class?" I shake my head. "Come on, I insist. We could all use a distraction today."

"Guess I won't be selfish," I say, lifting my notebook to show the class.

Someone says, "There's like fifty trees on there." Someone else: "Didn't know you could draw, Aria." Another: "Are they wisteria? I love wisteria trees. Never seen them that color."

I'm too tired to pay any attention to them, but Derek turns in his seat after the last comment. He catches sight of the page and goosebumps rise on my flesh as he stares at them. A knowing glance passes between us before Mrs. Dolly demands our attention.

When sixth period ends, my feet move on their own. Even though my heart is thrumming hard, even though I wasn't planning to talk to him yet, I follow Derek. He has his headphones in and I don't know how he'll react if I tap him so I press my shoulder against the locker beside him instead. He flinches back like I've scared him and pulls an ear bud out.

"Hi," he says, careful, soft.

Because I wasn't expecting his tone, it takes me a few seconds to say, "We need to talk."

He nods down at me and shuts his locker. "Yeah, we do." Another surprise.

I don't have the patience to pull him away from here, and I'm not sure he'd follow me for privacy, so I waste no time. "What happened the other night in the forest?"

Derek opens his mouth, closes it. He examines me for a while. I cross my arms to my chest, take deep breaths while I wait.

"We were in the forest?" he asks. "Together?"

Anger rises in me; my voice trembles a little. The entire world is gaslighting me, the other side too, or maybe I really am losing a grip on reality, maybe there are more side effects to stopping the tea than I realized. "After the party, when we went to Neutaconkanut and saw . . ."

"Aria," he cuts in, his voice shaking now too. "I never went with you to Neutaconkanut Park. I never went to a party. There's something . . ." He stops and brings two fingers to his face just as dark red blood begins trailing from his nose.

My mouth goes dry at the sight of it. "Derek."

I reach for him, but he shrugs me off, cups his nose to cut through the crowd, and disappears down the hall while my heartbeat drums in my ears.

⁓

Derek never got on the bus at Kennedy Plaza like he usually does after school. I've been home for three hours and don't know where he is or if he's okay or what else he was going to say. I pace my room, make and unmake my bed, rearrange my bookcase by color. Finally, I sit down to write a list.

Things that are possibly happening to Derek:
-It didn't seem like it, but maybe he was drinking the night of the party ... or worse.
-He's decided he hates me enough to be cruel and play games with my heart.
-A spellworker has him in a trance.

Puzzle pieces move around in my brain. I think back to the dream I had before the rosebush died, how he was in the gray with me. Then I add the most unlikely item to the list:

-He's messing with dark magic and somehow not himself.

Suddenly, my phone rings. My pulse races. I shiver. It's him.

"Aria, it's me. It's me, Derek." He says it like I didn't know. Like I don't have his new number saved in my phone. "Can you come over so we can finish talking? There's something you should know."

I bend under Derek's window to examine the fresh soil there before knocking on it. Memories of the rosebush blooming in different seasons resurface, and my heart aches for the loss all over again. But last night, Derek was digging something up or planting seeds here. I'm not sure which one and I can't see anything and he'll probably notice me standing out here like a stalker soon. I sigh and straighten out, look up at the window, chew my lip.

Derek would leave his window open for me every night. We'd sprawl out on his bed with chocolate and chip bags to talk about the difference between black holes and supernovas. I'd tell him about my dreams and he'd tell me about new plants he was growing with his mother. We made promises to visit The Wave in Arizona, stand under the aurora borealis in Alaska, ride the train across the country, and stop in random cities to try the food.

The promises meant we'd do it all together.

I raise a fisted hand to knock, then hesitate. Derek opens it before I have to.

"You came," he says, sounding relieved and confused all at once.

"I told you I would."

He makes room for me to climb through, and once I'm inside we both stare at each other until I pry my eyes away from him and glance around. I'm in his room. For the first time in too long, and so much has changed. His bed is neatly made, he has a desk with a lamp on it, which is the only light in the space. The wall above his bed is covered in photo prints of anime characters and old-school skateboards, and there's an old vinyl record player on his nightstand.

He clears his throat and runs his hand through his hair. He seems so different than he did the other night. He doesn't have that cool smile on his face. He's going to tell me. He's going to tell me he went to see someone who does witchcraft with his dumb friends and . . .

"What exactly were we doing when you were supposedly with me at Neutaconkanut Park?" he asks.

"Supposedly? Is this a joke? And weren't you supposed to tell *me* something?"

"Humor me, please."

I cut my eyes at him. "We were at the party, we played spin the bottle. You spun the bottle and it landed on me. By the way, I swear you wanted that to happen so it did." His brows lift and heat flashes across my chest. Why did I say that out loud? "Then we took off through the window and went to the forest and we saw . . . you showed me the wisteria trees."

He takes a sharp breath, starts pacing his room. "You weren't with me, Aria."

My blood boils, simmers. All the other theories fly out the window. "This again?" His head snaps in my direction. "I'm not playing these games with you, Derek. I told you that night and I meant it. Just because . . . I hurt you in the past doesn't mean you can treat me bad. What did you call me over to say?"

He covers his face with his hands, then, "Can we please sit down? I'm dizzy."

We sit, but I wasn't expecting to be so conscious of it. I'm on his king-size bed. We could sit on opposite ends, but just like two years ago Derek chooses to sit so close his leg touches mine. I become acutely aware of every part of my body and every part of his on this new bed. I'm seventeen now. Would Mom be upset

I'm here or figure Derek is the same boy she let me run around the neighborhood with years ago? I think she'd be okay with it. But the thought reminds me of one of the last times I was alone with him.

I had just bombed a math test two days before and Derek was trying to teach me trigonometry after school. He leaned close to me and stuck his pencil through one of my curls when I complained about not understanding. "You'll get it," he said. I could smell the gum on his breath, could feel my stomach do a somersault at his proximity, even though I wasn't supposed to feel those things with him. "And if not, well, I'll tell you how junior year is." I nudged him with an elbow and he pinched me, but the fun was over when his dad opened the door. I knew something was wrong as soon as I saw his face. Especially because Derek had a bad feeling all day. He hadn't seen his mom after school and she wasn't answering his calls. Derek went to talk with his dad in private, and I waited for so long, trying to study with my stomach turning. When Derek came back he had tears in his eyes and a letter from his mom he made me read out loud because he couldn't bear to himself. I knew I needed to do it for him, but it was the hardest thing I'd ever done. I still remember that letter. It's cataloged into my brain.

> Dearest Gerald,
> I'm sorry to do this, but I need my own life. All I've ever been is someone's mother, someone's wife. I need some time to just be me. Please take care of the kids. I'm sure Derek will help you. He's such a good boy. I don't know what else to say. There is too much, and nothing feels like enough. I love you all. But if

I don't do this for me, I'll never know peace. Please take care of yourself for our children. And please, please don't waste your time looking for me.

Love, Shelley

Derek shifts and suddenly he's even closer now. The memory vanishes and all thoughts leave me as he looks down into my face. "The person you were with last night," he says carefully, the words punctuated, "wasn't me. I don't know who it was, but it wasn't me."

As soon as he says it, I fight off flashes. Derek in Adelia's room. Scaring the neighbors. Asking me to dance at The View, then forgetting about our matching scars. Bluebird. He's been calling me Bluebird. He touched my cheek under the wisteria tree and brought down the gray. But there are so many other possibilities, I can't hear him tell me the one I need not to be true.

"It had to be you," I whisper.

His face falls, and he looks away. "You know what, maybe you should go. This was a bad idea. You haven't changed at all."

His words sting. I stand to leave, frustrated with him, with me for stopping the tea, with this whole situation and the constant back-and-forth. But I don't move. I can't go anywhere. Not with him looking the way he does right now. "Derek, please tell me anything else. Tell me you're involved in some kind of witchcraft, tell me you were drinking the night of the party, say you're just playing games with me because you think it's funny, but don't tell me it wasn't you."

He stands suddenly, takes a few quick steps, and cups my cheeks with both of his hands. I gasp at the feeling and he makes a similar sound. Surprised by his own actions, maybe. But my brain reminds me it's not the first time we've touched since we stopped talking. Except, it's different from the shocking electric chill the last few times he touched me. This touch is softer, delicate yet firm. Warm and cool. It's all things at once. My skin grows hot under his fingers, but he doesn't let go, he tilts my head to look up at him.

"Stop with your theories and listen to what I'm telling you." His tone matches his touch. "Look me in the eye, Aria." Brown eyes. Not dark, not black, just round and pleading with me. I feel his words deep down in my bones and know what's coming. "I need you to listen this time."

This time. Because I wasn't listening all those years ago when his mom left. I bury hurt feelings, my pride. Take a breath, even though I'm terrified. "I'm listening. Please tell me."

He sighs like he's needed me to say those words his whole life, then breaks the contact between us by stepping back. He lets out a short laugh, and my gut tells me he'll confirm the only conclusion that makes sense. The one I fear most. Because he can't be . . .

"Aria," he says, "this is going to sound crazy, but I think I'm being possessed."

TWENTY

The world spins when Derek says it. My heart beats wild in my throat. I knew, I knew, I knew he wasn't himself. Not the Derek Johnson I've known my whole life. Breaking into houses, being so mysterious . . . flirting with me. But I still wasn't ready to hear it.

I'm winded when I sit on Derek's bed and blink up at him. The memories bombard my brain, rework, rewire, give me a headache because I'm not ready. He's waiting for me, examining my face for signs. But I'm not sure what to say, so I say nothing at all. He sighs and begins to pace. All I can do is watch his feet make tread marks on the rug while I listen.

"It's been happening for weeks. First, I started losing slices of time. Then blacking out for hours. Early on, it was always after I went to sleep. But now, I can hear him in my head, asking me questions, peeling away layers to know me better, and I feel like I'm trying to keep a grip on myself while I'm awake. I keep getting glimpses of you. Our hands . . ." Derek stops pacing, I can see his side profile, him swallowing. "Us dancing at The

View. And at Neutaconkanut, I was there, I saw you, but *I* wasn't fully there. Not until right before you ran away. I came to, in the dark under the trees, then I was gone again. But it's like he wants you close to me. Not at first, but now he does and it's . . . I don't know what he wants." Derek rubs his temples and turns toward me. I can tell he's desperate for me to believe him. "Feels like I've been a passenger in my own body. So you *were* with me, Aria. But you weren't really with *me.*"

I'm scared, shaking. Something has been wrong all along. I felt it. I knew. He was in my dream the night the wisteria crumbled, and something was wrong with him too. But if this is really happening, if I'm not dreaming right now, what's going to happen to him?

What does it mean for me?

"Derek," I start, I try, but can't find the way to my words.

"You don't believe me." His brows knit together, voice raw. Suddenly his face feels like a mirror of my own after Bri said she couldn't see the wisteria. "Of course not," he says, "I'm probably making whatever theories you've cooked up seem more valid. But after everything that's happened with us, I thought you would be the one to believe me because . . ."

Because of Lolo. Because of the spirits in my dreams. Because he's finally speaking to me after two years. He doesn't have to say any of it. My stomach clenches at the thought of him reentering my life—only for him to tell me it's because a spirit inside of him wanted to. But I stand up, try again. "It's not that. It's just . . . I don't know what to think right now. I need a moment."

He sighs. "I get it, but I need you to leave."

"What? Derek, no . . ."

I look at him and see my dreams and the forest and the shadows wrapping themselves around him. *Bluebird*, I hear in my head. *I've been looking for you.*

"I hope you can process this, but I can't be with you while you try. I can't. Leave, please," he begs. I want to argue but I walk to the window. While my back is to him he says, "And if you tell anyone about this, I'll never speak another word to you for the rest of my life."

His bedroom door opens, then clicks shut. He left me alone here. I lean up against the wall, trying to slow my racing heart and gather the strength to climb back out the window.

While Mom rushes to get ready for work, more memories flash across my mind: Derek dancing with me under the moon, him holding my hand as we walk through the streets, us under glowing wisteria trees before the whole world turns dark. Mom asks me to pin her hair back for her and she brushes her teeth. I do it on autopilot, rewiring, rewiring. If Derek really is being possessed, what does the spirit want with him? He's having blackouts, but is it hurting him? Is that why his nose was bleeding? How did a spirit come to possess him? And what does it want with me? What do any of them want with me?

Mom spits into the sink and looks at me through the mirror. "You okay, Aria?"

"I am," I lie. I need Lolo. He can make sense of it all. He can help Derek and fix this. Except, Derek told me not to tell anyone and I can't break his trust. Not again. And maybe Lolo's solution would be forcing the tea down my throat. Maybe he wouldn't even let me be involved in helping Derek because whatever is going on is connected to me too.

"You can tell me whatever's on your mind," Mom says, moving from the mirror.

I catch my reflection and turn away. I don't want to see the colors in my eyes right now. Not with my head already spinning. "Can I really?"

"What's that supposed to mean?" She snatches her ChapStick from the sink.

"Nothing," I say. Then, "Do you think the spirits would hurt me? If I stopped drinking the tea, what do you think they would do to me?"

She tilts her head, surprised. "We haven't talked about this in a while."

"We should."

"I'm not sure what they'd do to you, Aria." She shifts on her feet and pulls her coat off the hanger on the door. "I just know it's safer for you to take the tea. It protects you."

"But from what exactly? They're always there, in the background. Why me?"

Mom doesn't speak for a few seconds, then moves forward to kiss my forehead. "Because you're special, Aria." Derek said the same thing the night under the wisteria . . . Or maybe that wasn't Derek. A shiver climbs my spine, and Mom pulls back with a frown. "Do I think they're around to hurt you? Probably not. But you still shouldn't suffer every day of your life with them bothering you because there's something they're attracted to inside of your soul."

Everything hits when she says it. Tears burn the back of my eyes. I let them free. I can't tell her about Derek or the tea, but I can tell her this: "I'm tired of not knowing everything about myself, Mom. I don't know what makes me special to them. I'm just tired."

She wipes the tears from my face with her fingers. "I'm sorry. I didn't realize you were thinking about it so much. Feeling like this," she says. "But sometimes it's the not knowing that saves us from ourselves. Your father always used to say that."

"He did?"

She nods. "He struggled with a lot of things while working for your grandfather, things I never even knew about. He wanted it that way. And I was fine with not knowing, I liked not knowing all of it. But you're like him and you've always been so curious, Aria. You might not know everything about yourself, but I wish that didn't feel like a punishment." The work alarm on her phone goes off, but she doesn't silence it or leave. She stays and brushes the hair out of my face. "You drink your tea and ignore the spirits. Live your life, baby. We only get one."

TWENTY-ONE

While processing, I don't have to avoid Derek at school because he avoids me just fine on his own. Still, I take measures to make sure I don't pass by his locker between periods. It's not like we're normal teenagers and something embarrassing happened between us; this is an otherworldly awkward situation, which means I should act accordingly.

Bri follows me. "The longest route to the cafeteria possible today?"

"Yep," I mumble, tired. I forced myself to stay awake last night because I was nervous about seeing Derek in my dreams. Or is it the hypothetical spirit I've been seeing in my dreams?

"You've been particularly moody. Annoyingly moody," Bri says, then grabs my hand. "Is it because I didn't see the trees? I'm sorry for . . ."

"It's okay, Bri. I shouldn't be dragging you into these things anyway." Especially if there are spirits on the loose snatching bodies. "But annoying and me in the same sentence, really?"

"You're always annoying, now it's my turn." She points to a

sign hanging on Mr. Shepherd's classroom door. "I invited Val to the haunted estate as a safe kinda-sorta first date."

"And you're giving me your best pouting face, why?"

"I want you to come with us to the event, and it's the last day for sign-ups."

Every year, Mr. Shepard takes his little adventure club to visit old cemeteries, haunted houses and abandoned buildings, and every year there's one event he opens up to the whole school. I've thought about being a part of the adventure club, particularly because Mr. Shepard is the kind of cool dorky teacher who wears vampire teeth year-round, but Derek's in the club and I never wanted to seem like a stalker. Not that I succeed in that department often. But he'll definitely be at the yearly event next week, and we will or won't be talking about possession and what the ghost inside of him wants—if there really is a ghost. Maybe Derek wouldn't even be able to attend an event. Maybe he'll be dealing with an exorcist. I'm so confused my brain hurts.

But I don't know if I can refuse Bri with the look on her face. "So you want me to come to make this already kind of, sort of first date more awkward?" I ask, arching an eyebrow. "Val doesn't even go to our school, and is this really your idea of a date? Does she like to be scared?"

"She said she'd come, so I'm guessing, and Mr. Shepard won't notice she's not a student. He'll be too distracted with the fun of it all. I'll forge a permission slip for her. It'll be fine."

I don't have much argument left in me. "How about we just go do something else?"

"No, Aria. I need it to be *this* event. It's a buffer in itself. You bring someone, I bring someone. It's like a double date, except no one calls it that. You owe me after the contract."

"So what you mean is: I'm basically bringing everyone that attends the trip?" I say.

"That's exactly what I mean, lots of buffers." She gives me the side-eye. "But you should try to make a friend while we're there. Lord knows you could use some action since you keep denying those feelings for Derek. Worse comes to worse you can hold Val's other hand."

Just as she says it, Derek walks down the hall and she snickers something about being psychic while his gaze lands on me before he goes into Mr. Shepard's class.

"Please, Aria. I'm begging you. I'd get on my hands and knees if the rug wasn't crusty."

I sigh. "Fine, but don't be mad when I'm sitting between you and Val on the bus."

TWENTY-TWO

My lola smells like spice and sinigang and everything I need after thinking of Derek all day at school. She just got home last night from her yearly trip to the Philippines and decided to surprise me at Lolo's.

"My baby," she cups my face with her small wrinkled fingers, "you've grown."

"It's only been two months, Lola," I say. But it does feel like forever. I've missed her.

"You've somehow gotten over your grudge against your grandfather. I call that growth."

I laugh and glance around the kitchen. "Yeah, because he let me work here."

"Speaking of," she turns to call out to Lolo, who's busy organizing paperwork in his office, "you don't have her messing with any dangerous plants, eh, Zackary?"

I wonder what Lola would say if she knew I was slicing belladonna berries the other day. I wonder if Serena's husband is okay.

"You don't work here anymore, Felise. Don't worry about what we do," Lolo calls back.

"For good reasons," Lola says, then pinches my cheeks. "I have so many stories for you, Aria. I sat with some other old ladies and they told me the good stuff."

My heart picks up. My grandparents know I love hearing stories from their countries. My mom's father is from Cape Verde and when I visit him he tells me stories too. I've been asking for myths and folklore from Cape Verde and the Philippines since I was a child. Sometimes it feels like there's a thick wall between me and my heritage. I am mixed with so many things; hearing these stories feels like thinning the wall. And besides, ghost stories have always made me feel less alone with my own ghosts. Maybe I should ask Lola what she thinks of possession.

"I'll tell you the stories later," my grandmother says. "Right now I have to scold your grandfather."

Lolo walks out of the office right after she says it. "What is it now, Felise?"

"What is it?" Lola treads through the kitchen, opening and slamming cabinets and banging pots and pans together. It looks like Filipino New Year's Eve in the shop.

He throws his hands in the air. "Stop that, you're going to do damage."

"Maybe you'll pay attention if I do," she says. "I just got back and you couldn't take the day off? If you don't start spending more time at home, I'm filing for a divorce. I will be the cutest little old lady on the dating apps. Aria will help me do Tinder."

Lolo shoots me a look. I laugh and say, "Don't put me in this, I'm begging you both."

He takes Lola's hand. "I'm there every day, my love. What more do you want from me?"

"You are a ghost, Zackary," she says, and my mind runs straight to Derek. "You appear quickly, then slip out again. I'll just move to the Philippines. Is that what you want?"

"Of course not."

"You'll come home at a decent time, or you'll sleep here with the mice. Understand?"

Lolo lets go of her hand and leaves for his office. She follows, and they bicker until . . . Ew. I've been through enough lately, the last thing I need is to hear my grandparents kissing.

I'm outside of the shop yanking weeds from the front garden and trying to decipher how I feel about Derek's situation. Is it our situation? From my peripherals, I notice a car pull up in front of the house and park. I stand, tuck a pair of shears in my pocket, and stare at the car until a man gets out. At first, I can't place him, but it doesn't take me long to remember his clean-shaven face and pale skin. He's bald, slinky; he's the man Lolo wants us to stay away from.

But he's walking up the path toward me quicker than I can think to move.

"Hi," he says. "Hi there."

"Hi." I give him a careful smile. "My grandfather is inside. I'll go get him for you."

He doesn't respond, just stares. Something about him makes me shiver. My fingers flit along the shears in my pocket. "Wait," he says when I turn. "Are you his youngest grandchild?"

"I am." I shift back, tilt my head at him. "Why?"

His eyebrows dip down to meet his round eyes. "Do you remember me?"

"Um, no. Why would I?"

"I worked with you when you were a little girl."

He examines me, scanning my body, my face, my hands. Goosebumps skitter up my arms as we lock eyes. I recall the defense tactics I've learned on murder TV and move backward toward the door. The knife Adelia gave me is in my backpack, but the shears should do damage; I don't even ask what he meant by saying he worked with me.

"I'm going to go get my lolo," I say again, firmer this time. Louder. But the front door swings open and Lolo comes out. Lola is right behind him. Neither of them look happy.

"Levi," Lolo says to the man with a small nod of his head. This lasts for several tense seconds before my grandfather orders me inside.

He doesn't need to tell me twice.

Safely behind the door, I peek out the window. Levi is getting frustrated. Lolo's raising his voice, but I can't make out the words. Lola gets between them, shoves her little finger in Levi's face. My chest is so tight I can barely breathe. If Levi does anything to hurt her I'll go out there and . . . He backs away, says something in a softer voice.

My mind races, in and out of memories, but I don't remember Levi at all. Maybe he made a mistake when he said he worked with me. I never worked with Lolo as a child. But then my stomach tightens because there might be someone else who knows more about me than I do.

Will Lolo even tell me what was going on when he comes back inside? I run my hands through my hair, knowing the answer to my question, and take one last look out the window before walking to the kitchen. Lolo wouldn't leave his office door open. Not for anything. Not even because a creep ex-coworker was talking to his granddaughter alone outside. Except . . . he did. I stare at the open door for a second. There are two things I could do right now: abide by the contract or find some answers myself. The latter is necessary. I just need to be quick about it.

The manila folders are still laid out on the desk when I sneak into the office. These files are for customers, but maybe there's an old one in here for Levi too. I lift a folder and the one right under it makes me go still. It's labeled G. JOHNSON. A coincidence? I flip it open and the first thing I see is a signed contract. The signature belongs to Derek's dad. What could Mr. Johnson possibly need Lolo's help with? My eyes scan the contract and the list of ingredients—most of which I don't recognize. But in the tiny scroll at the bottom of the page there's a note from Lolo and it says, *for the boy*. Derek. Does he mean Derek? I take a deep breath, ready to flip through the rest of the file, but hear the front door open. I fix all the files and rush to slip into the kitchen. I make it as far as the stove before Lolo comes limping through the door, catching me in midmotion. His eyes flick from his office to my face and back again.

"Tell me about Levi," I say as a way of distraction. "He told me he knows me."

Lola comes into the kitchen too. She sighs and pulls out a chair to sit down. Lolo's face softens, and he sits as well. "He doesn't know you anymore," he says. "Maybe he once did."

My heart is still beating rapidly. "He said he worked with me as a child. What does that mean?"

A knowing glance passes between my grandparents, but I'm not in the knowing. Lola's the one who speaks up, which strangely feels like a spark of betrayal after she says, "He probably just means you were running around the shop when he worked here with your lolo."

I raise a brow, unconvinced but ready to play their games. "Is he a creeper? Did he do something perverted in front of me? Because I get the creeper vibes from him."

Lolo stiffens. "He'd be dead, Blue. I'd shove belladonna down his throat myself."

My grandmother puts her hand on top of her husband's. "He's just not a good person, Aria," she tells me. "We'll explain when you're older, but you don't have to worry about seeing him anymore. We made it perfectly clear what would happen if he came around again."

The aching betrayal is on my tongue. I swallow, but it doesn't travel to my stomach where it can settle, it gets stuck in my trachea and makes it hard to breathe again. So many secrets. So many lies. What exactly is my family keeping from me? "Okay," I say.

"Okay?" The wrinkles on my grandfather's face draw together. "No fighting? No whining about it? No saying we treat Adelia better than you?"

"None of that," I confirm.

He gives his wife a small smile. "Blue's learning already, can you believe it?"

While my grandparents share a little laugh, I think about Mom telling me to ignore the spirits and live my life. I'd listen to her, some part of me wants to, but the stronger part of me aches to learn everything no one else wants me to. If I was alone I'd write this in my notebook:

Spirits slip through the cracks in our realm and cause chaos for others, but they've always been quiet inside of my head. They've made a home there without knowing whose home it was, but now the barrier is gone and they can see me too. I won't ignore them and put the barrier back up because I need to trust myself. My instincts tell me the only thing that is possibly happening to Derek Johnson is he's absolutely, undoubtedly possessed.

TWENTY-THREE

Derek doesn't answer my knocks on his window so I knock on his front door. Mr. Johnson answers with surprise on his face and I realize he probably doesn't know Derek and I are sort of speaking again. He also doesn't realize I'm cataloging everything about him after finding the file. "Hey, kid, how are you doing?" he says. His voice is deep and silky.

"I'm good, Mr. Johnson," I say. "Just have to talk to your eldest son."

He passed his highly expressive eyebrows down to Derek. "He's not feeling very well today, made me send his friends away when they pulled up on the skateboards earlier."

My stomach twists. Derek seemed fine at school. He seemed fine when I was with him last night. Or was I too worried about my own feelings to notice?

"Please, Mr. Johnson," I say. "It's really important."

He gives me a small smile and jerks his thumb to the side. "He's in the yard. The fence should be open, but don't tell him I sent you."

I find Derek crouched in front of a small patch of garden behind the house. The backyard is beautifully lined with plants and flowers and growing fruit, but the section Derek is working in seems new, something he must have carved out for himself. He sees me letting myself through the gate, sits on his butt, and wipes sweat from his forehead with his sleeve. When I drop to my knees beside him, he grips the trowel in his hand tightly and asks, "Why are you here?"

"Pleased to see you too, Derek," I say. "Move aside and let me work with you."

He looks up at the darkening sky. "I'd rather not."

"So it's definitely you." His eyes meet mine. "I'll know it's really you now because *ghost you* doesn't speak to me that way," I say.

Something flashes across his face. He flicks his tongue over his bottom lip. "Aria . . ."

"I believe you," I cut in. "I don't need you to feel bad for being cold to me right now. I just need you to know I believe everything you said. Okay?"

He doesn't speak, but he moves to the side a little to let me sit in front of the small plot of dirt with him. We're quiet while he digs small holes. I use my fingers to dig a few too.

"What made you suddenly believe me?" he asks.

"It wasn't sudden," I tell him. "I think I believed it as soon as you said it, even though I didn't want to. Maybe I had a feeling before that, but didn't want to acknowledge it."

He laughs. "Typical you."

I stop digging and tilt my head at him. "What does that mean?"

"It means you decide to validate someone's experiences and how they experience them when you're ready to, the way you want to, when it makes you more comfortable."

Here in the garden, his words dance in my mind, stir up dust from a memory I've tried hard to forget. Derek's mom had been gone for a month and he seemed even sadder that day than on previous ones. Maybe he figured out what I hadn't yet: She wasn't coming back. The sun was bright, and for the first time since she'd left, we sat together by the garden she'd helped him grow. He examined the ripening tomatoes, and even though he was quiet, it was summer; there was music floating to us from backyard barbecues, his brothers were playing on the swing set across the yard, the wind made the trees blow, and all of it helped me ignore how loud his silence was. Derek's eyes were red-rimmed so I knew he'd been crying before I came, but I said nothing about it, just asked if he wanted to walk to Lemon King. I'd scraped together a couple of dollars in change I found around my house for us to go grab some frozen lemonade in the hope that he'd want to. I thought he'd say no, but instead he smiled and said, "You gonna let me have your lemon wedge?" I always got lemon flavor while Derek was a blueberry fan, but the boy would bug me for my wedge. I stood and held out a hand to pull him up. What I didn't say was he could have every single one of my lemon wedges forever if he'd smile at me the way he just did.

But while he was still sitting and his hand was in mine, he looked at his brothers, then up at me. "Aria, why didn't my mom love us enough to stay? Why couldn't she do that for us?"

I was just shy of sixteen but I'd spent years not knowing how to handle grief. When my mom would cry over my dad in her bedroom, I'd pretend I didn't hear her, even though it hurt. Derek and I were still touching when I said to him, "She does. She loves you all so much. You'll see. We're going to find her and bring her back. She's going to fix all of this. You'll be planting zucchini and strawberries and she won't ever leave you again."

It wasn't the first time I'd said something like that. I had been searching the internet and trying to find clues about where she went for weeks. But I should've known all he really needed was for me to hold his hand. To tell him we'd go through the pain together. Instead, I watched him shut me out at that moment. Though I didn't quite understand what it meant yet when he dropped my hand. It was the last time he ever mentioned her to me.

"Can we go get ice cream tomorrow?" he had said. "I want to be alone right now."

I didn't know tomorrow would never come, and he'd have one excuse not to spend time with me after the next, until our friendship was just a phantom of something that used to be alive.

His words sit between us now and the air grows thick. "I'm sorry," I whisper.

He shakes his head, sighs. "No, I am. That was unfair of me to say. I told you there's a ghost in my body and I couldn't expect that you'd . . ." He laughs, trails off. "My life is a joke right now, but I'm glad you're here."

My heart beats a little faster. I feel flutters in my stomach. "Really?"

He clears his throat, looks away, and begins digging another hole. "Yeah. Now you can help me figure this all out, Detective."

I'm only a little sad that he's glad I'm here because he needs me. He just called me the nickname he gave me years ago and I'm storing the new memory in my head and heart. We'll figure everything out together, and maybe he'll forgive me eventually.

"Good," I say, "because I think I know what's going on."

He drops the trowel and braces his elbows on his knees. "I'm waiting," he says.

I spent the bus ride here thinking of what happened at the shop, of Lola complaining to Lolo about the little time he spends at home; comparing him to a ghost slipping in and out made me think of Derek. "I think the spirit isn't tied or bonded to you," I say to him.

Derek breathes out. "Keep going."

"And I think its energy must also be causing other supernatural disturbances like the rosebush dying and the wisteria trees growing. And the longer it can inhabit you, the more it does, the stronger it probably gets. So I think it's not all the way connected yet. It's able to slip in and out." Night falls around us and makes my words heavier. Derek wraps his arms around himself. I stare at him more closely. "And maybe," I say, careful, slowly, "you're allowing some of it to happen. From everything I've been told, spirits aren't able to possess humans easily."

His brows dip. "What are you talking about?"

"Not consciously," I say, chewing my bottom lip. "But maybe the spirit has a stronger hold on you because you have a lot on your mind, and maybe it gets stronger when you're feeling . . ." I trail off. What I need to say feels sensitive and I'm scared.

"What, Aria?" The bugs begin to tick in the grass beneath us while I gather the words, but Derek isn't patient enough. "Just say it."

"Sad," I say, and hold my breath. Derek doesn't respond, and I don't want the conversation to lag too long because I'm scared he'll tell me to leave. "I don't know. It's just a theory. My guess is it wants to bind itself to you, but it's still trying to figure out how. I know this sounds weird, but have you ever been to my grandfather's shop with your dad?"

Derek looks up at the house, his words come out in almost a whisper. "No, why?"

"There's . . . there's this file at the shop and it has your dad's name on it," I say.

The whites of Derek's eyes widen in the dark. "What does that have to do with me?"

"I think maybe he bought something from my lolo . . . for you," I say.

I don't explain the note in Lolo's handwriting at the bottom just in case I'm wrong.

Derek lets out a dry laugh. "Like he bought something to make me possessed?"

"No, no," I say, "I just feel like the file is connected to you somehow."

"Your feelings aren't always correct," he says, but the dig doesn't faze me as much this time. He stands up, doesn't offer me a hand. I'm fine with that too. One step at a time. "My dad might've wanted something for luck with his new job, maybe even a silly love potion."

I wonder if he thinks of his mom the way I do at this moment but won't say. What if Derek's dad tried locating her with magic? What if Mr. Johnson went there for Derek and his sons to have a chance at getting their mom back? I'm not sure what it is, but I have to trust my gut. "I think we'll just have to go see the file for ourselves." Before he can protest, I ask, "Do you remember being in Karina Wilson's backyard the other night?"

Derek laughs. "What? As in Mrs. Annoying Wilson from across the street?"

"Thought so," I say, and sigh. "So you have no idea what the spirit is looking for?"

"The spirit is looking for something . . . from Mrs. Wilson?"

I shake my head. "From lots of our neighbors apparently."

Derek scratches the back of his neck. "Is that why everyone's been acting funny with me? What exactly have I been doing?"

I reach into my pocket and hand him the wrapped wisteria stem I found in Adelia's room. "I'll explain everything I can make sense of on our way to my lolo's."

TWENTY-FOUR

Derek parks his dad's car a street over from Lolo's and we walk the rest of the way. The lights are out at the shop, which means Lola was successful in getting her husband home. I'm mostly relieved I didn't waste our time.

"Hurry up before someone sees us," I hiss.

Derek is several feet behind me. "Are you sure he doesn't have an alarm or some kind of poison in his grass that'll sink into our shoes and coat our skin, make our eyeballs burst?"

I choke back a laugh but look at the gnomes that have been guarding this house for more years than I've been born. "They might follow us home," I tell him, "but I'm sure about the rest."

When we make it to the kitchen window on the side of the shop, I tell Derek to give me a boost and he puts his hands out for me to step on. I purposely kept this window open doing lock checks for Lolo before we closed up shop. If he found out, he'd never let me work for him again. My heart races considering the risk, but we won't get caught, we can't. I lift the window and Derek boosts me through it. My feet are now in Lolo's sink.

Yeah, maybe he'd do more than ban me from the shop, maybe he'd use my toes in tonics for his customers.

I manage to get myself out of the sink without stumbling, around the table, and through the small sitting room in the dark while going to open the back door for Derek. Lolo keeps his birds in this room and I can hear them stirring awake from under their cloth covers. One begins to chirp when Derek steps over a crack and we hurry back into the kitchen.

The key is still there, waiting for me under the snake statue on Lolo's fridge. This has all been easy, so convenient, I convince myself we are meant to be here. But we have another problem when we get into the office. I don't know where Lolo keeps the key to his filing cabinet. I didn't consider that he might not keep it here at all. Was it in his pocket the last time he opened the cabinet in front of me?

We search all the statues, carefully look through the books on the shelf, and then I pull a bobby pin from my hair and try to pick the lock.

"You're so damn bad at this," Derek says, shining his phone flashlight on me. We didn't want to turn on any lights in case we triggered attention from Lolo's neighbors, but Derek's being so loud the birds are chirping in the back. "Why didn't you tell me you're still bad at this? That you didn't get any better over the years? I wouldn't have come."

"Shhh," I say. "Quiet down. And it's not helping with you hovering."

I try again, then kick the bottom of the cabinet when it doesn't work. Derek pushes me aside and takes the bobby pin. Two minutes later, we both hear the lock click.

"Some things never change," he says, and I can't see his smug face well, but his white teeth flash in the dark. He moves for me to be the one to open it, but my nerves make me shake. Lolo will know. He's going to see us here by using some kind of super-powered divination bowl. He'll feel the files have been touched by hands that are not his. Derek places two fingers on my lower back; the contact surprises me and I gasp a little when he pushes me forward. "Hurry up."

I open it with trembling hands and everything happens quickly after that. Derek takes the bottom stack of files and I take the top. We lay them out on Lolo's desk and use our phone lights to sift through them. I search for Levi's file and the one for Derek's dad at the same time. I don't find Levi's but do find Mr. Johnson's while going through my second stack. "Got it," I say.

But Derek is staring down at a file he took from his stack. "And I've got one for you."

He hands it to me. The initials on the file are mine, but they're also Adelia's. We both have A names to match my dad's. When I open it, there's a picture of me standing behind the church, near my dad's shrine. I'm around four years old with pigtails in my hair and dirt on my cheeks. A feeling flickers in my chest. I trace the picture with my fingers, flip it over. My breath hitches seeing Lolo's writing on the back. *First time it happened or first time we noticed? 6.1.2005.*

Beside me, Derek spreads out the papers in his file. Part of me is aware he's taking pictures, that I should probably do the same. We can't take these files with us, but I'm too stunned over the thickness of my file. There are so many pictures of me from over the years. My heart starts to beat faster as I tear through obituaries of people I've never heard of and random newspaper clippings with headlines like DIES AT 69. There are lists and lists of different ingredients and photos of plants and torn-out pages of books and even a bunch of sloppy-looking drawings I must've done in crayon. Too much to digest without enough time to dissect what any of it means.

But two photos steal the air straight from my lungs. The first is of the rosebush when it was lively, thriving, crawling toward the sky at the side of Derek's house. The second makes my hands tremble. A picture of the rosebush when it first died, still dark out, tar on the vinyl siding, a heap of mess on the grass. Lolo acted like he didn't care about it at all. When did he take this? Why didn't I see it? And why is it in my file and not Derek's dad's?

The last thing I see is a letter in a sender's name I don't recognize, but something stirs in my stomach. Touching it causes static to shoot to my fingertips. It's just paper, but it feels heavy with magic. I unfold the letter, then hear Derek take a sharp breath beside me; something in his file shocked him, but neither of us have time to speak because we hear a car pull up in the driveway. Headlights flicker through the window.

Derek panics, puts the papers back in his file and shoves his folder into the cabinet. "Aria, hurry," he whispers, but I didn't even get a chance to take a single picture. Derek pushes me out of the way, snatches my file, fixes it, and shoves it back into the cabinet right before we hear the front door open. I move toward the office window, ready to open it and climb out, but Derek is smarter, quicker. He pulls me by the arm and drags me under Lolo's desk with him.

We both fit, but not well. His body is draped over mine while I crouch low. His chest presses against my back, his breathing warm against my neck. With us this close, shivers dance up my spine and a heat grows in my belly. Every time he shifts against me, my body betrays me. All I should feel right now is fear.

"You okay?" Derek's breath kisses my ear, but before I can answer I see a piece of paper on the ground a few feet away, close to the cabinet. Evidence. If Lolo sees something from the cabinet on the carpet he'll know. I crawl out from under the desk quickly, ignoring Derek's warning whispers while snatching up the paper and crawling backward. I make it back to the desk right before Lolo opens the office door. Derek snakes an arm around my waist and pulls me under again; this time we're flush, there's no space between us. I can feel the erratic beating of his heart against my back. He holds me and doesn't let go.

For several seconds it's eerily quiet, we're both barely breathing, but finally Lolo flicks on the lights and moves through the room. I can see his shuffling feet, him messing with books on his shelf. He makes a satisfied humming sound when he pulls out a book, but accidentally drops it. The book clatters to the ground and lands too close. Derek curls us a little deeper under the dark of the desk while Lolo curses in Tagalog, then bends to pick up the book. Lolo's hand is just inches from mine, and I fear he'll hear two hearts beating a foot away from him, but he grunts as he straightens on bad legs and puts the book on the desk. I would take a breath, but Lolo just stands there in front of us, flipping through the pages. I'm close enough to reach a finger out and poke his ankle. In this moment, I wish I knew magic. We need a cloaking spell, a miracle, something. I should've thought this through.

Suddenly, one of Lolo's birds flies into the room. Divine timing to save us. "*Putang ina mo*," the parrot cusses in Tagalog as it flaps around. Just the other day Lolo brought two parrots to the shop, and they're already speaking the language better than me.

Lolo groans and steps away from the desk. "God dammit, how did you get out the cage?"

The parrot repeats the Tagalog phrase and Lolo moves to chase it out of the room.

This is our chance. I try to crawl out from under the desk, but Derek wraps a hand around my jaw from behind and leans down so far his lips brush the skin behind my ear. Everywhere we touch is static charged, scorching cold. I know before he speaks that he is no longer himself.

"Is this the kind of adventure you like, Bluebird? Did it get your little heart pounding? I know Derek's heart is racing with you under him."

This is the first time I've been in contact with Derek's ghost since the wisteria trees, the first time we've spoken since I found out he's not really Derek. He grips my jaw a little tighter, then uses his thumb to stroke my neck. All of the bones in my body throb. Shadows float across my vision, but we don't have time for this.

Lolo is still in the kitchen, trying to catch the parrot, and we need to move.

"We have to go," I whisper.

"Is that really what you want? Are you not enjoying the feeling of us close?" he says, playful almost. "I know we like being close to you."

There's a fluttering feeling in my belly, but I need to ignore it and act fast or Lolo will come back. Besides, I can't be this close to the spirit. I have no idea what it wants from me. So I reach a hand up and dig my fingernails into Derek's neck. When he hisses and lets me go, I crawl out fast and crouch to look at him under the desk.

"Get up right now or I'm leaving you in this shop for my grandfather to deal with."

I don't wait for him. I head to the window and slide it open, looking down at the drop I'll have to take and panicking at what it might sound like.

Seconds later, a warm hand grabs my shoulder from behind.

"It's me," Derek says, and a sigh runs through us both. He moves me aside and climbs out the window first to help me down. "Come on, Aria."

But before I follow him, I take one last look at the filing cabinet and all the secrets I'll have to leave behind.

TWENTY-FIVE

We hardly spoke on the way home. Too stunned by everything that's happened, I think. And here in Derek's room, with the fan droning above our heads as we sit on his bed, I find myself quietly tracing the edge of my jaw while having flashes of Derek's fingers there. Except he wasn't him for a few seconds. I try not to let it cloud my brain while searching the internet for a certain herb listed on his dad's contract from Lolo, but I can't find the herb anywhere.

"Maybe it's not an herb at all?" Derek says, leaning on his elbow to look at the laptop.

I chew the skin around my nails, then, "Wait, you're right, it has to be a mixture of different things. Lolo loves making all sorts of concoctions, he's also stealthy and slick for an old man. I bet the letters all stand for something different . . . maybe the P is for pig's feet."

Derek crinkles up his nose and I laugh. He grabs me a notebook and pen and we both begin listing possibilities for the letters. Derek's knowledge of plants helps us narrow down a huge list we make. We decide that three of the ingredients must be gotu kola, blue lotus, and ginkgo biloba. Besides having healing properties, the only thing they each have in common is they all open the third-eye chakra and allow for spiritual growth. It can't be a coincidence.

"Do you . . . do you think he fed these to you?" It feels even scarier saying it in Derek's house while his dad and brothers are sleeping in their rooms down the hall.

While Derek tries to decide, he goes to lie back on his bed with a frustrated look on his face. "Maybe," he finally says, "but how? I think I would've noticed some strange-tasting herb in the three dinners he knows how to make. He tries, he really does, but . . ." Derek trails off, the realization seeming to dawn on him. "The tea," he says, stands up and heads for the door.

I follow behind him and wince as he starts opening and closing cabinets. I remind him we're not in the house alone and he stops slamming things, but he's still searching frantically. When he finally opens a small tin jar he finds above the microwave he smells it before handing it to me. There's only a very small pinch of tea leaf left, but it smells strong, so pungent.

"Whoa," I wince. Something in it is familiar. I inhale again, deeper this time. It doesn't smell exactly like my tea leaf, though there must be a shared herb between them. A chill travels through me, and I'm upset I didn't take pictures of my own file. But Derek takes a few steps backward till he hits the counter with a thud. It doesn't even seem like he feels it.

"He was making me drink that every morning. Basically

forcing it on me, saying he'd read a study, something about pre-existing conditions and health and . . . Why did he do it?"

I put the top back on the tin and place it on the table before cupping my elbow with my hand. "Maybe we could ask him."

Derek seems to consider it for a moment but shakes his head. "Not right now. We have other things to worry about besides asking my dad if he knew he was opening me up to a spiritual attack." He laughs, runs his hands over his face. "Isn't that what he did to me?" We're both quiet for a few seconds because I'm not sure how to answer, or if I even should. I'm relieved when Derek speaks again. "And I don't want anyone to know about the spirit anyway. Not until I can prove it or fix it. I can't risk my dad thinking I'm just having a breakdown. He's already on me enough about . . ." Derek trails off and I fill in his words: being sad.

My chest tightens. I've watched Derek skateboard with friends, excel in sports, debate in class, even date girls, but I wasn't close enough to see how he battled the sadness behind closed doors. "What if my lolo can help?" I offer. "He'll believe you."

"Aria," Derek says, "did you read the file? He's made it clear he's not responsible for adverse reactions. No way are we telling him right now. Besides, can we really trust him? He has a file on you too. What the hell was that about?" I hug myself and Derek sighs. "Sorry, I'm not trying to be disrespectful."

"I get it," I say, because even though it hurts to hear someone else talk about my grandfather that way, he's right. Zackary Cayetano can't be trusted. Not right now.

I follow Derek back to his room and watch him examine

himself in the mirror on the wall. "Did I hurt you when he took over?" he asks, meeting my gaze behind him.

"No," I say, feeling the urge to trace my jaw again. "You didn't hurt me."

Derek turns around and walks toward me. We're inches apart now and he reaches forward to softly tilt my chin, checking for markings there. My eyes flutter shut at the feel of his gentle fingers. When I open them again, Derek is staring down at my face.

"If he's able to slip in while I'm awake now, I don't know if you're safe with me."

I flush at his words, not because of what he's saying, but because he's saying them like he still cares about me. "I don't think you have to worry," I say. "Pretty sure I can kick your ass if I have to."

Derek laughs, lets go of my chin, touches the marks on his neck. "You got me good."

"Oh," I say. I was too caught up with the way he gripped my jaw under his desk that I didn't even think of how hard I dug my fingernails into him. "Should we clean it? I'm sorry."

He smiles. "I give you permission to snap me out of his hold any way you can."

I nod. Then look down at my dying watch. "It's really late. My mom's going to be coming home from work soon. I should get home. We can talk more tomorrow."

"Talk about whatever you remember from your file?"

The pit in my stomach grows. I feel like a failure for not taking pictures. "We should."

"We need to." His tongue flicks out to wet his bottom lip.

"Aria, whenever you're around, I get this buzzing feeling in my bones. Like every fragment is moving, pulling me . . . toward you."

His words float around us, make my heart thrum fast. We were only friends before. We might become friends again. But for a second, I can't help wishing he was saying those words to me for another reason. "The spirit inside of you," I say, and swallow.

"Yeah," Derek smiles just a little, "I still don't like you much, but I think he does."

The corners of my mouth twitch. "Well . . . I guess I'll have to thank him for reconnecting us the next time we speak," I say. Derek shifts his gaze from me. I wonder if I made it awkward, so I keep talking. "Maybe I can find out what he wants with the both of us."

"As in speak to him? You think he'll actually tell you?" Derek questions. "Because I don't know a thing about him. He's not letting me over on his side. It sounds weird, but there's this layer, some kind of barrier, and I can't get past it. But he knows everything about me."

His words make me think of the filmy barrier in my room last night, and I make a mental note but don't mention it to Derek. In the car on the ride to Lolo's, I told Derek about how intense my dreams have been getting since I stopped taking the tea, but I didn't tell him about the weird things that have been happening to me. Something in my gut told me to wait to tell him, just in case the spirit was listening. After the incident under the desk, I'm glad I did.

"It doesn't sound weird. I think he knows mostly everything, but he didn't know . . ."

"Didn't know what?" Derek asks.

"Nothing. Forget it."

"Tell me."

The wind blows through his window like a warning to get home. To not open more doors between us right now. I wrap my arms around myself and start walking backward.

"He didn't know about the tattoos. *Our* tattoos," I say when I'm close to the window.

Derek's hand automatically goes to his shoulder blade. Seeing him do it makes me touch mine. For a moment, we are a mirror. Staring into each other's eyes from across the room, but he blinks and the moment is gone.

"See you tomorrow, Aria," he says.

I throw myself on my bed and stare at the ceiling, willing my heart to beat slower, but my brain won't let me rest. I try to envision my file again, remembering a picture of a kava plant, bigger than any I'd ever seen. On the back of the photo, Lolo drew a symbol of a snake eating its own tail. I know it symbolizes the cycle of birth and death, but I wish I knew more. I don't know if I should keep what's happening to me from Derek. I don't think I want to try to figure it out alone. Will Lolo notice the unlocked window tomorrow morning and watch me closely now, or will I get another chance to look at the file? There was so much I didn't get to see, but . . .

I shoot up in bed and reach into my pocket. With all the adrenaline of possibly getting caught and Derek's ghost and trying to figure out what his file meant, I forgot all about the letter. But it's here, in my shaky hands. The only solid thing I have to learn more about myself.

My phone vibrates on the bed, a text from Bri blinks on the screen. **So nervous about my haunted estate date with Val. Happy you'll be there, but . . .**

I hit the button on the side of my phone. The screen goes black. Then I open the letter.

Dearest Zackary,

Someday someone will come for her. When that day comes, I might not be able to help. I wish you'd take my offer, but my father always said you don't listen to reason. I left a gift for her with a certain botanica owner we know. You'll find it fascinating in your line of work, but Aria's the only one who can retrieve it when she's ready. I've had it engraved to help her understand, but the engravings are a code because, as you always say, tricky spelled objects shouldn't fall into the wrong hands. I'm sure you'll be able to decipher them. Keep it safe. Keep her safer.

L. Rivera

TWENTY-SIX

"What do you think it is?"

I'm bent over the soil in front of Derek's window and he's waiting for me to speak. But I'm still grasping for words. There is something growing and spreading aggressively in the soil. Its roots are wide, anchoring farther out than the rosebush did. Something is alive here when just yesterday there was nothing. I stand and look up into Derek's eyes.

"I'm not sure," I say. "But I did see you, or not you, planting something the other night."

He frowns. "Wonder if the neighbors saw too. They'll have whole theories about me."

We walk to the bus stop in silence after that. Both of us know whatever is growing is another otherworldly occurrence, but neither of us know what it means. My eyes flick over to Derek's face, and even though my mind is preoccupied with many things, that doesn't stop it from realizing this is the first time in two years we've walked together to catch the bus to school. The sunlight hits his skin so good I fight the urge to reach up and touch him.

He catches me looking and I swear he smiles just a little. We spent the morning doing research on his file, and I decided to tell him about the letter. A quick Google search turned up too many L. Riveras to start with, but Derek printed a list of all the botanicas in the Rhode Island and said we'd go to every single one if we had to. I'm not sure if it was the right thing, but he made telling him about my dreams changing and feeling like the spirits have been creeping into my world easy to do.

We're still quiet when we arrive at the bus stop, but the sounds of Derek's ragged breathing cuts through the silence. He shifts away so I can't see his face. I reach to turn it back and he grabs my hand. We're both out of breath as we stare at each other.

"Don't," he says.

"Is the spirit . . ." I swallow and examine his glossy eyes. "Is it hurting you?"

Derek's attention moves from my face to our clasped hands, but he doesn't let go. "I'm just really tired. But I feel better now, with you close." For a second, I feel like I've stepped into some future time, where Derek would say things like that to me followed by his lips brushing against mine. My belly squeezes when he meets my gaze again. "Has to be the spirit," he says.

"Yeah," I say, embarrassed by where my thoughts went. "Yeah. Has to be."

Derek's mouth parts and his face scrunches up. "Aria, your eyes," he says. "They . . ."

My eyes. There are two things I still haven't told Derek: that I've been dreaming of him in the gray space and about my eyes. I've felt weird admitting he's in my dreams, though I know I need to tell him soon. And I was too nervous he would say he didn't see anything in my eyes.

"What about them?" I ask quietly.

With our hands still touching, he pulls me closer. Staring intently. Both of us barely breathing. "I see so many colors," he finally says.

Everything comes rushing to the surface. The time I've spent feeling delusional, the years I've spent without him. I blink back tears. It's real. It's all real, and Derek sees me. I let go of his hand, breaking our contact to keep my composure.

"No one else can see them," I tell him. "But something is going on with me. Something other than being able to see spirits, maybe bigger. I just wish I knew what it was."

Suddenly, the city bus pulls up in front of us and we both jerk back.

When the door opens, Derek looks down at me with a worried expression before getting on the bus. For a second, I think we'll sit together, but Derek heads to the back with his friends and I take a seat up front. Hurt stirs somewhere in my heart. I can't help but wonder if he's embarrassed to be seen with me, what he's told others about our relationship over the years. I wonder if there really is a chance we'll be friends again after this. Then my phone vibrates.

Derek: We'll figure it all out, Detective. Including your kaleidoscope-looking eyes.

I take a breath, type back. So they're dizzying huh?
They're actually kinda pretty, he writes.

There are a dozen swallowtails in my stomach and their wings are beating at once.

Ok <3, I text back, then click out of the conversation to send one to Bri. I want to tell her everything but remember the promise I made to Derek about keeping his secret. And I don't know if Bri would believe me anyway, not until I can prove it. But there are some things I can still tell her: **Derek and I've talked, and I'm starting to think we can be friends again.**

Bri: Details. Now. And we'll need a new contract. He can only have you Mondays.

After school is over, Lolo picks me up and we go to India Point Park to meet with a customer like we're selling something illegal. I guess we *are*, but outside of Lolo's shop it actually feels that way. I've been on edge ever since I got in his car earlier, wondering if he noticed something out of place in his office, or if there really was some kind of magical ward up that told him Derek and I snuck in, but he hasn't mentioned a thing. He seems normal while we wait in the park; we watch people walk their dogs by the water and Lolo tells me about the plant mixture in the bag I'm holding. There are a few I've never heard of, but most are herbs I'd use in the kitchen. Until he holds a finger up and says, "Ah, yes, gotu kola." The name strikes me. This was one of the possible herbs we decoded for Derek's file. Maybe I should ask him about it. Or maybe . . . he's testing me. Before I can speak, something moves in the corner of my vision.

I turn my head slowly and see the slight shine again, the same thin, filmy layer I'd seen in my bedroom the other night. Behind it the world has gone darker, the water black, the sky dull.

"Blue," Lolo calls, and when I blink the world is bright again. He narrows his eyes, but then his customer walks over to us. The customer is a fidgety one, says he's uncomfortable with me being here, asks Lolo who I am while my heart is still a frantic thing in my chest from the filmy layer.

"Do you really think I'd tell you who she is?" Lolo asks with a gummy smile. "All you need to know is that we have your product. Are you ready for it or should I feed it to the dogs?"

The customer digs into the back of his neck with his nails before passing Lolo an envelope. "I'll see you next Tuesday," he says, grabbing the bag from me and walking away.

I look around, trying to spot the layer again, but Lolo's got his eyes on me. To distract from his questions back in the car, I count the money in the envelope while he drives. "Six hundred dollars for one bag of tea?" I ask. "What does it do? What does he need it for?"

"Who knows what he uses it for, but he probably doesn't need it," Lolo says, and he must be feeling generous because he bangs a left at the stop sign and keeps talking. "That mixture can do many things. But mostly, it can bring the other side into focus."

I think of the connection with Derek's tea. "Why would anyone want that?"

He glances at me. "You don't think people want to talk to the dead?"

"I mean . . . I'm not sure. You've always said *I* shouldn't want to."

Lolo quickly gets serious. "Aria, there's nothing over on the other side for you."

"Then why is it natural for me, when other people pay you to see it?"

"Some are naturally inclined," Lolo says, rolling down his window. "Some are foolish."

I wait for a few seconds, then say, "But even with the tea, I still dream of the spirits. The dreams are fuzzy," I lie, "but the spirits are still in them. And I'm not scared of them, Lolo. So what's so wrong with letting them in all the way?"

"The tea doesn't just make your dreams *fuzzy*. It keeps the spirits from spilling over to your conscious state, and you have no idea what it would be like for you because you don't remember how it was before. But I do. The tea is good. I wouldn't do anything to hurt you."

"Never thought you would," I say, and silence fills the space around us until he puts an end to the conversation by turning up the radio.

When we pull up in front of my house, I drag Lolo out of the car and force him to walk across Derek's lawn with me. Lolo's eyes widen when he sees it. We both squat low, staring at all the thick roots that seemed to have super-spread in the hours since I've been gone. There's no denying it by the look on his face. "What kind of roots are growing here, Lolo?"

His voice comes out in a whisper, like he's talking to himself. "Wisteria."

I want to be unnerved, but part of me already knew. I spent the school day scribbling wisteria roots in my notebook. "Why is it growing here? In this season? So aggressively?"

Lolo stands and reaches out a hand to help me up. He crosses the street and gets in his car. I stand over him outside the window, watching as he does calculations inside his head. When the silence goes on too long, I sigh. I can't talk to Lolo about Derek or about what's happening to me; I can't ask about the letter or where the gift L. Rivera left for me is, but I can talk to him about this. "Say it," I demand. "Say that this is some sort of magic or otherworldly thing—and then admit the rosebush dying the way it did wasn't normal either."

"Have you asked if they planted something?" Lolo says, treating me like a dumb child.

"Why would Mr. Johnson plant wisteria months before winter when he just got the rotting smell from the rosebush under control?"

"Wisteria is a very tough plant," Lolo says, but he's tapping the steering wheel nervously.

"It wouldn't grow *that* fast. Why are you being so weird about this?"

"Because, Blue. We are not detectives." His eyes move past me to Derek's house. "Even if there was something going on, it's not supposed to be our concern. The truth is, there are things like this happening all over the world, at any given time, but that doesn't make it our job to figure out why. There are more important things for you to be doing."

His words hit me weird. They have me thinking about how

much time I spent searching for Derek's mom after she left. I feel a twinge in my chest. "What kind of things?"

"Being able to identify the plants we sell in the shop and successfully make an elixir, anticipating the needs of our clients so teaching you feels like less of a chore."

He might be joking, but it hurts to hear. Bet Adelia never made it feel like a chore, but I can't compare myself to her. "So you don't think anything dangerous is happening here?"

"Out of the ordinary? Maybe. Dangerous? No," he says. "Will you let it go? You should be having fun outside of the shop with those friends you supposedly have. Be normal."

I roll my eyes at him but think of how, just two weeks ago, Brianna and I were talking about prom and college. Mom was coming home to warm dinners. I missed Derek so much, but everything was fine with me. Normal. But not for Derek. Two weeks ago he was still possessed.

"I thought our family wasn't normal," I say. "Whatever, though. What was the name of the poisonous plant your customer bought yesterday?"

Lolo squints his eyes at me and says, "Pokeweed. It can induce vomiting." Then he takes something from his pocket to hand to me. It's a bobby pin. "Found this in my office."

Damn. "I . . . uh. It must've fallen out of my hair while we were in there the other day."

We stare at each other. I'm not sure if he knows the truth and is waiting for me to admit it. But then he puts on his sunglasses and says, "Stay out of trouble, Blue," before driving away.

I walk across the street and knock on Derek's window. He

answers but doesn't move aside to let me in. "I'm a little busy," he says through the screen. "Did you need something?"

This catches me off guard. Makes me feel like maybe I should've texted or called first. "Oh, I . . . uh . . . no, not really." I start to turn away.

"Aria, wait," he says, "I noticed you're going to the haunted estate event tomorrow."

"I am. Is that . . . is it weird?"

A smile creeps up on his face. "Why would it be weird?"

I'm flustered now. "Well . . . I don't know, really. I guess because it's your thing."

He's still smiling like he knows he can affect me. "That's what I wanted to talk to you about. I'm not going and I was wondering if you'd cover for me with Mr. Shepard. He takes these events seriously and expects me to be there to help him with it."

I try to keep the disappointment from my voice. "Is it because you don't feel well?"

Something shifts on his face. He looks disappointed now too. "No, Aria, it's because I'm literally living with a ghost and don't want to be around more of them willingly."

"That makes sense," I say, feeling guilty that I'm going. And deep inside I can't help but think about how I've been inviting my own ghosts into my world more each day. I wonder if Derek will want someone like me around after we get rid of his. "I'll give Mr. Shepard a good excuse. But I'm wondering if I should even be going. Maybe we should do research and find a way to help you get rid of the spirit instead. Or maybe we should go back to see the wisteria trees tonight. There could be clues there too."

Derek grips his windowsill. His arms shake a little. This morning he told me the spirit didn't take over his body last night. I wonder why. It's been taking over every night for weeks. Is it waiting for something? Has it found someone new to haunt? "I just need a night alone, Aria."

The sinking feeling I get when he says it stays with me even after I smile and leave.

TWENTY-SEVEN

Bri and I decide to kill time at Providence Place mall before the event. Mr. Shepard told us to be back at school at six P.M. on the dot or the bus would leave without us. We go half on a plate of Chinese food and Bri shovels her half and some of mine into her mouth. She's buzzing with nerves over seeing Val tonight and making *my* nerves sharper than they already were, especially when she throws a shrimp tail at me and says she's still mad I ignored her text the other night. After eating, we go to try on clothes we can't afford at Macy's. Bri makes me try on a black dress with studs beading the bustline. It hugs my waist and flows out like a bell at the bottom. I run my hands along the curve of my thigh, remembering that the belladonna berry is shaped like this. Serena Bettencourt crying in the living room flashes in my mind. Is she happier now?

"You look stunning, madam. Might be a good choice for prom," Brianna says from behind me. The bright colors of her dress pull my eyes away from my own. A huge neon flower sits on her shoulder and the skirt looks like the blue curtains in Lolo's windows, but Bri still spins in it. "Do you think I should've offered to go pick Val up?"

"With the RIPTA bus driver?"

She cuts her eyes at me. "Sarcasm doesn't suit you, even though you swear it does."

We sit on the dressing room bench in our overpriced dresses. Bri plays with the flower on her shoulder and wonders whether she should make some kind of move to let Val know she's interested tonight. From the mirror, I watch her fingers tangle in the petals as she talks. I watch as a thin ribbon of a shadow starts to form around the flower. It stretches out from the petals like a snake and slithers around her wrist. My heart thrums. I reach for her hand; my fingers flutter along her skin, trying to feel what I see, but I only feel her.

She pulls back from me and the shadow slinks away slowly. "What's wrong?" she asks.

My throat is sandpaper dry. I wish I could tell her about what's happening, but I'll never forget the look on her face when she didn't see the wisteria.

I scrub my eyes with one hand. "I think I'm just tired."

"Well, get it together because you'll need to be alert in this haunted estate. If not to try to see the supposed ghosts that are there, to make sure I don't say anything stupid to Val."

When we leave Macy's, we stop at Auntie Anne's with new pins on our shirts from Spencer's, and Bri goes to order us two pretzels while I hang back with our backpacks and run my brain ragged. I've gone a while without the tea now, but I'm still only seeing wisps of shadows in my conscious state. Lolo said I have no idea what it was like for me before and I wonder how much clearer it'll get. Maybe the tea isn't fully out of my system.

Someone brushes by me. "Sorry, excuse me," they say.

That voice. I know that voice. I turn just a little, enough to catch the side of his slender face. Chills creep up my back as I watch him disappear through the crowd. Levi.

It's starting to get dark on the walk back to school and I can't help but look between buildings and turn to make sure we're not being followed. I don't know if Levi saw me standing there. We could have been in the same place at the same time because Rhode Island is small enough for these kinds of coincidences, but Bri catches a chill and wonders out loud if someone is watching us.

"I'm probably just spooked early," she says, wrapping her arms around herself. "I'm not ready for this event. Do you think Mr. Shepard would hire people just to scare us?"

"No," I say. "And I don't think he'd have to do that in a place like Belcourt Castle."

Bri doesn't believe in ghosts, but for a second she looks at me like she does. She shimmies to shake out her fear just as we turn the corner and see Val standing at the edge of our school building. She tucks her phone in her pocket and waves at us. She really is cute.

"Ahhh, I'm going to vomit," Bri says.

"Act cool. Remember your name. Remember hers . . ." I pull a stick of gum from my bag. "Don't embarrass me, my child."

"God bless you," she says, snatching the gum. "She looks beautiful, doesn't she? I should've made sure to look beautiful."

"You do that effortlessly," I tell her. "Now get over there and say hi to your date."

We file onto the bus, and I tell Mr. Shepard that Derek had a family emergency. He looks as disappointed as I feel. Bri and Val take the seat right in front of me. The door to the bus closes and I almost expect Derek to knock on it, say he's changed his mind. I hate that this is happening to him, that he can't be here doing something he loves, especially because I'm here. There's a ghost haunting him, but I'm out having *fun*. Being *normal*.

Bri turns back in her seat. "Wow. He really isn't coming?"

Val turns too, and smiles. "Who?"

"Her ex–best friend turned enemy turned lover," Bri says.

"Ou, like a romance novel," says Val.

"Gross," I say, but my face is hot as I lean back in my seat. A seat I'm suddenly sharing with someone. Bri's eyes go wide and she grins before I look beside me.

"Mind if I sit with you, Aria?" Sean says, and he's got this cool kind of look about him that makes me shake my head.

Bri and Val peek over at us from their seats, but I pay them no mind and shoot Derek a text. **You feeling OK?**

Resting 😊, he replies.

I should feel better seeing that little smiley face, but I don't. When the bus starts to move, Sean's thigh presses into mine and he keeps it there the whole ride to Newport.

When we arrive at Belcourt Castle forty-five minutes later, students from my school file out of the bus in a rush with Mr. Shepard yelling not to act like fools. Though his crew is waiting for him, somehow Sean ends up next to me while we gather around Mr. Shepard and a woman who will be our tour guide. Brianna gets close to me and she's getting no better at whispering.

"I knew you'd manage to find someone for a double date."

In my mind, I try to pinpoint some moments that may have made Sean interested in me, but I'm met with blanks. I deduce that he didn't want to be scared in front of his real friends and since we were bus buddies he thought he might be able to be scared with me. But whatever his reason, he's pretty decent company, has a few good "would you rather" questions, and also a really nice smile. A smile that happens to be directed at me as the woman giving our tour introduces herself as Ms. Sharon and tells us the owners of the estate are away, that we will have to respect their wishes and try not to touch anything.

Mr. Shepard does another head count, looking warily at Val a few times, surely wondering if he's ever seen her before. Then he lays out his own rules and regulations. We are to stay close to a buddy, no wandering off, and if by any chance one of us gets lost to make sure to meet back at the bus in an hour. "I'm trusting you," he says, his eyes alight with a childhood-like joy as we walk into the darkened building.

As adrenaline rushes through my body, I decide one night of

fun can't be a bad thing. I'm already here. Maybe I'll be able to see a real ghost or two. "I hope it's scary," I say.

Sean laughs. "You're wild."

Maybe my deduction about him being nervous was the correct one.

"Why didn't you say you were scared on the phone?" Bri asks Val, who's terrified enough for everyone here. "We could've done something else."

We're entering a hall with wooden walls when something cute happens: Val links arms with Brianna and says, "No, I'm excited to do this with you."

Suddenly it feels like Sean and I are interrupting something private. We're the last students to walk through the grand entry into the hall, but I turn back to check again because it doesn't feel like it. My thoughts shift to Levi and all I can think about is Lolo telling me to stay far away from him.

Val and Bri cling to each other while they trudge through the darkened halls and into the gothic ballroom where our class is gathered. "This is where parties have been held since the 1890s," Ms. Sharon says. "You can't see it now, but the floor below us is a mosaic tile, imported many years ago from Italy."

She shows us a large cathedral room with stained glass and the highest ceilings I've ever seen. In it stands medieval armor brought here by the original owners ages ago. Sean wishes we could try it on, and Ms. Sharon overhears him and lets us know the man who wore it died an agonizing death. "It's said that his screams still ring through the castle every night."

I'm not scared, but this seems to make Sean move a little

closer to me. We start walking through another hall into a room with a lot of relics. Lolo would love these. Ms. Sharon shows us two chairs that are believed to inflict pain for unwelcome guests.

"The former owners said seventy people saw a bolt of lightning strike the chair for the quickest second on a tour here." She runs a finger along the top of it. "And they say if you sit, the chair will forcibly remove you if you don't have the right energy. Any volunteers?"

Mr. Shepard practically runs up to the chair. Students gather around him, but my eyes flick to a mirror at the opposite side of the room. It's large and antique with a rusty gold lining and distressed glass, and it calls to me. I leave Sean and the group and slink toward it.

When I look into the mirror, the room behind me starts to slowly spin. I blink, trying not to feel sick, because when I open my eyes the room is still spinning. But before I can tear myself away from the mirror, I see something else. A dark figure is standing in one of the doorframes behind me. Maybe they really did hire people to scare us.

Or maybe it's a spirit.

As the figure retreats into the shadows, I feel the familiar pull in my limbs again and I have to know. Everyone is busy trying to get the chair to do something spooky, and no one seems to notice me slipping into the darkened hallway.

TWENTY-EIGHT

The silhouette stands at the end of the hall. "Hello?" I call out, but it turns left and disappears. I start to follow, but someone touches my arm and my heart leaps into my throat.

"What are you doing?" Sean asks me, voice hushed, eyes wide.

I let out a breath. Relieved it's him. "I saw someone," I say. "Or something."

His gaze flicks to the darkness at my back. "And?"

I swallow, smile. I can't tell him my bones are literally aching to go after whatever it was. "Don't you want to see the real reason they say this place is haunted?"

"Aren't you even a little scared, Aria?" He sounds more relaxed now, even entertained.

"Everyone always feels a little fear in these kinds of situations," I say, then link my arm with his the way Brianna did with Val. "But if you want to come, I'll protect you."

He laughs but looks back toward the relic room before he says, "Alright."

We walk through the hall and into a space with statues and

hardwood floors. The figure is in front of us, then it turns toward one of the walls and suddenly just . . . vanishes.

"What the hell?" Sean says, right before the sound of a snake hissing echoes through the large empty room. It seems to be slithering above us on the ceiling, getting closer and closer. We're so still at first, movement an opportunity for the snake to sense us, but then my bones throb and I hurry to the wall where we watched the figure disappear. It's smooth. Sean is at my side feeling the wall frantically, but there's no opening to let us through. Maybe the figure was a spirit. The sound above us gets louder and Sean wants to turn back. But then I remember the research I did on this place.

"There are hidden rooms," I whisper, and start pushing on the wall. Finally, I hear something click under my hands. I push that spot one more time and the door creaks open enough for me to peer into a pitch-black space. Sean turns his phone's flashlight on, and in this moment, even with my fear creeping up, I'm thankful he's here and didn't listen to Mr. Shepherd's rule about leaving our phones on the bus. The hissing sounds so close now. I turn to look back, but Sean slips his free hand into mine and pulls me inside the room.

It's a decent-size space with an old claw-foot bathtub in the corner that reminds me of the old hotel horror movies, but other than that it's completely empty. There's a smaller door across the room and I take a step toward it, but Sean squeezes my hand.

"I think we should stop here. Go back to our class," he says. "Maybe the snake sounds were on a speaker to scare us. Either way, we're not supposed to be here."

"I'll be fine," I say, removing my hand from his to turn the doorknob. "You should go."

Sean sighs but stays by my side as we walk into another room. I choke as dust motes dance in the air. Sean shoves them away, swats at cobwebs, says things under his breath. There's furniture covered in cloth and too many doorways to choose from. While Sean is lifting a cloth to look underneath, I walk over to one of the doorways, but then the room goes entirely dark.

"Shit, my phone died." Sean's voice is too many feet away. I don't remember the direction.

Brianna warned me not to leave my phone on the bus, but I didn't listen. I turn to head back to where I think Sean is, but something shifts and stands right in my path.

I flinch back at the sound of breathing. Something or someone touches my hair. My voice trembles as Sean's name spills from my lips. "Sean . . . Sean. Is that you?"

"Aria," Sean says, worried. Still across the room. Still far from me. My pulse rushes in my ear. "No. It's not. What—where are you? I can't see anything. Is someone here?"

My body pricks everywhere, a shiver climbs my spine. I walk backward, away from the person or the spirit, slowly heading for one of the doorways. Sean's voice grows farther away. And I'm silently listening to the footsteps that are echoing my own, until my adrenaline takes over and I break into a run.

I stumble into another hall, see dim light coming from a room ahead, but before I can make it there, someone tugs my arm back and turns me around. Air doesn't exist. My lungs give out. Time stops for just a second. But then I see what's in front of me: a guy wearing an old cartoon mask resembling a baby. The kind you would see in a slasher movie.

Levi, my mind screams, but I have no time to reach for my father's pocketknife because the masked person clamps their hand around the back of my neck. My body buzzes; his touch sends electricity swirling through me. I try to scream, but he shoves something soft into my mouth. A flower? Tears build in my eyes as he forces me to swallow it. Even though it's smooth, I still choke, dry heave, cry. He lets me go and takes a few steps back, giving me space to run, but then something happens.

Suddenly, I can feel every atom I'm made of. All the pieces of me burst with energy. A power thrums in my veins; my skin scorches hot and cold and everything between. Then, the darkness around us changes color. The ceiling is the aurora borealis; my body is the source. Every inch of my skin glows with a fluorescent blue light.

For a few seconds, I am nothing I once was but everything I've always been.

Levi makes a guttural sound and removes his mask. The blue light from my body spills onto him and . . . he's not Levi. He's Derek.

I'm hurt. Scared. The light coming off my limbs goes away in an instant as shock floods through me. Derek grabs me and pulls me close to him in the darkness. Together, we are a blazing fire and there are traces of blue light in the air around us.

I start to sob, my body shakes, I can't breathe. This isn't Derek.

"Shh," the spirit says into my ear. "It's okay, Bluebird. I've finally found you."

"What did you do to me?" I push away from him, touch my lips with trembling fingers, and realize the flower I ingested must've been wisteria. "What did you do?"

Wisteria from the glowing trees. It did something to me the night in the forest and it did something to me now. Before the spirit stealing Derek's body can answer, Sean's voice cuts through the dark room. "Aria." He sounds scared, more terrified than he was.

"Sean," I call out, clear my throat, try louder. "Sean, I'm over here."

Not-Derek smiles at me, then I watch him slink into the shadows.

When Sean taps my shoulder a few seconds later, I swing a fist out on first instinct and miss entirely. My limbs don't feel like they belong to me; I nearly fall forward.

"Whoa there, Pacquiao," he says, breathing heavily and helping to steady me by the shoulders. "It's just me. What happened?"

I throw myself at him, wither as I sob.

While he rubs my back, the last of the buzzing under my skin fades away.

"Let's get you the hell out of here," he says.

TWENTY-NINE

Val and Bri are waiting for us outside the mansion. They're hyped, but I still haven't spoken more than two words to Sean so I don't know what to say to any of them.

Sweetness sticks to the roof of my mouth, bitterness sits in my esophagus, a phantom of blue light builds behind my eyelids. There are no words.

"Where the hell did you two sneak off to?" Bri asks, narrowing her eyes and glancing between us like she knows exactly what happened. She doesn't. Neither do I.

"We were following someone planted by the estate to scare us, seemed like a ghost," Sean says, sending a tingling sensation up my spine. *Seemed like.* "Your little friend here decided to go on an adventure by herself. I'm not sure what spooked her, but maybe she'll tell you."

Bri's eyes shoot to mine and for a second I think I see some understanding in them, but she smiles and throws an arm around me. "Did your curiosity finally catch up to you in there?"

All I can do is nod. While they laugh and talk about the estate, I focus on finding Derek in the crowd, behind trees, somewhere in the distance. I can still feel his fingers in my mouth, pushing wisteria down my throat. I wonder if he's watching me right now.

When we're back on the bus, Mr. Shepard gives Val another skeptical look before shrugging. "I'm sad Derek wasn't here," he says. Derek *was* here. In body, not in spirit. I hug myself. "If any of you talk to him this weekend, tell him to email me. But I want to say I'm proud of you all for following the rules . . ." He pauses, points to three students up front. "Correction, I'll be discussing your little extracurricular activities with your parents."

While he goes on, Sean leans over to ask if I want to talk about what happened. I shake my head and he says, "This is gonna sound weird, but I saw these colorful lights in the door-way of the room you were in. Felt like they led me to you. Did you see them?"

Relief pours through me. He saw the lights too. I let go of myself, allow my arm to brush up against his. But then I remember that he doesn't know the lights came from me, or why, and the relief I feel starts to dissipate. There's only two ways I'll know what happened to me: I can talk to Lolo or I'll have to ask the spirit. Both options weigh me down. Derek wasn't in control, but every time I close my eyes I see his face and feel him shoving that flower down my throat.

Sean is waiting for an answer, so I say, "I saw them too, but I don't know what they were." He seems to accept this and scoots a little closer to me. It feels nice to tell someone the truth, even half of it. Especially because I've been robbed of truths for years.

"You're alright, Aria. Even though you almost got us eaten by ghosts or whatever."

I swallow and say, "You're not so bad yourself."

"Are you going to Gary's party tomorrow?" He grins. "Maybe we could hang out there?"

"Definitely not," I say. Gross Gary *and* another party after what just happened to me?

Sean places his hand on top of mine. "I really hope you change your mind."

Something twists in my stomach. Sean likes me. My face flushes with blood, but I gently pull away from him. There's no time to think about boys right now. Unless that boy is Derek. As the bus starts up, I look out the window and wonder where his body is right now.

⌁

My heart is still making me aware it's in my chest as I sit cross-legged on Bri's carpet. We are painting our toes with her mom's brand-new gel polish and I'm doing a really shitty job. Black streaks everywhere, missing the edges, a glop of it on my pinkie toe. Brianna asks me what's got me so distracted, but there's nothing real I can tell her right now so I shrug. I'm happy to be here with her tonight, away from my house and Derek, not alone while Mom works. I'm tempted to go to Lolo and tell him everything, but even if I was willing to betray Derek's trust, I know Lolo might take control of the situation and leave me in the dark again. So I texted my sister earlier instead, told her to call me tomorrow. I'm hoping she actually comes through.

"Shit," Bri says, and scrambles toward me, grabbing the tipped-over bottle off the floor. But it's too late. Black polish has already pooled on her carpet.

"Your mom's gonna flip." I stretch out my shirt to wipe it away, but it smudges instead.

"She told me not to touch her new polish." Bri gets to her feet, hurries out of the room, comes back with acetone and we try to work on the stain, but we don't get far. "I'll throw something over it for now," she says, resigned. "But if she sees and I get smacked up, you owe me a large square from Silver Lake Pizza and some fried lumpia from your kitchen."

"Deal." I laugh. For only a second, things feel normal, they feel okay. "I'm sorry, though."

"Is it Derek that has you so distracted?" Bri asks. "Why do you think he didn't come?"

A breath gets caught in my lungs. I duck my head to avoid her eyes. I can't lie to her. I don't want to, but what choice do I have? Maybe another half-truth. "Derek does have me distracted," I say. "He hasn't been feeling well. I hope he's alright."

"Hmm, is it the flu or something?"

"No," I say, then change the subject. "How was it with Val and your hot half date?"

"Magical," Bri says, throwing herself down on the carpet. "We screamed and held hands. I think I'm falling in love."

I lie down beside her. "Tell her she can only have you Mondays from now on."

She laughs and looks over at me. "Maybe we need some

rules for Sean too. He's so damn cute. Had heart eyes for you the whole night."

"He did, didn't he?" I say, and feel a little warm thinking back to our conversation on the bus. "He wants me to go to Gary's party tomorrow night."

"And so do I," Bri says. "I'm taking Val. We can have another double date."

"Not gonna happen," I tell her. I need to figure out what happened to me. I feel different now, something circling around in my soul. But I can't pinpoint exactly what the feeling is.

I lift my phone, look at my last text from Derek.

Resting ☺, the spirit said.

While Bri snores on her bed, I try to write notes in my journal but find myself staring into her vanity mirror. The small lights make the blue in my eyes glow the same color coming from me at the estate. My hand shakes. I put my pen down and examine the rest of me. My nose, my neckline, my throat. I mostly look like me, but I *am* different.

Shadows slink on the wall behind me and above Bri's head. I tear myself from the mirror with a sigh and crawl into bed beside her. For the briefest moment, before sleep comes for me, I wonder if I made a mistake when I stopped drinking my tea.

I drift right into the gray.

The shadows are silver, black, white threads weaving and intermingling, tangling and growing. They glow and so do I. My hands are wispy, almost translucent, then sparkling before becoming moonlight. I'm not afraid when I reach out and grab for the shadows, but they suddenly become solid in my luminous hands. They don't just take on shapes, they become people without color. Black-and-white like an old movie. They stare into my eyes, ask me to help, they cry, pull at their hair, they're scared.

We see you, they say. *We see you.*

Behind me, the abyss forms. Slowly spinning, pulling, eating everything around me. Colorless spirits get sucked into its gaping mouth. They try to cling for something. They try to cling to me. The abyss takes whatever it wants. But it doesn't take me.

And it doesn't take Derek's body.

There you are, Bluebird, the spirit inside of him says from beside me. Startling black eyes staring into my soul.

I wake up right then, gasping for air, choking on my saliva, gripping the sheets.

Sound floats across the room. A whisper, singsong. "Ariiiiiia," someone calls. Once. Then again. Brianna is still asleep beside me and the wind brushes up against the window and I can't shut the sounds out. I sit up, swing my legs off the bed and head for the light switch. Bri doesn't flinch when the room goes bright. I remember the faces of the spirits, but can't see them right now, even though it feels like some of them see *me*. I brace myself against Bri's desk, knowing my whole life will be different. My heartbeat slows in understanding.

The spirits are a part of me and I am a part of them.

I am changed. Was this what I was asking for?

I need something for my burning throat, to splash water on my face, to speak to Derek.

I'm careful not to make too much noise walking through the house to the kitchen. Brianna's mom is a light sleeper, but she has her bedroom door closed and I've mastered using quiet feet. But then I hear a creaking sound behind me. Like someone's walking in the shadow of my footsteps. I walk fast through the living room and click the lights on as soon as I make it to the kitchen. I'm never usually scared like this. I'm not scared, I'm not.

I splash water on my face from the sink and try to catch my breath before opening the fridge to pull out the bottle of orange juice, but as soon as I shut the door something shifts to my left and startles me. But it's just the curtains rising.

Wait. The curtains are rising. The window is wide open.

Brianna's mom always makes sure to shut them because of *thieves and killers*, but the window is open enough for someone to fit through it. I bend to look out at the backyard and can see the leaves rustling in the trees and the faint glow from the neighbor's driveway light, but nothing else. It's good. I'm good. I shut the window and start to straighten, but then someone taps my shoulder and I drop the orange juice bottle on the floor.

"Boo," Bri says, voice flat, right up against my ear. She bends to pick up the juice bottle while I try to regulate my breathing. "Good thing this was closed, you klutz."

"What the hell are you doing scaring me like that?"

"Since when are you so scared?" Bri asks, rubbing her eyes.

"The window was open," I say.

"No way," Brianna replies. Then, "Wow. That woman stays getting on me for everything and she's over here messing up. I can't wait to talk junk about this tomorrow morning."

When we go back to the room, all I can hear is Derek's voice in my head. *There you are, Bluebird, I've finally found you.*

THIRTY

I walk home from Bri's early to make potato, eggs, and cheese while Mom irons our outfits. It's rare for her to get a Saturday morning off, but it's like she knew I needed to be with her. We decide to make it count with pedicures and the flea market before she has to sleep for her overnight shift and before I have to pay closer attention to the constant vibration in my bones since eating the wisteria. I'm relieved we don't see Derek across the street on our way out.

It's been a while since we hit the flea market to buy cheap stuff we might not need. As we walk through, I keep seeing flashes behind my eyelids: the faces of spirits, people, some only children, in the gray space with me last night. I try to shake off the thoughts and have fun with Mom. We watch the fighting fish in their bowls, check out bamboo plants and the knockoff purse section that's always packed with people. Mom is giddy while looking through the dollar earrings on a table. It's strange to see her this way.

"What? A woman can't smile?" she asks when she sees the look on my face.

"Are you . . . dating?"

"No, are you?"

I think back to Sean saying he hopes I'll come to the party tomorrow, then an image of Derek staring at me from a seat over on the bus crops up in my head. "Definitely not," I say.

"Well, I'm not either . . . not yet."

I snatch a hoop earring pack off the table and hand it to her. "These. Now tell me."

"Well, there is this one person from my job and he's so kind. The nicest person I've ever met. He helps me when he's done with his shifts and takes extra desserts from the cafeteria for me. He offered to cover one of my shifts today so I could spend some time with you."

Her words make me feel warm. "Maybe I like him already."

"Let's not get ahead of ourselves. He's just a friend for now. No one I'm pushing for you to meet. But if it goes someplace special, would you consider it? I'd need your approval."

Mom tried dating before but no one was ever worth taking seriously. Sometimes, I wonder if she misses my father so much no one else can measure up. My stomach forms a knot when I think of Derek again. This time, it's us at fifteen, writing letters in class because we were assigned seats on opposite ends of the room.

I clear my throat. "Oh, you'll definitely be needing my approval. Can't have an evil stepfather around the house eating my Lunchables and possibly the neighbor's flesh too."

Mom swats at my arm and laughs. "I can assure you he's not a cannibal."

"And I promise you wouldn't know that kind of deep, dark secret," I say.

Bri texts while we walk, begging me to go to Gary's party with her and Val, but I ignore it because I see a CARD READINGS sign on a door two rooms down from the perfume shop. My heart thrums a little faster. It seems like a sign here just for me. Mom doesn't appear to notice. She pulls me into the perfume shop and starts sniffing open bottles. While she's entrenched in conversation with the perfume seller, I can't fight the urge.

"Mom, I'm going to go look at the hats," I say. I shouldn't go anywhere. I should stay and have a normal day. But part of me knows I'll never have a normal day again.

As I walk through the crystal-beaded curtain in the door-frame, someone calls, "First few minutes are free. If you like what you hear, it's twenty dollars for a full reading." She's look-ing down at the deck of cards she's shuffling. "My name's Sheila. Tell me yours."

"Aria," I say, and her owl-like eyes shoot up from the cards to my face in an instant.

She has a spread of freckles over her taupe-colored skin. When she tells me to sit, she doesn't break eye contact. She's mes-merizing. "You have an energy about you, Aria."

I laugh nervously, wondering if Sheila is a fraud. Isn't that the first thing they always say on TV? And she can't be much older than me. Her early twenties, I'm guessing. The mediums Lolo has talked about in the past all had years of experience. Still, the color of her irises are startling, more yellow than golden. I wonder if they're contacts or if there really is something different about her like there's something different about me. "What's my aura like?" I ask.

She puts her deck down and grabs my hands, pulling them

across the table. Her firm grip surprises me. "I don't even need a card reading for this. Your hands are thrumming with enough energy. There's also a veil surrounding you as well." I think of the gray and shadows of spirits, the black abyss, the thin filmy layer I've been seeing lately. I think of the dark things that hide inside of me. She runs a finger down one of the lines on my palm and we both seem to shiver.

"You are a magnet, Aria. Things are attracted to you. You find them easily, but they also find you. You're solid, a . . . fixture." She quirks an eyebrow at me and I shut my open mouth. "You're on the verge of discovering how special you are." *Special?* I lean forward, my breath caught in my throat, waiting for her to say more, but then fear sparks a thought: What if she says the special thing inside of me is evil? "You've been running toward it lately."

"But what is it? What's wrong with me?"

"Oh, my love," the frown on her face is enough to make my eyes sting, "there is absolutely nothing wrong with you. You have a gift. Don't be scared of it."

Oh. Tears burn the backs of my eyes and threaten to slip. "Are you sure?" I ask. "Do you know what it is?"

"I'm sure." She runs a finger in a circle on my palm, her eyebrows dip together, a humming noise comes from her throat. "I see earth and trees and a serpent in a circle . . ."

For a moment, I try to register her words. Then I whisper, "Death and rebirth."

She looks up and folds her fingers around mine. Her irises suck me in. "We have company coming, and you'll need to get going, but you should know your aura is unlike any I've ever seen. It glows like moonlight but has more colors than life has to offer."

Chills travel the length of my spine. The hair on my arms rises. I almost ask her if there's blue light in my aura, but Mom comes storming into the room, the crystal beads in the doorway clacking against one another. "Aria, that's enough. Let's go," she says.

Sheila lets out the smallest sigh. It's probably only audible to my ears, but I can tell she wishes we weren't being interrupted. She gives my mom a smile, then releases my hands. "Thank you, Aria," she says to me. "I'm sure I'll see you again soon."

On the way out the door, I watch her bring her palms to her cheeks and close her eyes.

I'm still flushed with what just happened when we get in the car, and Mom's persistence to get us out of there has my mind running wild. How much does she truly know about me? She fumbles with getting her key in the ignition. I ask her what's wrong, and she says, "Nothing."

I'm tired of it. "It's not nothing," I say. "You're hiding things from me. So is Lolo. If you know something about me, then you should tell me now. I'll find out myself. Sheila . . ."

Mom turns sharply; the look on her face rips my words right out of me. "Is a fraud," she finishes. "People like that don't know what they're talking about. Sometimes they say things to lead others in the wrong direction, down a whole path of trouble from predictions that aren't even real. And if we are hiding things, it's for your own good, but nothing *she* says is real."

"She said I have a gift," I confess. "Is the fact that I see spirits a gift, Mom?"

"No. It's not a gift. It's a curse," Mom says, and her words hit my heart. "That's why you drink your tea, Aria. And Sheila might be trying to make you see that curse for what it isn't. She's a scammer wanting to feed you lies so you can keep paying her to send you traveling dark paths with her guidance. You're seventeen, it's time you stop being so naive and trusting."

I'm crying again. She mumbles something, frustrated, and I laugh through the tears. "You're the one always telling me I have too many theories, that I watch *The First 48* like it's breakfast and need to stop spying on the neighbors. Suddenly I'm too trusting? The person I shouldn't be trusting is *you*, and you've just admitted it to me."

Mom's lips twitch. I worry I've said too much. She smacked me across the face once, and I feel the same energy between us now. But then she narrows her eyes as she stares into mine. My stomach squeezes in panic. What if she sees the new colors poking through? I shift in my seat, away from her gaze, exhale sharply. She grabs my chin roughly and examines me.

Her voice is low when she asks, "You are drinking your tea, right?"

She can probably hear my heart racing. "I am," I whisper.

It's not convincing enough. "Aria," she starts, but then I'm saved by her cell phone. "Shit. My boss is calling." A pause, and then she says, "We'll talk about this later, but I don't want you to think of Sheila ever again. That's an order."

I feel like screaming but settle in my seat and stare out the window.

While she talks on the phone, I think about how Sheila told me more about myself in three minutes than my family has told me all my life. I shoot a quick text to Lolo, lying about having a big test to study for this weekend, and ask if I can return to work Tuesday.

Wish I didn't have to see your face tomorrow morning for church either, he replies.

As we drive home, the colors of the world blur and that thing inside of me burns.

THIRTY-ONE

I'm sprawled across my bed, ready for sleep so I can see what it's like in the gray space today. *Don't be scared of it*, Sheila said. But the sun is far from finished for the day, and Adelia finally calls me. She sounds as exhausted as I feel. "Everything alright, Aria?"

My heart does a nervous thing hearing her voice. "Is everything alright with you?"

"Yeah, yeah, everything is fine," she rushes to say. "Anyway, talk to me."

"If you're sure," I say, and tell her as much as I can while leaving out the wisteria flower being shoved down my throat and Derek's ghost being the shover. "Do you happen to know anything about the file at all? The letter?" *If I have a gift?* I can't force myself to say it out loud again right now after Mom called it a curse.

Adelia is quiet for a few seconds, then, "Do you know that little botanica on Atwells Ave I'd go to? The one in the basement?" I sit straight up in bed. "The letter you mentioned makes me wonder if L. Rivera was referring to that botanica."

"Why?" I hold my breath, wait.

"Lolo used to say the family who own it are very special. I'd do deliveries to and from the botanica for him all the time. I think maybe," she pauses, seems to consider what she is about to say and how she will say it, "maybe you should go there and introduce yourself to a woman named Isobel. But you'll have to be discreet about it if you don't want Lolo to know."

I smile. "He'll realize his perfect little Adelia is far from perfect for telling me."

She sighs. "He'll find that out sooner than later regardless."

Her tone catches me off guard. "Tell me what's wrong, Adelia. I know something is."

"Nothing I can't handle," she says. "But listen, I'll come home as soon as I can, okay? Sorry I haven't been around, but I love you and I'm doing my best. For now, please stay safe."

When we hang up, I make a list.

-Go to botanica Monday, talk to Isobel
-Find Sheila again. Weekend? Talk more about my gift...or curse?
-Check the growing wisteria on Derek's lawn tomorrow + go back to Neutaconkanut
-Call Derek. When?

Just as I write it, a knock on my window startles me.

I open the curtain. He's standing outside with his hands in his pockets. We stare at each other through the glass. I should be scared to let him in after what happened last night. I was nervous thinking of it this morning, but seeing his face only brings me relief. He's alright. I'm alright. For now, we both are, and we have each other, no matter how messed up everything is.

When I open the window, Derek lifts himself up and inside with ease. All 6'3" of him is towering over me in my small room with its slanted ceiling on one side. I'm suddenly aware of four things: my door is shut, Mom is sleeping in the next room, my own bed is a few feet away, and I'm only wearing a T-shirt that hits above the knees. Derek doesn't seem to notice any of it. He just takes a tentative step toward me; his Adam's apple bobs in his throat. He looks sick as he searches my face. His skin seems leached of some color, and he lifts a shaky hand like he's going to touch my cheek but drops it.

"You're safe," he breathes. His shoulders slump, he closes his eyes. I watch him shake just a little. "I didn't know if . . ." I reach to touch his arm without thinking and his eyes flutter open. He glances down at my hand and frowns.

"I fell asleep," he says. "I tried so hard not to fall asleep, but I did and he went after you."

My stomach sinks. That's why the spirit hadn't taken over the other night; Derek hasn't been sleeping. I slide my hand down his arm and squeeze his wrist. "You can't just not sleep. This isn't your fault. We need to get rid of the spirit."

He pulls away from me and tugs at his hair from the scalp. "It's not just sleeping now. Since last night . . . Aria, I don't remember anything from today. He let go, and I came here."

My brain jumps back to the spirits in my dreams. How fleshy they looked there. I wonder if the spirit feeding me the wisteria changed things, tipped them in his favor too. "He's stronger," I say.

Derek chews his bottom lip. "Just tell me you're okay. I know . . . Ugh. I was in and out at the estate when he . . . when *we* made you eat the wisteria. What even was that? Why?"

"You didn't . . ."

"Aria," he says, quieting me. "I'm so sorry."

I feel his words in my chest. They make me heavy. Ache. Bring back the fear and sadness. "I know it's not you," I say. "But if he uses your body for something like that again . . ."

"Use that knife you've been keeping in your pocket," he says with a straight face.

"If I have to," I say. "I thought I could kick your ass myself, but I don't know anymore."

"Use it," he says again, then his features soften. "Are you feeling okay? Did the wisteria make you sick? I saw a bright light. Glowing. Was that . . . coming from you?"

I release a breath. I didn't know how much I'd have to tell him about last night, and even though he'd believe me, this is another person who saw the light. That makes two. I think of Sean briefly. He's probably getting ready for the party right now, doing normal teenage things while I'm doing this. I start to explain what happened and Derek's eyes go wide hearing about Sheila, but before I can elaborate or tell him about Adelia and the botanica, he stops me.

"Don't tell me any more. Not yet. He could be listening and I don't think he should know anything else about you. I don't want to hurt you, Aria. I can't." He covers his face with his hands. "Maybe we should go to your grandfather. I don't want to hurt anyone else either. If I can't get my body back and he doesn't believe me, I'd rather my dad commit me someplace."

"Don't talk like that," I say. "He'd definitely believe you. They did this to you."

We sit there in silence for a moment, me thinking of the options we have, Derek probably trying to convince himself that telling our family is the right thing. I'm just not so sure anymore. What have they told us? Nothing. They just made a mess for us to deal with. "Not yet," I say.

He uncovers his face, looks at me. "I need my body back. What if my passenger does something worse with it? What if he takes it over for good?"

"I don't think he can do that without some kind of spell, but we should try to talk to him," I say, "find out what he wants from the both of us. I think we need more answers for ourselves before we go to my grandfather with facts and force him to fix this. Okay?"

It takes Derek a moment to speak. "Alright, Detective," he finally says. "But how do we get him to talk to us? He comes out when he feels like it now."

An uncomfortable thought nags me. "We could go to Neutaconkanut, see the wisteria."

"After he made you eat a flower?" Derek makes a face. "No.

Besides, I don't trust him to talk to you alone there. I barely trust myself with you alone at all."

His protectiveness brings flutters to my belly. And after what happened, I'm not ready to go back there just yet, even though we should.

"I have another idea," I say, "but you might hate it."

THIRTY-TWO

I'm on FaceTime with Brianna, trying to find something to wear while she's fully dressed and eating a burger provided by the school cafeteria for our trip yesterday. Mr. Shepard passed them out on the bus and Bri packed mine and Val's both in her bag. She makes a face as she examines the burger after a bite. "Do you think they even cooked this right?"

"Will you eat it regardless of my answer?"

"Yes," she says, and takes another bite. "Ooh. That one!"

"This one? Really?" I hold the white dress to my body. "It's a little plain and short."

"Short is fine. And do your hair like you do with those clip thingies," she says.

I throw the dress down on the bed and my eyes flick to the letter from L. Rivera. I can't wait to get to the botanica on Monday. I hope my sister is right.

"Thinking of how you're going to handle meeting up with Sean while bringing Derek as a date?" Bri asks.

"What? No." I shake my head and laugh. "Neither of those things truly apply here."

She rolls her eyes, makes a smacking noise with her mouth. "I can't believe Derek's coming to Gary's party with us. What the hell is up with you two anyway? Are you both ready to admit that you've been pining over each other for years?"

"Pining for our friendship, maybe," I say.

Bri uses a fake jealous voice. "Just friendship? Then what does he give you that I can't?"

My stomach sinks. I don't want to compare them like this, and Bri might be faking jealousy right now, but I've been leaving her in the dark the past couple days, lying to her. There are things that I can talk to Derek about but can't tell her as easily. It doesn't mean her friendship matters any less to me. It's just different. "I need you both," I tell her.

"Good answer, darling," she says.

Derek is a smart-ass. I watch him through the window as he makes a dramatic entrance to the street, waltzing down the stairs, hands in his pockets, dark shades on even though it's night. I move away from the window and a few seconds later a car horn beeps outside. Mom comes into the living room. We didn't talk after the flea market; she went straight to her room to go to bed. She sees me dressed up and asks who's outside waiting for me. I don't want to talk to her, but I tell her I'm going out with Derek. She eyes me suspiciously. "You're friends again?"

"Umm . . . I think so."

"Hmm. Well, I can't believe I'm saying this, but when I was your age there was lots of funny business going on between me and my *friends*. So no funny business with him, okay?"

The thought of doing anything *funny* with Derek makes my cheeks hot. Her light tone would normally get a laugh, maybe an *Ew, Mom,* but I'm still upset with her so all I do is nod.

"I see the way you look when you say his name. All red in the face and . . ."

Derek beeps the horn again. "Anyway," I say. "Have a good work shift, Mom."

When my hand is on the doorknob, she says, "Aria. I'm sorry for what I said in the car. I just want to protect you."

"From myself," I say, my back still turned to her, throat gone dry. "I know. Love you."

She sighs. "I love you too, baby."

I notice right away that Derek's wearing cologne. It's soft and airy and smells so good. I missed the stage where he started wearing it and feel bitter for a second. He's looking at me, so I fidget. "I hope this isn't weird," I say. "There will be two other people with us. You only know one of them, though. But once we get to the party, there will be shuffling feet and teenagers dancing, but not us, and possibly food there in case you're hungry. It'll be four friendly people going to a friendly place together."

He laughs. "You are still the same awkward little human. You don't have to make sure I know this isn't a date. We came up with a plan to draw my passenger out, remember?"

"Good, because that would be gross," I say. "I mean, we bathed together in rain puddles when we were kids. So yes, we're only ghost hunting tonight."

"Fine," he says, smirking.

I lift an eyebrow at him. "I think we need some kind of system."

"A system?"

"Yeah, like how do I know it's you right now and not your passenger?"

"Because I'm telling you it's me."

"Not good enough," I say. "There has to be a way you can prove it."

He looks out the window. His voice is lower when he finally speaks. "One night, you woke up from a bad dream and couldn't go back to sleep. It must have been three in the morning when you crawled in my window and into my bed." I hold my breath, but there's a floating feeling in my chest. "You were shaking and I held your hand and told you about lilacs and growing onions, boring stuff, until you fell back to sleep." He breathes out and looks at me. "Proof enough for you? Since my passenger doesn't know everything, are memories good?"

I'm trying to get my heart to beat in a steady rhythm. I clear my throat. "Yes. Memories are good for this," I say. "And it was never boring stuff."

Derek smiles. "If you say so, Detective."

As we wait for Val to come out of her house, Bri catches my eyes in the mirror and does a little shimmy. "This is so much better than RIPTA right now," she says, and leans forward. "Please thank your dad for letting us use his ride. He came through for our double date."

My mouth goes slack. I'm going to pinch her stomach so damn hard at the party.

Derek lets out a laugh and glances at me. "Just four people doing friendly things, huh?"

"That's what it is. We talked about this."

He decides to crush my feelings a bit: "I hope so. I think we'd be better as friends. *If* we get there."

"If we get there," I repeat. The crushing feeling eases and is replaced with something lighter. Derek, my Derek, just referred to us as friends. Kind of. Possibly. But it's enough for now.

From the backseat, Bri claps. "Was that a burn? Derek, don't be rude to my best friend," she says. "Just so you know, she doesn't even find you attractive."

"Perfectly fine with me." Derek shrugs. "So is your girl getting ready for prom or something? We've been out here a while."

Bri sucks her teeth, but she's smiling. "She's not my girl yet. But you're over here talking and wearing dark sunglasses just to look cute. How are you driving like that? Are we safe?"

"I can see perfectly fine," Derek says. "And if you need to know, my eyes hurt earlier when I looked at the moon."

"Okay, werewolf," Bri says. "You should get that checked."

I look out the window at the huge hunter's moon. I have a feeling it's the passenger inside of Derek making things difficult for him. And I didn't notice it before, but he keeps tapping the steering wheel with shaky fingers. Val comes out of her house, and while Bri is nervously adjusting her outfit, I ask Derek if he's alright. He nods, but I'm unconvinced.

Gary's party is packed with more people than usual. He seems to have invited half of Central High School and maybe Mount

Pleasant too. There are people sitting on top of his dad's pool table and there's someone hanging off his staircase bannister. I can tell Derek is the Derek I know because he shoves his hands in his pockets and looks stiff when Gary and the gang come up to him. Sean isn't with them, so he must be around here somewhere. Val and Bri leave to get drinks in the kitchen, but Derek's already got a beer that Gary shoved into his hand. He hasn't sipped on it once. "You hate this," I say.

"I do," he admits at the same time some kid falls off the coffee table and lands close to us with a thud. Derek startles and spills some of the beer. "Do you really think my ghost friend shares your love for this crowd?" he says.

"I don't love this crowd," I tell him, "but I don't completely hate it either. Sometimes it's an interesting way to people watch." A smile spreads over Derek's face. Before he can say something slick about me, I ask, "Do you want to go out back? Get some air?"

"Yes please," he says, but then—

"Aria, you made it," Sean says, suddenly beside us. He looks so happy to see me, my face flushes.

Derek says something that I can't hear over the music, then cuts around Sean to head out the back door. Sean follows Derek with his eyes, then looks at me with a question on his face. He knows better than to ask why I'm with someone else when he invited me here. "We could go talk somewhere? Or dance?"

He says it right when the song changes and people start slow grinding around us. My throat thickens. Brianna's right. I don't know how to flirt. And I don't think right now is the time to be doing it either. "Can I get back to you on that?"

"Oh." He blinks. "Yeah, sure. I'll be waiting."

I give him a smile and slip away to find Derek.

The smokers are messing with one another's shirt collars under the trees in the yard and Derek is sitting at the bottom step of the small deck watching. I take a seat beside him, play with the hem of my dress. "You, umm. Sean. He," I try.

"Aria," Derek cuts in, "remember how we said this isn't a date? That it's definitely not, for sure, no way a date. You don't need to explain the Sean thing."

"It's just . . ." I trail off, my ears burning with embarrassment. "Sorry."

Derek throws a small rock off the deck. "You don't need to be sorry either. We're cool."

"Got it," I say, watching the smokers make wispy shapes that remind me of spirits in the night sky.

Derek tilts his head and stares at me, but I pretend not to notice. Until he says, "This isn't a date, but if it was a date I'd tell you that you remind me of moonlight tonight."

A breath gets caught in my throat. Sheila's words bounce back; so does my dream after the haunted estate. I tilt my head at him. "Hurting your eyes?"

He doesn't laugh. "Your dress is pretty. And I like what you did with your hair."

I touch one of the dozen small clips in my curls. Glued to them are different-size pearls on top of white daisies I found in our neighborhood. My cheeks burn. Did he really just say all of that to me? "You smell good," I say.

"Thanks, but you should learn to take a compliment."

"I'll try," I say, then, "So, what can we do to make your passenger come out and say hello?"

He scratches the back of his neck, then quickly reaches to slide his fingers over my palm.

Woof. Goosebumps trail my skin at the feel of him. His touch doesn't need to be startling, ghostly and almost painful, to make my body do things.

I swallow. "Thought you said this wasn't a date."

He rolls his eyes, and rubs circles into my skin with his thumb. "I'm testing something."

We stay like that a while. Me, having a tough time breathing, hoping he can't feel my sweaty palms. Him, looking up at the sky like he's completely unfazed.

He removes his fingers from my hand and curls them in a ball. "Well, guess touch isn't it," he says. "He must not like you in a romantic way. I thought he might because he took my body out to dance with you and that was ridiculously romantic."

Shit. He remembers. I laugh, but inside I'm screaming. How much of it did he get to see? How did it feel watching himself dance with me when he wanted nothing to do with me at the time? I want to ask him, but instead I say, "What other theories do you have, sir?"

"None," he says, "but I'm sure you have some, Detective."

"Just a few."

THIRTY-THREE

Derek and I walk on top of the thin porch ledge, balancing like fools because my first theory is that the spirit inside of him likes when he lives on the edge. But even when his foot almost comes off the ledge and he sways, the passenger doesn't come out. We try everything from a mini outside manhunt with the smokers where my heart is racing and Derek is calling out stuff like, "Come out, come out wherever you are," followed by him doing backflips off the porch while our new friends use their fingers to score his landing. Derek even pulls a muscle doing it, but the passenger doesn't care.

"Maybe you should take a nap on Gary's bed," I suggest.

Derek scrunches up his nose. "Who knows what's happened in that bed."

Back inside the house, Derek says he'll consider going to his car and attempting to nap but he's wired, too awake, and he needs a little break from me and my theories. We part ways. At first, I feel this desperate worry that if I don't help him with this we'll go back to not speaking at all. But then I realize this is good. Parting ways for a bit gives me time to think of everything I haven't thought of without the pressure of him being anxious beside me.

And I'm hungry and tired. I need Cheez doodles. My eyes land on Bri and I watch her give a fake bow before asking Val to dance. Bri's hand moves to Val's back, and they're both smiling so big it makes me want to take a picture. So I do. On Monday, we'll eat cafeteria chicken patties that manage to taste like garbage *and* hit the spot while sitting in the hall at school, and I'll show her this picture so we can talk about how cute she and Val looked together, but tonight, I have a mission. Before I head to the kitchen, I see Derek at the beer pong table with a disgusted look on his own face while watching Gary beat on his own chest over winning a match.

Sean's here with a group of people, but his eyes meet mine when I walk in the room and he parts the crowd quickly to get over to me. He's definitely interested, and I think he's interesting to look at, maybe not as interesting as Derek but . . . I bite my lip hard to try to clear the thought.

I'm on a mission. Must stay focused.

"Hi." Sean sounds exasperated. "You look beautiful."

It doesn't make me feel the way it felt when Derek mentioned my hair, but it brings a smile to my face. I thank him, and he says he's going to get me a drink without waiting for my response. When he comes back, he hands me a red plastic cup, but somebody calls him from across the room and while his back is turned, I dump my drink into the cup he put on the counter for himself. He turns back and he's stunned. "Whoa, you chugged it?" Then, "You're wild. You want another?" I shake my head and he shrugs. "Well, would you please, please dance with me?"

His voice is so sweet I tell myself the mission can wait three song minutes.

Sean sips on his drink as we walk through the crowd to find a spot for a dance. He tries to pull me in beside the wall, but I know what people do on the walls and we will not be doing that. We move past Bri and Val, close enough to see the beer pong table in the next room. Sean is happy when a reggae song starts to play. He's a better dancer than me, and I hope I don't look ridiculous, but I move my hips and swing my hair and Sean seems to like it. He gets behind me and locks our hands. We start dancing with him pressed against me and everything suddenly feels sharp. His cologne has a strong smell and the music is perfect for this type of dancing, but nerves bubble in my belly as he pushes into me a little harder.

When the beat drops and my favorite reggae song plays, I let myself forget that there are people around us, that this is my first time dancing like this with someone. His body sways to the beat, and then his fingers brush against the back of my thigh right before I feel that unmistakable tingle at the base of my neck.

My eyes shoot up, land right on Derek's. He takes a drink from his cup and averts his eyes. Is he still him? I slow my sway before Sean's fingers find the hem of my dress. I feel them dance along my skin there. I start to pull away, but he snakes an arm around my belly, brushes hair out of my face. I smell the liquor coating his breath as he whispers, "Let's go upstairs. There's something I want to show you."

I stiffen in his embrace. "What?"

He stumbles over his feet and we both lose balance a bit. "Gary said we could use his room," he says, slurring the words. The alcohol must have hit him.

I pull out of his arms. "Use his room for what?"

"You know exactly what I want," he says.

I turn sharply; we're face-to-face. My heart skips a beat.

He gives me a sloppy smile. "I can put on a mask from a horror movie, or we can do it out on Gary's balcony or in the grass in the backyard. You get off on that weird kind of shit, right? He told me he thinks you probably do."

"What the hell are you talking about?"

"You like the games. Being scared. We could make it a game. I'm down for whatever."

"Well, I'm not down for anything. Ever," I say.

He grabs my arm. I regret leaving my knife in Derek's car, but I yank free of him and push him so hard he bumps into the person behind him. He barely has the steadiness to straighten out. When he finally does his words come out a jumbled mess, but I make out every one. "I'm going to lose the bet," he says, nostrils flaring under the fluorescent lights spinning on the ceiling. "You're just a weird bitch. I can't believe I chased you through a haunted house for this." He pushes through the crowd, tripping the whole way over his own two feet until he finally disappears.

Everyone's still entrenched in their dancing, in their drinks. It was a bet. He wasn't interested in me. He faked the whole thing and all he wanted was sex. My stomach rolls, and the room spins to match, even though I'm sober. I look for Bri in the crowd but can't find her.

Then I feel the lightest tap on my shoulder and it still sets a fire to my skin.

I turn to face Derek. He's impossibly close. His eyes are black as he bends his head low to look better into mine. There's a current that rips the whole room away and pulls me closer to him. Our bodies are touching and I shiver when he says, "I could kill him if you'd like."

THIRTY-FOUR

The ghost inside of Derek is looking at me so seriously I'm scared his offer to kill Sean is real. "That's not necessary," I rush to say.

"No," he bares his white teeth in something like a smile, "but it'll be fun."

"Not for Derek," I whisper, and somehow the spirit still hears me over the music.

He tilts his head, mischief blinking in his eyes under the lights. "I am Derek," he says.

"You're not." I try to step back, but there's no space to put between us. He reaches to lift my chin. Gentle, touching with just the tips of his fingers. But I feel him everywhere, invasive, all over my body. I traded one monster in Sean for another in Derek.

He speaks against the shell of my ear, says, "Are you sure . . . Detective?"

I open my mouth to respond, but the sounds of sirens hit and everyone starts to scramble.

⚶

The cops break up the party, and Gary tries to sweet-talk them into keeping it from his parents while the rest of us leave. Bri is shaken up and Val keeps saying, "If my mom finds out about this, she's going to kill me." We couldn't find Derek anywhere. I lost him in the crowd, and his dad's car wasn't parked out front by the time I made it out. The spirit isn't answering his phone and I've got a bad feeling.

But Bri's pissed. "So cops come and he just bails on us? That's selfish as hell."

I open my mouth, but it's Val who comes to his defense. "I don't know, maybe he was scared and couldn't find us."

"That's bullshit," Brianna says, "and extremely naive."

Val looks taken aback. She doesn't know this fiery side of my best friend yet. With my eyes, I warn Bri to tone it down, but she's not going to stop being who she is for anyone.

Val stops walking, pushes a strand of straight hair behind her ear. "You think I'm naive?"

"Definitely."

Yikes. Val shakes her head and starts walking again, faster, trying to get away from us.

Bri lets out a breath and hurries to catch up. "Sorry, but you can't go around . . ."

The bus turns onto the street. Val holds up a hand to cut Bri off. "If you want to think the worst of people, do that, but I'll believe whatever I want." She says goodbye to me, then leaves us to get on our bus with some people from her own school.

Bri groans and looks at me. "I messed up, didn't I?"

I wrap an arm around her and pull her toward the bus. "I

mean, yeah, and your apology wasn't really an apology. But I think it'll be okay."

"Really?"

"Yeah," I say, then add, "hopefully." She pouts. "I do think it's better to show her how passionate you are now. Even so, maybe be less aggressive with the passion next time?"

"I'll work on it," Bri says, and we flash our passes to the bus driver. "You okay?"

"Yeah, why?"

"I know you like Derek and he's an absolute asswipe, so."

"I do not like Derek," I whisper, wishing I could tell her everything. I wish it with all my heart. "But there is someone I thought I possibly could like and I gotta tell you about it."

Her eyes narrow. "What did Sean do?"

"Sean *and* his little friends," I say.

"Oh, see. Now I'm going to have to beat some boys up."

"See? This passion is perfect. Just needs to be directed at the right people."

We slide into seats and she turns back to look at Val, but Val doesn't even acknowledge it. Bri leans on me, her face screwed up. "Tell me what happened with Sean please."

⌒⌒⌒

At the end of my street, something stirs in my chest and I break into a run. I'm out of breath by the time I reach Derek's. His dad's car isn't in the driveway and all the lights in his house are off. I text him and call him. On repeat. No answer.

I stay awake most of the night waiting to see when Derek

will pull up, thinking of the alcohol on Sean's slimy breath and hating his and Gary's guts for making a bet about me. My eyelids are so heavy by the time dawn cracks through my blinds and Mr. Johnson's car pulls into the driveway. I'm blinking back sleep while watching an unharmed Derek get out of the car and walk inside. I want to call him, but I barely make it to my bed before I'm dragged into a dream.

The gray looks different. Brighter. Like the sun is trying to break through clouds. I can hear faint sounds in the distance— waves hitting the shore, rustling leaves—can smell grass after the rain. Only one spirit comes to me in human form. She takes my flesh-colored hand into her colorless one. I feel nothing. Nothing at all from her touch. But I do feel the pull of the abyss against my back. I shift to see it's only feet from us. Where did it come from so fast? It begins to pull the spirit, her hair swaying into the gray, moving around us like wisps of smoke. Her body goes up next. I try to tug her hands to anchor her down with me, but it's like trying to touch a shadow. "I'm scared," she tells me. Right before she's sucked straight into the belly of the abyss.

I wake, panting and pulling on my sheets, searching for her in the sunlight of my room. My face is wet with tears and my heart aches. I remember her face: chin-length hair, eyes bigger than Adelia's, a tiny mouth. What happened to her? What is the abyss? Where does it take spirits? Why doesn't it take me with them? I couldn't help her and it hurts.

My phone lights up on my nightstand. I have two texts from Derek. The first is a video, the second says, *You're welcome, Bluebird :)*

Derek answers the knock on his window and holds out a hand to help me in.

I don't take it. "How do I know it's you?" I ask, throat thick, voice shaky.

"Seventh grade," Derek starts, but he stops to lick his dry lips. He's tired, so tired. "You were scared to go to school because your mom cut your bangs too short. Someone joked you looked like Dora the Explorer, but after that you started singing *backpack, backpack* whenever someone stared at you in class. I thought you were so brave."

I laugh, even though now is not the time to laugh. He holds out his hands again and I'm filled with relief to feel his warm skin as he helps pull me through the window.

We sit side by side watching the video. It starts out shaky and dark but focuses in, the camera flash capturing metal bars. It's the Pedestrian Bridge in downtown Providence, easy to recognize by its lights. "Please stop," someone says. The voice is easy to recognize too. It's Sean's. He's blindfolded, a gloved hand grips his shirt, pushes him against the bars. Sean grunts, and the cameraman leans in to whisper, "Stay right there," then flips the phone to reveal a horrifying baby doll mask. The same one he was wearing at the estate. "Are you ready for revenge, Bluebird?"

Hearing the nickname gives me chills, even worse because the spirit makes Derek's voice high-pitched, singsong. I take a breath, and Derek stiffens beside me as the spirit in his body props the phone on a bench and we watch him walk back over to Sean. He wastes no time, just shoves Sean so he's halfway off the ledge, then grabs hold of his lower half to keep him there. I gasp again, feeling the fear like it's the first time I watched it. Sean screams and cries while he's nearly dangling headfirst. It would be a painful, possibly fatal drop into the water below.

"Say you're a pervert," the spirit orders. Sean just cries. "Say it!"

"I'm a pervert," Sean screams.

"Say you'll treat women with respect and keep your nasty hands to yourself."

The spirit lets his grip go a little bit; Sean squeals. "I will. I will."

"You'll what?"

I think about the blood rushing to Sean's head, wonder how winded he is, if he's ready to pass out. "I'll keep my nasty hands to myself. I'll treat girls good. I will."

"Just good?" Derek's spirit asks.

"With respect. I promise. Let me down!"

The spirit loosens his grip again and I almost choke, but he doesn't drop Sean. He pulls him up and pushes him on the ground. Sean lies there gasping, then turns on his knees to dry heave. The spirit picks up the phone again and shoves it into Sean's face.

"Tell Aria you're sorry," he says. "A sincere apology just for her. No one, and I mean no one, will try to hurt her ever again. Do you understand?"

Sean's snot drips down his face. "I'm sorry, Aria. I'll never try to hurt you ever again."

The spirit leans down and gets in the screen with Sean. The mask gives me goosebumps. Sean is crying again. "If you tell any-one about this, what will happen?"

"You'll cut out my tongue." Sean inches away. "You'll feed it to Gary."

One beat. Two. "And it'll be fun," the spirit says, echoing his words from the party.

The video cuts to black and Derek pushes off the bed to pace the floor. "He threw the mask into our firepit in the yard. The smell of the smoke is still clinging to me. Then he . . . we slept good. But I'm still so damn tired." He runs his face over his hand. "I remember all of it, Aria. I was the passenger, but I remember. Like he specifically wanted me to watch."

My mind races. What was the spirit trying to prove? What would make him think I would appreciate this? Is he completely out of control or does he have a mission? Will he start using Derek's body for violent acts? I'm not sure how I feel about any of it, but Derek looks rattled.

I stand up and walk over to him. "Hey, it's okay. You're not like that. You wouldn't . . ."

Derek shakes his head. "I'm glad he did it." His admission steals my breath. "Am I a bad person for being happy Sean may never treat someone else the way he treated you again?" I'm not sure if he's asking me or God because he looks up at the ceiling, but I grab his hand, squeeze.

"Sean and Gary, they're bad people," I say.

"You're not upset?" He laughs, pulls away from me. "The spirit inside of me took it too far, but the only thing I keep thinking about is the fact that while he was controlling my body, I was helpless to scare Sean myself. What even is that?"

I shake my head, give him a small smile. "I'm not upset, but our teachers might call it toxic masculinity."

He laughs but frowns after it fades. "Do you think Sean knew it was me?"

"I think even if he suspected it, you'd never hear a word about it from anyone," I say.

Derek nods, then says, "Aria, what happened between you and Sean . . . I'm sorry he did that to you. That they did this to you. Are you okay?"

"I'm fine," I say. Though I'm not sure it's the whole truth. There's been so much going on, it's hard to process all of it. "I have to go get ready for church. Will I see you there?"

He sits on his bed. "I think I'll just stay home and rest."

On the way out, I wonder how much of a toll the spirit is taking on Derek's body. How much longer do we have to uncover the truth before we have to get him to an exorcist?

THIRTY-FIVE

My grandparents come by to take us to church today. It's been a while since my mom saw her in-laws, and Lola is excited to help us get ready *properly*. This means changing from what we were going to wear into dresses she thinks we should wear. Lola fixes my hair into a bun and fusses when the short strands come loose in the front. She picks out my mom's shoes and tells me to brush my teeth again.

"Helena, are you done using the bathroom?" Lola calls. "We need to get going."

Mom groans from behind the door, but I know she secretly loves it. She always says Lola reminds her of her own mother, who passed away years before my father did. From the window, I watch Lolo talk to Mr. Johnson across the street. I wonder if it's about the wisteria growing. But Mr. Johnson seems frustrated and I feel it in my gut: They're not just talking about the dead rosebush and the new wisteria roots, they're also talking about Derek.

Hearing the church choir sing calms my nerves but doesn't stop my thoughts from pouring in. How can I keep the video of Sean on the bridge from Bri? I need her help to sort through my feelings. Maybe I can show her and tell her I don't know where it came from. That won't work. She'll know it was Derek, and she can't know it was him. I lean my head back; a sick feeling settles in my stomach just as Derek slips beside me on the church pew.

He was supposed to be resting. Maybe he is. My skin tells me it's his passenger in the driver's seat before he leans in to whisper, "Should I give you a childhood memory now?"

"We don't have to pretend," I say without looking at him.

"You may be astute, but I bet you don't know all that goes on in your neighborhood." Not-Derek taps me, demanding attention with his burning touch, then nods toward the pew in front of us. "Your neighbor there is a racist. She mutters things under her breath when *colored kids* walk by her porch."

I straighten out, the hairs on my arms begin to prick. "How do you know?"

"Oh, when you wander around the city searching for something as long as I have, you're bound to know a thing or two. And I like it, knowing what they do. Just like you do. We're so much alike, Bluebird. We're both detectives. I'm just better at it."

"I don't think we're alike at all."

"Why's that?" He leans so close our cheeks could touch if I moved an inch to the right. It's a confusing feeling to see Derek's body and hear his voice but know it's someone else giving me goosebumps. Before I can answer, Lola turns to us with a scowl and raises her finger to her lips. "Uh-oh, I think we're in trouble," not-Derek says. "Too bad I don't care."

"Aren't you supposed to be in hell or something?" I whisper.

This shuts him up. His body shifts away from mine, shoulders tense. But then a few minutes later he grabs my hand the way Derek did at the party. His large fingers fold over mine and touch the topside of my wrist. They're slender, delicate, and soft. Derek takes good care of his skin, and his earthy complexion compliments my tawny tone. Our hands fit. Except while not-Derek is in control, my palms sweat and tingle. They ache.

I pull away, look up into eyes as dark as the abyss. "What's your name?" I ask, needing him to not be Derek any longer. Not when I get the truth out of him.

He stares at me for a while; the choir creates a melody to mask my heavy breathing while I wait. I think he's going to laugh, but instead he says, "Marcus, my name is Marcus."

It comes out so soft I wonder if he's been waiting to say it for many years. It hits me for the first time: the ghost that snatched Derek's body had a whole life we know nothing about. He had parents who gave him a name. A small sigh escapes his lips before he stands in the middle of the song and manages to slip off without attracting too much attention.

The rest of the service is a slow torture with me itching to go after him.

At the end, my mom, grandparents, and Mr. Johnson talk in hushed voices about what's growing where the rosebush was. I know there isn't any information I'll gain here when Lola cluelessly asks Lolo, "Can't you find out what it is? You're the plant expert," and he just shrugs. I excuse myself from the group and slip off to where I saw Marcus heading.

The hallway is dark, and it leads to a large empty space.

He's facing the wall, staring at the stained glass windows. "Hello, Bluebird."

"Marcus," I say, and stand beside him. We quietly admire the beautiful view as the sun breaks colors through the room, bouncing off of the walls, our skin, making my eyes feel sensitive. "Why can you see the color in my eyes, but most people can't?"

"Dead things can see beyond what the living can. The exception is that the living beings who are somehow touched by death can see it too." He winks at me. "Like Derek."

I think about Sheila. Is it because she's a medium or because of something else?

Marcus closes his eyes. "Do you believe in heaven, Bluebird?"

"I am Catholic," I say.

"I asked you a direct question."

"I do."

"Me too," he tells me. "Too bad I'll never get there." There's a wistful sound in his voice, but when his eyes flutter open, he smiles. "You're not scared of me. Even after the estate."

"I am a little scared," I admit, fingering the knife in my pocket. "What are your intentions? Why did you make me swallow the wisteria?"

He turns and softly cups my face, sending an icy chill through my cheeks. I stop touching the knife. "You should be more than a little scared," he says, "and so should Derek."

He lets me go and my skin grows cold. "You won't hurt me."

"What gave you that impression?"

"Because you want something from me," I say.

"You know, you're annoying, but I can see why Derek found you fascinating before I did." I don't know if he's trying to get a rise out of me, but it hits my belly, makes warm feelings bubble there. "You're both pretty fascinating to me, actually. When you talk to him, ask him if he's the one who's been enjoying holding your hand or if that was me. I really can't tell the difference, but maybe he can. Just like seeing you dance with Sean. I'm not sure if he was jealous, or I was. Maybe it was the both of us."

Marcus is grinning now. He can probably see the flush on my face, so I change the subject. "That stunt you pulled with Sean? Derek could be in serious trouble if the cops found out."

"Oh, he'll be just fine. But did you not enjoy that?" Marcus tilts his head and studies me. "I did it especially for you, Blue. I felt the way Sean made you feel from across the room."

"You felt it?"

"I can feel you constantly." He means to make me shiver. I can see the way his eyes dance. "We're connected now. Tell me you enjoyed it. Tell me the truth." I hesitate to answer and he turns to the stained glass, whistles. "Yeah. We're just alike, you and I."

A feeling flicks across my chest. Am I like him? Did I enjoy it? I swallow and try to keep my voice steady. "If we're alike, why are you doing this? You don't want to hurt me, but you're hurting Derek. He's not like Sean. He's a good person."

"I mean Derek no harm," Marcus says, strumming his finger

along the glass to sweep away the dust. "But it does seem like he's getting tired of our long nights. You should tell him to stop fighting me. I'm getting stronger and he's just making himself sick. It'll be a waste of such a beautiful body." His words make my chest hurt. "And, Aria, deep down you know the answer to your question. I came into this body to find *you*."

The way he says it makes my heart race, but some part of me feels the relief of a puzzle piece clicking, something I might've already known but needed to hear. He was looking for me while scaring my neighbors with the wisteria stem. Except, a thought hits that makes my stomach sink. He's hurting Derek because of *me*. "Tell me what you want," I say.

He reaches out to twirl a lock of my hair before bending close enough to suck my soul through my mouth. "What I *need*." His words make me nervous, nauseous, his proximity makes me sweat, but some part of me feels bound to him. Pulls me closer. "I would've preferred to do this away from judgy eyes," he looks up at the stained glass and smiles at Jesus Christ, "but . . ."

I suck in a breath, wait. But then Marcus closes his mouth.

"Aria," my grandfather calls from behind. I turn around. Marcus doesn't. Lolo is across the room, looking between us with narrowed eyes. "We're all waiting for you."

Marcus leans in to whisper, "I'll catch you later, little bird."

I cut my eyes at him and follow Lolo out, still fighting off chills from Marcus's creepy words when Lolo stops at the end of the corridor and says, "Is there something I should know?"

"Why would there be?" My voice trembles some. "Unless *you* know something I don't."

Lolo's lips turn down. "If you're good, I'm good."

THIRTY-SIX

12:25 P.M.: Derek doesn't come back with his dad from
church.

7:04 P.M.: Stalking his phone instead of processing my
feelings, recapping makes me anxious, ill. I have to see Sean
soon.

What might happen when I see Sean in school tomorrow:

-He'll apologize.

-I won't see him there because he'll be busy begging his
parents to switch schools.

How I'm feeling about what happened with him:

-disgusted

-like maybe I did enjoy seeing the video a little

Things Marcus might possibly need:

-For me to get Lolo to help him with something. A spell to
stay in Derek's body?

-Connected to the ghosts in my dream who cry for help?
The abyss?

Will I get any answers at the Botanica tomorrow? I search the internet, trying to find some information on a dead Marcus, but there are many people in the area named Marcus and no recent deaths. While I'm reading old archives, a text message from Derek comes through: *Aria, I'm fine. You don't have to keep calling. I'm with a friend.* I want to throw my phone across the bed. I've been waiting, worried, and this is all he says? But then: *And whatever the hell Marcus wants from you, we're not giving it to him.*

THIRTY-SEVEN

Green is shooting up from the ground and the wisteria growing in front of Derek's window is attracting attention. Mr. Johnson is talking to a neighbor from up the street while I walk over to inspect it, careful not to touch anything after Marcus forced wisteria down my throat. I hear Mr. Johnson tell our neighbor he planted something, but it'll be a surprise. When our neighbor walks off, I ask, "Why'd you lie to him? You didn't plant anything."

Mr. Johnson's head snaps over to me. He frowns. "Better than having to keep answering questions about things I know nothing about."

"So," I say, "you're not suspicious that this whole thing is . . . somehow supernatural?"

Mr. Johnson laughs, but I can see something shift in his eyes. He dodges my question. "Derek slept at a friend's house if you were here looking for him."

I nod, look at the wisteria roots one more time, then turn to catch my bus.

"Wait," he calls, voice wavering, "have you noticed anything off about Derek lately?"

The question takes me by surprise and I struggle to lie. "He's ... I ..."

Mr. Johnson shakes his head, says, "It's alright. I'm just glad you're friends again. Maybe he'll talk to you about it. He's had a rough couple of years."

The guilt stays with me the whole way to school because Derek had a rough couple of years and I wasn't there for any of it. And now, whatever is inside of me has attracted Marcus who is making things worse for him. A theory forms in my head: What if Mr. Johnson went to Lolo for help because he was worried about Derek? What if the tea was to help Derek open up to his dad, but instead it opened him to the spiritual world and allowed Marcus to slip right in?

At lunch, Bri lays out a checklist she's gone through with her parents on how to prep for getting into her top school choices early. My mom pressed me this morning about meeting with my titi to do the same thing. But I lied and said I'd talk it over with my guidance counselor. I have no idea what I want to do with my future, not when it comes to college anyway, and it feels like so much pressure to make a big decision right now.

"You could be a cop or an FBI agent," Bri says, biting into her apple. "You'd be good."

"Would I really? I'm not so sure I'm good at finding things out anymore."

Besides, I might be another crooked cop in the world if I continue selling magical objects on the side. I think about how natural it feels to work beside Lolo in the family business, and I imagine how much better it could get if I wasn't worrying about the secrets he's keeping.

I glance down at my phone. Derek didn't show up at school today, but he did send me an upside-down smiley face when I texted him, which didn't help because it felt like confirmation that Marcus is in control right now. I wonder what he's up to. The only thing keeping me focused is getting through the school day so I can go find Isobel at the botanica.

"A crew of trash," Bri says as Sean and his gang walk into the cafeteria. Gary and the rest don't even seem to notice us in the room; they're play fighting and racing to the lunch line, but Sean hears Bri and walks a little slower. He wasn't in first period today, and as soon as he saw me in the hall this morning he turned around and went the opposite way. When his eyes meet mine, images of his hands on my waist push to the front of my mind and bile rises in my throat. But I hold his gaze and lift my chin. He'll never try to hurt me again.

"What the hell are you looking at?" Bri says to him, making heads turn.

Sean quickly bows his. I know his hands are shaking in his pockets, I know he can't think of anything besides dangling over the Pedestrian Bridge. I wonder if he'll ever go near it again. I link hands with Bri and she squeezes mine a little.

Even though my chest is tight over what happened, I picture myself writing another feeling on the list: *Sean got exactly what he deserved*.

After school, Bri picks lint off my shirt while we walk to Kennedy Plaza. She's upset that Val hasn't texted her, and she's worried I'm sad over Sean. "Let's go get a large Italian grinder from Dee's Deli and binge-watch horror movies at your house."

I lean into her; my body feels heavy, my heart too. I wish I could say yes, but I have to go to the botanica and can't bring her with me. "That sounds nice, but . . ." I trail off because Derek's posted up against a building in front of me. Seeing him, after spending the day worried for him, and sick from seeing Sean, makes my heart beat faster and my bones wake up. Everything in me comes alive at once. I needed to see his face but wasn't prepared for the way it'd make me feel. He has his sunglasses on but his head jerks up from his phone like he senses me in the distance.

Brianna lets go of my arm and begins to walk slower beside me.

"Hey," I say when I reach him. "You're okay."

He doesn't get to respond before Bri catches up to us. She isn't her usual self; there are no quips. She stares between the two of us. Then says, "We're going to miss the bus, Aria. I'm hungry."

Derek's gaze flicks from her to me. "I need you for something. It's really important."

Bri sucks her teeth. "Seems to be a lot of that lately."

"Hey," Derek says, "I'm sorry for the other night. I didn't mean to leave like that."

I didn't even tell him she was mad about him leaving us at the party so it takes me by surprise, but Bri probably thinks I made him say it. I wish she knew he was taking the blame for something Marcus did, but I can't defend him.

She takes my hand. "Come on, Aria."

"Can we please have a movie marathon another night, Bri?" I ask. "I meant to tell you earlier that I have something else to do."

Her mouth falls open a little, but she doesn't say anything. She drops my hand, turns, and walks away. Derek and I quietly watch as she disappears from sight.

"I'm sorry," he finally says. "I don't want to mess with your friendship."

My stomach is a mess. I hate to hurt her. "I don't know how much longer I can hide it from her. I doubt she'd believe it, but . . ."

"Tell her," Derek says. "If you trust her, tell her everything."

I can't even express my shock because he pulls me so we're standing under the awning of the building, hidden by shadows. He lifts his shirt and the sight steals the air from my lungs. His rib cage is covered in pinpricks of red dots, they reach down his stomach. My hand shakes as I touch his skin there. The dots feel like nothing but look like blood spots.

"Petechiae," I whisper.

Derek nods. "I tried to keep . . . Marcus away all night and they started spreading."

"Why did you do that? If it's hurting you, then why?"

"It hurts regardless," Derek says. "I'm exhausted all the time, I feel sick, dizzy. If it hurts regardless, then why wouldn't I try to keep him away from you?"

My hands are on his chest when I look up at him. "I need to give Marcus what he wants."

Derek lets his shirt fall and pulls away from me. "No. That's final."

"You're not the boss," I say.

His jaw clenches. "And neither are you, but we have no idea what Marcus wants. I'm not letting you risk your life for me. We need to tell your grandfather."

"He'll just make me drink the tea again," I say. "And what if he can't help you? What if the only way to help you is by giving Marcus what he wants?"

Derek doesn't seem to care; his mind is made up. I don't want to put him in danger any longer either, but how do we know what the right thing to do is? My gut tells me we're close to figuring it all out. "There might be someone at a shop who can help us," I say. "But if she doesn't have answers, then we can go to my grandfather. Does that sound alright?"

Derek swallows but doesn't break eye contact. "Whatever."

The shop on Atwells Ave is empty when we walk in, but it's bright and loud. Reggae music booms through the small space and makes it feel bigger somehow. There's a woman up on a ladder, dancing, her long brown braid swinging back and forth as she stocks shelves. She turns toward us with a smile, huge dimples carving her cheeks, but makes sure she hits those last notes on the song's verse. She looks like she's in her midtwenties when she comes down the ladder and walks over to us.

"Love seeing fresh faces in the shop. Can I help you find something?"

"We're looking for an Isobel," I say, wasting no time.

Her eyebrows jump high. "Is that right?"

"Yes. Do you know her?"

"I am her," she says. "Who sent you?"

Isobel waits for us to answer with a smile on her face. It's a little creepy, but maybe that's her way of being intimidating. "Adelia," I say. "Adelia Cayetano."

She tilts her head, asks, "Why did she send you here? Or did she ask you to pick something up from me? Because you can tell her she'll have to come herself. She shouldn't still be messing with that stuff alone anyway."

What stuff? Is my sister at school messing with strange oils and herbs? "No, no," I hurry to say, "she said you might have some information for me."

"To help me," Derek cuts in, frustration and exhaustion thick in his voice. "There's a spirit inside of me, and we want to know if you can help us get it out."

He doesn't want me to keep searching, he knows whatever I might find could be the key to helping Marcus. It feels like we both played with each other coming here, knowing we'd be asking for different things. But Isobel's eyes go wide.

"Oh," she says, and I'm surprised she doesn't laugh or tell us to leave. "Oh, I see."

"So, can you help me?" Derek asks.

Now she laughs. "I don't do spirit work. I don't mess with magic at all. Adelia sent you to the wrong place. But good luck with your . . . situation."

"We can pay you," I say. "I don't have a lot of money, but . . ."

She starts to turn and waves a hand in the air. "Please see yourselves out."

"Adelia is my sister, but I'm here because of an L. Rivera," I say, hoping the name resonates while Derek shoots me a look. "She left something for me."

Isobel turns, stares at me for so long I think she might be stuck like that. My heart races while I wait for her to speak. "You're Aria Cayetano," she finally says, frowning.

"I am."

She exhales. "Lindy Rivera has been waiting for you to come for a long time."

THIRTY-EIGHT

We follow Isobel as she leads us through a back room packed with boxes and spiderwebs and into another room. This one is smaller and has a shelf in the corner and a table with white chairs in the center. She closes the door behind us and reveals a safe built into the wall. Locked inside could be the answer to everything we've been searching for.

"How do you know Lindy Rivera?" I ask Isobel.

She has her back turned while she touches the dial to the safe. "She used to be a regular here, but now she'll only call from time to time to check that what she left is still safe with us. And to make sure no one but you touches it."

"Safe with *us*?"

Isobel stops turning the dial, her shoulders stiffen. "I meant with me. She left your gift to my father a long time ago, but he passed away, so I own the shop now."

Derek tenses beside me. I clear my throat. "I'm sorry," I say.

"It's alright. It's been years."

When she works on the combination again and the lock

clicks, something sings under my skin. Whatever is in there is calling to me the way Marcus does. I take a deep breath while Isobel riffles through it, pushing things to the side and finally pulling out a small square box. Her hands shake as she holds it. Derek looks at me, and I wonder if we're both trying to imagine what could possibly fit in a box that small, that shape, and have the power to help us.

Isobel gives it to me with the softest smile. "Be safe on your journey. I'll see you out."

My stomach sinks. "Wait, what? Don't you want to know what's inside of it?"

"Heavens, no." She laughs. "Not with Lindy being able to spy inside my head."

There's a moment of silence before I realize what she's saying. "Lindy's a telepath?"

"A telepath with more complicated, very dangerous abilities. And she left specific instructions," her eyes flick between us, "no one else should see the gift besides you."

Derek covers his mouth with his hands and takes a few steps away from me.

"But that can't be it," I say. "What if we need your help with this . . . gift?"

"There's nothing I can offer in my little basement botanica to help. Trust me, girl," she says. "And anyway, I've had enough of dealing with Lindy and her family to last me a lifetime."

"Is she a bad person?"

"I wouldn't say that, but I'm happy you have this now." Isobel points to the box. "It's a weight off my shoulders to know my family's debt to her has finally been paid."

This gift, whatever it is, was important enough for Lindy to erase a whole family's debt. The knowledge suddenly makes me nervous. It feels like a responsibility I'm not sure I'm ready for. But there's a vibration coming from the box and seeping into my fingers and all I want to do is tear it open to find out what it is.

Derek sways on his feet. Isobel notices the unsteadiness and straightens her back, her smile falling away. "I think it's time for you to get going."

I nod. "Thank you for this. But before we go, do you have any idea where Lindy lives or how we can get in touch with her?"

Isobel has pity in her eyes. "You won't find that woman unless she wants to be found. You won't find any of the Riveras unless they want you to. And even if I could help with that, I wouldn't."

A shiver runs through me. Just how dangerous is Lindy? Is her reputation the reason why Lolo decided to never tell me about this gift? Has he been protecting me from her?

When we leave the shop, Derek refuses to let me open the box in front of him. "Whatever's in that isn't for me. But it's especially not for Marcus to see," he says. "He's probably been listening in this whole time. I never should have come with you."

On the bus ride home, I'm aching to open it, but he's beside me and there are too many people here anyway. The silence between us becomes uncomfortable.

"Let's open it together," I say. "Who cares if Marcus sees? We need to do what he wants, maybe this will help somehow."

"We don't need to . . ." His words are lost when blood begins to trickle down his nose. I watch him wipe it with the back of his shirtsleeve. My skin pricks all over. My bones pull toward him. I ache. "Derek should really stop fighting me," Marcus says.

"You're hurting him," I whisper, watching the blood build under his nose again.

"Derek's the one who invited me inside." Marcus smiles. "He was so lonely, our Derek. But he's not lonely anymore. Not with the two of us here. Think he's grateful for me?"

"You're evil," I say. But his words reverberate in my mind, and a thought makes me wonder if there's evil inside of me too: Derek and I might not have ever talked again if it wasn't for his possession. If it wasn't for Marcus.

He shrugs. "Sticks and stones may break Derek's bones, but words won't hurt either of us. Now, let's talk about what I need from you, Bluebird." He leans close, reaches for me slowly. I think he'll touch my cheek, but he snatches the box out of my hand instead. "We're already off to a good start with . . ."

I panic, my heart thrums. I snatch the box back and shove his chest with all my strength.

He makes a winded sound and other passengers look over at us, but I don't care.

When he rebounds, he's even closer, eyes dancing in challenge. An inch away from me, close enough to kiss. He runs a finger over my bottom lip, asks, "Did you like the way the wisteria tasted when I shoved it down your throat?"

Before I can answer, his hand starts to shake, his nose bleeds again. He takes a sharp breath, suddenly his dark eyes brighten and his mouth goes slack.

Derek is the one who pushes away to give me space. "Sorry, I . . ." His voice is hoarse. He looks at the box, then into my eyes. "Did I hurt you? Did he hurt you?"

My bottom lip tingles. "No," I whisper. "No, I promise."

Derek sighs and stands to pull the stop cord. I didn't even realize we were three blocks past our usual stop.

There isn't a sound around us as we walk up our street. It's just us, blanketed by fear for everything that has happened and everything that can. Our energy is a storm cloud. I see no sun. All I hear is my heartbeat and his breathing: two beats, a breath, two beats, a breath. The world doesn't come alive around us until we're in front of his house and see the roots of the wisteria curving and twisting and growing their way aboveground. Making its home here.

We stare for so long I start to forget what happened, but the box in my backpack calls to me. Then Derek steps away, walks into the middle of the street and covers his face with his hands. I want to pull him to safety, but I follow him there instead.

"I think I know why your dad got the tea from my lolo," I say just to hear one of us speak. Derek doesn't look at me, but I keep talking. "Maybe he wanted you to open up to him. Maybe he didn't want you to be sad about your mom anymore."

"I figured," he says.

My heart squeezes. "I wish you would've talked to me," I tell him. "I wish you didn't pull away from me years ago. I would've been there for you." I reach up and touch his shoulder, right where our matching scar sits. "We could've gotten through it together."

"Like we're doing now?" His bitter tone catches me off guard. He turns to face me. "You dragged me to Isobel's. You keep baiting Marcus. Now he knows about the box. You never listen to a word I say. You never have." A car beeps as it passes us, but we don't move. Sadness shifts in his eyes, his voice softens. "You really hurt me, Aria."

While we've been searching for answers, I selfishly hoped we wouldn't have to discuss it, that time together would heal his hurts, but I've been naive. "Derek . . ."

"No," he shakes his head, "you really hurt me, and you need to hear it. I needed you when my mom left. You said together, but I was alone."

"What do you mean? You weren't alone, I was with you every day. I tried . . ."

"You were playing detective. Trying to figure out why she left me, where she went. Find her for me. But you weren't look-ing *at* me. You weren't listening when all I needed was to know that you were there. She left me and my brothers, Aria. She didn't want us anymore. That's it. She didn't want to be our mother anymore. That's what the answer was."

Having already had these suspicions, wondering if this is what broke us, and hearing him confirm it hurts differently. I open my mouth, but can't conjure a single word in response.

"I was trying to deal with that. And I needed you to be my best friend and you . . . you needed to do something to make yourself feel better about it. You couldn't even look at me the same way anymore. I became a project you had to figure out, and that's what I am to you now."

I take a step forward so I'm almost pressed against him, my hand still on his shirt over his scar, but another car passes and Derek moves us both out of the way. We are on my side of the street now, safe on the sidewalk, but he separates himself from me.

"Derek, you weren't a . . . project." The word feels sour on my tongue. "I just didn't want you to be in pain."

"Neither did my dad, but look at what good that did for me." Derek closes his eyes. "At least he was trying to talk to me."

The two feet between us feels like miles, but I can see the tears slipping down his cheeks. My own face is wet with them too. He breathes out, stops crying.

We stand in silence for a minute, two. So long I wonder if we'll be here till sunset.

"I wish I didn't need you right now," he says, the words cutting like a serrated knife. He opens his eyes and takes a few steps toward me, towers over me. "I wish I didn't need you, but I do. And I'm trying not to put you in danger, but just like back then, you do whatever you want."

"But we have to . . ."

He swallows. "Do you know what it'll mean if you're hurt because of me?"

His tone sounds so tender that my temperature rises. My cheeks burn. My heart grows hopeful. "Nothing will happen to me," I say. "And if something does, it won't be your fault."

"God, Aria. You're so damn difficult. You don't even know what it'll do to me."

These words aren't tender; they're heated and heavy. They take so much space between us. My heart is somewhere outside of me. I drift above us like a ghost. Count his heavy breaths.

"What will it do to you?" I hear myself say, but my voice doesn't belong to me anymore.

He throws up his hands. "Forget it," he says, and starts to walk away.

I grab his arm to spin him back around. "Wait. I . . ."

But the second our eyes meet, he closes the distance between us and I descend down, down, down. I'm back in my body. The world slows to a stillness again.

Not even the wisteria grows while he kisses me.

There's fire behind it at first, a burning heat. But with each brush of his lips, it softens to something like a sigh. His hands find the small of my back and he pulls me flush against him. My whole body vibrates when his tongue finds mine. Warmth builds and builds in my belly. He moans into my mouth and it makes me ache, but then, then . . .

The sound breaks something for him.

He pulls back suddenly, I whimper, he touches his mouth.

We are a mirror again. Wide-eyed.

"I don't know why I did that," he breathes out, bites his bottom lip. Then, he leaves me.

I stand there, so still, barely breathing while staring at his front door with my fingers against my mouth, willing my feet to move.

PART THREE

WHERE THE FLESH
GOES TO ROT

THIRTY-NINE

How fast can a young person's heart beat before it's considered dangerous?

My Google search doesn't tell me exactly what I'm looking for. I'm lying on my hardwood floor under the light of my window and it does nothing to slow my pulse. Derek Johnson kissed me. His lips were against mine.

My belly grows so hot I have to sit up and try to force the memory away.

I'm shaking when I pick up the small box from the floor. I should open it now, even though there are already a hundred feelings I'm trying to process; Derek's words repeat in my head and I know there's no choice. I can't waste any time. He might not want me in danger, but he doesn't know what it'll do to me if *he* gets hurt and there was something I could've done to stop it.

I unwrap the delicate gold ribbon on the box and lift the lid. The first thing I see is a small piece of paper with five words written on it: *Open me all the way.* Waiting for me underneath is a golden compass. As soon as I touch it, the same electric feeling I get with Marcus sparks my skin, but it only lasts a second.

The compass fits perfectly in my palm. Like it was made specifically for me and no one else. There's even a butterfly engraved in the center, reminding me of the wisteria tree circle and my dreams. I can tell by the weight and the color that it's real gold. The edges catch the sunlight. I think I could stare at it for an eternity.

I flick it open and gasp at the engravings inside. They twine and tangle like the roots of a tree. But then I notice something else. The compass doesn't move when I shift on the floor. I stand up and walk around the room, but the needle stays in place. Is it broken? I search for a button, some kind of switch, but what I find is two thin slits toward the bottom of the compass. If I wasn't standing directly in the sun, I might have missed them.

The note. *Open me all the way.*

I find tweezers to stick in the slits and rotate them one way. Nothing. Then the other. A clicking sound. A small compartment springs open at the side of the compass and inside there's another piece of paper folded in a small square.

Lindy likes leaving letters.

Aria Cayetano,
Did you enjoy the compartment? Clever little compass, this is.
Came across it on my travels, and I know it'll be of use to you
when the time is right. After it's decoded, they say all seekers
have to do is speak to it to make the magic work. I'm not sure
exactly what that means, though I wish we were learning it
together. Your grandfather won't approve because of the part I

played in a big imbalance done with a spell for my family a while ago, but you should know you were born with this gift before that. Zackary will have to approve of us connecting eventually. I've been told I'll play a part in your future and I'd like to think it'll be a special one.

L. Rivera

The tea Mom made me grows cold on my nightstand while shadows slink across my walls and weave around my bed frame. I've been trying to ignore the whispers in my room, the spirits wanting to catch my attention tonight. I read both of Lindy's letters over and over in case I might've missed something while simultaneously searching the internet with questions like *What's a seeker?* Mostly I'm awarded with elementary school definitions attached to pictures of kids playing hide-and-seek. I text Adelia, tell her I need to see her in person as soon as possible. I'll drive up to URI and stalk her on campus to show her the compass if I have to. Right now, I'd pay to have been a fly on a wall when she worked with Lolo, learning all the secrets she did. Maybe she'll know where to find Lindy. I get up to look at the snake plant in the corner of my room. It hasn't died, even though I've poured countless cups of tea into its soil, but I now notice color is leaving from a couple of the leaf tips. They're going gray. I grab the teacup on my nightstand, crouch down low, and slowly pour the liquid over the leaves. Then I watch, waiting to see if the color will drain before my eyes. It doesn't. I grab my journal and sit on the floor near the snake plant.

Dear Journal,

An ugly question I'd never ask out loud: Was Lolo killing something inside of me with the tea? Before I thought he would never. But I never thought Derek would kiss me either. Except he did. It was a good kiss too. The <u>perfect kiss</u>. But he hasn't texted me, and I won't text him. He still hasn't forgiven me for the way I acted two years ago, and even if he does, friends shouldn't be kissing. But every time I close my eyes I see it again. I feel it. How soft his lips were, how good he was with them, the way my chest hurt when he said he doesn't know why he did it.

What Derek could mean by that:

-He didn't enjoy the kiss.

-He was delirious because he hasn't been feeling good & reacted in the heat of the moment.

-Kissing me made him realize we can only ever be friends.

-Marcus took control and made him kiss me. Why? A sort of parallel to Gary and Sean's bet? ☹ yikes.

-Derek wanted to do it, but doesn't think I deserve it.

My phone taunts me from the floor. I'm itching to call Bri, but I can't. There's so much to tell her and it needs to be done face-to-face. For a moment, I imagine things are different, less complicated, not otherworldly. I'm just a normal girl who kissed her *platonic* best friend. What would Bri say if all of this were true and I told her I liked it a little too much?

I sigh and start to get up, my knees cracking like I'm thirty, but then I see it: the filmy layer right in front of me. It wavers, nearly shimmers under the moonlight coming through my window. And the snake plant behind it has gone completely colorless. But there's something more, something different. Perched on one of the leaves is a butterfly. A black butterfly like the one from my dream. Seeing it there brings a bitterness to my tongue, makes my throat tight in memory. It beats its black wings, slow and steady, and then it stills. I hold my breath, waiting for it to move again, but it doesn't. When I reach a finger through the filmy layer it starts to dissipate like dust, and the butterfly blinks out of existence. But life doesn't seep back into the snake plant.

What am I seeing if not the gray while I'm awake?

I sleep with purpose: to search the gray and be welcomed with answers. It responds in kind and says *Change*. I'm inside of a shape I've never seen here. Walls form with each step I take, a ceiling, doors, windows. I'm standing in a colorless house. And inside of this house, I can open doors, hear them creak, feel the knobs against my fingers. But each room is empty until I get to the one farthest down the hall. Under the doorframe, a purple hue glows to invite me inside. When I walk through the door, the spirit is waiting for me in the form of wispy purple smoke. I reach to touch it and a face configures beneath my fingertips. Then a neck, arms, a whole body. He takes my hands, tells me, *Sit, sit*. We are cross-legged and facing each other, him gray, me full color. He smiles, then leans forward to place his hands on my head. Soothing. It feels soothing. Then suddenly, bookcases form along the walls, posters, a rug, a bed. The spirit smiles and closes his eyes, hands still on my head. When he disappears, his purple hue spreads through the room, coating all the things here with color.

FORTY

The compass was warming my cheek when I woke up. I tucked it under my pillow last night, but now I want some silence from it, from my dreams and whatever they mean, from having to talk to Bri and see Sean again at school, and from thinking of Derek's lips. His hands on the small of my back, pulling me closer, making circles against my skin through the fabric. A heat rises from my toes and sends me in a spiral. I scream into my pillow. In a few minutes, I'll have to face him at the bus stop.

Mom opens my room door. "What have you been screaming about all morning? Clearly that pillow isn't doing enough because I hear you down the hall."

Half-truths for her only. Just like she tells me. "I thought this boy liked me at school, but turns out he made a bet with his friends that I'd hook up with him."

"What the hell?" Mom's pissed at first, until she sees the look on my face. She walks over to fold me into her arms. "I'm so sorry people are like this, baby. Are you okay?"

I breathe in her scent, let her rub my back. "I'm okay," I say. "Just feeling uncomfortable. Hate that I have to see him."

"Is he harassing you? Do you need me to go down to the school?"

My mind runs to Marcus in the baby doll mask. "I don't think he'll bother me again." A few seconds of silence pass, then I say, "Mom, do you think I'm too difficult for someone to like?"

She pulls back to look at my face. "Oh, Aria, you are impossible *not to like*. You're quirky, smart, beautiful, passionate, adventurous. You just have to find someone to mirror that. Well . . . eventually, when you're twenty-five. You don't need to date anytime soon."

I laugh and grab my backpack. "Thanks, Mom."

When I get to the bus stop, Derek doesn't avoid looking into my eyes. "Hi."

My stomach does somersaults. I pull on my backpack straps, trying not to stare at him. Why does he have to look so good today? Can I still be his friend if I feel this way? "Hi," I say.

He doesn't wait for the awkwardness to eat us. "Can we talk about the kiss after this is all over? When I'm the only one inside of my head? When we're both thinking straight."

"Of course," I say, but I wish he'd rip off the Band-Aid. Tell me he acted on impulse or that Marcus did it so I can try to forget the way it felt with his mouth on mine.

After school, I take the bus to Lolo's and before I get off, I write:

Dear Journal,

Derek and I were okay after the bus stop, but he was so tired he kept laying his head on the desk in class and I couldn't help but worry. Bri didn't want to talk to me at all. She even took her lunch tray to another table. The only good thing that happened was Sean pretending like I didn't exist today.

As soon as I step inside the shop, I feel relieved. This place is always brimming with good energy, untainted by the questionable things Lolo does here, and I can ignore everything else. He's currently cooking Filipino food and shuffling on his bad legs while dancing to hip-hop.

"What's all this food for?" I ask him. "You feeding customers?"

Lolo stops dancing and makes the most horrified face. "Absolutely not. We're closing up shop and going to your auntie Maria's house for dinner. Sasha just got engaged."

I have to hide my disappointment. It's not that I'm not happy for my cousin Sasha, but she's never treated me very well. Adelia used to wonder if it's because her mother, Auntie Maria, was upset that my dad didn't marry a Filipino woman and instead ended up having mixed kids with my mom. So I can't help but feel like we're the outcasts or outsiders at her parties.

Lolo hands me a spoon and has me turn the rice while he packs up the tinfoil pans.

It feels strange to have the compass in my bag on the table three feet away when Lolo probably had no intention of ever bringing me to pick it up from the botanica in the first place.

"How come you don't deal in any inanimate objects, Lolo? Do you not know how to spell them?"

He gives me a funny look, laughs a little. "Of course I do. But putting spells into inanimate objects requires a level of care for my customers that I can't afford to have."

"What do you mean?"

"First of all, it's a different level of *magic*. Spelled inanimate objects can be far more dangerous. You'd think it was the opposite because objects in nature have their own energy, which can be tricky, but objects that aren't alive can hold an infinite amount of spell. And because nature isn't there to balance out the spell, the power is in the person holding the object; I don't like the idea of giving my customers access to infinite power. That would mean I'd have to be more responsible for their actions and we all know how I feel about that."

"But you've done it before? Spelled an object?"

Lolo points to the watch on his wrist. "This watch right here tells me the time."

I raise an eyebrow at him. "Isn't that what all watches do?"

"Yeah, but this one says we better hurry up before your greedy cousins eat all the pancit."

Family gatherings always look like this: big ceramic pots to keep the food warm filled with rice and meat, someone in the living room setting up the karaoke machine, my aunties saying *Why you put on so much weight* and *make another plate of food* in the same sentence. I probably have thirty cousins and at least twenty-eight of them think I'm weird. But today, squished inside Auntie Maria's house, everyone seems happy to see me—and excited we're all together again.

The second surprise of the day comes in the form of my sister. She shows up for this, but couldn't show up for me? I ignore her while we pray for our cousin Sasha, who is gorgeous in a traditional Filipino dress. I can't eat much, too preoccupied over the fact that most of my aunties are smitten with their golden child Adelia, who has a tattoo on her neck and three face piercings they somehow don't see because they're swooning while she talks about plans to be a chemist. She's here, being perfect, smiling so much her face must hurt, and she didn't even tell me she was coming.

I'm staring at one of our aunties when my sister finally comes up to whisper in my ear. "I see Auntie Rina still has impeccable style for parties, but I hope she doesn't wear that new outfit in church." I hate to laugh at Adelia's jokes right now, but Auntie Rina is wearing bright green leather pants and cheetah print heels and she has a feather dangling from her head.

"I'm not happy with you," I tell her. "I tried to get in touch with you yesterday."

She gestures for the door. "Come on, let's talk out back. I can't stay long."

Outside, Adelia and I sit on the swing set and I tell her to give me her lame excuse.

"I don't have one, but I came here for you," she says. "Lolo never misses parties. I knew you'd be here."

I pout at my sister. Soft. I'm so damn soft. "You swear?"

She kicks her feet. "I swear. Now tell me what the emergency is." I take the compass out of my bag and she stops swinging, long hair falling into her face. "Where did you get that?"

"You recognize it?" I hold it out to her and she hesitates before taking it.

"Not the compass, but the energy." She looks toward the house windows, even though it's a half acre away and Lolo wears glasses to see twenty feet in front of him. When she looks at me again, she whispers, "This is a spelled object, Aria. I'm guessing a very strong one."

The confirmation causes something to stir in my chest. "It's what Isobel was holding for me at the botanica, but it doesn't work. Are you sure you've never heard of a Lindy Rivera?"

"I'm sure," Adelia says. "Lolo has some special customers he never introduced me to."

"Well, she said I needed to decode it first. Maybe that's why the needle isn't moving."

Adelia flips it open and moves her finger along the engravings. It only takes her a few seconds to say, "There's nothing here to decode."

"Wait, what?" I point to the small symbols around the edges. "These?"

"I know seven different languages, and I've decoded things with Lolo before. These are just . . . swirls. Pretty designs." My stomach sinks, but my sister smiles. "Don't trip, little sister. I think Lindy meant you'd have to decode the spell, not the etchings on the compass."

Lindy's letters feel like riddles, so that sounds right. "But how would I do that?"

Adelia looks over at the windows again, then behind us like spirits are listening. "Spelled objects usually run on blood. And if this spelled object is for you, then it needs yours."

"Okay," I say, so anxious to know that it works I can feel my heart beating like it'll come through my chest. I pull out our dad's pocketknife. "How much do I need?"

She swats at my hand. "I said you could only use that when you *really* have to. I wouldn't *ever* use it on yourself, Aria."

"Because it's another spelled object?" I examine Dad's knife, the black blade glinting in the sun. "You should've given me clearer instructions. What does it even do?"

"I'm not one hundred percent sure because I've never had to use it, but the energy isn't pleasant."

"Got it. Do you have something to take my blood?" I'm careful while closing the knife.

My sister frowns at me. "You're in a rush to feed this thing. Are you sure you want to?"

"I'm not sure of anything anymore," I tell her.

A look of understanding crosses her face. "Fair enough." She places the compass in my lap, then reaches for my jean jacket and starts to unfasten the pin there. It's of Satoru Gojo smiling in his blindfold. Derek gave it to me on my fourteenth birthday. "But I am little nervous to unlock this thing, then leave you with it. We don't even know what it does."

"I'm more nervous of how deep you'll have to cut with that thing to draw blood." She narrows her eyes, so serious, and I sigh. "Well, is the energy of the compass unpleasant?"

She shakes her head. "No, no. It's almost . . . soothing."

I think of the spirit in my dream last night, how soothing it felt to sit with him. "Alright, then," I say, holding out my hand. "I'm ready."

"When the time comes, you better not tell Lolo and Mom I helped you with this."

"I wouldn't dare taint the name of their precious little Adelia Cayetano."

My sister doesn't even warn me after that. She drives the pin into my thumb. Pulls back, does it again, then squeezes and squeezes to get the blood up. I wince. That hurt like hell.

"Dear lord, it burns," I complain while she pushes my thumb along the engravings, coats the glass frame, and squeezes as much blood as she can into the two slits. After, she shoves a napkin from her pocket at me. "Ew. Did you eat your lumpia with this?"

"Aria, stop being a damn baby cry."

"I'm not a . . ."

She points down to the compass in my lap and my words leave me.

The needle moves counterclockwise. Slow at first, then faster and faster.

I pick it up and suddenly I'm in the gray. My sister is too. The house in front of us is dull, the grass dark, the sun has left the sky. A kaleidoscope of black butterflies descend from it, swarming above our heads. And then a rush of energy shoots through my body, the butterflies disappear, and color coats the world around us again.

I have to catch my breath, but Adelia doesn't even seem to notice.

"That's strange," she says. "The compass is still moving wild."

She takes it from me and stands up, and I can't get the words out to tell her what just happened to me. How dull she looked in the gray. That the blood must've worked.

"The needle doesn't move for me at all. I'm a little jealous," she says, frowning. "I've never had a spelled object react to only me before. This one must be special."

"Adelia," I start, but someone calls my name and sends me out of my skin. Our little cousin Frankie runs into the yard. He's only six but has the menacing energy of double the toddlers.

"Adelia, Aria, if you don't play tag with me you're butt-ugly," he says.

My sister gives me a kiss on the cheek, slips the compass into my hand, and says, "That's my cue to get going. But you have fun with little Frankie here and let me know what happens with the . . . thing."

I give her the dirtiest look I can manage before she leaves me with Frankie and a mysterious compass I have to hide.

"Why's your thumb bleeding, ugly Aria?" Frankie asks. "Did you get hungry?"

FORTY-ONE

It's like Mom knew exactly when I'd be home from Auntie Maria's to make sure there was a hot cup of tea waiting for me. She has her work scrubs on and she rushes to find her keys.

"I'm old enough to remember to fix my own tea," I say.

"I'm your mom and I'd do anything for you. I love you."

Even though her motives might be shady, her words make me smile. My mom thinks what she's doing is protecting me. The thought propels me into a memory. Derek making sure his cell phone volume was turned up in class just in case his mom decided to call after she abandoned him. Me, leaning over to whisper a theory into his ear: *Maybe she was in trouble and left to protect you.*

"Aria?" Mom's voice cuts through. I didn't realize she was standing so close. With the memory still making me sick, she hands me the teacup. "Are you okay?"

"I'm fine," I lie, but she's still standing there, her eyes flicking from mine to the cup. She doesn't move to go to work until I take a sip in front of her.

My body alerts me to his presence before I step into my room.

"You don't look frightened." Marcus smiles, white teeth flashing as he sits on the edge of my bed in the dark. "Maybe I should've tried harder."

I toss my backpack by the door. The compass is in it, but I don't want Marcus to notice me keeping it close. "The one good thing about our supposed connection is the fact that you'll never take me by surprise again," I say.

"There's one thing better than that." He taps the bed beside him. "Derek's been fighting me for control every time I try to talk to you, but he's too tired tonight, so come over here and I'll finally tell you." I shake my head, but he insists. "Oh, Bluebird. Don't be like that."

I leave at least a few feet between us, but he scoots over so our thighs are touching. And then he tilts his head, his face so close we could kiss. I take a breath. He isn't Derek.

"Aria," Marcus says, and the use of my real name grabs my attention. "I need you to help me move on."

"What?" I let out a little laugh, but Marcus is still staring at me with a straight face. "What are you talking about?"

The whites of his eyes glow. "You need to find my resting place and the compass you *think* you're hiding will assist you." He must see the shock in my eyes because he smiles. "Don't look so surprised. I knew what it was as soon as I touched the box. We're all connected. You, me, the compass. I have flashes of you, I can feel you, I see you whenever you dream of the other side. It's fate that we didn't even have to go looking for the compass together. Thank your sister for me, okay?"

His words make me feel exposed. I put distance between us on the bed. Is he really in my head? How much can he see? *Wait.* "You want to rest?"

"Don't be dense, Bluebird." He lets out an exasperated sigh. "We don't have to play the repetition game. I need a resting place. You know, like your father has with his shrine."

My bones tighten at the thought that he's watched me visit my father. Then I wait for him to tell me he's joking. He runs a hand through his hair. His body begins to vibrate but he braces himself on the bed. "Can you focus?" he hisses to himself, or to Derek, or me. I'm not even sure anymore. "This body . . . I like this body, but I need out of it. Let's focus on that."

"So get out of it," I say, anger suddenly swelling inside of me.

He lets go of the bed and grabs my face. My cheeks catch an icy chill under his touch. "Ha," he says, looking into my eyes manically for a second. "Not until you help me."

"You need to let him go, Marcus. Maybe I can help you after . . ."

He pushes my face away. Giggles low. It's a haunting sound that will sit with me forever. "This is my body until you find a resting place for my soul. The problem is, you have no idea what you are. What you can do. It's a shame, you'll have to learn fast."

Answers. Marcus is going to be the one to give me answers. The thought makes me squirm, but I lean in with need. Desperate to know. "What . . ." I can't keep my voice from trembling.

"What am I?" I ask, though the word is already circulating in my brain before he says it.

"You are a seeker, Bluebird. At least, that's what Lindy calls it. I've been looking for someone like you for sixty years."

At the mention of Lindy's name, the hairs on my arms rise. "You've talked to Lindy?"

"Something like that," he says, a grin splitting his face. "She said a seeker is someone who can find resting places of the dead. We find you for you to show us the way through the in-between. The other side. Whatever you silly humans want to call it these days." *The gray*, I say inside my head and Marcus nods. "The gray. The veil there is too thick sometimes. Or we get trapped there for other reasons, but people like you can be in both places at once and pull us through the veil."

I hear what Marcus is telling me. I hear it and feel the words in my body, the gray, the veil, the filmy layer I've been seeing. I know they're real. But I can't believe he thinks I can do something like *this*. Then Sheila's words from the palm reading reverberate through my mind.

"Abilities," I whisper to myself. "Sheila called it a gift."

Marcus must've watched my reading with Sheila because he doesn't ask who she is. "I wouldn't call it a gift," he says. "It's probably a curse, actually. I mean, who wants to be the guide for dead people? To spend time with the weeping to connect them with their dead loved ones? Pretty morbid gift, if you ask me. But it remains the same. You have the compass now and all you have to do is concentrate and . . ."

"Marcus, I've never . . ." I stand up, my limbs shake, I'm

weak. "I haven't even had a second to process what you're saying. I don't even know if it's even real."

When I look over at him on the bed, he's wiping blood from his nose. "Well, Bluebird, your friend is going to suffer until you figure it out. Don't you want to help Derek?"

My throat grows thick, my chest burns. "Of course."

"The longer you spend in denial, the longer I have control of his body and I promise it's not going to be a pretty sight."

My mouth doesn't belong to me at the mention of Derek being in danger. "Tell me what I have to do. How do I do it?"

Marcus lets out a ragged breath. "I don't know how your ability works. You'll have to find that out on your own." He's frustrated. I just don't know what he expects me to do. I've seen things, dreamt of spirits, but those things have always felt like something happening *to* me.

"How do you know I'm the one you've been looking for?"

"Oh, right." He smiles again. "Well, you see, before taking over Derek's body, I was drawn to this fluorescent blue light on the other side, and I knew it was the aura Lindy spoke about. The light was coming from this city, this area, but it almost looked like watercolor running. You were cloaked under it for some reason. I had fun in Derek's body testing the neighbors, but it was a waste of my time. When I got the inclination that you were the one I was looking for, I tried to confirm."

"The forest. Neutaconkanut Park. The trees," I say.

"You ran. And then Derek . . ." Marcus rolls his eyes, stands up and strides over to touch my cheek. "He's been making things difficult. But one night while he was too tired, I shoved that beautiful wisteria flower down your throat to speed up the process. Thanks to me, your powers are coming back quicker. Thanks to me, we're connected again."

Everything clicks into place. Lolo saying the tea hides me from the spirits. The way they weren't able to touch me or see me before I stopped taking it. My eyes.

The glowing light inside of me.

I am a shaky mess by the time I find my voice. "Why wisteria?"

"Wisteria can act as gateway plants. An anchor between this side and the other. Sort of like you. Except, you're more here and the wisteria growing on the hill are more there." Marcus runs his thumb down my jaw and goosebumps rise in the wake of his touch. "Don't waste our time, Bluebird. You know deep down in that little heart of yours everything I'm saying is true." The moonlight cascades across his face. "And if you don't come through for me soon, you'll have to get someone to bind me inside of Derek with a spell."

"I won't do that."

Marcus places two freezing fingers against my lips. "Then I'll stay until he dies."

All that's left of my energy crumbles when he climbs back out the window. I collapse on the bed. If Marcus is right and I can help spirits find space, why would Lolo keep it from me?

FORTY-TWO

The gray is quiet. Shadowy, colorless. Something about the stagnancy steals my breath, makes it feel as if all the oxygen has been sucked from the room my body sleeps in. I'm completely alone until he appears in front of me and puts a hand on my shoulder. I'm not scared. He doesn't speak. We are melded together in time and space with nothing but silence surrounding us. But then he opens his mouth and I can't hear what he says. The light goes from his eyes when he realizes. He tries again. Nothing. Then we both feel the pull of the black abyss before it materializes. I don't even have a second to react before it begins to drag him into its belly. My feet are shackled to this place, bound by all that I am, but Marcus clamps down, digs his nails into my shoulder. I feel no pain when he's sucked away like a wisp of smoke.

I wake in utter silence with red marks on my skin.

At school, I find Bri sitting in the hall, leaning against the lockers and FaceTiming Val. I drop down beside her. Val smiles at me through the phone. "Oh, Aria! How are you?"

"I'm good," I say, then shake my head. "Actually, I'm not. Nothing is going right. So, Val, I need you to ask my best friend if she'll talk to me since she refuses to even look at me."

Brianna scoots across the rug so I can't see Val anymore. "And, Val, I need you to tell Aria that she has another best friend to go to for her problems."

Val sucks her teeth and says, "Stop acting like a toddler. We talked about this when we made up."

Bri sulks, but her eyes dart over to my face. "Yeah, yeah, practice listening and forgiveness and patience."

"And having an open mind. Talk to you later, babe," Val says, and hangs up the phone.

Brianna sighs and breaks off half of her chocolate bar to hand me. "I don't like you right now, but I know food is part of your love language, so I guess I'll return it and listen to you."

I move closer to take her offering. "You love me."

"You're pretty annoying, all those damn phone calls and texts begging me to talk, the creepy staring in class, trying to get me in trouble when you threw that balled-up note at me in second period. But you're . . . also pretty hard not to love."

It's everything I needed to hear. "Awwwww, lemme just . . ." I grab her and rub my face all over hers like a cat, but she shoves me backward. "Too soon, huh?"

"Yes," she says. "I'm happy you found someone to be with. I don't like Derek much after the party, but I guess I can give him another chance if he treats you well. Except, I'm not sure he does. He really pulled you out of your plans like he got it like that . . . and not only did you diss me for some boy, but I don't want you being with a controlling dude."

I laugh so hard I almost choke on a piece of chocolate.

She scowls at me. "This isn't funny."

"It is," I say. "Firstly, because Derek and I are not together. Well, there was a kiss, but that's not important right now."

Bri gasps. "What? A kiss? And that's *not* the most important thing to talk about?"

"There are far, far more serious things," I say, hiding my smile because now is not the time to be thinking of Derek's lips on mine. Even though it's been impossible not to. "There's so much I've been wanting to tell you. But I need to know that you can handle it. And not just that, but you need to promise to take it all to the grave."

"Remember that time you told me about the embarrassing thing that happened to you freshman year? I never told a soul about it. Not even my diary, and believe me I've wanted to."

My cheeks flush. "This is so much bigger than that."

"Don't you trust me?"

"With my life, but I'm just not sure you trust me as much."

She sulks again. "Is what you're going to say life changing?"

"Yes. And I realized I can't go through it without you."

"So don't."

"You'll love me no matter what?"

"Cross my heart and hope to die."

"Don't do that," I say.

"Your superstitious ass." She rolls her eyes, then says, "I'd help you clean up a homicide."

"That's real love," I say, "but would you believe me if I told you I really do see ghosts?"

Bri is silent for a moment before she breathes out. "I'm not sure, but it might be possible to be convinced," she says.

So I smile and start at the very beginning again, but this time with everything I know now. Telling Bri makes my heart race. It's like going through the motions with open eyes. I pull the compass from my bag and goosebumps shoot up my legs. No one's watching while I hold it in my palm and talk to her. Her eyes were already wide from my storytelling, but they bulge as the compass spins wild. When I'm done, she throws her head against the locker.

"Well, shit."

The bell rings, and I quickly tuck the compass away. "Do you believe me?"

She starts to gather her stuff, stands up, and says, "The truth is, I don't want any of this to be real. Life is scary enough."

I stand too, dust my pants off. "I know, but . . ."

"Listen, Aria. Figure out how to get me proof, more solid proof than that compass and I'm all in for whatever madness you have to go through, but I need to be able to *see* it first."

During fifth period, while everyone else is researching for the essay we have due next week, I'm researching my situation. The same as looking for Lindy Rivera, it seems like there's nothing online about humans having the ability to find a spirit's resting place. But my research isn't all in vain. I glance over at Derek. He's up front talking to the teacher so he can't see my face when I find the article. Marcus told me he's been searching for someone like me for sixty years, and I think I found him too. Or a very old article of him in an archive.

Marcus Herrington, 18, cause of death: drowning

My stomach twists as I read the details of this boy's death. Eighteen, strong and healthy, very loved. Even though my gut tells me this is him, I don't want to accept it. My eyes sting a little, a swell of emotion sparks inside of me. I've been feeling them heavier lately, feeling more emotions than I usually do and I don't know what to do with them. I don't want to know this much about the ghost that's threatening to destroy Derek's life and his body because it makes Marcus feel more human, and that's scary. This thought propels me into another: If I'm going to prove any of this to Bri, I should do it in a way that's not scary for her.

When Derek sits back at his computer, his legs shake and I feel the emotions rise up again. I want to tell him about the article, but something tells me to keep it close for now.

acayetano52407@gmail.com: R you feeling ok?
DtheSorcerer401@gmail.com: Fantastic.
acayetano52407@gmail.com: Really?
DtheSorcerer401@gmail.com: No, not really, Aria.

My stomach drops. I peek over, but he's focused on the screen.

acayetano52407@gmail.com: I'll learn to use the compass and we'll fix all of this.
DtheSorcerer401@gmail.com: Or we can go to your lolo and

have him help. If he knew how to bury your abilities, he should know how to help you use them. Safely.

I grit my teeth, thinking of my last dream. Derek knows about everything . . . except for the marks on my shoulder. If I show him he'll probably go straight to Lolo himself.

acayetano52407@gmail.com: You know how he is. He's not going to let me do a thing.
DtheSorcerer401@gmail.com: Maybe that's for the best. How do we know what Marcus wants won't have repercussions for you? Just saying. We both have to be alive if we're ever going to talk about the kiss.

Heat shoots up my neck. I see him smiling from across the room and hide my flushed cheeks behind the computer screen. The bell rings and I'm thankful I don't have to write back.

FORTY-THREE

Bri doesn't complain about the hike up the hill this time. She's ready for proof and I'm ready to have her by my side. When we step into the clearing, she doesn't see anything. And for a second, this moment that's supposed to not be as scary for her is terrifying for me, but then I remember what Sheila said about my eyes, and what Marcus said about Sheila.

There are things humans can't see unless they're touched by death. I place one hand against a wisteria tree trunk.

Bri looks at me strangely because she can't see it. "You're not ready," I tell her, before touching her face with my other hand.

I can see the moment it happens: the purple glow reflecting in her irises makes *her* look magical. Swallowtails flutter down from the trees and surround us like fairy lights. She gasps and clutches my hand. When she looks at me, there are tears in her eyes and now I'm crying too.

"Oh . . . ," she whispers. "I . . . I didn't believe you."

I pull her into me, press my face against hers. "It's okay. I'm sorry I couldn't show you sooner."

A butterfly lands on Bri's shoulder. We smile and wipe

each other's tears. She spins around, examines every single tree, eyes wide. "How is this possible?" She keeps saying, but she's not looking at me. She touches bark with a trembling hand, hums. "Wait. That was rhetorical. It's not really possible, and yet . . ."

I reach to touch the same tree, and though it doesn't give me the scorching feeling it did the last time, it does give me a rush of heat. I close my eyes and let it move through me, working my body till I shiver. I bite down on my bottom lip then pluck one of the flowers off the tree. It glows a fluorescent blue in my hand, but it's gone before I can blink. I don't need any other proof but my body and the magnet that pulls me to this place to know one thing for certain: somehow, I'm one and the same with these glowing wisteria.

I'm connected through blood, earth, bones, to the layers of each realm surrounding us.

Bri is staring at me, her mouth crooked on one side, a few swallowtails in her hair. She tilts her head and says, "So . . . what are we standing around here for? We need to go learn how to use that compass."

The compass didn't move at all around the wisteria trees. Because it's an anchor and not technically on this side of the realms, I wonder if it makes the earth's magnetic field void in that area. We move around the forest, but the compass becomes erratic. We try different things to trigger my ability or my attachment to it, and now that it has my blood it should be working, but Lindy did say I'd have to speak to it. Maybe I have to calibrate it too. So

I say stupid things like *Work for me, Show me the way, Abracadabra.* Brianna bites back a laugh.

I close my eyes and try to let it lead me, but bump right into a tree. "You could've told me it was there," I say.

"What if you walked through it like a portal?" says Bri. "I can't mess up your flow."

We chant to spirits, but it feels weird. I'm not a witch; I'm something else. Bri runs the compass along my forehead, then hits me with it after I insist maybe pain triggers my "powers."

"Oh! What if you need to feel the way a spirit would?" She runs her hand over tree bark. "How do you think a spirit would feel if they were trying to get your attention?"

I frown. "Desperate? Sad? Lonely?"

"Maybe focus on all of that? Try to . . . I don't know, be empathetic." She gives me a pointed look. "I know it's not one of your strong suits."

I want to protest, but my mind drifts to Derek and all that's happened between us after his mom left. I sigh. "What if there are no spirits here?"

"Shhhh," Brianna says, finger against my lip, British accent in full force. "They can hear you. Just try it, darling."

But what Bri's saying scares me the same way I was scared when I read the article about Marcus. The same way I tried to avoid Derek's sadness so I wouldn't have to feel his pain when his mom left. I don't know why, but it's always felt like there's a wall between me and the pain of other people, their loneliness, their grief.

I clear my throat and admit, "Maybe something shook me

up when I was a kid, maybe seeing the ghosts and feeling their emotions scared me off, made me *numb*."

She's silent for a second, then places both hands on my shoulders. "Or maybe you handled it just fine because this is what you're built for, but the tea didn't just hide you from the spirits, maybe it made you less empathetic so you wouldn't be able to find them either."

At first, I can't accept her words, but an ache grows in my chest. What if I was different? What if I could feel these things and my grandfather changed me? I move to cover my mouth with my hand, but a loud cry comes from my throat without my permission. Pieces of my life flash before me: Adelia being sad when she first came out of the closet and people were mean, my mom crying over my dad, Derek over his mom. My brain dreams these moments differently and I choke on a sob. Feeling all the things my sister felt, holding my mom's hand while she told me about my dad, letting Derek be sad. Letting him lean on me. Us, never missing any moments.

Bri doesn't hug me. She takes a breath and says, "That's good, my love. Let it out." She lets me cry for as long as I need to. When I'm finally done, she pinches my chin. "You're going to be okay, but you need to focus on those feelings to figure this out, alright?"

She folds my fingers around the compass. I take a breath and try to imagine what it would be like wandering for years, for sixty, for a century. I think of all the things the spirits must see, the people, the places, but always on the other side of a layer, a film they can't push through, dull and dark. No one to hear them scream or speak, no one to listen, no one to comfort them. My eyes burn again and it's almost too much—until the compass vibrates in my hand.

Something moves. I hear the soft crinkle of leaves, my eyes dart toward the trees, but nothing is there. I breathe in the energy around me, listen to the sounds of the trees whistling in the wind, smell the faint scent of wisteria not far from here. And then they start to whisper, and I think I can see something. There's a fog that blankets the space between *us*. A young girl, pigtails, standing by a log on the right of us. There's a gray bunny unmoving at her feet, and I think it's staring at me too. In my mind, I speak to her, call things, try to get closer, but when she opens her mouth to answer no sound comes out. I can't move. The layer is too thick. Sludge, weighing down my feet, shackling me. Suddenly shadows wrap around my chest like I've been sucked into the gray. The compass won't slow or lead us anywhere. The girl looks behind her, then back at me. She's scared. She squats down and places a protective hand on the bunny, and I know it's the abyss coming for them before they both disappear.

The fog leaves, the shadows go. All that's left is me, Bri saying things I can't hear, and the compass slowing till it stops spinning. My breathing comes out in spurts, my throat is dry, my bones feel heavy, like they don't even belong in my body.

"Did it work?" I can hear Bri now, feel her hand on my arm.

I'm barely comprehending what I just saw, my body trying to play match with my mind, and it takes me a minute to gather myself. To know that what I just saw was real and in front of me. More solid than it's ever been. "The compass wasn't leading us anywhere, and I couldn't talk to her. Or she couldn't talk back. I don't know. But . . ."

"She?" Bri covers her mouth with her hands. "Oh."

We both feel the weight of the meaning in the moment. A girl in the woods. One that only *I* saw. Bri takes the compass from me. "It'll be okay. You made progress; you did it."

It takes me a bit to rein in my emotions. "Because of you," I breathe out.

She smiles just a little, then checks her watch. "Shit, I need to get home."

"Already?" The sky is dimming above our heads, but it's early for her.

"Ever since my mom found out about Gary's party from a friend, I've been on curfew."

I can't blame her for leaving. Mom insisted I be home by a certain time too, but she's at work, and she won't know I'm not there until she calls on her dinner break in a couple of hours.

We walk back down to the bottom of the hill, but when we reach the stairs, I stop and tell Bri I'm going to stay here a little longer.

She narrows her eyes. "You probably need the rest so you can keep working."

"Probably," I say, "but I want to sit with it."

She shakes her head. "I'm not leaving you alone. We'll figure it out together tomorrow."

"I am pretty exhausted," I admit, and she opens out her arms to hug me. "Thank you for believing me. And thank you for being the best friend in the whole world."

"Better than Derek?"

"We're not best friends again yet, but maybe it'll be a tie."

She sucks her teeth but rubs my back. "Thank you for trusting me with all of this. But on the walk home you're telling me every single detail about the kiss with Derek."

FORTY-FOUR

Dear Journal,

For two days, I asked Lolo if I could work shorter shifts
so I could "study." He didn't mind and I was happy not
to be around him for long anyway. I would watch him make
elixirs and wonder if he knew taking my empathy would be
a symptom but felt like he had to, or if he did it purposely
to disconnect me from the spirits. After work, Bri and I
practiced with the compass. The little girl didn't come back;
neither did the bunny. I didn't see any spirits. Bri keeps
offering to make me cry, but it doesn't help. On the third
day, Derek practiced with us and it was the same. Nothing.
He left early, said he was tired. Bri said he looked like he
had the flu.

    I wonder if he's in pain, if there are things happening
to his body he's not telling me about. I wonder if I'm
making the right decision by not telling Lolo yet.

What I'm feeling:

-Scared that Derek's getting sicker

-Nervous that Marcus hasn't spoken to me in days. (What's he doing? Would he really kill Derek by staying? Does Lolo know someone who can do a spell to bind Derek and Marcus?)

-Exhausted. My brain hurts.

-Hungry, literally all the time. (Is it the compass work? Is it that the tea is finally gone from my system? I'm never like this.)

-Selfish. (I hate the feeling, but it hits whenever I think of Derek.)

FORTY-FIVE

I'm a mess because Derek left school early after Bri spotted him in the nurse's office. He finally texts during third period, says he's at the emergency room with his dad because he fainted on the ride home. He doesn't explain, just tells me he's getting scans done. Insists he's okay. I ask what kind of scans, but he doesn't text back the whole day. I spend most of the night waiting by the window, wondering if the scans were of his brain. Did his dad think they'd find something festering there? How can he not know this is partly his doing?

When Mr. Johnson pulls up and into the driveway at five in the morning, I hold my breath while he gets out of his car and goes around to the passenger side door to help Derek. My heart beats furiously when I see him, and I'm heading outside before I can stop myself.

Derek needs his rest, I should let him rest, but his window is already open. He was waiting for me too. I'm careful not to stumble inside because his dad might hear, but there's an old song floating from the record player to muffle some of the noise. I know this one. "Time After Time," by Cyndi Lauper. My mom plays it a lot. Did Marcus put this on?

The thought stills me for a second, but as soon as I'm close I know it's Derek who's curled into a fetal position on his bed. I blink back tears and drop to my knees, reaching to push his hair out of his face.

His eyes flutter open. "Hey," he says, voice achingly soft for me.

"Hey," I say back, give him a small smile. "I was so worried about you." He opens his mouth, but his lips are trembling. My fingers move on their own. I touch him unflinchingly, and the contact seems to soothe us both. "You don't have to speak if it's hard," I say.

He nods and closes his eyes. His lips are warm and unmoving against my fingers.

"I'm going to find his space and then he'll leave you alone, I promise."

It's such a big promise. For a moment, I regret making it. I think about how impossible it all seems. Something has always been off about me; the spirits have been with me this whole time, suppressed by the tea, but what good is an ability if you don't even know how it works?

Derek takes soft breaths, and I find myself counting them. "I'm just so tired," he whispers through my fingers. "But they didn't find one thing wrong with me." I watch his chest rise and fall. "For a moment, I was hoping they would because maybe it'd be better than all of this."

I sit back on my heels, trying to figure out what to say, what not to say. I have no words.

Then someone knocks on Derek's door. "Coming in," Mr. Johnson says.

I panic, drop to the ground and crawl under Derek's bed.

Mr. Johnson comes in to ask his son how he's feeling, and Derek makes his voice sound like it has more life when he reassures his dad he'll be fine, but I can hear the exhaustion in it. Mr. Johnson is clearly having a rough time too. He sighs and sits on the bed, shaking his leg back and forth. "Yeah, of course you'll be okay," he says. "But with the blackout and headaches, all the dizziness. We don't even know why you have petechiae. I'm going to call a neurologist tomorrow, just to be sure."

My stomach sinks. Derek told me the petechiae went away. I didn't know about the headaches. I'm sick while they talk above me, but Derek drops his arm so it's dangling off the bed. His hand is in front of my face and I know he did that for me. I swallow the thickness in my throat, reach slowly, quietly, to touch the tips of his fingers. Derek doesn't pull away from me.

There is a thread of invisible strings connecting us. When he sighs, I sigh inside.

The conversation he's having with his father fades behind this blood rushing through my body, this heartbeat in my belly, this feeling that I could stay under here forever if it meant I'd never lose this. And when Derek opens his hand and laces our fingers, a spark of heat goes through me. It travels from my toes, wraps around my thighs, glides up my back. A strong ache blooms in my bones and fills me with need. I never want to lose him again. I can't.

When I hear the bed move, see his dad stand and leave the room, it feels like I'm watching from elsewhere, from inside a bubble that protects me and Derek with a song playing just for us. At this moment, I know it with my whole heart: I am in love with Derek Johnson.

Maybe I've always been.

I don't move right away and neither does he. He might not love me back, but I need him in my life. There's still so much work to be done in healing what we had, and right now the door feels open for it. Right now, Derek and I are connected and my soul tells me it'll be forever.

We stay like this, hands clasped, Derek stroking his thumb over my skin, and *oh*. I hope I'm not too heartbroken if he only wants a friendship. I can't be.

"Derek," I start, trying to form the words on my tongue, trying to find a voice when I feel like it's far from reach. "I'm really sorry for . . ."

The contact between us catches static. Then, "Sorry for what, Bluebird?"

His touch goes icy, hot electric, a sharp burning sensation.

"How cute," Marcus says, the bed shifting under his weight. He leans his head off, his smile is upside down, he stares at me with big dark eyes. "Are you enjoying this, Blue? I know we are. This beautiful song. The way your small hand fits perfectly in ours."

I stiffen, pull out of Marcus's grasp, but at the loss of contact we both seem jolted.

"Come out from under there." His voice is singsong. "We should talk. You and I."

The tender moment with Derek leaves my body in a rush and I fight to lock it away for later, but Marcus peeks under again, this time the smile splits Derek's face like I've never seen. "Or I can come under there with you. Might be more exciting to talk in the dark."

I groan, slide out from under the bed, pushing my clothing back into place when I stand.

"Thought I'd never be able to surprise you," Marcus taunts, then gets up slowly. "What's taking you so long with the compass?"

"I'm trying, okay? I don't know how it works."

He walks toward the mirror hanging on Derek's wall. Stares for a few seconds. "He's not looking so good, our Derek."

"He's not *your* Derek."

"Well, he's not exactly *yours* either." Marcus eyes me through the mirror. "But you'd probably like him to be."

I hope he can't see the red in my cheeks. "How are you more energized than Derek?"

"Oh," he waves a hand at me, "I'm able to push his body past its limits."

"You're going to . . ." I bite down on my lip. "He'll die before I can figure it out."

Marcus shrugs and turns to face me. "Then so be it."

"You don't mean that," I say, touching my shoulder where he left his nail marks. His eyes flick to it and I can see him swallow. "You hurt me in the dream, how?"

"Guess your dreams aren't really *just* dreams, Aria. And the closer you get to connecting with the other side, the closer we get to you."

I swallow and step toward him. "Be honest with me. You

don't really want Derek to die because you're scared of the abyss." His eyes go wide. "What's in it?"

He opens his mouth, shuts it. I can feel his fear clouding the room around us, going deep down into the marrow of my bones.

"Nothing," he finally says. "Nothing, forever."

We share a breath. Connected again like we're back in the gray. Nothing, forever. That's what happens to spirits who wander for too long, who never find space.

"I'd rather burn in hell," he says, taking another step so he can tilt my chin, "than be nothing at all." I feel the weight of his words. The nonexistence is heavy. He strokes my chin, leans low so our lips are nearly touching. "Figure it out. And tell Derek to stop fighting me for control. He's a tough one, but he's killing us quicker."

My mind turns while the puzzle pieces continue to snap and glue into place. Then I say, "I can't promise he won't fight you. So maybe you should fall back, let him control his body while I learn to activate my ability. You don't want something to happen to him before I do."

He grasps my face with both hands. "You're a slick one, Bluebird." My body betrays me, calls to his energy. I close my eyes and let his voice seep into my soul. "But the next time we speak, you better have something good to tell me or I'll use the last of Derek's energy to do far worse than what I did to Sean. Maybe I'll start with your racist neighbor. Maybe your sister."

Marcus blinks rapidly, and then the electricity is gone. Derek stumbles forward. I catch him but I can't bear the weight of his body. We collapse together on the rug.

"You are pretty slick," Derek breathes against my neck, warm and on top of me, bringing ripples of good feelings through my body. He pushes himself up and stares down at me, looking stronger already. I try not to think about everywhere our bodies still touch. Or Marcus's threats. "I'm sorry for being a bad friend," I whisper, the words slipping out. "I'm sorry for everything."

Something flashes across Derek's face before he gets onto his knees and holds out a hand to pull me up. Then, he wraps his arms around me, my head is flush with his heartbeat. He doesn't say he forgives me, but this is more than enough. He pulls back to look into my face, about to say something, but the door to his room swings open and his dad stands in the doorway, confusion contorting his features. I wonder what it must look like: the two of us on our knees, wrapped in each other. I'm not supposed to be here.

"Derek? Are you okay?" he says.

Derek pulls away from me and stands slowly. His dad is at his side in an instant. "Don't worry," Derek says. "I'm feeling a little better."

"Better?" His dad's voice shakes. "Uh . . ."

"I just . . . I'm really hungry for a cheeseburger."

"A cheeseburger?"

"Yeah . . . maybe two?"

"Oh . . . okay, I'll fry some up," Mr. Johnson says, then his eyes flick over to mine. "Aria, how did . . ." He shakes his head. "You know what? Never mind. You should get going."

"Yeah, alright." I smile and head to the window, but Derek's dad clears his throat. "Uh. Maybe I'll just use the front door this time."

"You do that," Mr. Johnson says.

I take one last look at Derek, tell him, "It'll all be okay. I know it."

There's a flicker of fear in Derek's eyes; he frowns. But I don't wait for him to respond.

I know exactly what I have to do.

Lolo answers the phone with a sleepy voice. I can hear Lola in the background asking who's calling so early, but he doesn't tell her. "What is this about, Blue?"

"I need you to help me and Derek," I say. "If you don't, something really bad can happen to him. You gave him that tea and you allowed a spirit to slip right inside of him."

"What?" I can hear him take a breath, shift in bed. His next words are sharp, sure. "I never did anything to that boy."

"You *and* Mr. Johnson, and now Derek is being possessed."

"You must be mistaken. And even if you weren't, I'm not a spell worker. I can't attach a spirit to him."

"His tea had repercussions," I say. "It opened him up to the spirit world."

Lolo doesn't let a beat pass. "Gerald Johnson signed a contract. And so did you, Blue. You said you wouldn't get involved and here you are coming to me with this nonsense. Derek is probably lying to you for fun. My advice would be to let this go for your own sake. This conversation ends right here."

Before he can hang up, I say, "I'm a seeker." The words feel true; there's a power in saying them with certainty for the first time. I feel like I can finally breathe.

A beat. Three. Then, "You are no seeker, Aria Cayetano. You're just a kid." His tone is final. "Don't call me, don't come back to the shop. I won't speak about any of this. We're done."

When he hangs up, I make my heart steel. There's no time to cry. It's all on me now.

FORTY-SIX

The smell of bacon frying wafts through the house. Mom is cooking breakfast. She never makes breakfast. She has a smile on her face and she's wearing cute new work scrubs. I snatch a strip of crackling bacon from the pan and nearly burn my fingertips.

"Aria, don't be so reckless," she hisses.

I hot-potato the bacon while blowing on it, then shove it into my mouth. I'm not hungry, but I have to pretend to be normal after that call with Lolo. But then Mom points to a cup on the counter and says, "I already fixed you your tea."

There's only so long a person can pretend and I've reached my limit. All I hear is Lolo calling me a kid and Derek's ragged breaths as he deteriorates on his bed. What I see when I pick up the cup and dump the tea into the sink is me, a seeker, someone who is capable of creating great change. What my mom sees, with her wide eyes, is a defiant daughter who is asking for a slap.

"What the hell, Aria?" She turns off the stove and stalks over to me. "What the . . ."

"You're not poisoning me with another drop of that," I say.

She blinks, her eyes darting over my face. She opens her mouth, but no words come.

"I know what you and Lolo have been hiding from me, and I'm done letting you decide what I'm going to do with my body, my mind, and my soul."

"Aria . . . ," she breathes. We stare at each other. Tense. "You need that tea. You . . ."

Her phone buzzes on the counter. An alarm. I nod my head toward it. "What I need is to get to school, and you need to get to work. Like always."

I turn to walk away, but she grabs my arm and spins me around. "You will not speak to me that way, Aria Cayetano." I sigh and her expression softens. "Stay. Let's talk."

"I can't miss school," I say, shifting out of her grasp. "We'll talk later."

When I turn to walk out the door, she lets out a strangled gasp and I try to shake my guilt, wondering if she'll cry on the way to work.

⁓⁓⁓

Bri texts back, says she'll take the attendance sheet down to the office so she can erase my absent mark, then I bunk school to spend the day at Neutaconkanut Park. I shoot Derek a text every hour to check on him and he doesn't seem to mind. When my mom messages, telling me to be home early so we can talk, I lie and say I'm heading straight to work after school. If Lolo calls her, so be it. Around four P.M., Brianna finds me at Neutaconkanut. We work at the compass for hours, but the only thing I manage to see is faint fog, the glimmering of the veil, nothing more. Why did it work the other day, but not now? Not when I really, really need it to.

It's past Bri's curfew and her parents keep calling, so I walk her down the path and sit on the stone steps there. She starts to protest, pulls out her phone. "I'll just tell my mom . . ."

"No," I say. "Please, Bri. I need some time. I'll just sit here."

Bri pulls on her cardigan and her British accent, then kisses my forehead. "Alright. I know you're worried for Derek, darling, but please stay out of the forest. It'll be dark soon."

As soon as she makes it out of eyeline, I get up and start walking the path again. I want to listen to her, but I can't. Not with Marcus being impatient and threatening to take Derek's life one way or another.

Before I break through the canopy of trees at the end of the path, the wisteria call to my body, wanting me closer. It's transfer time in the sky when the compass starts to move. It gets faster as I approach the trail that leads to the wisteria trees, and I'm wondering why it's moving so erratically in this area when I hear the sound of a twig cracking. I shift, scan my surroundings, searching for a person or an animal. But all I see are trees, the day growing darker underneath them. So I keep moving. A little faster because there's a raw feeling in my stomach and a tingling at the back of my neck like someone's watching me.

Then I hear a twig snap again. This time, when I turn back I see someone coming out from behind a tree. My body goes rigid. He's about twenty feet away and the shadows from the foliage aren't in my favor, but I know that face. It's the man from Lolo's shop. It's Levi.

There's a moment of hesitation before I slide the compass into my pocket and touch my knife there. But I can't stand my ground. I can't. As soon as Levi takes another step toward me, before he can make a sound, I turn and run.

My name is acid on his lips, seeping through the ground, making the grass and leaves wet, dense, the brush under my feet sticky and corroded, slowing me down. I am slipping and falling and getting back up as he calls my name from somewhere behind. Too close. He sounds too close. I jump over a tree stump, try to find my footing while stumbling over some rocks, dirt, earth. I keep running. My chest burns, my heart threatening to burst right through it.

For a few seconds, my life flashes before my eyes. He's going to kill me. He's going to kidnap me. He's going to burn my body or bury me here. He'll take my teeth. No one will ever find me.

There are two hiking trails and I can't remember which one leads closest to the street so I go left and pray Levi goes right. He doesn't. I can hear him creeping closer. The sky getting darker, the buzzing of bugs louder. There's a walking bridge just up ahead, but I trip and fall before making it there. My knees and hands take the impact and it sends sharp pains through my body. But I turn as quickly as I can and flick open my pocketknife, thrusting it up toward Levi.

He doesn't back away but he raises his hands in the air like he's scared of me.

"I just," his breathing comes out ragged; he looks worse off than me, "want to talk to you. You . . . you didn't have to run."

What? I scoot back before standing on shaky legs and securing my stance with the knife. "Leave me the fuck alone," I say. My phone. Where's my phone? I can hit the emergency button, send out a distress call. Maybe someone walking the trails will hear me screaming. Levi takes a step toward me. "I'm warning you," I tell him, "I'll slit your throat."

If he gets close to me, I'll do whatever it takes to stay alive.

Levi's eyes crinkle a little, and I think maybe he's amused. "Aria. Let's talk."

"My lolo will . . . he'll cut your hands off."

"I have no doubt he would." Levi takes another step. We play the dance. He comes forward, I move back. We're crossing the bridge slowly. "But I'm not going to hurt you."

"So why did you chase me through the woods?"

"I knew my only shot to talk to you was getting you alone. And that hasn't been easy."

Sickness threads through my belly like tapeworms. I swallow a lump in my throat. Look around. Ready to make another run for it. "You've been watching me?"

"I have."

"You followed me to the mall. What do you want to talk about, sicko?"

Levi stares directly into my eyes. His face softens and his voice follows with, "About you finding my wife." I don't know if I've heard him right. "I'm begging you. Please find my wife." My hand holding the knife falters; I almost drop it. This can't be happening right now. Levi stops moving and says, "She died months ago, and I need you to find her." My throat burns, my vision blurs. "I need to know where she's resting. I can't move on until I know. I'll pay you."

"How . . ." I can't keep the tremble from my voice. "How do you know I can help you?"

It's like my body knows what he's going to say before he does. There's a moment where everything stops except for the beat of my heart. "Because I've seen you do it before," he says.

I don't speak. I can't. Who is this man? What exactly did he see me do? Why does he suddenly feel familiar?

"You were just a child." Levi smiles. "Maybe three or four. We were behind the church. Me, you, your grandfather. We were letting you play, while . . . while we did some business together. But you disappeared. Ran off across the churchyard. It was a mess back then, lots of big trees. Your grandfather was so scared. And then . . . then we found you inside of the shrine."

My throat doesn't belong to me. The world turns gray then white then colorful. I blink and pieces of me come down from the sky and begin fitting together again. "My dad," I choke out.

Levi nods. "You climbed inside the shrine, but you weren't playing there . . . you were . . . you turned everything blue. The stone, the grass. A bird in a tree. Even your body."

Blue. Bluebird. Blue.

"Not blue like the ocean. Glowing, fluorescent." He exhales like he's needed to for months, watches my face to see if he should keep going. "Your grandfather pulled you out quickly and everything regained normal color. But your hands took a while, they were red and raw like you had been burned. No one saw you except for us. And then he—Zack—he touched the stones and he knew. He knew his son's spirit rested there. We wept together that day."

I drop my hand holding the knife to my side and think of

Derek. What this means. I could do this for him, I really can. For Marcus too. I could put an end to their pain. I think of my sister and my mother and all the memories we've made at the shrine. I've felt my father there.

The knowledge makes other memories of childhood creep back in. But I'm dizzy. It'll be work to rewire them all, and I can't just yet. Not right now.

Levi looks worried when I raise my head and look into his face, but he doesn't come any closer. I'm thankful for the space between us. I pocket my dad's knife. "Do you know how I did it?" I ask.

He shakes his head. "I don't. Why?"

The disappointment rises inside of me again, but I push it down. I know without a doubt now that I'll figure this all out. I'll save Derek. There's something special inside of me, and I once knew how to use it. I'll learn again. I clear my throat and say, "Because I have no idea how I can help you right now. I've been trying to figure it out for . . ."

"What?" Levi breathes out, his face falling. He starts walking toward me but stops when I stiffen. "You don't know how to use your own ability?"

"No," I say. "I didn't even know about this . . . I had no idea about any of it until recently."

Levi looks like he might crumble for a second, but then he regains composure. "Your grandfather should've told you." He sighs. "I'm sorry you had to find out from me. He made me keep it a secret too, you know? For all of these years, I swore I'd never tell anyone. And I haven't . . . even after we fell out years ago."

His words make something tick in my chest. Because of what he told me about myself, I almost forgot that my grandparents said he was a bad person. "Why did you fall out?"

"That's not important." Levi smiles. "What's important is you returning the favor of keeping your secret and helping me find my wife. But I need you to do it *now*."

I take three steps back. "I just told you, I don't know how it works yet."

Suddenly, his eyes morph like a monster's and he says, "There must be a way to trigger it."

"Maybe." I take a step back, back, back. "Listen, I'll try to help you, but first, I need to figure this out. I need to talk to my grandfather."

"That won't work. Zackary can't know about me." Levi grips the rail of the bridge as he comes toward me. "Let's try to trigger it now."

"No." My voice is firm, eye contact direct, my head is high.

Levi stops, cups his hands over his mouth and laughs through his fingers. My nerves jitter, but he turns like he's going to walk away and leave me alone. Then he pivots back and we lock eyes. It takes only a second for my hormones to make my body run.

I'm faster this time; my feet move over the brush and the rocks like it's all flat ground. The woods are dark now, shadows push through the open parts of the forest like they're trying to catch me too. I scramble down a small hill, over thousands of little pebbles, and so does Levi. I can feel him right behind me. But he grunts, trips and falls at the bottom of the hill. And I think I've caught a break, I can get away, but then his hand cups around my ankle and he yanks me down with him.

I stumble over him and hit the ground with a thud. My bones feel broken, the air knocked out of my lungs. I'm trying to catch my breath when Levi says, "I'll force it out of you." But as soon as he grabs my shirt, I reach into my pocket, release the spring and shove my dad's knife right into his hand. Then I twist hard.

Blood as black as tar splats onto my shirt, my neck, runs down my cheek. Levi can't move. He cries out—a grotesque sound comes from his throat. The birds scatter from the trees.

The knife has teeth. I watch it sink deeper into his skin on its own, pulling black blood with it, deteriorating all the flesh there. The smell of rot rises and images of the rosebush resurface. He begs for my help, but I'm already up and running.

By the time I make it to the mouth of the hill, it's so dark I can hardly see my feet in front of me. But I can still hear his screams. He's calling for me somewhere in the distance. When I hit the stairs and lay eyes on the skate park, I almost collapse right there. Too relieved to see bright lights, people, my body ready to give out, but I'm not safe yet.

I keep going, heart in my throat, sweat drenching my back.

My adrenaline is on one thousand when I make it to my front door, looking over my shoulder like he's still following before barreling inside. I'm leaning against the side of the couch, catching my breath, examining the locked door like he'll break right through it when my phone buzzes in my pocket again, then again. I don't look at it. Everything aches. The world around me trembles. I drop to my knees and my mom comes running into the room.

"Aria, I was calling you," she says, but when she sees me on the floor she drops down too. With shaky hands, she touches the blood on my cheek. "Aria. What happened, baby?"

I'm drifting out of my body when she says it again, when she shakes my shoulder. Her words blur together. But she kisses my face and pulls me into her arms and brings me back to my body. I sob when I make it there, and she's still asking what's wrong.

"Just hold me, Mom. Please . . . please hold me."

FORTY-SEVEN

My bedroom door is open. I'm too nervous to be closed in by myself, so my grandfather steps right inside. He doesn't know I just got out of the shower, how long it took to clean the black blood from my face. His voice is softer than it usually is, but I can hardly look at him.

"Blue, tell me what happened," he whispers. "I need to know."

"You failed me," I say.

He swallows, looks me over like he'll notice something out of place. "Tell me."

So I do. I tell him about Lindy, the letter, the compass, about Derek going to the hospital, and Levi. I speak so fast, jumbled and disoriented, I'm not sure how much he understood.

"Dad's knife, it's like," my voice quakes, "it has its own soul," I say. The images of Levi's skin getting torn apart seep back into my mind and bile rises in my throat. "You should've told me." I repeat Levi's words and make myself sicker for it. "Why didn't you tell me?"

Lolo walks over, sits on my desk chair while I'm on my bed.

From here, I can see the shine of tears in his eyes. "I'm sorry, Blue. Please forgive me," he says.

I laugh, swat my own tears from my face. "Why? Why'd you keep it from me?"

"To protect you." His tone is so sure.

"From what?" I dig my fingers into my sheets. "What was so bad that . . ."

"We used to be friends, Levi and I," Lolo cuts in, his eyes darting across my face, "but then he tried to use you. Wanted us to make money off of your gift. I should've ripped out his heart then, but I let him walk away with the promise that he'd stay gone," Lolo says. "I didn't tell you about your . . . abilities to protect you from people like *Levi*." Lolo spits out the name like it's disgusting on his tongue.

"You think . . . you think this could happen again?"

His lips curve down. "I do, and worse. Far worse," he says. I think of Sheila's words, how comforting they were, and he seems to read my mind. "Blue, you have a gift, but because of that, people will want from you, try to take from you and force you to use it. And the spirits on the other side, they get desperate. They've been trapped there for a long time. Who knows what they could do to you if you refuse to help them."

I touch the nail marks that are fading from my shoulder and swallow. "No one else needed to know about it. But at least I would've been prepared. I wouldn't have thought there was something bad inside of me or wrong with me all this time."

Lolo looks like he wants to hug me but doesn't know how. "Maybe I'm wrong, Blue, but I've always figured if you knew about it, you'd be inclined to help people. You'd want to help the spirits too, which means you'd be constantly at the hands of wishes that aren't yours. Forever trapped doing this work that you never asked for."

I think about Marcus and tell myself it's different. Derek is my best friend. He needs this and so do I. But then there's Levi. If he wouldn't have come off like that, I might've helped him too. I felt the urge. But he was desperate. How many more will there be?

"What good is having a gift if I can't use it?" I ask.

"Not every ability is meant to be used, Blue. Some people I know with complicated gifts have learned the hard way. I won't allow that to be you."

I throw my head back and laugh. A delirious feeling trickles out of me, expanding, clouding over us and thickening the room. I can almost see the gray here. Like I brought it down just to see the look on Lolo's face. He's frightened because I can't stop laughing.

"*Tama na*," he says, his Filipino accent thick.

"You don't get to tell me what to do," I say. "Not anymore."

"Aria, quiet." My real name sounds funny coming from him.

I chew my lips to keep from laughing, then say, "You haven't told me even a quarter of everything I need to know, and you think you get to tell me what to do with my life after I found this all out for myself?"

Lolo stands abruptly, the chair rolling back. I laugh again, and he looks like he might slap me. "I won't allow you to lose parts of yourself to the other side."

All of the laughter drains out of me. "What?"

He pushes silver hair from his face, huffs out a breath. "We don't know if there are other repercussions for you using your gift. Every good has a bad. That's the balance. The best way to protect you is to keep you from it."

"I need a real explanation."

My grandfather sighs. His worse-off leg shakes a little. "There's not much history on people who can do what you do, but there are rumors that each time you help ferry a soul into a resting place, you leave something of yours on the other side."

The words are hard to digest. I'm still trying to wrap my head around everything that happened in the forest, the news about my dad's shrine. "As in . . . a personal item?"

"I'm not exactly sure, and you need rest. I'll tell you everything I know tomorrow."

I stand up and shake my head. "I need you to tell me now. How do you expect me to rest knowing Levi is out there, looking for me?"

"He'll never bother you again," Lolo says. "I promise that."

"Because of Dad's knife?" I ask. "Will it kill him?"

Lolo doesn't blink. "He'll wish for death."

A shiver climbs my spine. But Lolo turns to leave and I clear my throat. There's one question I need answered before he goes.

"Did I really guide Dad's spirit to the shrine?"

Lolo doesn't turn to look at me. "You did, and it was one of the happiest days of my life."

My heart hums with something bigger than happiness.

Something I can't put into words. "Because of what you did, Derek needs help," I say. "You need to teach me to use it."

"I'll do what I can," Lolo says, then disappears into the hall.

While I'm pouring bags of tea in the trash, Mom comes into the kitchen. I think she's going to yell, but she doesn't.

"I felt you get out of bed. It's the middle of the night."

"Couldn't sleep," I say.

She walks over and gently takes the last bag of tea from my hand, then goes up on a stool to put it high inside of a cabinet. While she's up there, she looks down at me. "There are some incredibly rare ingredients in here. We'll save one in case you change your mind someday."

I want to tell her I won't, but how can I be sure? "Are you sorry for keeping it from me?"

"I'm not." She comes down from the stool and touches my face. "Let's go back to sleep."

I am in the darkness of the gray, but his voice creeps through it like color.

"Aria," he says, low, faint, but getting louder and clearer with each call.

My small feet move toward the sound. I am four. Scared of being here. "Daddy?" I call out again, glancing around the void space. "Daddy, where are you?"

"I'm right here," he calls back before a small circle of yellow light forms in the distance.

I walk until the circle gets bigger, closer. I stop when it's big enough to fit through. Yellow, orange, and green, fluorescent lights dance together like glow sticks. I reach through the circle until the world forms around me. Suddenly there are trees and sky and people in the distance.

There's my church. And my father, standing above me.

He kneels down to get on my level. "You found me, Aria."

I bolt forward, jump into his arms, cry, "I missed you, Daddy."

He strokes my hair, tears trailing his cheeks. "And I missed you."

Two people sit on a bench behind us. They look like they're talking about something I don't need to know about. I know who they are. Lolo is much younger. His hair is peppered silver and the man with him is Levi, who actually has some hair. My dad holds my hands and sits on the grass with me. We play with sticks and rocks. We laugh. He tickles my armpit and I grab his wrist and see the strawberry birthmark there, big and round. I show him the one on my belly.

"Like mine," I say.

"A connection." He smiles. "You always have a piece of me with you, right there."

Then he pulls me in for another hug and says, "Aria, Daddy is tired. I need to rest."

We stand and I look back at Lolo and Levi, but they don't see me walk away with my dad. He and I stop at a shrine. It looks different. It's filled with rainbow light. The yellow shines down on my father's skin, makes him glow, makes me giddy. "It's so pretty," I say.

"You made it look like that." He kisses the top of my head

and lets go of my hand. "You have all these colors right inside of you. And I have to go to them now or they'll disappear."

"No," I cry, clinging to his shirt, his leg. "Daddy, don't go again."

He wipes my tears and pokes my belly through my shirt. "We're connected, remember? Daddy will be here whenever you need me. Sleeping with one eye open."

He walks into the yellow by the shrine and disappears when it turns fluorescent blue.

I shoot up in bed, clinging to my sheets. Almost call out for him, but the name gets caught in my throat when I look down and see my mom. She stirs beside me on the bed, then blinks awake and sits up to touch my forehead like I have a fever. "Baby, what's wrong?"

"I remember him," I say, my shoulders giving out, fresh pain from missing him hitting me like a wave. Would I have remembered him sooner if I never took the tea?

"Remember who?"

"Dad. I remember Dad."

She takes a startled breath. "Did you have a dream?"

I don't answer right away. I am buried in all the things I forgot about him. His smile, his laugh, the way he'd chase me around the yard and play hide-and-seek and take me on walks in the city. I suffocate with all the memories, with the grief they bring. But then I remember the way it felt as he walked into the light of the shrine, and it slows my racing heart. That feeling spreads through me, calms me. I lie back onto the pillow and so does Mom. She strokes my hair.

When my voice finally comes, it's faint, a whisper. "He had a strawberry birthmark like mine." I lift my shirt. It's too dark in the room to see it, but I touch it with my hand. "And his voice was soothing and soft. He sounded like he could call to the moon."

The whites of her eyes grow large and she's trying not to cry, but I can hear the tears thicken her throat. "Was it a memory?"

"It was *the* memory," I say. "The one where he found peace. He looked . . . happy."

She rubs my back, but I grab her face. "You can cry, Mom. It's okay, I'm here."

She leans her forehead against mine. "Tell me everything," she sobs.

FORTY-EIGHT

The sound of Levi howling in the woods has haunted me for two days, but I feel calmer at my father's shrine. It's just me and Derek. We didn't come here to learn anything, to trigger my abilities, or to talk about Marcus. We came here for me. Derek thought visiting my father would ease the ache in my heart and he was right. We don't speak much. I dance my fingers up the stone, feeling the connection like a calm vibration under my skin. Out of the corner of my eyes, I watch Derek hunch forward, bracing himself on his knees. He looks better than yesterday but still sick. Marcus is letting him take the lead, but we need Marcus gone completely.

He catches me looking and his sharp canines flash when he smiles. "What?"

Butterflies spread through my stomach, bringing a burning sensation to my cheeks because we're here together, but I can't tell him that. "I'm happy you're okay for now," I say.

His face falls, but then he moves my hair from my shoulder and makes me shiver. The nail marks from the dream with

Marcus are gone and all that's left is our matching scar there. His fingertips are soft when he grazes it. "I'm happy *you're* okay. What happened . . ." His Adam's apple moves in his throat. "I can't stand the thought of anyone hurting you. I hate that I wasn't there. That you were put in that situation because of me."

Just like that, we aren't human anymore. We are wispy: the air moving through the trees, a mass of gravitational energy, right before he pulls me to him. My mouth falls against his shoulder, I close my eyes, let myself smell him, and kiss him there. We pull back after a few seconds and stare at each other. I wonder if he's thinking about the way he kissed my lips.

I turn to look at the shrine, so he can't see how red my face must be. "How'd the talk with your dad and my grandfather go?"

Right before we came here, Lolo was at Derek's house, breaking the news about the tea and the possession to him. I wonder just how many ways Lolo had to explain it to Mr. Johnson.

"It was interesting," Derek says, sighing. "I mean, who knows how long it'll take him to really believe it. Do you think his own guilt will even let him?"

I think about it for a moment, then nod. "Yes, he'll process, and then just keep processing until he realizes it's been there all along . . . Did he say why he did it?"

Derek's eyes flick up to mine, then toward people playing soccer on the grass. "He confirmed that he just wanted me to be happy, to be able to open up to him."

I don't know what to say to that so I say nothing at all. Still scared I'll get it wrong.

"Anyway," Derek finally says, and I stress because I probably should've said something. "I still don't understand why we had to get him involved at all."

My hand finds his. I squeeze. "What's happening . . . what's happening is dangerous and he should know. He was scared you were sick with something else. He's your father."

Derek squeezes back, but I'm nervous I did the whole thing wrong. Until he asks, "Do you think she ever thinks of me? My mother?"

My eyes begin to burn. I swallow and say, "I think she thinks of you and everything she walked away from all the time. I think it haunts her. How can it not? Nothing and no one else in the world is going to fill that space for her. But maybe . . ." I chew my lip. ". . . maybe you should pay attention to the people who show up for *you* every day. It might be good to let your dad in. Your mom walked away from your family, but he put the pieces back together. He was wrong for the tea, but he's so strong for everything else, and he absolutely loves you."

Derek is quiet for a long time. I try to breathe through it, but then he moves closer, his arm presses against mine, we both watch the birds walk on the grass. "Thank you, I needed to hear that," he says, then tilts his head to look at me. "Did anyone fill my space in your life?"

My body tingles. I breathe out. "That's not possible, Derek Johnson."

He flicks his tongue over his lips and laughs. "Good, because you stuck to me, Aria Cayetano. Little pieces of you attached to parts of me and I've been picking to get you out, but it's not possible. I'm . . . I'm sorry I didn't give us a chance to talk about it sooner."

I wrap my arms around myself like I can pull his words in and keep them closer. He goes into his backpack and takes out a box to hand to me. "You got me something?"

He smiles shyly. "Just open it, Aria."

When I look inside, my heart sings. There are dozens of enamel pins. Ones from different horror movies like *Scream* and *Halloween*, there's *Avatar: the Last Airbender*, and a ghost in glasses.

"I got you that one last week as a joke," Derek says, finally meeting my eyes. Is he blushing? "I never stopped thinking of you. It's why I don't ride my skateboard to school. I like to see you in the morning on the bus. Even when it's hard to be around you."

Now I'm the one blushing again.

The weight of our separate years falls away and suddenly it feels like we've never not been two energies colliding to become this one thing. And I swear his gaze flicks down to my lips, but then his phone rings and breaks us from the moment.

I steady myself, try for a joke. "You actually use a ringtone? My phone lives on silent."

"With the way trouble seems to find you, I'm sure it would make us all feel better if you kept it on," he says, then answers the phone to talk to his dad.

I turn toward the shrine with the box of pins in my lap to speak to mine. I tell my dad that I'll consider turning my ringer on just for Derek. And when I put my hand back on the stone, for a second, my fingertips turn fluorescent blue.

⁕⁕⁕⁕⁕⁕

Before heading home, I stop by the shop. Lolo opens up the cabinet drawer and pulls out a knife. My knife. He slides it across the table and I'm trembling when I pick it up. I never thought I'd see it again. I flick it open, examine it for black blood, for tar stains and Levi's skin, but the knife is cleaner than ever. It even glints like it's new.

"How did you get this?"

"I'm only answering necessary questions, and that's not one of them," Lolo says, but he doesn't turn away. "All you need to know is Levi is out of your life for good."

He's back at the stove now, pulling a pot from the oven to start cooking an elixir. While he goes to work, my mind runs to dark places. I can't bring myself to fear him for the things I'll never know, but it gives me goosebumps to imagine Levi rotting somewhere with a purple tongue and bulging eyes. I wonder if he still has his hand.

"Are you sure this knife is safe for me to keep?" I ask, knowing I'll keep it regardless.

"It won't hurt you. Like the compass in your pocket, the spell on it will only release to its owner. You're the only one it'll protect because you're a Cayetano. It's been protecting us for generations. Now that you've foolishly chosen to embrace your abilities, you might need it in the future."

A chill races up my spine. I close the knife and pray Lolo's wrong and that I won't have to use it on anyone else ever again. "What exactly does it do?"

"It's different for everyone," he says. "It seeps into a person's blood like a window to view their soul. And then, depending on the darkness there, it unleashes a punishment. Slow death, endless nightmares, hallucinations, it might even have the power to collect their soul and leave them without a chance to find space when they finally die."

It reminds me of the abyss. Of *nothing, forever*. And I wonder if a knife that could lock away souls should be in the hands of someone who is meant to free them. So, I make a promise to myself: I'll lock the knife away until I figure out how I feel about it.

"Which fate do you think Levi got?"

"I'm hoping he got them all," Lolo says.

I'm not sure I don't feel the same way, so instead I ask about the rumor for seekers. It's been heavy on my mind. This theory that I can lose things to the gray. A trade for lost souls.

"Like I said, I don't know much, but what if it's true and the other side takes something special from you? What if it messes with your body, soul, or mind somehow?" Lolo says.

I narrow my eyes at him. My grandfather could have made this all up just to scare me from tapping into my abilities. How do I know for sure? I sigh. The energy in the room has gone somber, and the last thing I need is more dullness in my life. "What if it takes my lashes?"

Lolo groans, unappreciative. The joke is enough to make him crack and start talking about where we go from here with my abilities. He tells me my connection to the spell in the compass has already been made, but I need to reconnect to the earth and then to the spirit world. I can recalibrate the compass by recalibrating myself. Right now, it's probably just as confused as I am. He pours the elixir he was making into a mason jar and places it in front of me.

"We'll need to find a really good spell worker to help, but

we can start with you drinking this in order to further clear the buildup of tea from your system."

"What's in it?" I stare at the gloopy-looking brown liquid and frown. The tea was more powerful than I assumed.

"I'll make you a list." He smiles. "But you'll wish I hadn't."

I take a sip and my stomach gurgles. "Are you sure there's nothing else I can ingest?"

"Enjoy your fate, Aria. You chose it."

"It was chosen for me the day I was born," I say.

Lolo is quiet for a while, then he tells me a story: I was three years old and couldn't articulate what was going on with the spirits I was seeing so he called Lindy in for a favor. She's a telepath, although she never calls herself that. He thought she could work to get inside of my head, and she did. She was able to tell him it was true, that I could see the dead. I connected with her like no one else, followed her around, wanted to be close to her.

I find myself slouching forward now. A couple of weeks ago, I had no idea Lindy existed, but we had a bond at one point. I wonder if memories of her will start to come back.

Lolo leaves for his office and returns a few minutes later with a kava plant. This one has the distinctive heart-shaped leaves and roots with hairs like a spider, but its color is so green I'd think it was fake if I didn't know any better. He carefully trims off a stem, then a leaf, and hands both to me. I feel the familiar spark of Marcus and the wisteria trees when I hold it.

Lolo watches me play with the stem. "When you were four years old, I left you with Lindy for a while, and she said you slipped away from sight and ate the plant in her back room."

My eyes flick to his. I laugh. "I was one of those kids, huh? Just chomping on a leaf."

"You ate a whole kava plant, Blue." Lolo's face is so serious. "You ripped the roots out and ate those too." *Oh.* "Lindy says she swore she didn't mean for it to happen, but I'll never know." He takes a breath. "You were sick for some time. And then when you weren't anymore, you were changed. You were connected to the veil in a different way. You were making plants glow and freaking out your mother when your bathwater turned blue."

I lean back against the counter. "So . . . I'm kind of like Spider-Man?"

Lolo looks like he'll cuss me out. "Huh? What are you talking about, God dammit?"

"Never mind," I tell him, then look down at the plant. "You think that if I eat kava again it'll help me connect to the other side? But why? What's special about this shrub?"

"Regular kava has been used sparingly to help facilitate psychic connections and healing for ages, but the kava I curate is special because it's grown specifically for spell workers to be able to use in rituals to call on the dead. This one has been growing with my enhancement recipe for twelve years. But I never thought I'd be feeding it to you." He sighs. "A little each day."

"Here's to being Spider-Man," I joke, then bring the leaf to my lips to take my first bite.

FORTY-NINE

The spirits are Peter Pan shadows playing on my wall, but each time I ingest kava they become sharper, more distinct. Except it's not enough. While Lolo searches for a spell worker he trusts with the knowledge of my gift, Derek's getting sicker. He's coughing up blood and hiding trembling hands, and the purple under his eyes deepens each day.

My mom had a doctor friend write us a fake note to spend the week out of school.

I chew on a kava leaf before we practice in Lolo's yard. My thighs tingle as they press against the ground. With kava in my system, my body feels more alive. Derek is sitting across from me with one long leg stretched out and touching my own. We've been practicing with physical contact, trying to see if Marcus's spirit will help facilitate my connection to the other side, while I'm actively trying to connect to the earth. It's a lot and nothing all at once. I hold the compass in one palm and dig my hands into the ground with the other. My fingers burn. The feeling travels up my wrist, my arm, all the way to my neck. I concentrate for so long. Try so hard sweat drips down my forehead, but I still can't slow the spinning of the compass.

Derek's leg twitches and takes my concentration from me. I lift my head and open my eyes. Then flinch back at how close he suddenly is. He snatches my wrist and pulls me closer.

I haven't felt this burning chill in days. "You're failing, Aria," Marcus says.

The words cut me open like only the truth can. "You're not supposed to be here," I tell him, yanking my arm free and standing to put distance between us. "Leave me the hell alone and let me work."

I walk across the yard and bury my face in my hands. *Work? Is that what I've been doing?* How can I find Marcus's resting place if I can't even see the other side? If the earth isn't welcoming me the way Lolo says it should be.

When Marcus crosses the grass, I feel it. He stands right behind me, his chest brushes my back. I turn so we're face-to-face. He lifts his hand and places it around my throat. Just the tips of his fingers flex around my neck. He's hardly touching me and still sends a sharp shiver up my spine. I calm my breathing, but I know he hears my heart thrumming. He feels it.

"I'm not hurting you, but I can," he says. Except, I can see the conflict on his face: him wrestling with parts of himself as he looks down at my neck like he wants to bite it.

Maybe he's wrestling with Derek. How do I even know?

"Bluebird, your sweet Derek is going to die," he says.

"No, he won't," I breathe against his fingers, looking into

his eyes defiantly. "You can let him go. You've already lived your life, but he has to be able to live his."

Something shifts on his face. "What life did *I* get to live?"

His words rob me of mine. I think of the article. Him being a boy when he died.

He drops his hand, releasing me from his icy touch. I trail my fingers over the burning skin of my neck. "Tell your grandfather to find a spell worker strong enough to bind our spirits together," he says. "You clearly can't do this, and it's the only way Derek and I both get to live."

"You'd really do that? You'd keep his body?"

His dark eyes grow wide, his pupils dilate. "I won't go into the dark . . . I won't." There's a vulnerability to his tone before a smile tugs at his lips. "If I can't make it to the afterlife, I sure as hell won't be taken by the abyss. I'll live again at the cost of Derek. His life is better than nothing. We will share this body, if that's what it comes to. Maybe you'll learn to love us both."

When Marcus vanishes from Derek's eyes, I feel the comedown hard in my bones, like a whole other realm leaving me. We're more connected than ever. Derek starts to choke, bends over, and coughs out dark red blood. After I lay him down on Lolo's couch, I take out my journal and write down the date.

Then, *Did Derek hear the last thing Marcus said?*

FIFTY

There's a spell worker coming over, and we wait for her in the shop living room. Lolo doesn't like that I got Bri involved but said no one would believe her if she told them because she talks *so damn much*. Every time she comes over she annoys him with her British accent. Today she says, "Bloody hell, what is that awful smell?" and Lolo groans, then leaves for the kitchen. She taps the box of Edible Arrangements in her lap. "Hope Val's not allergic to fruit."

"Can't you just talk to her?" I ask. "You know, apologize for making her mad again?"

"I will . . . with this box full of chocolate-covered strawberries. It'll soften her up."

"That's what I'd do," Derek pipes in from beside me.

Bri looks pleased. "Yeah, food always makes us women happy." But then she opens the box of strawberries, picks one up, and bites it. I screech. She hums with happiness.

Derek reaches to take a strawberry when Bri offers it to him, and then he says, "Pretty sure Val's going to be confused as to why her gift is open and half the slots are empty, but I could use one."

"Oh please," Bri says. "Do you know I had to sell two of my PS4 games to have enough money for this? Pretty sure Val will be okay with six strawberries instead of twelve."

"You're a shame," I say, shaking my head at her.

"Agreed," Derek mumbles, mouth full of strawberry.

Bri shoots daggers at us. "What do either of you even know about relationships anyway?"

"I know plenty," says Derek, leaning back on his hands to brace himself.

Bri sucks her teeth. "Ones that have lasted longer than two days? Hasn't happened. Right, Aria?"

Their eyes both land on me. Derek looks amused waiting for me to answer. "There was that one girl, Megan," I say, and drag my nails across the hardwood floor we're sitting on. "Seemed like you two were good together."

Derek reaches over me to take another strawberry, but Brianna swats his hand away.

"That's right," she says. "Whatever ever happened to you and ol' Megan? Did that hallway kissing get tiring? You were sick of smelling like saliva, huh?"

My chest grows hot remembering him and the PDA with Megan last year. It was like no one around them existed. Especially not me. But when he laughs, I smile. He's been so exhausted this week, I've hardly heard his laugh. I want to hug Bri just for making it happen.

"We were too different," he says. "Had nothing to talk about. Never laughed like this."

Bri clicks her tongue. "So it was only sexy?"

"It was only sexy," Derek repeats.

I wonder if that means he's had sex. Not that there's anything wrong with that, but it's still weird thinking of how many important things I've missed. Bri hums and opens the chocolate-covered strawberry box again. She passes Derek another strawberry and tries to hand one to me, but I shake my head. Ever since starting the kava I've lost my growing appetite.

"I guess I do have to get another gift, huh?" she says.

"I mean, I'm sure she'll enjoy the lone strawberry in that big box," I say.

"This relationship is about to make me broke," she whines.

Derek's eyebrows knit together. "Aren't you already broke? You don't have a job."

"Well, neither do you."

"I'm possessed, so I get a pass."

They go back and forth cussing each other out, and I'm so happy to see them getting along. But a fear washes over me thinking of how fragile this is. How strong Derek seems right now when just yesterday he was coughing up blood. I say a silent prayer that he'll fight long enough for me to figure this out without us having to decide on the binding ritual. Lolo says there's a chance we can tear Marcus's spirit away from Derek, but it might require time and a system cleanse and he's not even sure that the spell worker will agree it's the best option.

"Is it strange that I keep wondering what it'll mean for Marcus if we do exorcise him?" I say. "Will the abyss snatch him right up? Will he have time to haunt me in my bedroom?"

Both of their smiles fade. Bri drops a strawberry back into

the box. I am the moment killer. "Can't you help him from over there, though? Isn't that how it works?"

"But what if the abyss already got its claws too close to him? He says he's been there so long and he sounds terrified. Once he's out of Derek's body, what if I can't find him in time?"

"Well, then let it suck him away," Derek says.

Sadness coils in my stomach. I have to remind myself of Marcus's threats, of his fingers flexing around my throat, the way he's been torturing Derek, so I don't imagine him being sucked into the belly of the abyss where nothing lives forever.

When the spell worker knocks on the door, I jump up to answer it. Happy for a chance to help Derek, and happy for the distraction. But as soon as I see those bright owl eyes, shivers climb my spine. "Sheila," I say. "What are you doing here?"

She smiles. "I knew I'd see you again, Aria."

In the dim light of the living room, we all sit in a circle and Sheila tries to talk to Marcus. It's futile. Derek pushes away from her and digs his nails into the hardwoods. "You'll get hurt, Spell worker." He sounds half him, half Marcus. "Stay away from me."

I crawl over to him, take his hand. His breathing settles, but he's still looking at Sheila like he wants to gouge out her pretty eyes. She frowns and tells us that a severing spell to break the bond between them won't work, and not just because it's one of the hardest spells to pull off, but mainly that there wasn't a binding spell to sever in the first place.

"The spirit has his claws in deeply, but it's just another freak accident." She narrows her owl eyes at Lolo. "Probably because of the veils you helped drop years ago. My mother told me you assisted the Rivera family and some teenagers with unbecoming magic. You disturbed the balance back then. Made the veils weaker and the spirits stronger. Now we all pay for it."

Lolo smiles. "I'm glad I'm important enough to talk about in my old age."

She sucks her teeth, and my mind runs. Isobel spoke about the Riveras like they're all dangerous. What did Lolo help them with years ago? Why was it so bad? . . . Teenagers?

"That's a story I'd like to tell my granddaughter another day," Lolo warns Sheila. "On my own time. When this is all over."

"Fine." Sheila sighs, then sets her sights on me. Derek stops tapping nervously at my side. "I can't do anything to help him. But I can help you connect with the earth, Aria."

Lolo crosses his arms over his chest like he suddenly doesn't trust her. "How?" he asks.

"Essentially, the tea cut her off from nature like a slow death. Now she'll have to be reborn." She smiles—looking more cat than owl. "I'll just need to bury her."

The whole space goes silent, cold creeps into my bones, then Bri cries, "Bloody hell?"

"Do it," I insist without hesitation. Derek tries to protest, but I don't even look at him.

"Tomorrow night," Sheila purrs, "when the moon is at its apex, meet me in Roger Williams Park. We'll do it there. Today, I need you to get ready for it."

FIFTY-ONE

Dear Diary or Journal or God,

I liked Sheila better before "getting ready" meant that I'd be eating only dandelions and have to take three ice baths while sitting on dozens of tigereye and rutile quartz crystals within twenty-four hours. At least the dandelions taste good cooked. My first ice bath was brutal. Mom held my hand when I sank into the water. The crystals hurt my legs. The cold made my body convulse. I shook until the numbness hit. The second one was just three hours later and twice as bad. Mom tried to hide her tears while I trembled. She said she hates all of this for me. Asked me to focus on school and let the grown-ups deal with Derek. She wants me to be the girl she tried to keep under control, but I told her I'll never be that girl again. It's three in the morning, and I'm feeling better after the third bath, my breathing is easier, any aches in my body have gone, my central nervous system seems happy. Mom worries I'll catch hypothermia doing three in one day. She keeps coming in to check my temperature.

Derek just texted me. You better be alright, Detective.

And I feel guilty that he's worrying about me because something has been on my mind. Something I will only confess here. I'm doing all of this, about to get buried alive, but I keep thinking of the rumor Lolo told me about. What if it is real? I want to do this for Derek, and as someone with a gift, for myself too, but I don't want to lose anything in the process.

When I drift into sleep, I don't see spirits in the gray. I see a woman with thick hair that falls below her bra strap. She turns to someone and says, "People like us are different, and sometimes different can be scary, but that doesn't mean it's bad." Then she holds out her hand and I'm there. Just a toddler lacing my fingers through hers before we disappear into darkness.

My phone rings at four A.M. and wakes me from the dream. The caller ID shows an unknown number. I answer but don't speak.

"Oh," says a sultry voice, enthralling, soulful, "you're still fascinating."

The words are similar to Marcus's. My chest tightens. "Who is this?"

"You know who it is. Isobel said you'd been by the shop. Took you long enough."

"Lindy," I whisper, glancing around my dark room. "How did you get my number?"

She doesn't answer my question. "Wish we could meet again in the flesh, but unfortunately for you I'm out of the country.

It would've been fun to help you connect with the spirit realm, though." She hums. "Your mind is so loud now. It was quieter when you were a child, easier to sift through. You're brave for those ice baths, couldn't be me. Wow. How do you think so many thoughts at once? Dark ones too. You sensed me before I called. Interesting."

The dream. Was it a memory of us? "If you can't help me, why are you calling?"

"Never said I couldn't help you," she says, then is silent for so many seconds I think she hung up. "Aria?"

"Yes, Lindy?"

"Tell me in your own words what you need from me."

I hesitate because I'm nervous to *need* anything from her. Before what happened with Levi, I don't think I hesitated enough. But I do need her. "Even though I fed the compass my blood, even if I can connect to the earth, none of it will be enough if I can't see the other side."

"There are two things you need to do. One of them is ingest the kava."

"I've been doing that."

"A whole spelled plant?" She doesn't wait for me to answer. "You have to reactivate your gifts. Kind of like the reboot you're about to do by being buried alive." It's creepy when she reaches into my mind, but I don't have time to complain. "How can you show the compass the way if you can't even see it? Yes. I pulled that thought from your brain too. It's correct."

"But . . . but I almost died when I was young," I say, then, "*you* know, you were there."

"I was." It sounds like she's smiling. I shiver. "What's that saying? *What doesn't kill you makes you stronger?* You'll prosper if you survive. Tell me what else you're afraid of. There's something hiding from me."

I lick my lips. "My lolo says there's a rumor that seekers lose things to the other side."

"Ah. That. There have been some whispers of it, yes."

So it *is* real. "Would I . . . lose things that I'm traveling with when I cross realms?"

"Maybe a pen, maybe your phone, maybe your dad's knife, maybe . . . a memory."

Her words take my breath. I was thinking about Dad's knife. But, "A memory?"

"Or maybe nothing at all. Rumors, whispers, I've never been one to believe in anything unless I see it for myself. We seem to have that in common, Aria."

I swallow, but my throat burns. Would I be willing to sacrifice memories if it meant helping people? I'm only seventeen and I've already lost memories to the tea.

"You only have one person to think of right now. Are you willing to sacrifice for Derek?"

Nothing felt as intimate, as intrusive, as her pulling his name from my brain. "Yes," I whisper, even though my heart is thrumming.

"Then I'd put that silly rumor out of my mind if I were you."

Seconds pass. I clear my throat. "Besides eating the kava, what else do I have to do?"

"You're a seeker, but have you even tried to connect with the spirit inside of Derek?"

My insides twist. "I've spoken to him, yes."

She laughs. "That's not enough for a seeker, silly. You'll need to form a personal tie. You know . . . really *see* him."

Suddenly I can feel Marcus's fingers tapping my throat again. *Maybe you'll learn to love us both.* "He's impossible," I say. "Evil."

"Well, in order to find his resting place, you'll need to facilitate some kind of transfer. So that you can see his life, *see* the space for him. Just because you can see the other side doesn't mean you can see where *he* belongs. And is he really evil?" Her voice softens. "Marcus has been wandering for a very long time, Aria. I had the pleasure of connecting with him during a séance years ago and he seemed more in tune with his humanity than most spirits who wander for that long are. If he was evil, you probably wouldn't be alive to have this conversation right now. And besides, no one is inherently evil. Nothing is. Something you'll learn over time."

I lay my head back against my bed. "So eat the kava plant and connect with Marcus?"

"I'd certainly reverse that order, but yes." Lindy smiles. "I look forward to spending time with you in the future, Aria. We had a special bond, you and I. It won't be long before we have something greater, I'm sure."

The question spills out of me. "Why is everyone scared of you?"

"They'd be foolish not to be," she says. "Oh, and I wouldn't go running to Zackary to tell him about this phone call until after your burial. He might get worked up. Sleep well, little bird."

When the line goes dead, I call the number back, but it says the recipient is unavailable. So I lie back in bed and think about all the things I have to do.

The first on my mental list: Forget that a rumor about losing things to the gray exists.

FIFTY-TWO

The hole they're digging isn't deep enough for my body.

"Ay, you're talking nonsense," Lolo says to Sheila. "Her body will definitely fit."

The night air is crisp. I've never been to Roger Williams this late while it's this dark. And they're arguing about how deep they have to bury me. I wrap my arms around myself, trying to still the shakes but can't stop shivering. Derek glances at me, then his eyes flick away and he wipes blood from his nose.

"Are you sure this won't kill me? Being reborn sounds a lot like having to die to do it."

Sheila's yellow eyes blaze like small suns in the dark. "You only have to be under there long enough for nature to accept you." Lolo drops his shovel and she finally nods, pleased. "Once it does, it'll show me a sign."

But Derek spits into a bush. I wonder if it was blood too. He turns to me, the lines on his face sharp under the moonlight. "Aria, you'll be choking on dirt down there."

"I'm doing this," I say, then watch him shift away from me. I wish Bri were here, but her mom refused to let her out the house, even for a *friend emergency*. Mom would've come, but Sheila refused to do the burial with overbearing mother energy around.

The rest happens so fast. One moment I'm standing by the huge hole in a patch of woods, the next I'm closing my mouth and watching as Lolo and Derek bury me from above. Derek's hands shake as he piles on the dirt. I wonder if it's Marcus or if he's really that worried about me. The last thing I see is his face before he covers mine with earth.

Dirt finds its way into my nose, my eyes sting and burn. I shut my mouth so hard that I might run out of air before Sheila even gets a chance to start chanting from above. I tell myself that it takes five hours to run out of air in a coffin, but this is different. What if something happens? What if they don't get me out in time? What if the cops come and arrest them? I'm panicking. I don't even know Sheila. But . . . I do know Derek and Lolo. They'd protect me from anything. And if I don't relax, the earth won't accept me and I'll have experienced all of this for nothing. So I breathe through my nose the best that I can, and try and try.

Suddenly, my body feels like it's back in the frigid water of an ice bath right as the numbness kicks in. And here, underground, all the physical pains fall away. I don't feel the dirt putting pressure on my chest or the way my lungs are begging for release. I only feel the way the earth moves around me. I can hear it growing. Every atom I'm made of warms with energy. I become grass and leaves and water and rock. I don't need to breathe, the earth breathes for me. Invisible vines wrap around my ankles and wrists, flowers grow from my fingertips.

I don't know how long I'm under when the light starts to break through from above.

They pull me from the ground, and the physical feelings come back at the same time as the rain comes down. The dirt caked in my eyes turns to mud, but it doesn't hurt when I try to open them. My body is weightless and heavier all at once, and every drop of rain on my skin cools the nerves there. I've never felt like this.

They usher me into the frothy water of Roger Williams and even that doesn't disgust me. They take turns wiping me down, but I can barely hear anything they're saying because the earth is speaking to me. My heart is pounding in a rhythm to match its words. *There you are*, the earth says. *I've been waiting.*

Sheila and Lolo leave the water to talk, but Derek stays in, waist-deep, and washes the dirt from my hair. My skin is still prickling when he moves closer and uses his shirtsleeve to wipe my cheek. "Hi, you," he breathes out, "tell me how you're feeling."

I close my eyes and he runs his sleeve down the other side of my face. How do I tell him I can feel every single fiber of the cotton in his shirt? That all of me is on the brink of becoming something bigger? When I look at him again, he's tilting his head and chewing his top lip.

I place my hand on his chest, tell him, "I've never felt so alive."

His heart speeds up under my palm. He pulls me in, wraps his arms around me, puts his mouth in the crook of my neck. We float.

But Lolo walks back over and clears his throat. "Time to go."

Derek doesn't care that Lolo's watching. He dunks his sleeve again and uses the water to clean my shoulder. The scar sitting there sings with feeling. I wonder if his matching one does too.

Lolo smacks mosquitoes away while Sheila holds both of my hands. She doesn't use a flashlight, just examines me with her owl eyes. "You seem . . . happy? Not sure how long that'll last after you decide to connect with the spirit realm too. You'll be seeing them left and right. They'll take a bit of the happiness, but at least you'll have the earth to comfort you."

"Do you have any idea how I can connect with the spirit realm?" I ask Sheila, and Lolo grunts from where he stands by a tree. He doesn't know that I'm hoping she'll have other suggestions, that there's something besides what Lindy told me to do.

Sheila shakes her head. "I've offered all I can here," she says, then leans to whisper in my ear. "Aria, your gift is more important than you know. I won't lie to you; I see lots of trouble in your lifetime, but I hope you'll always remember this life was made for you."

FIFTY-THREE

There's a breeze today and even though it's warm, when the wind rustles my hair goosebumps rise on my arms. I'm still feeling nature all around me. Still getting used to its presence like it's right in my bones.

"I won't let you do it," Lolo says from beside me on his stoop. "We'll figure out another way to help Derek, but you're not ingesting a whole kava. Bottom line."

He didn't talk to me for a whole day after I told him about Lindy's call, so this many words would be progress if we had time to waste. "Like what? You've said it yourself, his body can't handle this for much longer. What if he . . ." I shake my head. "I did it once before."

"And you were in the hospital for a week."

"I was a child then." I squeeze my fingers into a fist. "I can do it now."

Lolo stands and blocks out the sun with his shadow. Warmth leaves my body in a rush. I shiver. "If I have to tie you up until this is all over, I will," he says. Then, "Give me a couple days to figure it out. Don't be thickheaded like your father."

"I didn't get buried alive for nothing," I say. "You're not binding their spirits."

"It might be all we can do to save you both."

We stare at each other until he shifts away and heads inside the house, slamming the door shut behind him. He's worried about me, but he's not worried enough about Derek. If Marcus managed to cling to Derek like a virus *without* a binding spell, how strong will he be *with* one? The only person I can rely on for doing everything it takes to save Derek is myself.

Derek is on his front lawn, lying in the grass beside the mound that was the rosebush, which is now growing into a wisteria tree. The buds forming on the stems are calling to my body.

He shifts his head to look at me when I lie down beside him, and knots form in my stomach. I can't stand to see him with hollow eyes, shaky as he sways to the music. But I steal one of his headphones and let myself sway to "Stand by Me" by Ben E. King. I love this song but briefly wonder if Marcus's influences will remain long after Derek is alone in his body.

Derek and I are connected by time, memory, by the universe. Our lives dance somewhere above me in the clouds. I can see us growing and changing and becoming more than we are right now. But that can only happen if I help Marcus. Derek is already becoming less and less of the boy he was before. If he binds with Marcus, one day he won't be that boy at all. It's like he knows when he looks back at me because the song stops playing and suddenly he is Marcus.

"Hi, Bluebird," he says softly. He's tired too. The part of me that's connected to him aches hearing it in his voice. But then something shifts on his face. "What do you want?"

This is going to be as difficult as I imagined it. "Marcus, you need to tell me about when you were alive. We need to . . . connect."

"So you can fall in love with me too?"

"I knew you'd be ridiculous." I sit up, pick some grass. "But I can't do it alone."

He follows my movement and sighs. "Connecting might be difficult because I don't remember much from my past. I don't even know how I died."

There's a moment where I wish someone else could sit in my place, tell Marcus what he needs to know for me. But then I take a breath and pull a paper from my pocket to hand to him. It's a printout of the article I found on the internet. "I think I do," I say.

Marcus hesitates before taking it. When he reads the head-line, his eyebrows dip, mind going deep into someplace I've never seen but need to. I remember the article word for word and I try to go there with him.

BOY DROWNED TRAGICALLY

Marcus Jenkins caught in the sandbar at Conimicut Point Beach trying to rescue DROWNING CHILD. HIS BODY FOUND, BUT . . . still searching for the girl. His parents . . . devastated. Marcus Jenkins was an artist. A floral painter. His mother says he enjoyed singing and dancing and so many people loved him . . . Only eighteen years old.

Marcus runs his shaky hand over the page and reads it again. I clear my throat and he looks up into my eyes. "This is . . . this is me," he says.

Relief runs through me, but when tears start to fall from his eyes I struggle with the urge to make them stop. I tell myself I want to comfort him because he looks like Derek, because we're connected in the gray, but I'm not so sure that's all it is.

He looks shocked to feel the tears, reaches up and touches them.

"It's been so long since I've been able to cry," he says, and in a flash of a moment I can feel that he's grateful for Derek. It's complicated and sad, and it makes me feel so many things. But deep down, I'm grateful he can cry through Derek too.

His bottom lip trembles and he looks away. "I was good," he says to himself.

"You were a hero," I tell him.

His shoulders buckle. His voice is so quiet when he says, "And someone loved me."

FIFTY-FOUR

We notice the connection between me and Marcus is working when his memories start to come back. But not just for him—I can see them too. I see flashes of him at four, six, ten, twelve. He is running in a field of sunflowers with a sibling, he's painting a rose vine that resembles Derek's, playing in the mud, singing his momma to sleep instead of the other way around, he thinks he can fly. Lolo theorizes that if we use the compass in places where the memories happened we might be able to find his resting place without me ingesting the kava plant.

We try to dissect the memories, figure out matching landscapes from sixty years ago, but the longer Marcus leads Derek's body, the worse off Derek is for it. I try to keep my resentment away, try not to let it deteriorate whatever little bond Marcus and I have, but sometimes it simmers close to the surface. And he's anxious too. Snaps at me, curls his fingers into fists, and digs the nails into his skin till they bleed. Into *Derek's* skin.

Lolo's traveling to Massachusetts today to speak to another spell worker. This one is supposed to be practiced at exorcisms.

While he's away, Marcus, Bri, and I visit the land Marcus lived on as a child. It's been bulldozed over, along with any other houses in its vicinity, and is now a hotel. I'm overwhelmed with emotion as we stand outside of it, knowing that at some point, Marcus was a baby in this space; his mother and father probably died here. But ever since then, many lives have walked and slept in this place. Marcus and his family are bones for its structure, but they aren't the whole of it. He looks taken aback too. Like he's trying to search his mind for what it means that this space used to be his. But now it's a business.

"You sure you want to do this?" I ask him.

Marcus picks the skin around his nails. "You have a better idea, Bluebird?"

"You both fill me with agony," Brianna groans, and starts walking toward the entrance.

She's not as creeped out by him as I thought she'd be, but every so often I catch her cradling herself when he passes. We walk around the hotel for an hour, even though the staff glares at us, wondering why three kids from Providence would choose their hotel to do a school project on. Nothing special happens with the compass, but more of Marcus's memories filter through him and into me while we're here. One flashes in my mind and sparks it with a blue glow: trees, green grass, rocks, the sound of a steady stream. It's one memory among many we'll have to sift through later, but Marcus doesn't bring it up.

I wonder if Lolo's right and the compass could work regardless. I wonder if we're standing in Marcus's resting place right now, but since my abilities aren't fully awakened there's no way for us to know. But Marcus says he doesn't feel anything here and neither do I.

Back in the car, while Bri and Marcus talk about other possible locations, I look at a short list in my journal:
Connect with the earth, connect with Marcus (ugh), connect with the spirit realm (eat the damn kava plant).

Two of those items are already crossed off, I just need to be brave enough to do the last one. Except I'm not just nervous about possibly dying anymore, I'm nervous of living with missing memories too. The thought makes me feel selfish when I look over at Marcus and see how strained Derek's body is. But after we drop Bri home, she texts me.

Saw your journal over your shoulder and let me tell you I will literally grow magic powers to bring you back from death just to beat you down if you eat the kava.

I send her a heart emoji, then put my phone away. It's been fourteen hours since Derek's spoken to me. But Marcus doesn't notice how worried I am because he leans his head against his window and closes his eyes. I think of the kava, how Lolo's been guarding it with his life and how my mom refuses to even acknowledge it as an option. When Marcus lifts his head from the window and looks at me, the chill of his energy falls away and it's Derek who says my name.

Everything in me settles to a calm. I pull into my driveway and shut off the engine.

"Hi, you, how are you feeling?"

"Happy to be in the front seat of my body right now." His voice is low, gravelly.

"I'm sorry we have to do it like this," I say.

He shrugs. "Sometimes it's nice, actually. You know, letting him work to carry us for a little bit." I open my mouth to say something, but Derek shakes his head. "Are you ever going to be able to look at me like I'm not pitiful again?"

My chest tightens. "I don't now. I never will."

He leans to grab my hand and presses two fingers to the pulse point in my wrist the way he used to. My heart is beating so fast in my chest I wonder how it feels against his fingertips. "Aria, you have to promise me you won't eat the whole kava."

"I can't promise that, Derek."

"Please." He huffs out a breath that can undo me. "I can't lose you."

Butterflies flutter in my stomach, but I need to be strong for him. "You won't lose me."

"So promise."

"I can't lose you either. So this promise isn't a fair one."

"If we can't figure it out soon," he says, "I'll bind with Marcus."

I pull away from his grasp. "No."

"Maybe it won't be so bad; we can make a custody agreement. I get sixty, he gets forty."

"That isn't funny at all," I say, but my smile betrays me. "And you know he'd want a lot more than forty."

Derek frowns, then tucks a fallen strand behind my ear. "I'll still need that promise."

He cups my face. "I promise," I breathe out.

We stare at each other. "Aria, about the kiss . . ."

"No," I say. "We'll talk about the kiss when this is over. When you're *you* again."

He smiles just a little, and I know he doesn't think he'll ever be just him again. "Alright."

We don't move from the car and we don't speak another word while we sit here. Derek turns up the radio and we let Frank Ocean's *Blonde* album run straight through.

When Mom comes home, she's shocked to see all the old family photo albums scattered around me on the living room floor. "Aria? What are you looking for?"

"A sign." I hold up a baby pic, then another. "Do you notice anything off about these?"

She crouches low, looks at them good. In one of them I'm sitting on the grass, blowing a dandelion. In the other, I'm running toward the camera with chocolate all over my face. Mom smiles down at it. "What am I supposed to be looking for?"

"Something in these that confirms I wasn't born with a magic ability, that I was just a kid who saw ghosts and ate a magical plant that made me do one little magical thing."

She sits and takes a photo out of my hand, then tucks it back into its sheet. "Aria, I think what Lindy meant was the plant helped bring forward what was already there."

"But how do we even know for sure?"

She leans forward and runs her finger over a picture of my

dad holding me. "He knew it the day you were born. Said you had it in your eyes. Something different about your irises," she says. "I've never told you this, but, your dad, he used to see them too."

"The spirits?"

She nods. "Somehow that got passed on, but he liked to say his sight was just a higher frequency of what humans are capable of. Some people have it and some people don't, some can work for it. You, your eyes . . . I can't explain it well, but he said they didn't just turn colors when you were a baby, they reflected the world in rainbow light." She laughs. "I sound silly."

"You don't," I whisper. "My dreams were always dark gray before, but now colors are breaking through and . . ." I sigh and lay my head against her shoulder. "Just, thank you."

She kisses my forehead. "After you ate the kava, you found your dad. You could see the spirits. Fully see them. I had to watch your every move or you'd wander off. It was so scary. It didn't calm down until we started giving you the tea."

I didn't consider how that might make her feel. "I'm sorry, Mom."

She shakes her head. "You were happy. Brave. You wanted to help them all."

I blink back tears. "I want to help Derek, but I'm not so brave anymore."

"You're the bravest person I know," she says. "But we don't know what the kava would do to you now. And, Aria, you can't spend your whole life helping every spirit or every person who crosses your path. If you did that, you wouldn't even have a life. And that's not what I want for you. I want you to go to college, find something you love to do, and meet someone someday, maybe have children, maybe not, but I want you to have a future that's just for you."

"I'm so scared of doing the wrong thing," I say.

She wraps an arm around me. "So am I."

FIFTY-FIVE

It's quiet in my house when I wake up. Mom doesn't work today, but she's not here. Her car is gone, and so is Mr. Johnson's. I call Derek, Lolo, Mom twice, text them all. No one answers. My stomach sinks. I grab my things and bike faster than I ever have in my life.

There's a fire blazing in my chest, my legs burn too, but all of their cars are here when I arrive. The shop door is locked so I pound on it, praying I made it here before they ruin Derek's life. But he's the one to answer and his face falls when he sees me.

I throw myself at him and he wraps me in his arms, holds me so close. Breathes into my hair.

"Did they do it?" I pull back just enough to reach up and touch his face.

"Not yet," he says, and we're hugging again. If I could choose an ability it would be to still time. I would be able to keep us safe for a bit, locked in this bubble we've created.

Lolo says my name from behind and breaks us apart. I push past Derek, angry, betrayed. Lolo throws a hand up to silence me.

He tells me it's not my decision to make. He says things about how sick Derek is, how his dad almost dialed an ambulance this morning after he collapsed; he gets right in my face, doesn't care that it's wet with tears.

"If you don't like it, you can leave, but look at him. Really look," he says.

I see my mom standing at the door with a sorry expression. Lolo ushers her back into the kitchen and leaves me alone with Derek. I don't turn to look at him. I stand there listening to our parents talk to another person. A new spell worker. They are debating and discussing Derek's fate, but their words run together. All I hear are bits of pieces that cause me pain: *the binding, separation, detachment, permanent, it might be permanent . . . are we sure?*

My eyes flick around the room, land on the kava plant in a box in the corner. Was Lolo getting ready to throw it out? Give it away? I hear Derek move behind me, the cushions on the couch give under his weight. When I turn, I make myself *really* look. And my heart breaks. The underside of Derek's eyes are purple. His stomach caves in when he breathes. He's lost weight and can hardly hold himself upright, but he gives me a half smile anyway.

"It's okay, Detective. The spell worker says he knows someone else who will be able to help him try a severing spell down the line. The binding will be okay for now." I sit beside him and stare. He averts his eyes. "I don't want you to see me like this."

The invisible thread between us pulls again. I move closer. I don't want to see him like this either. Derek, who backflips off porches and jumps off roofs and does tricks on his skateboard all day, *my* Derek deteriorating. I take his hand, don't stop looking.

"Maybe it won't be that bad," he says, quiet, so quiet. "Marcus isn't completely awful, I guess. And I already told you that taking a back seat when I'm tired is pretty nice."

"You don't mean that," I say.

"I just want to feel better," he admits. "And if binding our spirits helps my body handle it better, then yeah, I do mean it."

"That's not fair for either of you. Marcus doesn't even want it. And none of this is fair for anyone else." My voice cracks. "It's not fair for me."

He laces our fingers and swallows hard. "Maybe you'll be able to help other spirits eventually, but at least you can get there on your own."

I swat at my wet face and put distance between us. "So, I can help people down the line, but I can't help you now? Do you know how much that'll haunt me? How much it'll hurt?"

He's giving up; he doesn't believe in me. But someone else does. My eyes flick to the kava, then to the keys on the coffee table, and back up to Derek's face. His own eyes grow a little wide with knowing. He starts to shake his head, tries to speak, but I get so close to his face I can feel him breathing against my own. I stare straight into his brown eyes. "Marcus," I whisper.

Derek closes his, and when they open again they're that familiar blackness I've grown used to. I snatch the keys off the table and pull him up off the couch.

"My girl," he says, something glinting in his eyes. "Where are we going?"

"I'm not your girl," I say, but I'm smiling. "And less talking, more movement."

He doesn't need to be told twice. He heads for the door, and I hear the spell worker tell everyone he'll do the spell tonight. I grab the box with the kava. They can't do the spell if they don't have Marcus, and he'll be long gone before tonight's moon.

We manage to get a mile out in my mom's car before our phones start going off. I silence them while Marcus drives. "Have any ideas, Bluebird?"

I pluck a kava leaf off the plant. "Think about it . . . What's the one place we always find ourselves at? The place you've lingered for a while?"

He raises an eyebrow at me. "You're not actually suggesting Neutaconkanut, are you?"

"I am. There's a reason the wisteria chose to grow there."

"But we've searched the park. I've been there so many times. Wouldn't I have found my own way by now?"

I won't tell him there's a memory he's been blocking out, one that's been trying to slip from my grasp. Last night I realized why that may be. "It has to be more difficult than that," I say. "If I'm wrong, you can gloat in Derek's body tonight. But we've never been there while my powers are unlocked."

When we hit a stoplight he watches as I eat two leaves at a time. They taste bitter and my throat itches and burns. I made him drive even though he's tired because I don't know what'll happen to me.

"Why do you really want to do this, Bluebird? It's not just for Derek. It's definitely not just for me."

My stomach starts to grow queasy after I swallow another kava leaf. I brace myself against the dashboard and glance over at him. "Because nothing's ever been right," I say. "I've always been searching for something outside of myself. I didn't know I should be searching within. And if I can help people while tilting my own world right, I want to do it."

"What else?" He smirks.

"You're really gonna make me say it?"

"I'm waiting."

I sigh. "The thought that I'll be solving mysteries for spirits gives me . . . adrenaline."

"I know it does, Bluebird."

Neither of us say anything else for the rest of the drive.

FIFTY-SIX

The sun is just beginning to set in the sky, filling the area with a golden hour light and making my skin tingle. But it's moist out. I'm sweating while ingesting the plant, bit by bit, as we walk up the stone path. Marcus keeps looking back at me like he thinks I'm going to change my mind, turn, and leave him. I consider it a few times.

When we finally make it to the clearing, the sensation under my skin is supercharged. I'm aware of every nerve ending inside of my body. I sit in the grass under one of the trees and let the butterflies land all over me. Be brave, I tell myself before shoving a handful of kava into my mouth, but I'm growing dizzy. There is one Marcus, he is Derek, and then there are three of them on the ground with me, watching as I finish the last leaf. It feels like more than enough, like too much when the last bit goes down my esophagus. But it's not. Bile rises when I rip at the roots and eat some of those too. I don't know how long it takes me to eat them, but it feels like some of them are trying to crawl back up my throat, others attach to the lining of my stomach, prick me there. Maybe I'll grow kava inside of me.

"You okay, Bluebird?" Marcus asks, kneeling and hovering over me with a bottle of water. I try to take a sip, but it spills down my face. His big hands cup my cheeks. "Look at me," he says. Or I think he says, but he has six eyes, two mouths, his limbs spread out like a spider's. There is pink and blue and yellow and green around him. Black butterflies fall out of his mouth when he opens it again. And I blink and blink and then I. Can't. Breathe.

For a moment, time stills. A new superpower. Then everything goes gray.

There are no shadows. I feel nothing. No energy around me. No static. No pain. I can't hear my own footsteps, can't feel my feet hit the ground as I walk through this void space.

Is this death? This must be death.

But out of the darkness come small wisps of white. They form a shape. Solid. They become the little girl I saw in this same forest. But she is different now. She can speak.

"You see me?" She's holding her bunny. "Can you see me?"

The air around us turns thin, the filmy layer between us falls away. I watch color drip into her eyes, change her skin, brighten her hair. She looks very much alive.

"I can see you," I say.

She is quiet at first, but when she smiles I feel all of her in my chest. But I feel me too, my aching bones, the exhaustion, my head splitting.

"We can go slow," she says, but while we walk through the darkness together, pain pierces the heels of my feet. For the briefest moment I wonder if she's walking me to my death.

But soon, I'm the one leading her. I turn to see she's a few steps behind me, and each one of hers makes a ripple in this void, bringing with it a burst of color, a leaf floating across the space, the warmth of a sunray shooting from somewhere above us. We build fresh flowers and tall trees. When I reach down and run my finger over a flower, I feel a little stronger.

"Am I almost home?" she asks from behind.

I see it then: a small brick house with a wreath on the door. The little girl laughs and holds the bunny close, then bounces on her feet. She's a prism of light. A suncatcher.

My feet stop moving a few feet from her door. She looks back at me and suddenly her eyes are fluorescent blue. "Thanks, Aria," she says before fading in front of me.

The voice doubles back, but it's not her voice anymore. "Aria. Aria, wake up." It's Derek's. I come out of the void choking on air. Derek is above me, or maybe it's Marcus. A worried look on their face, their phone in their hand, tears in their eyes.

"I'm calling an ambulance," they say. And I realize it's definitely Derek.

I sit up and shake my head. My body is transitioning hot, cold, hot, cold; my mind is full of fog. Derek doesn't stop, and it takes all of my strength to pull his hand away from his ear. "I'm okay," I say.

Derek drops the phone to the ground before pulling me to his chest. He breathes in deep. "You promised me."

"I'm alive," I say, the earth shifting back. "I'm alive, Derek. And I did it."

"You weren't breathing." He pulls back to look at me like he just needs to be sure. Our faces are inches apart. He brushes my cheek with his thumb and then leans his forehead against mine. "Don't ever leave me like that again." I close my eyes. My heart is erratic in my chest. Our lips are a breath away. Almost touching. "You hear me, Detective?"

"I hear you," I whisper.

When I open my eyes again, he pulls away and a sensation moves through my stomach. I push myself to my knees slowly, trying to regain my strength.

"I need to finish this with Marcus."

Derek's face contorts. "Hell no. He was going to let you die."

"He gave you control so that you could make sure I was okay, didn't he?"

"Not without some force," Derek says. "I don't trust him."

"You don't have to trust him. You just have to trust me, believe in me."

"I've always believed in you. But this . . ."

"You gave up too soon," I cut in. "You were going to sacrifice yourself."

Derek stands, but I can tell he's trying to keep from swaying. "To protect you, Aria."

I let him pull me to my feet, but say, "Now let me protect you."

He sighs, so tired, then presses his lips to my forehead. "Bring us out of this alive."

When his warmth turns to burning, I know it's Marcus staring down at me. But he doesn't tease or taunt, he doesn't make smart remarks. He just pulls away and asks what I saw in the void space of the gray, the other side.

"Darkness," I start, and Marcus's face falls, "then more color than this life can offer."

He reaches into his pocket and places the compass in my palm. We both spend several seconds suspended in sadness and hope and uncertainty. "I'm ready to see it," he finally says.

Nothing happens when I hold the compass at first, and with Marcus staring at me I'm even more nervous nothing will. But then we move away from the wisteria trees, just at the edge of the clearing, and the tips of my fingers start to buzz and it fills my whole body with a vibration. Then the compass starts to move.

"If you could see your eyes right now." Marcus exhales. "You're glorious."

I can't see them, but I remember the girl and her fluorescent eyes: a reflection of me.

I'm still weak, but my legs move deeper into the forest. Marcus is close behind me, breathing heavy as we wind through trees. There's no path for us to take. We follow the compass through bushes and mud. Marcus carefully pulls apart a spiderweb in our path. My pant legs brush against poison ivy leaves, my ankles turn in when I stumble on rocks, but Marcus is there to steady me. We finally get to a place that converges into two unmarked trails and the compass begins to burn my hand. Then it stops moving. Marcus is barely breathing beside me.

"I don't know which way to go," I tell him, glancing back and forth between the two paths, then up at him. I know he's scared, I know he's holding back. "You have to help me."

Marcus slowly extends a trembling hand and places it under

mine. We both clasp the compass and his energy threads through me until our fingertips start to glow faintly.

The compass begins to move again. It points in the direction with a narrower path, darkened by the crowns of trees. Marcus's hand stops glowing when he moves away from me, but my hand gets brighter. He looks at the path the compass wants us to take, and I can see the fear cross his face.

"Well," his voice is low and light, "I did say as long as it wasn't the abyss, it didn't matter where I ended up."

We share a breath before we head into the darkness.

There is little room for us to move together so Marcus walks behind me, trying to swat away the tree branches that cling to us, but they cut me as I walk, and the burning of the compass makes me wince. Sweat drips down my face and stings my eyes, but I can still see everything around us. And when the darkness starts to open, I hear the sound of water and walk quicker toward it, squeezing between two trees and into a small glade.

Marcus staggers to a stop while I watch the water run down a watershed and into a small creek. It's beautiful. I've never seen it here before. I turn back to look at Marcus, but he's still hidden under the canopy of the trees. "It's okay," I tell him. "Come on."

When he steps toward me, the faint glow in my hands turns a radiant fluorescent blue. They no longer burn. The color travels from the tips of my fingers through my arms, making the veins stand out in my skin. A soothing, cooling feeling flows through my body and brings moisture to my eyes. I inhale deep, welcoming whatever is swelling inside of me.

Marcus gasps when he looks at me. He's mesmerized by me until his eyes sweep over the area.

My words come out in a whisper. "Does this place mean anything to you?"

He walks slowly over the grass and rocks, then touches the running water. He speaks without turning back to look at me. "We loved this part of the watershed. My little sister and I . . . We'd skip over these rocks right here," he sits down on one of them, "and try to keep our feet dry before we were ready to go play in the creek. I'd spend so long here, just watching the water run."

The glow surrounding me gets brighter as it extends onto the rocks, giving them an otherworldly glow. Marcus's eyes flick up to my face and in them I see his spirit. He's beautiful. "But the water," he whispers, eyes shining with tears.

He doesn't have to say any more. He died in water, but it's where his spirit wants to rest. I feel the conflict twisting inside of him and drop to my knees so we're face-to-face when I tell him, "It's okay to be scared." I close the compass and slide it into my pocket, then take his hands. We burn together. "But your family is here, Marcus. I can feel their energy. They've been waiting for you. They said you're safe now. To come home."

His face is a watershed. His bottom lip trembles. I wipe the wetness from his skin, and then blue tears start to trickle from his eyes. I cup his face the same way he has cupped mine. The blue light envelopes us both. We are shrouded in it like a bubble.

"Close your eyes and tell me what you see."

He does as I ask. "It's dark." His voice trembles. "The abyss . . ."

"No, keep looking." I try to guide him with the thing stirring inside of me.

Finally, he takes a sharp breath and says, "More colors than this life has to offer."

My heart races. I think it's done, that he'll leave without another word, but with his eyes still closed, he reaches out to touch my lips. "Will you sing to me, Bluebird?"

Images of lying on the lawn come to me. We listened to Ben E. King right before I told Marcus he was a hero. The song slips out of me now. I stroke his face with my thumbs and sing about the night coming and the sky falling and the mountains crumbling. I sing about being brave because he's standing with me.

He smiles and his hand falls from my face.

The bitter chill I've grown to know fades first. Then the blue light seeps out of Derek, before it leaves me. It settles in the water and runs down to find a home in the creek below.

I choke on my cries as I feel Marcus go.

FIFTY-SEVEN

It's only been two weeks, but the flowers are already growing on the wisteria tree, coating the front of the Johnson house with a pretty purple. The neighborhood has finally stopped going feral about how fast it grew, but I think it's because Karina has been spreading rumors that the Johnson family does witchcraft and no one wants to mess around and find out.

A monarch butterfly feeds on a cascading vine. I pluck a flower, carefully so it doesn't fly away, and the memories of Marcus come flooding back in a rush to press on the aching spaces inside of me that our severed connection left behind.

Derek comes outside and my face burns wondering what he's thinking when he watches me tuck the wisteria between the pages of a new notebook. But then the sky turns ashen and color leaves the earth. In the gloomy light of the gray, joy is sucked from everything around me. Somber spirits wander the street; some see me, some don't seem to see anything at all. Derek becomes a dense shadow of himself. And I can't blink away any of it.

Until he shakes me by the shoulders. "You good, Aria?"

I get dizzy shifting back but appreciate the brown of his eyes. They're so easy to focus on. "I'm good," I finally say. "Are you?"

"I'm not the one dealing with dual realm limbo," he says.

Ever since setting Marcus free, the other side has been blinking in and out of existence while I'm awake. One moment, I'm in school with friends, the next I'm in the gray with spirits. It always looks like a dull, dark version of the living realm. Derek might not be dealing with what I'm dealing with, and things are returning to normal for him, but sometimes I catch the far-off look in his eyes and know he's thinking of his former passenger. I wonder if he misses Marcus the way I do. But when I tease him he always shakes his head and laughs.

"Why would I miss the ghost who stole my body?"

Why would either of us miss Marcus? And yet, it's there. Some deep tenderness embedded inside of me. I hope it won't be like this if I help another spirit. I hope they won't leave seeds in my heart. It's not easy for me to let go, and I need enough space in my heart for me. I tell myself Marcus was special. It was different. I know it, and so does Derek.

I put the notebook in my backpack and zip it up. Derek looks down at all the new pins he gave me. Soon I'll be running out of space. When he smiles, my face flushes again.

"Did you ever find your old journal?" he asks.

My stomach sinks something awful. My journal, containing all the memories and questions I've had over the past few months, is missing. I think I might've lost it trudging through the forest with Marcus the day he moved on, but searching for it has proven fruitless. "No, but I'm praying it turns up soon," I say, raw, honest. I'm sure he can hear it in my voice.

He frowns, but then says, "If there's a memory you're unsure of, if I was there . . . as Marcus or as myself, I'd be happy to help you remember."

The offer is gentle, kind, reminds me that he's still in my life. That he'll be here. It also makes me wonder how much he could see and hear when Marcus was in control. The last moment we were together, when Marcus touched my lips and I sang to him, crosses my mind. Derek ducks his eyes shyly, but we start walking to catch the bus and he nudges me with his elbow. I laugh and jam mine into his side. He pushes me.

We haven't talked about the intimate moments between the two of us. We haven't mentioned the kiss. But I know he'll be sitting beside me on the bus.

My hands are still bandaged up, but just days ago they were bleeding and crusting over. Lolo's healing balms have been the only thing to make the pain bearable. Will they always burn when I use my gift? *Every good has a bad. That's the balance*, Lolo had said.

Lindy contacts him while I'm trying to string garlic together, and he swears in Tagalog but passes me the phone. "Are you calling for a favor?" I ask. "I know I owe you something."

She does nothing for free, nothing out of the kindness of her heart, I've been told.

"You don't owe me anything, Aria, but I'll be in the States

soon and there are so many great things I can show you." She's smiling. "And I know you're worried you won't have control as an anchor, but I can help with that too. For now, think of the other side as a constant presence that you can make fade into the background whenever you choose to."

I consider Lindy's words, then say, "Sort of like being near-sighted and choosing not to wear my glasses because I can kind of see fine without them? But knowing that if I do put them on, the world might look different?"

Lolo rolls his eyes from across the table and Lindy cackles. "Yeah. You're definitely fascinating," she says. "And tell your grandfather to relax his head over there. Worrying about you will only make him grow old faster, and he hasn't been able to bottle the fountain of youth yet." Her words make me smile, but then she says, "It's okay to miss Marcus. I know I did."

My stomach squeezes, but before I can respond she hangs up the phone.

Lolo makes a sour face. "Do I even want to know what that wretched woman said?"

"I think I'll spare you," I tell him.

"Fine. We need to collect slug slime for a healing tonic anyway."

Lolo let me work back at the shop, but only with the agreement that I won't go running around finding space for every single spirit who crosses my path. After Marcus moved on, our family found us at the mouth of the hill. It was dark and cold, my mom was a sobbing mess examining my eyes, my raw and reddened hands. Mr. Johnson was crying and apologizing, but

Derek just held him. Lolo wasn't happy with me, but he told me I saved two lives.

There's a pang in my chest remembering the day. I hope Marcus knows I'll never forget him. I hope one day Lolo realizes that Marcus and Derek saved me too.

FIFTY-EIGHT

Fall weather is perfect for backyard camping. Bri and I are bundled up in sleeping bags, sipping hot cocoa, and trying to guess constellations in the sky. I'm happy my mom finally agreed to let me spend a night out. She's been working less lately to keep an eye on me since I'm struggling with finding my place as an anchor. She's not the only one; Adelia has been calling more. She's always asking me to describe the other side, and sometimes we FaceTime so I can practice trying to make it fade to the background like Lindy said. It's not easy. Even out here, the inky night sky will randomly pale to something dreary. But Bri is a good distraction. She's falling in love with Val and has the cutest stories to tell me. It's nice not to worry about the dead for a little bit. Even though there are always going to be other worries.

"Do you think I'll have someone to love someday soon?"

Brianna looks at me sideways. "So we're going to pretend you don't have Derek? He's been with us almost every day. He even laughs at your horrible jokes and believe me, they are bad. I mean, I wouldn't laugh at them if someone paid me."

"Enough already." I swat at her. "You don't have to be so cruel. I like my jokes."

"I know you do," she says, scrunching up her nose. "And so does Derek."

"That doesn't mean he likes me. We haven't talked about the kiss like he said we would." I play with the hem of my sleeping bag. "Maybe he forgot it even happened."

"Girl . . . retrograde amnesia? You serious?" She rolls her eyes. "Remember when he was saying Megan never made him laugh? You're not paying enough attention. Why don't *you* talk to him about the kiss?"

"Because . . ." Bri is beyond invested now. She gives me big puppy dog eyes and scoots closer. "Well, what if it was just the intimacy of being put in a crazy situation together, having to be close and comfort each other? What if part of the magnetic pull was Marcus? What if he . . ."

"Had a ghostly crush on you?" Bri laughs, and my face burns. "Or tried to play matchmaker? Actually, I wouldn't doubt either of those things, but that doesn't mean Derek doesn't like you."

"What if he does, then he breaks my heart? I can't risk us losing our friendship."

"Why don't you stop speculating and try giving him a chance to talk to you about his feelings for once? And just because you want to try a different type of relationship doesn't mean you'll have to lose your friendship if it doesn't work out."

I turn the thoughts over in my mind, then say, "Sometimes you say good things. Even when they're kinda low blows. You know that, right?"

"Oh, I definitely know, but you should tell Val that because the girl stays trying to argue with me, saying I'm difficult. I am not difficult."

"A little bit."

She pinches me through the sleeping bag, and the night is everything I've needed.

FIFTY-NINE

After school, Derek lets me off the bus at the end of our street first. "Like gentlemen do."

"Why thank you, good sir."

"Anything for the lady."

We fall into banter as we walk. His English accent is a wash, but mine is particularly on point. Better than Bri's, but I'll never tell her that. "Do you think I'm funny?" I blurt out.

He looks like he wants to take a stab at me, say no, but then, "You're the funniest person I know. Truly, I missed this perk of friendship."

Even though he says *friendship*, my stomach still flips. "Are you lying?"

"I am. You're actually so dull, Aria Cayetano," he says, smiling with his whole eyes.

I catalog that smile to bring home with me. We stop in front of his house and he grips his backpack straps. The smell of wisteria wraps around the two of us.

"Aria," he says, voice so soft I think he's going to mention the kiss, but instead, "I feel like I haven't thanked you enough for saving my life."

"You thank me every day, Derek Johnson." I smile. "Honestly, it's getting tiring. I might have to put you in the ground myself. Or worse, use the Cayetano family knife."

He laughs hard, then says, "Don't get tired of me yet. I love having you in my life." Words get caught in my throat. He walks backward to his front door. "And don't forget to study for AP Calc, wouldn't want to be a college freshman without you."

I watch him disappear inside and take my heart with him.

Sitting by the window is an unhinged level of stalking now, but I don't care. I'm a ball of nervous energy because I can't stop thinking of Derek using the word *friendship*. I open my new journal and there's a pang in my chest realizing that I probably won't find my old one. But before I can write anything, a text makes my phone vibrate against my thigh. Derek must've felt me thinking about him.

We should've had a slasher movie marathon today, it says.

We had one a few nights ago.

Yeah, but I kind of miss you already.

There have never been so many butterflies in my belly.

Really?

Really. Sleep well, Detective.

I won't sleep, I can't right now.

When I tap on Derek's window, he opens the curtain with a surprised look on his face, even though I've done this countless times. We stand there, separated by glass, protected from each other's feelings. But as his chest rises and falls, I imagine he's feeling the same as me.

Finally, he lifts the window to let me inside. He doesn't ask why I'm here, just walks over to his bed and nods for me to join him there. I take off my shoes and crawl over him to the side near the wall. We lay face-to-face, looking at each other until he closes his eyes.

His breathing is heavy to match mine.

He whispers my name, and doubt creeps in. Is he going to tell me to leave? Is he going to break my heart? But he opens his eyes and lifts one of my hands to undo the bandage. My breath catches when he traces the rawness there with his pointer finger, then leans down to place a kiss on my palm.

I am glowing blue, but he can't see it.

His gaze flicks to my face. "Why did you come here?"

"I . . ." My voice is unsteady, I can barely breathe. "I wanted to be with you."

He exhales before brushing his thumb across my bottom lip. "What else do you want?"

I'm brave for everything else—why not this?

"I want you to kiss me," I tell him. "Do you want that too?"

Derek doesn't answer with words. He smiles and leans to press his lips to mine. He's gentle, tentative, as he softly traces the outline of my mouth with his own. Until I sigh into him. Then we are tongue and teeth and touching skin with needy hands. He flips me to press his body into mine, my fingers find his hair, and we melt into each other.

When we finally break apart, my whole body vibrates. His kisses are magic.

He puts his mouth against my neck, groans out, "Oh, God."

My lips are still tingling when he moves to kiss my shoulder where our matching scar is. The act feels more intimate than anything else, so I'm already trying to catch my breath when he blocks the moonlight and covers us both in shadow. His brown eyes call to me in the dark.

"I've been in love with you all my life, Aria," he says.

My stomach twists and tangles at how sure he sounds. Still, I can't stop the words from spilling out. "As a friend?"

His laugh makes my chest warm. "As a friend and everything more. I love you all of the ways someone can be loved." His eyebrows meet in the middle. "Is that okay with you, Detective?"

I nod because I love him every single way you can love a person too. "I've been in love with you all of my life, Derek Johnson," I say.

He smiles and he leans his forehead against mine.

The space around us dances with colors that are too bright for this world.

When the vision comes, my body feels like it can levitate: Months from now, the two of us are under the wisteria tree as it grows new tendrils. I'm sitting between his legs, his arms are wrapped around me, we make summer plans, talk about mastering my abilities, about college coming, and what it'll be like being in the dorms and about growing in love.

We remember Marcus each time the wind blows, and we're thankful he left something sweet for us.

EPILOGUE
THREE MONTHS GONE

Lindy Rivera knows how to apply pressure with only her eyes. I know the look she's giving me means we aren't leaving The Hill at Neutaconkanut Park anytime soon.

The cold is sharp, but we sit together on dormant grass—dead from hibernation season—and she tries to teach me things. No matter how far within the forest we work from the wisteria trees, it seems like the butterflies find her. Glowing green swallowtails sit on her shoulder and she doesn't even seem to notice.

"Go back in," she says, like the other side is a door I can walk right through.

It's not, but I'm getting better at balancing both realms. I close my eyes, regulate my breathing, and try to bring the gray into focus. Once I'm there, Lindy makes me walk the lackluster land while she tries to dip inside my mind and see what I see. But the other side is dark and gloomy, the same spirits wander the forest, and I'm tired today. I miss Derek.

I get ready to push the gray away, but something shimmers

in the corner of my eye. As I walk, I can hear Lindy's voice, distorted like static. "Something new," I think she says.

When I'm close enough, I notice the shimmer is coming from a small notebook lying between two leafless trees. It glints, blinking in and out of the gray like something that doesn't belong.

And I realize right then that it doesn't.

"Breathe, little bird," Lindy warns.

I drop to my knees and reach for it with a trembling hand, but the tips of my fingers disappear through the cover like it's permeable.

When I come out of the gray, I'm gasping for air. I take one look at Lindy before I get up and run, fast through the clearing, down one of the marked trails and deep into the forest.

She slowly follows, and by the time she reaches me I'm digging through dead leaves.

"Where is it?" I say, spinning around, scanning the area with my eyes.

Lindy places a hand on my shoulder, her brows knit together, she tilts her head at me.

"Aria, your journal isn't here."

"But . . ." It hits me then, makes the world fall silent. All I can hear is my heart beating.

My journal isn't here because I lost it to the other side.

ACKNOWLEDGMENTS

The sophomore slump is real. It took three tries at different projects before Aria snuck into my mind and asked me what I was doing with my life. Once she found me, the words poured out and suddenly there was a book. I probably shouldn't confess this, but she has been my favorite character to write. Now I must let her wander off in the world.

One last list in this book:

—To my agent Jess Regel, who I adore very much: I literally can't imagine my career without you. Please be my agent, a friend, and my fiercest advocate FOREVER.

—Thank you to my entire publishing team at Holt, and especially my editor Mark Podesta. *Dark* was a zero draft, but you were prepared to tear it apart with me. Thank you for listening to me ramble on our calls and for the virtual hugs when I need them. The cover is a MASTERPIECE, truly. I'm in love with it. So, my undying gratitude to the incredibly talented team of artist Kenza Fakira and art director Aurora Parlagreco.

—To Rachel Menard and Lillie Lainoff for your unwavering support of my work, and for the beautiful words you both said about *Dark*. And to Lyndall Clipstone for the gorgeous illustrations inside of this book. Your dreamy style fits Aria's world so well. Thank you all for the gift of friendship.

—To the booksellers, librarians, reviewers, and readers who make it possible for me to keep putting work out into the world. And huge shoutout to the incredible booksellers Mads Vericker and Caroline Vericker, who are the founders of one of my very favorite local indie bookstores (Heartleaf in Providence; they have a shop cat named Penny and I adore her).

—To my author friends, especially my forever love Em North. To Isha Abreu and Madelfy Rodriguez, the very first people who listened to me ramble about DARK when the only solid thing I had was Aria spying from a window. Thank you! To my brothers Carlos Cruz Jr. and Troy Perry, Rochelle Baker (I love you, Ma), auntie Connie Bisignani, Emily Danforth, Shylene Lopez, Jenny Ramirez, Kathy Reyes, Nilson Abreu, and anyone else who has encouraged me or loved me and my children during the journey of writing this book. And to the family I've recently lost, including our sweet bunny Bo, whose spirit I swear I still feel sometimes.

—So much love to my uncle Jose and uncle Charlie for believing in me from the very start and doing all you can to spread the word about my books.

—My parents, Angelique and Antonio Gagnon: I love you both so very deeply. It makes me emotional thinking of how proud of me you are. Thank you for being incredible grandparents and giving me unconditional love at times I need it the most.

—Jadin Gagnon, my baby brother, who will spend hours with me dreaming up worlds I may never write, Thank you for *caring* about me and the things I do. My love for you is infinite.

—Yoli Rodrigo for the undying love, going with me to book signings and author events, for believing in me so fiercely I can physically feel it. Love you!

—Shirlene Obuobi: We are *star-crossed*. You've been here for every book (even the ones I left in a dusty file), every win, every complaint LOL. Love you and our writing sprint sessions between hours of conversation about silly things. I can't imagine publishing or my life without you now.

—My papa, Jose Rivera: I wouldn't be *me* without *you*, so I'm convinced my books and the worlds I build wouldn't exist if it weren't for growing up with you. Mahal Kita.

—To Philip M Johnston. Here we are again. Another wish. So much more to come. Thank you for our white board sessions. No one gets how my mind works the way you do, which means brainstorming together is literal magic. One day, we will be changing the opening of your books right before deadline and it'll be magic then too. For now, I'll see you at the cove. <3

—To my children, My'ah and Jada, who are old enough to brainstorm with. Thank you for being sweet kids (mostly, haha). Staring at my computer for so many hours a day would be a lot harder if you weren't. I'm hoping I feel the same way for the next book, and all the ones to come, so please behave, my broke besties. I love you both with every fiber of my being. Forever.

—To God for each day you gift me to put words on the page.